A
TALE
FOR THE
SHADOWS

A NOVEL OF DEATH AND LOVE

JOYCE SHERRY

First edition

Paperback ISBN: 979-8-9986378-0-3
eBook ISBN: 979-8-9986378-1-0
Library of Congress Control Number: 2025908224

For my fellow incubators.
Where would I be without you?

Millions of spiritual creatures walk the earth
Unseen, both when we wake, and when we sleep...
~John Milton

PROLOGUE

Stories like to be told in their own way. This one could have been different. If Sarah had listened to Stan. If she hadn't been so self-absorbed. If Kenny hadn't been so good-looking. Or if he'd had a shred of human decency. Certainly Sarah wouldn't have died. But then, I have to ask myself, would I trade her continued life for the beauty of my existence? I don't know that I would. I have two tales to tell you, both of which—I swear on my mother's grave—are completely true. As I said, stories like to be told in their own way, and this one wants to start here.

Sarah Sommers strode down a narrow hallway, her messenger bag hanging from her shoulder. She was about to duck into the restroom when someone called her name. Stanley loped toward her, a scarecrow in flapping Birkenstocks. He caught up and, resting one hand on her shoulder, leaned over, panting. "Let me … catch my … breath," he rasped in a voice that betrayed a three-pack-a-day habit.

Sarah watched him with concern. "You've got to quit smoking," she scolded.

He straightened up, hand to his heart. "Bubbala," he growled, "tell me about it. Peter has been nagging me since the day we met." He coughed wetly. "Okay, better. Listen, Sarella, I want to remind you: this show would be bupkis without you."

Sarah laughed. "It's okay—you don't have to stroke my ego." She rested her hands on his tie-dye-clad shoulders and stood on tiptoe to look him in the eyes. As if it were a mantra, she said, "We created *Blood Moon* together. We've believed in it together. We've won Emmys for it together. And now we're starting season eight together."

"Because of you, Sarah."

She stepped back, trying to get a better read on him. Under his untamed shock of gray hair, he looked worried—even a little pale. "Where's this coming from?" she asked. "This is beyond your usual impostor syndrome."

Stan leaned against the wall, rubbing at his forehead. For a moment, all he did was look at the floor.

"Stanley!" Sarah put a hand on his arm. "You're worrying me."

He took her hand and looked at her, then looked away again. "I'm afraid to say it," he murmured. "You're not going to like it." He looked back at her, his famously green eyes pleading. "Promise me you won't hate me forever."

"Jesus, Stan!" Crossing her arms, she leaned against the wall next to him. "You're my oldest and dearest friend, for god's sake. Of course I'm not going to hate you forever. I might be mad at you, but I'll never hate you!" Becoming conscious of the weight on her shoulder, she dropped her bag to the floor.

"I don't want you to go away this weekend," Stan blurted.

"What are you talking about? I cleared this with you weeks ago."

"I just don't want you to go." He pushed himself away from the wall and turned to her with a stubborn expression.

"That's not enough and you know it." Sarah couldn't understand what was going on. This was so unlike him.

"Bubbala, Peter and I … well, we decided I needed to be honest with you about our feelings."

"Peter and you? What? You've been discussing me?" She grabbed her bag and threw the strap over her shoulder. "Stan, I love you, but I'm late. Kenny's picking me up and we're heading out of town for the weekend."

A chatter of voices came to them as four or five actors left the rehearsal room. Stan grasped Sarah by the elbow and pulled her through the door behind them into a women's restroom. After a moment's hesitation, he locked the door and leaned against it.

Sarah gaped at him. "What the hell?"

"All right," he said. He stood up straight and squared his shoulders. "Here it is. I don't want you going away with Kenny."

"Uh, why? Need I remind you we're going away to celebrate our one-month anniversary this weekend?"

"Darling, I don't trust him."

"You don't—" She couldn't finish the sentence.

"And neither does Peter. We're agreed on this. Don't go."

Pressure mounted in Sarah's head. If she listened to this much longer, she would blow like Vesuvius. Reaching deep for all the patience she could muster, she steadied her voice. "Let me get this straight: you came to my wedding. You drank the champagne and ate the fucking canapés. You had your pictures taken for the gossip rags. And only now I'm hearing you don't trust Kenny?"

His voice softened to a quiet rasp. "Sarella. Darling. I know you don't want to hear this, but no, I don't trust Kenny. He's charming and a real smooth operator. He's too smooth." Sarah scoffed, but Stan persisted. "Where did he disappear to on the morning of your wedding? He didn't have a good excuse for why he was gone so long, did he? And he couldn't come up with a single groomsman to stand up with him? I know he told you it was too far for anyone to travel. But they couldn't come to his *wedding*? And what do you know about Kenny's practice?"

"Stop!" Sarah held her hand up as if to ward off the torrent of words. "I've heard enough. My life is not our TV show. There really isn't danger lurking around every corner. I don't actually spend my days staking vampires or melting down silver to shoot werewolves. This weekend I will enjoy being in nature—off the grid—with my husband. On Monday, you and I will sit down and have a good, long discussion about this. Don't interrupt!" She held both hands up and turned her face away as if not seeing him would prevent her from hearing him. When he didn't speak, she turned back. "Stan, I love you. But I'm leaving now. Have a good weekend." She eased him out of the way, unlocked the door, and left the bathroom.

Outside the building, Kenny waited in the idling car. Sarah felt her heart flutter at the sight of him: those dazzling blue eyes, his golden hair.

"Hey, sweetheart," he said, leaning over to give her a kiss. "You're late. Rehearsal go long?"

"Sorry," Sarah replied as she reached behind herself for the seat belt. "Stan wanted to talk about something."

"Oh, yeah? What?" Kenny navigated the SUV into the stream of traffic. "He got some new camera angles for the next vampire staking scene?"

Sarah found herself not wanting to tell him what Stan had said. Why did she feel guilty for listening to Stan's accusations? She'd dismissed them, hadn't she? Or was she trying to protect Stan from Kenny's outrage? She'd like to think Kenny would laugh off Stan and Peter's concerns, but she suspected he'd be upset. She told herself she didn't want to start the weekend with an argument.

Before she could come up with an answer, Kenny said, "Oh, hey, babe. You didn't change. I thought you wanted to get into your hiking gear before you left."

"I didn't have time." Sarah patted the bag at her feet. "I've got everything here. I'll change at a rest stop. How far is it?"

"About six hours. We should get there around midnight with a stop or two." He glanced at her. "What about your phone? Did you remember to turn it off like you promised?"

Sarah laughed. "I'll do it when we get up there. What if we need directions or something?"

"Babe, no! This is our weekend. Everyone can leave you alone for forty-eight hours, right? Like we planned. Just us, you and me. Romantic. Besides, I already know how to get there."

"But—"

"Nope! No buts. Hand it over."

"Okay, okay!" She reached into her bag and pulled out her cell phone. "Just us." She held it up for Kenny to see as, with a flourish, she powered it down. "Just us all weekend, no interruptions."

"Hand it over."

"Oh, my god! You're a nut." Laughing, she gave him her phone.

"Thank you." He grinned. "It'll be like a honeymoon." He reached back and dropped the phone into his bag resting in the footwell.

Sarah turned to take in his perfect profile and tousled blond curls. "It feels more romantic already."

"Right?"

"So, tell me about your day."

Kenny merged smoothly onto the freeway, then glanced at Sarah. "Oh, you know, same old same old. Not very interesting. Tell me about rehearsal. That's way more fun!"

Sarah realized this was how their conversations about work always went. Instead of answering her questions, Kenny tossed the topic back to her. And she was always willing to go along with it because, truth be told, she found herself far more fascinated with her own experience than his.

Goddamn it, Stan! she thought. *You're right—I don't know a thing about my husband's practice.*

She reached out and gave Kenny's earlobe a squeeze. He glanced at her and smiled. She said, "I want to hear about your day. You never talk about work. Or your colleagues."

"Because it's not very interesting. I mean, I think it is, but most people would be bored to death by it. It doesn't lend itself to stories the way your work does, you know?"

"Right," Sarah drawled, tapping a finger to her lips. "That's why you never see a courtroom drama on TV. What was that series that died after the pilot? Oh, yeah. I think they called it *Law and Order* or something."

Kenny laughed. "Okay, smartass. Oh, hey, look!" He pointed toward the side of the road up ahead of them. "Goats!"

Sarah turned to look. She loved goats and always enjoyed any glimpse she could get of them. She watched the flock chomp at the roadside grasses until the car rounded a bend and the animals were out of sight.

"It's so good to get out of the city, isn't it?" Kenny said. "You're gonna love this little place, babe. It's in the middle of nowhere, off the grid. No one can bother us. It's you and me and the wonders of nature."

Sarah leaned over and kissed his shoulder. "'A loaf of bread, a jug of wine, and thou beside me in the wilderness.'"

"Is that a line from a play you did or something?"

"Or something."

It wasn't until miles later Sarah realized Kenny hadn't answered her question about his work. Had he purposely deflected or was he being sweet in pointing out the goats to her? *Goddamn it, Stan*, she thought again. *You're making me paranoid. I didn't have these thoughts before you put them in my brain.* But wasn't that Stan's warning? He and Peter saw something she didn't? Kenny was … what had he said? "Too smooth." *What does that even mean? Forget it*, she commanded herself. *You can talk with Stan on Monday, but until then, you're going to enjoy your weekend with your husband.*

It was dark by the time they reached the old logging road, and they had to creep forward to avoid breaking an axle in the ruts. At one point, a fox darted across their path, flicking in and out of the headlights and making Sarah gasp with excitement. "See, babe," Kenny said. "I said you were gonna love this place!"

The woods grew thicker as they went, and the road became increasingly overgrown with weeds. When they had to drive over a tiny sapling growing in the middle of the road, Sarah asked, "You found this place on Airbnb?"

Kenny laughed. "God, no!"

"Where then?"

By the light of the dashboard, she barely made out Kenny twirling an imaginary mustache, trying to be funny as he said, "Oh, I have my ways."

"No, really." Her worry irritated her. "Where did you find it?"

Kenny glanced at her, then returned his attention to the road. "Babe! It's okay. It belongs to a client. I mentioned I wanted to take you away somewhere you could get some rest, and he offered us this place."

"Oh. That's kind of him." Sarah scolded herself for letting Stan's suspicions get to her. Kenny was always thinking of her. He took better care of her than she did of herself.

The road opened up into a clearing and the headlights illuminated the corner of an old wooden cabin. The porch had pulled away from the outer wall and sagged drunkenly.

"Oh. My. God," she whispered. "Is that it?"

"It must be." Kenny sounded doubtful.

"This place is really … rustic. And kind of creepy."

"It's not what I pictured," he agreed before returning to his usual cheerful tone. "But no worries! I have all the supplies we need to make it perfect. Let's check it out."

Unless you have a very big hammer and some ten-penny nails, Sarah thought, *no way are you gonna make this place perfect.*

They dug headlamps from their bags and climbed out of the car. A chorus of treefrogs greeted them in surround sound. The air smelled of redwoods, late summer, and nature long undisturbed by any human being. Looking up, Sarah saw a rough circle of open sky with more stars than she thought existed in the universe. Kenny stood behind her, wrapping his arms around her waist, and she pressed her back against him. They gazed upward. "I'm so glad you're getting to see this," he murmured in her ear. He planted a kiss on top of her head then pulled away and flicked on his headlamp. "Let's take a look inside."

Although Sarah would have liked to admire the Milky Way for a bit longer, she reminded herself she had all of tomorrow night to look at it, too, and switching on her own headlamp, she followed Kenny to the door of the cabin.

The door wasn't locked and swung open with a hint of a groan from its hinges. A layer of dust, decades in the making, blanketed the floor and sparse furniture. It swirled in little eddies where the breeze from the open door reached it. The place reeked of mouse, and Sarah heard the scuffling of tiny feet in the corners and even overhead as the light from their headlamps alarmed the cabin's denizens. She stood in the center of the cabin and turned in a slow circle, taking in the single room. Rodent nests in one corner, a dangerous-looking wood stove in another next to a block of derelict kitchen cabinets, a rusty ax jammed in between, and an old wooden table with two rickety chairs. Windows, dust clinging to their panes, reflected the shine of the two headlamps.

"Well," Sarah said, trying to look on the bright side, "at least the spiders are artful interior decorators."

"Oh, babe!" Kenny sprang into action. "Hang on. I brought some candles. I'll go grab them." He rushed out of the cabin and was back within seconds, carrying a candle, a box of matches, a bottle of scotch, and two plastic cups. He set the items on the table and lit the candle. As the light spread, Sarah noticed an old saucer that looked like it had been used before as a candleholder, given the wax remnants coating it. Kenny held it over the flame until the wax softened, then pressed the new candle into it. He replaced the saucer on the table so it was centered in the window and stepped back to admire the effect. "Not bad, huh?" he said, turning to Sarah with a grin.

"Kenny—" Sarah began. But she wasn't sure what to say after that. How could he think anything here was "not bad"? She wanted to label everything horrific. And he was standing there looking at her with a goofy, expectant grin on his beautiful face, and she didn't know what to say. "Sweetheart," she started again, "I–I don't think I can sleep here."

Kenny's face fell. "Sarah! Why not?"

"Well, for one thing, there's no bed. And there are mice everywhere. And the place is filthy. And it's eerie. Like, sinister. I swear somebody died in here. The whole place feels wrong."

He looked at her with a stricken expression that wavered until he smiled and erupted into laughter. "Babe, I can't do this to you. I had you going though, right? I'm sorry. I know … it's totally awful."

Sarah was overcome with relief. She reached Kenny in two steps and wrapped her arms around him, burying her face in the crook of his neck. "You jerk!" His neck muffled her words, but he caught the gist because he laughed again.

"I'll tell you what," he said, leaning back to look at her but not removing his arms from her waist. "I got this fancy bottle of scotch to celebrate. Let's have a snort—then we'll go make up a bed in the car for tonight. In the morning, we can look for somewhere else to stay."

"What will you tell your client, though? Won't he be offended we didn't stay?"

"I doubt it." Kenny opened the bottle of scotch and poured a couple of ample drinks. "I'll just tell him we were freaked out by his cabin. Somebody obviously died in it."

"Don't tell him that!" Sarah laughed. "He'll fire you."

Kenny handed her a plastic cup and held his own up for a toast. "Here's to a month of wedded bliss," he said. They touched their cups together. "Down the hatch, babe. You deserve it. Relax and leave the rest to me." Sarah downed her drink in two swallows, feeling a small twinge of guilt at chugging such expensive scotch. She'd sip the next glass, she told herself. Already she felt the warmth of the alcohol spread through her.

Before he could take a sip of his, Kenny snapped his fingers and set his cup on the table. "I totally forgot. You sit down, babe. I'll be right back." He left the cabin again, and Sarah regarded the two chairs with distrust. She tested one, pressing down on the back and wiggling it. It seemed reliable enough. She lowered herself into it, expecting the old wood to shatter, but it held her weight. She poured herself another couple fingers of scotch and leaned back with a sigh. This time, she took a sip and let the liquid spread on her tongue: the smoky, peaty smoothness of it transported her to the first time she'd met Kenny.

She'd been slumped at the bar in the Algonquin Hotel sipping a Hemingway Daiquiri, aware of looking like a ridiculous cliché of an artsy-fartsy actress. But it had been a long day of frustrating and fruitless rehearsals, and she was past caring what anyone thought. There was no one in the bar but an elderly couple tucked away in a dark corner, so her annoyance flared when someone took the stool next to her. She turned to say something snippy about there being plenty of other stools but had gotten no further than turning. She took one look at the man sitting next to her, and the desire to get rid of him evaporated. If she were going to make a film about a superhero whose power was to stop traffic with his looks, this would be the guy she'd cast: square jaw, his golden hair perfectly coiffed. He turned to her, and—dim bar light or not—she saw his eyes were a shocking shade of blue.

"Tough day?" he'd asked. "Daiquiris aren't gonna cut it. You need a shot of scotch." He had raised his hand for the bartender, and she had let him.

Sarah smiled at the memory. The smile melted into a frown. *Wow, this scotch is hitting me hard.* She felt woozy, far more so than she would have expected, even from the stiff drink Kenny had poured. It had been a while since she'd eaten anything. Maybe that was it. She tried to lift her arm to the table but her muscles wouldn't obey. She ended up knocking her cup over, spilling the contents. "Shi–" she mumbled. She watched the pool of spilled scotch form a tiny river to the edge of the table and drip onto the floor, creating a patch of dust-mud by her chair leg.

Kenny stood in front of her, looking at her with an unreadable expression. She was afraid she'd disappointed him, getting drunk on two drinks. She hadn't meant to. She tried to say, "Kenny, I don't feel good," but her lips were numb and her tongue wouldn't form the right sounds. She couldn't hold her head up any longer, and her chin fell to her chest.

Kenny squatted so she could see his face and tenderly took her hand. Why wasn't he teasing her for being such a lightweight? Why wasn't he asking her if she was okay?

Out of nowhere, Stanley's face appeared before her. His words, "I don't trust him." In a blinding, panic-inducing flash, she considered the inconceivable. She tried to pull her hand out of Kenny's grasp, but her arm wouldn't move. None of her muscles obeyed her frantic commands. *Stand! Run! Get away!* She was breathing hard, sweat prickling her forehead and dripping down her back.

Kenny regarded her with pity. "Try to relax, babe. The guy said it wouldn't hurt. I told him I didn't want you to suffer." He sounded like he thought this was noble.

This has to be a nightmare. Sarah willed herself to wake up. In a second, she'd open her eyes and see she had fallen asleep in the car and was having an appalling nightmare, brought on by her conversation with Stan.

Oh, god, Stan. Would he ever know what happened to her? *Wake up, Sarah. Wake up!*

Kenny's voice broke into her thoughts. "Knowing you, you're wondering why. You always want to know why people do things. Occupational hazard, I guess. People don't always have a well-defined why, babe. They just do things. I mean, not me. I have a why. I'm not a savage who murders his wife for no reason. But that's not important. Not right now." He stroked her hair and tucked a lock behind her ear. "That piece never stays in your hair tie, does it?" He smiled at her, dipping his head to look up into her eyes. "I guess it'll never get long enough now. Though they say hair keeps growing after you die. I don't know. Animals might get to you before it has much chance to grow, I suppose."

Sarah's mind revolted at Kenny's words. There was no way the beautiful man she had met at the Algonquin, with whom she'd fallen in love, woken up to each morning, there was no way he—

"So today was nice, right? You got to see goats and a fox. And the gorgeous stars. I'm glad you got to see that before you die. The important thing right now is not to be scared, Sarah. Here's what the guy told me. He said your muscles will stop working, so he seems to be right about that. First it'll be all the muscles you have control over—then it'll be your heart and breathing. Don't worry! He promised the decrease of oxygen to your brain will make you pass out before you feel like you're suffocating, so it'll seem to you like going to sleep. I'll stay with you the whole time. You know, until I'm sure your heart has stopped."

Sarah thought of Stan and Peter. They would know Kenny had done something. They'd pursue it. She was sure they would. *I'll never see them again*, she thought. A deep sense of loss swept through her, and her eyes prickled with tears.

"Aw, babe! Don't cry. It'll all be okay. It'll be over soon, I promise. I'm here."

Sarah didn't want to share her last moments with Kenny. She wanted to be with Stan. She allowed her heavy eyelids to close, to block out the sight of his blue eyes, his artfully tousled blond hair.

They nauseated her now. She thought of Stan lifting her and spinning her around after they found out their series was picked up. She pictured sitting with him, she and Peter squeezing his hands as they waited for his name to be called at last year's Emmys, the eruption of cheers all around when it was—his speech naming her the most dedicated, most inspiring actress he'd worked with. Things were getting dark around the edges. She thought of Peter's birthday party the year Stan had given him a kitten. It was hard to focus in the darkness, but she clung to her images of Stan. The year he'd made oyster stew for Christmas dinner and no one would eat it. The day she'd first auditioned for him, and they'd ended up talking until sunrise. Although she couldn't think anymore, she felt Stan there with her. He wrapped his arms around her and held her close. "Bubbala, it'll be okay." And when he said it, she believed him.

Kenny stayed until he was sure she was dead. He left her in the chair, her torso and head sprawled across the table. He picked up the bottle of poisoned scotch, the glasses, their headlamps, and scanned the room. Satisfied he'd forgotten nothing, he blew out the candle but left it in the window. The door groaned, stirring the dust as he closed it behind him and walked to the car. The dome light came on, illuminating his emotionless face. He climbed in, buckled up, and started the car. The dome light went out. He executed a three-point turn and headed down the logging road.

Deep in the shadows of the cabin, the ghost of Sarah Sommers watched him go.

This isn't real.

This isn't real.

This isn't real.

The words weren't thoughts—they were her substance. They created her. There was nothing else.

This isn't real.

She recognized she was wrong when she watched a rat devour the index finger of what had once been her left hand.

It was *very* real.

All right, then, why? Why did Kenny kill me?

Why did he kill me?

Why did he—?

Time passed. Was it days? Weeks? Years? Sarah had no way of knowing how long she remained fixed in this corner of the cabin, immobile, obsessed with the question of ...

Why did my husband murder me?

The only change that interrupted this thought was the arrival of one carrion eater or another to cart away a piece of her remains. Then there was nothing left.

At last, a new idea wormed its way into her awareness.

I will find him and I will make him pay.

For the first time in a long while—so long a tree had fallen, punching a hole in the roof, and been colonized by devouring fungus— the ghost of Sarah Sommers moved. She moved toward the door.

Rage built in her. She turned the handle and yanked the door open then took a step forward.

And couldn't cross the threshold.

She saw moonlight illuminating the forest floor. She heard crickets and tree frogs. An unseen force pressed against her chest. She couldn't step from the cabin into the overgrown clearing beyond it.

Is this all a ghost is: a being of feelings and obsessions, unable to act on them? Why did I stay in this world if I can't do anything about Kenny?

She swung the door closed before turning back to the room that marked the boundaries of her existence. *I won't give up,* she decided, *until I figure out how to make him pay.*

She began to think. First she thought about revenge, but as time passed, she thought about her life, her regrets, her joys. She burned with loneliness. She awakened to the rhythm of the seasons, the animals around her, the rain and the sun. Finally, she simply experienced what there was to experience.

Until one night, a long forgotten candle flared into life.

Chapter One

The ward is dark when I walk into it for the first time. The smell of antiseptic and vomit permeates the children's floor just as it does the adult oncology ward. I peek into each room, searching for my next traveler. Most of the children are asleep. A few watch television, which I have no reason to complain about.

A slight, pale child draws my attention, and I stop at her door. She huddles in her bed, unmoving, a ragged stuffed dog under one arm. As I watch, a man slips past me into the room. He bends over her and brushes the dark hair from her face. Her father, here to watch over her. She is very, very sick, but she'll live. I know these things.

I move past other rooms. Here, the child is too young to understand my story. In the next, there won't be enough time to tell it.

Halfway down the hall, I come to a room where a boy, alone, sits up in bed reading *The Martian*. A story of survival against the odds. He'll need that.

I'm guessing he's sixteen or seventeen years old. I stand in the doorway and watch his face. His thoughts and emotions dance across it like wisps of fog across the moon, and he laughs with just his breath.

On the whiteboard next to the door I find his name: Finn Swithun. A name with character.

Two bags hang from the IV pole wedged between the bed and the nightstand, tubes dangling like jellyfish tentacles reaching for the inside of the boy's right arm. The lower half of his body is encased in a fuzzy blanket decorated with baseball team logos, so it's hard to be sure, but he appears tall. Tall and lanky. A wild mop of sandy brown hair tickles the collar of his pajama top. It's the kind of hair that would look every bit as wild two minutes after he brushed it.

This is a boy who would live his life if he could. He'll need my help.

I rap on the doorjamb.

"Come in." It's a pleasant voice, warm.

"Hi, Finn." I swing the door closed, muting the beeps and murmured conversations from the nurses' station, and walk to his bed. "How are you tonight?"

"Not too bad." He looks at me, eyebrows raised in question.

I nod at his book. "You enjoy a good story?"

He glances at it, then back at me. "Yeah."

His eyes tell me he's wondering why I'm here after visiting hours, a woman in street clothes, not scrubs. I keep my tone neutral. "Would you be interested in hearing a story?"

"Like an audiobook? Those are okay."

"Not a recording. I'm a storyteller. If you'd like, I could come here every evening, to your room, and tell you one."

He narrows his eyes. "Is this a, like, a service of the hospital?"

I wag my head back and forth. "I'm freelance, but the hospital's okay with it." He doesn't need to know the whole truth; he'll figure it out at some point.

"What's the story about?" He crisscrosses his legs under the covers and leans forward.

"I don't want to give you too many spoilers. Stories like to be told in their own way. "

"How often would you come?"

"Every night."

"Every night? Like, when? After visiting hours?" Anyone who's been in a hospital for any length of time knows the hours after visitors leave are the longest.

"That's right."

"The hospital would let you?"

"I've done it before. It won't be a problem."

I can see him checking for downsides, a cautious boy. He looks up at me and says, "That sounds good. Yeah. Thanks."

"All right." For some reason, I feel relieved. Am I attached to this boy already? "Do you want to start now?"

"Right now?" He smiles and his tired face transforms; he looks younger. "Okay." He gestures to the chair tucked into a corner beside his bed. "Do you want to sit down?"

I settle in. "Right," I say. "Here we go." I clear my throat.

As far as anyone knew, the cabin in the woods had been abandoned for years. In fact, it had been so long since anyone had gone there by accident, let alone on purpose, most people had forgotten it was there. At one point, it had stood in the middle of a clearing, but nature was taking the clearing back. Saplings had crept in to sprout right next to the dilapidated porch. Bugs, rodents, and birds made nests in the roof and inside the cabin's single room.

Despite what people thought—if they thought about the place at all—it wasn't only animals and dust that inhabited the cabin. Another being existed there, trapped and alone.

Finn interrupts. "Is this a ghost story?"

"In part."

"Huh."

"Do you have a problem with that?"

"No." But he sounds surprisingly tentative. The result of years of fragility, maybe. "How did the ghost die?"

"Her husband killed her."

His eyes widen in shock. "Really?"

"Really."

He pinches his lip, wiggling it back and forth, and frowns. "Why did he kill her?"

"That'll come out in the story. We can't get ahead of ourselves." As much as I prefer to ease his mind, he needs to experience whatever he feels as the story unfolds.

"And the story likes to be told in its own way."

I smile, happy he heard me say that. "Yeah. It does."

"But now she's"—he hooks two fingers in the air—"a ghost."

"That's right. Ready to go on?"

He says, "Give me a sec to get comfy" and scrunches down in bed, pulling the blanket around his shoulders, a futile defense against the spirit world. "Go ahead."

Another being existed there, trapped and alone. She had lost count of how many years it had been. She had lost track of time altogether, measuring the passage of days and months by the angle of the sun or the color of leaves.

"Sounds lonely," Finn interjects.

"Yes. Horribly lonely."

One night, a candle flared to life. In all the time the being had been in the cabin, the candle had stood by the window, useless in its dusty holder. Now, it flickered, grasping at life, making the cabin smell like burning dust and casting a circle of light across the rickety table it stood on. Shocked, she withdrew into the deeper shadows where the light couldn't reach.

At the same moment the candle flared, the chill of a deep winter's night swept through the cabin. A man appeared in the center of the room, a silver-gray cat tucked in the crook of his arm. When he set it on the floor of the cabin, it slunk into the shadows. The man moved to the table, as if by habit, and sank into one of the peeling wooden chairs, its splintered back cracking dangerously. He let out a groan, almost too low to hear.

He was tall, with an athletic build, and wore an expensive-looking pair of jeans and an elegant cashmere pullover. As if he had a headache, he brushed his dark hair from his face. For a second, the being in the cabin could see his face. Early thirties, prominent cheekbones, thick brows lurking over vivid brown eyes, a sharp nose. He looked like an exhausted eagle.

A scuffling sound drew his attention to a dark corner of the cabin. It was followed by a thump and a high-pitched squeal that cut off with an unmistakable finality. The man stared into the shadows until the cat emerged, a small rat—held securely by the middle—dangled from its mouth. The cat padded to the table and leapt, seeming to float to the tabletop. He positioned himself in front of the man, and the two regarded each other. The cat blinked slowly before leaning forward and dropping the rat in front of him. The man stroked the cat's chin. "Thanks," he said, then picked up the rat and popped it, whole, into his mouth. A crunch, some soft slurping, and the man spat the corpse into his hand and laid it in front of the cat. It had been transformed into a bloodless sack of meat, bones, and fur.

"Cool!" Finn laughs.

"Sh. Listen."

The cat reclaimed its prey and carried it back to the shadows to enjoy in private. For some minutes, delicate crunching and gnawing sounds came from the corner.

The man put his head in his hands and stared at the tabletop. The curve of his back, the slump of his shoulders, the emptiness in his eyes broadcast his misery, though some color had come into his cheeks since he had drunk the rat's blood. The cat returned and resumed its seat on the table, giving itself a thorough post-dinner bath. At last, the man came to a decision. He nodded and tapped the tabletop, ready for action. "All right, Luna—"

Finn sits up. "Luna? I got the impression the cat was male."

"He was."

He scrunches his face. "Isn't Luna the moon goddess, though?"

"Yeah. I'm impressed you know that."

"I've read a lot of mythology." He studies the San Francisco Giants logo on his blanket. "One of my teachers had a female cat named Spencer."

"All of this man's cats were named Luna."

Finn snorts. "All of them? Not very original."

So judgmental, teenagers. But he's not wrong. It's too early in the process, but I test his willingness to believe. If I can't get him to believe, I can't help him. "This was his twenty-second Luna."

"That's a lot of cats. How'd he call one without calling all of them?"

"Each cat was an only cat."

He's silent for a moment, doing the math. "And he had twenty-two of them?"

"Yes."

He gives me a thin-lipped smile and raises an eyebrow. "Mm-hmm.

First ghosts, now a guy who's hundreds of years old. I'm kinda old for fairytales."

It's hard not to laugh at his sassiness. "Oh, this isn't a fairytale. It's one hundred percent fact."

"Sure." He's humoring me.

"Well, then, think of it as an allegory." For now, I add to myself.

He shrugs. "Anyway, twenty-second cat."

I have time to earn his belief.

At last, the man reached a decision. He nodded and tapped the tabletop, ready for action. "All right, Luna. We'll start over. Somewhere it will take him longer to find us." He picked up the cat, tucked him in the crook of his arm, and blew out the candle, plunging the cabin into darkness.

He was gone.

The being that inhabited the cabin separated from the shadows and walked into a shaft of dusty moonlight that had found its way through a hole in the roof. She stood thinking, hands in the pockets of her hiker's shorts.

Why didn't I say something to him? she wondered. *Let him know I was here?*

Other than the forest animals who lived around, and sometimes in, the cabin, the man and the cat were the first beings she'd seen in many seasons. She went to the table and laid her hands on the spot where the cat had been sitting. A slight warmth remained. She slid her hand to where the man had rested his arms. As she expected, against her more rational judgment, she felt no warmth there.

Well, why not? If I can exist, why can't he? "There are more things in heaven and earth, Horatio." How right he was, the Bard.

She couldn't help wondering if it was lonely, being a vampire. Or maybe she was projecting.

The sun rose, dispelling the shadows; daylight filtered through the forest trees, and the cabin welcomed the shadows back as the sun made its way behind the mountains. The whole cycle had happened so many times she'd lost count. She had watched as disoriented bugs trapped themselves behind the window panes, battered themselves against the glass for hours, and died with their salvation in sight but unreachable. She had seen deer and their fawns come to nibble at wildflowers, and observed those fawns grow into mothers, witnessed their fawns have fawns.

She welcomed the shadows. They were her friends, her protectors. They comforted her when memories and regrets pummeled her over the long days and nights.

Stanley.

She remembered.

"Sarella," he'd said to her. They hadn't seen each other for a couple of weeks, a long gap for them. She'd been filming on location and just gotten back to LA when Stanley called her to demand she meet him that afternoon, no excuse.

"Sarella," he'd said, "I've met him." He beamed; she'd never seen him look happier.

"Who?" she'd asked, like an idiot.

Him!" Stanley crowed. "Mr. Right."

"That's terrific!" she said, making the right noises, but she wasn't happy for him. All she could think was, *Where does this leave me?*

She'd always been able to keep herself from sounding like an asshole, but she was an asshole at heart. Now, she cringed at the memory. She'd give anything to see Stanley and tell him how happy she was he'd found Peter, how much she loved them both. And she wished she'd listened to them.

Remembering an afternoon when Stan had the flu and she tried to make him chicken soup, she snickered to herself, thinking of how he'd told her, with surprising kindness under the circumstances, "It was almost but not quite entirely inedible." She was shaken from her reverie by a sudden icy chill, and the candle in the window flared to life again. Immediately, she concealed herself in the shadows, as she had done before.

The same man, for lack of a better word, stood in the center of the cabin again. Except for his clothes, which were now dirty and torn, his appearance hadn't changed. This time he held a small ginger cat in the crook of his arm. He set it down and lowered himself into one of the rickety chairs. Through a tear in his shirt, she glimpsed an open wound, then watched spellbound as the wound drew itself together and healed. He looked exhausted, as he had before, but now, the slump of his shoulders, the way he hung his head and let his arms droop, spoke to a sense of defeat. Of despair and hopelessness.

While the man stared into the candle flame, the cat inspected the cabin. He was young, no more than a year or two old, and had a flair for drama, surprising himself with dead moths and leaping at the flickering shadows brought to life by the candle.

Without warning, the cat tensed. His green eyes, already large, expanded to the size of quarters. Whiskers bristling, ears forward, he arched his back and poofed his thick fur like a Halloween decoration. It would have been funny, given his size, except for the weird, guttural, rising growl that filled the cabin. The cat stared into the shadows, straight at the being hiding there.

The man twisted in his chair. On high alert, he peered into the darkness, but even his eyes could see nothing. The cat paused his wild growling to hiss, then picked it up again, running the octaves from low to high.

"Who's there?" It came out as a growl not much different than the cat's. The man stood, tipping the chair off its legs so it clattered to the floor. "Come out!" he ordered, like someone who expected to be obeyed.

The being in the shadows felt something whisper around her as if his command carried power. She hesitated. She didn't fear this vampire—assuming that was what he was. What she feared was she might move into the candlelight and he wouldn't see her. If she stepped out of the shadows and was still alone in the stifling pain of grinding loneliness, how would she bear knowing she would never again be seen? Because if someone like him wasn't able to perceive her, no one could.

An endless future of desolate sunsets rose before her, overwhelming her fear. She drew herself from the deepest shadows into the half-light.

The little cat hissed.

A flicker of apprehension crossed the man's face, but the being couldn't tell if he'd perceived her or if he was relying on his companion's warning. "Is it you?" he whispered, taking a step backward.

It was a question she didn't know how to answer. Yes, of course it was her. But no, she wasn't who he expected. She decided simple was the way to go. She reached deep inside herself to find her voice, unused for so long she wondered if it would be there. "No," she whispered.

She wasn't sure he heard her until he said, "Who then?"

Gathering her courage, she took a tentative step into the candlelight, watching his expression. His squint of tension changed into open-eyed curiosity as he looked straight at her.

Whatever else happens tonight, she thought, *I'm not unseen anymore.*

A new emotion flowed through her. What should she call it? Relief? That seemed too mild. Gratitude, without a doubt. She looked down at the cat and smiled. He had stopped his operatics and was licking one of his back paws, as if all along, he had known there was nothing to fret about.

"Hello. Are you Luna's successor?" she whispered. The man started, but the cat just paused in its licking to gaze at her and blink, then resumed his bath.

"You were here the last time I visited the cabin." He wasn't asking.

Once again, she took in the man's movie star good looks: wavy hair, high cheekbones, strong jaw. She guessed he expected her to respond, but she had no idea what to say. She was out of the habit of chit-chat.

"Who are you?" he asked.

The questions this man—no, this *vampire*—asked seemed simple, but again, she didn't know how to answer. She used to be Sarah, creative, fun-loving. Self-absorbed. So slow on the uptake it was embarrassing. But this description no longer fit her. At least, she hoped it didn't. She glanced around the room looking for inspiration. "You can call me Senka," she said.

The vampire tipped his head to the side, appraising her, she thought. "You've spent time in Serbia?"

"Yes."

Some decision made, he bowed very slightly and said, "Senka. My name is Silas." He gestured to the cat. "This is Luna."

"Luna? The same name?"

"Luna the twenty-third."

She considered the implications of the name. "I see." She moved into the room and sat at the table, keeping her eyes on him for the sheer pleasure of seeing someone else. "What are you doing here?"

"I might ask you the same question." He stuck his hands into his pants pockets. The gesture made him look so young, despite the obvious truth, that she had to stop herself from smiling, afraid of offending him.

"As far as I know, I have to be here," she said. Silas righted the chair he'd knocked over earlier and sat across the table from her. She savored the homey feeling of sharing a table with someone, but watching him stare morosely at the candle, she was touched. "You're sad when you come here, aren't you?" He lifted his head and met her eyes. *He's not sure he can trust me*, she thought.

Senka recognized her sympathy for this being was tinged with some distaste, like looking at an injured spider. She chastised herself; the feeling came from old stories about his kind. "You know," she said, leaning forward, arms on the table, "I used to wonder if beings like you were real. And if the books and movies and television shows had gotten it right."

As he smiled, his whole face changed from rugged beauty to the promise of wit and intelligence. "Mostly they do not, but every now and then it seems an author has met one of us. To be honest, I am not familiar with all the stories."

"Yeah. There are a lot of them." Senka offered him a half smile. "So what's going on? Can I help you somehow?"

Silas turned his eyes away from her and stared at the candle flame again. "It's a bit complicated."

"I'm finally realizing existence often is, you know?"

He nodded. "I do."

"I'm willing to listen to why yours is, if you'd like to tell me."

He looked at her again and nodded once more, as if acknowledging a decision to himself. Luna jumped onto the table and sat, regarding them both, eyes round. They were a trio, bearing witness to one another's existence in the world.

Silas spoke, still tentative. "I am in trouble with … my Maker." He paused, watching her. "Do you understand what I mean by the term?"

The idea of a Maker wasn't foreign to Senka, but how a vampire and a ghost were made had to be very different. She said, "So the writers had the Making part right, anyway."

"Some of them," Silas acknowledged. He grunted. "To a certain degree."

"How does that …" She waved her hand in the air, hoping to include the Making, the transformation, all of it. "How does that all work?"

"It is complicated," Silas said again. "Well, the Making isn't," he corrected himself. "The relationship between a vampire and the vampire's Maker can be complex. Mine is possibly a little more so than most."

"How?"

Silas glanced up at her, but retreated to his study of the candle. "He … disapproves of me. He'd like to terminate me."

In his brown eyes, she saw both pain and anger. She couldn't tell which one was winning. "Do you mean he wants to kill you?"

He waggled his head back and forth to suggest both yes and no. "We use the term *end*. In a sense, we cannot be killed, as we are already dead, though animate."

"Undead."

"As the writers designate us."

"And so you're hiding out here?" Senka gestured to the cabin.

"I'm *always* hiding from him. He is always searching for me. I come here if he gets too close."

"Judging by the state of your clothes, he got really close."

"This was not him." He gestured at his garments. "It was one of his servants."

If a minion could do so much damage, the Maker must be frighteningly powerful, she thought. "Why did you come back here? How did you find this place?"

"I was made here." Silas shrugged, then added, "Well, nearby, to be accurate."

Senka was surprised. "You were made in California? In this little cabin in the middle of nowhere?"

He waggled his head again. "There has been some kind of habitation in this spot since humans first came here. Once, I lived here, though our little hut rotted generations ago." He lapsed into silence, his expression reflecting unpleasant memories.

Senka prompted, "So you come here when your Maker has tracked you down … in the world?"

He looked up at her again, unhappy. "A Maker may not return to the place of Making without invitation. Luna and I are safe. We can take a moment to regroup before we start again. Though each time, I lose everything I have built."

"If he's just going to keep hunting you," Senka said, looking at Luna, "why don't you get to him first?"

Silas laughed, but it wasn't a happy sound. "That I am not able to do."

"Why?" An idea struck her. "Do you care for him?"

Silas sat back in his chair with a look of disgust. "I despise him! No, we are literally incapable of ending our Makers. In the same way he cannot follow me here, I cannot terminate his existence. Even if it weren't true for our kind, I am not convinced I would have the strength to beat him. He is enormously powerful."

"So you keep running, lying low for as long as you can." It seemed like a miserable existence. "Why don't you stay here?" Senka asked, trying not to be transparent in her hope. "You would be safe."

For all her effort, Silas seemed to see through her. He smiled, looking apologetic. "This is the longest I have remained in this place since I left after my Making." He glanced around. "Though the structure has changed, there are too many painful memories. I cannot stay."

"I get it." Senka shrugged, trying to sound like she didn't care.

Luna's deep growl jerked them from their conversation. His ears lay flat against his head and his whiskers were swept back tightly to his face. He peered into the darkness, his growl low and menacing. Senka felt a crawling tingle at the back of her neck. Silas leapt from his chair, scanning the dark recesses of the cabin. Senka stood too. "What is it?" she asked him. Not sure, he shook his head, but any response he might have made was cut off as Luna's growl mutated into a piercing shriek. Silas pressed against the table and put a protective hand on the cat's back. "He has found us," he said in horror.

Senka felt no new presence. Until the corner of her eye caught a blacker shade in the shadow under the cabin's broken roof. It slipped through the gaps of splintered shingles, coiling and twisting, a gray slime flowing toward the center of the room. She melted back into the darkest of the shadows. Luna, on the table, his back arched, uttered a long, low growl.

Outside, the world had gone quiet. The peeping of night frogs, ever present beyond the cabin's walls, had stopped, as if the frogs were trying not to draw attention.

The slime flowed on, swirling, twisting, forming itself into the figure of a man as the stench of fetid swamps flowed from it. Although it bore a human figure—head, torso, two arms, two legs—it blurred as it moved, leaving behind silken strands of darkness that stretched until the creature reabsorbed them.

Dragging gloom behind it, the creature raised its hand. Senka cried out a warning, but Silas stood immobile, paralyzed by fear or despair. Before he could raise an arm to block the blow, the creature's obsidian-sharp talons slashed his face.

The shattering blow lifted Silas off his feet and slammed him against the far wall. With a crack that reverberated throughout the cabin, his head dented the wooden boards and he crumpled to the floor. Luna yowled in fury, but when Silas gestured to him, the yowl cut off as if he had flipped a switch.

The creature looked down at Silas with sneering disgust. "You are useless," it said in a voice like the chittering of dry reeds. It turned its back on Silas and seeped away from him. "Fight," it commanded.

Silas stepped forward, snarling, eyes fixed on the creature. As he brought his fists up to strike, the creature twisted and kicked him hard in the ribs. Silas crashed into the opposite wall, his arm flying out and shattering the window. Luna leapt from the table and streaked to Silas's side as glass rained around them. A ragged triangle of window pane jutted from the back of Silas's hand, and blood spattered the wall and floor. Senka watched, horrified, as Silas pulled the chunk of glass from his hand. He whispered to Luna, and the cat slunk into the shadows to stand by Senka.

Silas hauled himself to his feet, squared his shoulders, and faced the creature. "Why have you come?" His voice sounded stronger than Senka expected. The creature laughed with the squelching sound of a boot pulled from the mud. It was on Silas in a blink, but this time he was prepared. He jumped, his head skimming the underside of the roof, and threw a punch like a thunderbolt. It should have been devastating; instead Silas's fist sank into greasy slime. With another laugh, the creature plucked him from the air and hurled him with such force, half of one wall gave way and Silas tumbled to the ground outside the cabin. A gash across his forehead exposed the bone beneath. Gaping edges of skin strained toward one another, but the more blood he lost, the more his wounds struggled to heal.

He dragged himself upright once more, but Senka was afraid she saw resignation in his posture. He climbed back into the cabin. "Are you bloodying me to amuse yourself?" he shouted at the creature. "Get it over with."

Senka wanted him to keep fighting. How could he value his existence so little he would accept its end? No matter how long he had been on the earth, he must have something worth fighting for.

The creature sneered. "The moment of your ending is near." It was a simple statement of fact; his scritching voice held no threat.

One huge paw grasped Silas's head, piercing his skull with its talons. The other hooked the meat of Silas's leg. It lifted him high overhead and hurled him to the floor. Thick floorboards splintered with a shriek of rending wood, the shards impaling Silas's arms and legs.

In the shadows, Senka wondered, *If a piece penetrates his heart, is that his end?* She had no time to wonder further.

The table, half its legs no longer supported, tipped sideways, sending the candle holder sliding down the tabletop to the floor. The candle dislodged and rolled into the corner. The flame found years of tinder-dry rats' nests and ignited them in a crackling rush. A vivid orange snake climbed the old walls, reached the roof, and spread into a raging fire. The creature yanked Silas free of the shattered floor, scattering broken boards, and flung him toward the flames. Silas hit the burning wall and tumbled through it, scorching his shoulder and one side of his face. The creature followed him, grabbed a fistful of Silas's long hair, and heaved him back into the cabin.

"This has gone on long enough," Senka muttered. Luna looked up at her, wide eyes reflecting the leaping flames. "Help me out here," she said, and turned her back on the chaos. Luna hesitated for a moment, watching his partner, then followed.

Silas lay on his back, exhausted. His wounds were no longer healing. He looked up at the creature towering over him. "Have done with it!" he shouted over the roaring flames. "End me!"

The creature opened its lipless mouth, razor-sharp triangular teeth arrayed in three curving rows. It lowered its head.

Silas turned away, waiting to feel a talon pierce his heart.

A thump made him open his eyes. He couldn't understand what he was seeing. The creature's head lay on the floor a foot away from him. Minus its body. Silas raised himself for a better vantage. He wasn't wrong. The head lay oozing its contents onto the broken floor. Not far from it, the creature's body evaporated to oily smoke and disappeared into the raging fire. Silas searched for the cause of this development. His eyes landed on Senka, Luna standing beside her, his tail raised like a flag of defiance.

Senka stood looking down at Silas, a rusty iron-headed ax gripped in her hands. She raised it over her head and slammed it down. With a nauseating squelching sound, the blade cleaved the creature's skull and embedded itself in the floorboard.

She hadn't been sure she could heft the ax; she'd never tried to hold onto a solid object before. As she extended her hand to Silas, she realized she hadn't felt another being in well over a decade. That she could touch his hand, cool and solid, thrilled her.

She helped him to his feet, and they stumbled out of the cabin.

Senka, Silas, and Luna watched as the cabin burned to the ground. When it was reduced to a pile of flaming planks, Senka asked, "Why did the ax work? You know, to chop its head off?"

"It is iron. Most of these creatures cannot bear iron." He looked at her, his brows knit. "You didn't know if you would succeed, yet you swung the ax?"

"I had to do something." This was a new feeling for her, and she liked it.

For several minutes, they watched the flames in silence until Senka turned to Silas. "So are you safe now?" She saw only confusion on his face. "Your Maker is dead, right? You don't have to hide anymore."

Silas turned a quizzical eye on her. "That was not my Maker," he said. "I told you, my Maker cannot follow me here. That was an emissary, sent to end me and return to my Maker with my head."

That powerful creature wasn't his Maker? "Then why didn't you keep fighting?" she asked with a touch of anger.

Silas retreated from her gaze, turning his eyes to the dying fire. "What would have been the point? I could not defeat it."

"The point?" she exclaimed. "The point would be to stand up for yourself. The point would be to go on." She was flummoxed by the need to explain. "I don't get you."

"That is because"—he sighed—"you are not me."

She looked at him for a long while, then said, "So your Maker is still out there, hunting you?"

"Oh, yes."

"What are you going to do now?"

"Start again," he said with resignation.

"Alone?" She tried to keep her tone neutral but suspected she had failed.

He turned to her, eyebrows raised. "Would—" he started, then stopped. He tried again. "Would you come with me?"

She looked around the clearing, at the smoldering remains of the cabin. "To be honest, I don't know if I can. In my own way, I was made here too. This is my first time outside the cabin since then."

"But now there is no cabin," he reminded her.

"Yeah. So maybe I'm free to go somewhere else. And you know," she added, "now that I've saved your … existence, I'm curious to see what you do with it."

"What if I choose to do nothing with it?"

Her mouth became a grim, tight line. "Oh, you'll do something. You owe me now."

Silas started to respond, but something in him hesitated. She wondered if he'd had the same thought she did: if they were able to leave together, existence might not be as lonely.

Silas picked up Luna and offered his other arm to Senka. "Shall we see what happens?" he asked.

She gave one last look around the clearing. "Oh, please, let me go," she whispered, not sure who she was talking to. "Let me not be left behind." She held onto the arm Silas offered and closed her eyes in wild hope.

At some point in the storytelling, Finn lay down again. Now, his eyes droop, but he's fighting to stay awake. "She went with him?" he asks.

"She went with him."

"Where'd they go?"

"It's late. It's important you sleep."

"So everybody says," he grumbles.

"They're right." I smile, then stand and start for the door. "Goodnight. I'll see you tomorrow."

"Wait!" he calls out.

I look back. "What?"

"The ghost. She wasn't sure she could pick up the ax? Or kill the monster?"

"No."

"But she tried anyway."

"Yes. There'd been a lot of times in her life she hadn't helped when she could have. She realized she had to try, even if she failed."

"Mm-hmm." He's silent for a moment, a crease between his eyebrows. Then: "You'll come back tomorrow night?"

"Wild giraffes couldn't keep me away." I smile at him.

He raises an eyebrow at me, but there's a twinkle in his eyes. "Don't you mean wild horses?"

"Them either."

He chuckles, and it's a charming sound, like rain after a yearlong drought. "See ya, Storyteller," he says.

I smile at the nickname. I like it.

Although he may not believe my tale's true yet, at least he's interested. I'm already glad I chose him. It'll be hard when it comes time to finish the story, but that won't be for days. There's no point in grieving until the time comes.

CHAPTER TWO

Finn isn't reading tonight. He's resting with his arms outside the covers, eyes closed. He doesn't stir as I walk to his bed. Dark circles ring his eyes, stark against his pale skin. I glance around the room and notice a game lying across the sleeper couch: Ticket to Ride. It's a cheerful box with a large steam engine flying across the lid. Finn stirs.

"Are you awake?" I whisper.

He manages a smile. "I was just resting my eyes till you came."

"Tough day?"

He gives a hint of a nod. "Tiring."

"How come?"

"Three friends came over. We usually play video games, but Adio brought that." His eyes indicate the box. "His mom wanted us to 'look at each other, not our screens.'" Finn rolls his eyes, a comment on the eccentricities of parents. "It was fun, though. We played for, like, two hours."

It's the most I've heard him say at one go. "Sounds wonderful, but I bet it took a lot out of you."

"Mm," he agrees.

"Takes a lot of energy to keep up appearances for friends, doesn't it?"

"Mm-hmm." His eyes are soft, grateful. "I was glad to see them, but they get, like, weird if I look too sick. I don't like to freak them out."

"No. They have no context for what you're going through."

"It was like we were pretending I wasn't in the hospital, which is kinda weird. I mean, I weigh about a hundred twenty pounds, and I bruise if you look at me funny." He sighs. "But I pretend like everything's just fine."

"That's exhausting."

For a few minutes, we sit without talking, which feels comfortable. Finn breaks the silence. "You ready to go on?"

"Sure. I'll back up a bit to remind you where we were."

He nods. I think he'll close his eyes, but he doesn't. Instead he watches my face.

Senka gave one last look around the clearing. "Oh, please, let me go," she whispered, not sure who she spoke to. "Let me not be left behind." Silas offered his arm; Senka took it and closed her eyes in wild hope.

She felt bitterly cold, colder than she had since her death. And then, sound changed. The susurration of the trees she had heard for years ceased. The rustling of night animals, the chirping of tree frogs, even the angry snapping of the fire were gone. In their place was an eerie silence, one that spoke of somewhere devoid of life. Well, perhaps not all life. Underneath the smell of dust and stale air lurked the all-too-familiar odor of mouse.

Senka opened her eyes. She and Silas stood in the expansive entry hall of a manor house. "I did it," she whispered, looking up into Silas's deep-brown eyes. "Or *we* did it. I guess you did it. I wasn't sure it would work. I'd never been able to get out of the cabin before." She surveyed the room. "This place is huge. It's so … different." Silas looked at her and smiled. Realizing she still held his arm, she dropped her hand and took a step away.

Luna, nestling in the crook of Silas's other arm, surveyed the derelict state of the hall with a disdainful expression. He looked up at Silas and meowed once, requesting to be set down. Once on the floor, he sniffed delicately, then sneezed at the dust tickling his nose.

"What is this place?" Senka asked.

"It belongs to someone I know." Silas rubbed the back of his neck. "I did not want to travel far from where we were as I have not traveled with a ghost before. This is only a thousand miles away." He looked around and added, "It was in better condition when I saw it last."

The size of the place overwhelmed Senka, who hadn't been outside a one-room cabin for a very long time. Shadows, clinging to the edges of the large room, provided the only normality. A shaft of moonlight, the sole illumination, flooded through a window high above them and splashed across the faded, broken parquet floor. "It doesn't look like anyone's here," Senka remarked.

Silas grunted in agreement. "I believe if there were, they would have come to … greet us by now. Still, it would be wise to make a brief tour of the house." He tugged at the cuffs of his torn sweater, resettling them at his wrists. "Luna and I will investigate. Please don't leave the entry hall. If it turns out we have to go, I'll want to be able to find you quickly." Senka nodded, trying to appear confident but failing. Silas looked down at Luna who was licking dust from a front paw. "It is a good sign Luna is calm," he remarked. "He wouldn't be if there were anything threatening." Remembering his reaction to her and to the arrival of the creature, Senka felt reassured. "Luna," Silas continued, "would you see if there's any cause for concern on that side of the house?" He gestured toward one wing. "You will find a billiard room, office, dining room, and kitchens. I will explore the other wing, the library, morning room, and music room."

Luna stalked away, leaving distinct paw-shaped prints in the dust. Silas's shoes struck up echoes as he crossed the once-elegant floor and disappeared into a side room.

Feeling wary but restless, Senka paced the entry hall, keeping to the shadows. Her footfalls made no sound and left no trace in the dust. She went first to the sweeping staircase, craning her neck to see what she could. A section of the wrought-iron railing leaned over the first landing as if ready to jump. Two stories, at least, though the ceiling was lost in shadows. As she explored the edges of the room, she saw sheets of peeling wallpaper and exposed laths. On one wall, an ornate golden frame hung empty and askew, the painting having been cut away, leaving a fringe of ragged canvas. Senka peered up at it, imagining what the subject might have been. Silas's returning footsteps interrupted her.

"Find anything?" she asked.

"It appears the house has been empty for some time."

"Several years, at least, I'd think," she replied, cocking a thumb toward the empty frame.

"Dust, spiderwebs, and decay." Silas swept his hair back from his face in a gesture Senka guessed was habitual. "Whoever caused this destruction"—he gestured at the mess in the entry hall—"had no interest in books. The former resident always kept a good library, and it appears to be intact. Only a few of the books show damage, at least on a cursory inspection."

A library? Senka was having trouble getting her mind around the transformation of her existence in the last hour. She couldn't imagine spending her days reading, rattling around a house so large her cabin would fit in the entry hall. *What about Kenny?* She hadn't forgotten her dream of revenge.

"What is it?" Silas's voice deepened with concern. "I believe we're safe, for now. The creature is dead. It cannot report to my Master." He rubbed at a knot in his neck. "Of course, when it doesn't return, my Master will know his envoy was unsuccessful, and he will start looking for me again. I didn't consider this earlier, but you might come into the crossfire." His shoulders sagged. "Perhaps you were better off staying in your clearing. It may prove dangerous for you to have come with me."

Senka shook her head but considered for a moment before answering. "Imprisonment in the cabin made my existence awfully small. I'm done with that, even if it means facing danger and uncertainty. There's something else …" She paused, grappling with how to put her thoughts into words. "Not everyone who dies becomes a ghost, right? I mean, otherwise the planet would be packed." She looked around the entry hall. "How many people have died in this house, do you think? But no ghosts. I stayed, I became a ghost, and I want to do something with my continued existence. I mean, Dickens said it's only in life you have a chance to make a change, make a difference, whatever. But he was wrong, wasn't he? We're proof of that. Aren't we?" She leaned in, needing his answer.

Silas rubbed his face, then, "I cannot attest to our change-making capacities. I have had nearly three hundred years to make a difference in the world, but I have not been successful."

"But now you have another chance."

"Another chance to do … what? I have been fighting and running for more than two centuries. When is it enough?"

Senka couldn't let that be his answer. "I don't know. I haven't existed for even fifty years yet, but I'm starting to think there's never a time we stop fighting. For freedom from persecution, in your case. For revenge, in mine."

He shook his head as if she were too naive to argue with.

She had another thought. "Why does your Maker keep hunting you?" Silas looked away from her, silent. "It seems to me," she went on, "you've managed to have an impact on him." He chuckled without humor. "Laugh if you want," she said, "but I'd like to have an impact on someone too."

"By making that someone as angry with you as my Maker is with me?"

"The guy I'm thinking of? I couldn't give a shit if he's angry with me. But I'd sure like to know why he murdered me. And what happened to him afterward." Silas, who had started to pace, spun on his heel and stared at her. "The chance of making sure I get my revenge on him has suddenly become real." She shook her head. This was more words than she'd spoken in over a decade, and she wasn't sure she was expressing herself so he would understand. She kept trying. "I was living a perfect life … I thought. Then one night my husband poisoned me, and I became a ghost, for Chrissake. Everything I thought was true … wasn't. It was like the world slipped sideways, and I was left to figure out how to put it back on its axis. But finally, finally, I found comfort and a kind of normalcy in watching the animals come and go, the raindrops sliding down the window panes, the leaves turning red and falling and coming back to life. I came to terms with what my existence had become." She paused, studying Silas, hoping he was understanding. His hair glowed in a shaft of moonlight. "All that's gone now, literally burned away. And right now I have no idea what my new existence will look like. In lots of ways, escaping the cabin, coming here, this is as big a change as going from living woman to ghost. And now I want to do something that has meaning for me. Dealing with Kenny—" She stopped. She was out of words.

Silas was quiet long enough for Senka to hear a family of mice scratching in the wall behind her. "I had no idea," he said at last. "I have been thinking only of my plight. If you will let me, I would like to help you find your revenge."

A powerful feeling of gratitude flooded her. With tears prickling the corners of her eyes, she said, "Thank you. Maybe we could be a team. Help each other? What do you think?"

He came close to her and softly touched her elbow. "I would like that."

Despite herself, as she thought of taking action against Kenny, Senka felt a writhing in her stomach. *I exist,* she thought, *because I've dedicated myself to getting revenge. If I succeed, will I stop existing? What's wrong with waiting a little longer?* She told Silas, "Our first order of business should be seeing what we can do about your … predicament. I imagine it's hard for you to focus on anything else while your Maker is hunting you."

"There is nothing we can do about 'my predicament,'" he said without self-pity or anger. With a strained smile, he added, "For now, let's go see what Luna has found."

They headed in the direction Luna had trotted and found themselves in a dining room. The table, its top liberally gouged, was big enough to seat twenty with plenty of elbow room. Burn marks showed where a vandal had tried but failed to set it on fire. The many arms of the chandelier stuck out like trees in winter, the crystals plundered long ago.

They moved through a butler's pantry, now barren, and into an expansive kitchen where they discovered Luna hunkered on the corner of a baker's table. From his mouth dangled filaments of intestines. His paw pinned a sizable rat to the wooden surface.

"Everywhere I go," Senka groaned, "always with the rats and mice."

"Am I correct in assuming you found nothing of concern?" Silas asked Luna. "Or did you stop your explorations for a snack?" Whether in answer or not, Luna dipped his head and ripped a chunk out of the rat's side. "He's in his adolescence," Silas told Senka, as if in apology. "Wait here a moment, please, while I confirm the other rooms are clear."

As Senka waited, she watched Luna's methodical deconstruction of the rat. By the time Silas returned, the cat had finished with the back legs. "I see no sign of anyone, though there's evidence of burglary and vandalism throughout the house. Anything of obvious value has been taken. If she resided here still, a human would not dare to enter the grounds, let alone the house."

"She?"

Silas waved his hand as if to erase the pronoun. "The owner."

Senka let it go. "I'd say even burglars haven't been here for several years. For whatever reason, this house has been abandoned. Why do you think she'd leave?"

"I don't know." Again, he rubbed the back of his neck.

He'd make a terrible poker player. Senka suppressed a smile at the thought of a table full of vampires, each with an obvious tell.

"Maybe she—" He shook his head and clamped his lips tightly as if to hold back the words. "I don't know," he said again.

"Was she a vampire too?"

A deep frown creased the bridge of Silas's nose. "Why?" he asked.

"I'm wondering if something scared her away. And if it did, what it might have been. And whether it's likely to come back. I mean, is that the only one of those creatures? The one we saw tonight?"

"No." Silas raised a hand to his forehead and massaged his temple. "There are many more. But I do not understand why she would leave. She was not easily frightened." He shook his head as if to cast off his worries. "I'm sorry," he said, slapping his thigh. "I can't remember the last time I ate, and I'm gut foundered." Senka smirked at the antiquated slang, although she wondered what he would be eating. He went on, "I believe we are safe enough for now."

"You know," she replied, straightening up from where she'd been leaning against the old kitchen range, "I just realized there's nothing those creatures can do to me. You didn't see me at first, and the creature paid no attention to me at all. I'm not sure he knew I was there. Until I chopped off his head, I mean. What can anything do to hurt a shadow?"

Silas nodded, thinking. "You may be right." Tension dropped from his shoulders as he added, "Yes, I believe you will be safe."

"It's the two of you I worry about."

Luna paused in his post-meal whisker cleaning and gazed at her, slowly blinked his eyes twice, then returned to dragging a damp paw along his cheeks.

Silas, on the other hand, took great interest in the floor tiles as he said, "I am not accustomed to the idea of someone worrying about me."

Senka shifted, searching for a subject change. "You'd better go find something to eat, you know, being 'gut foundered' and all."

Silas nodded. Turning to Luna, he said, "Would you care to accompany me?" Luna gazed at him. "Perhaps next time," Silas answered for him. With a glance at Senka, he left through the kitchen door, out into the overgrown herb garden.

The half-eaten rat lolled on the table next to Luna. Senka narrowed her eyes at him. "Are you going to leave that there?"

The cat looked at her. All he said was, "Prrrp?"

Senka made her way to the library, Luna trotting after her. He jumped onto one of the tattered wingback chairs and curled up, draping a ginger paw over his eyes and nose. "Can you breathe like that?" Senka asked him, but he was already asleep.

Two grand windows, one at each end of the room, reached nearly to the ceiling, admitting dusty moonbeams that illuminated a beechwood floor, scratched and chipped by vandals. The other walls were crowded with bookcases.

As Senka took in the spooky grandeur of the room, she giggled. *Oh, my god. This place would have been perfect for location shooting. I've even got the vampire precast.* The giggle drained out of her. "Oh, Stanley," she whispered, "you would love this." She crossed her arms over her stomach and pressed in, trying to dampen the pain of grief that had come alive there. She whispered again, "Oh, Stan, I miss you so much. I hope you're okay." *How is it possible to feel so much pain even though I don't have a body? That just isn't fair.* She chastised herself: *beware the creeping self-pity.*

Trying to stop the spiral, she bent down to Luna and stroked his chin. As she'd hoped, he opened his eyes, though he didn't move his paw from his nose. "Wanna explore with me?" she asked him.

They climbed the stairs together. The hallway stretched out in both directions. "Which way?" she asked. Without hesitation, he turned right and trotted to the first closed door. Senka opened it and they peered in. Empty. "Brutal. Whoever trashed this place took the furniture and everything." As it had in the entry hall, wallpaper dangled in strips while panes of window glass gaped in snaggle-toothed smiles. Below them, the floorboards were warped and stained where rain had come in through the broken glass. She looked down at Luna, who turned and stalked to the next door, his tail held high, encouraging her to follow. Also empty, as was the third. They moved on to the fourth. Senka opened the door, assuming it would be the same, then exchanged a look with the cat. "Did you expect this?"

Moonlight filtered through dirty window panes, showing a fully furnished bedroom. Inches of dust blanketed the floor, a cluttered vanity, the surface of a faded duvet. Luna trotted in and sprang onto the vanity before stepping neatly between clustered perfumes and makeup containers. Senka went to him, and as he sniffed at a silver-backed hairbrush and comb, she picked up the largest perfume bottle, the contents of which had turned brown and murky from sun exposure and time. "I bet that smells rank," she said. "Why didn't they empty this room like the rest?"

She moved to the armoire and opened the double doors. Chiffons, silks, a fur coat somewhat stiffened with neglect. These had once been fashionable, expensive clothes. "I don't get it," she said as Luna batted at the filmy skirt of a Halston evening gown. "They've been hanging here untouched for decades, judging by the styles. What self-respecting plunderer wouldn't have nabbed them?"

Luna growled, deep and savage, his green-gold eyes fixed on

something behind Senka. She froze; she knew what Luna's growls meant. *Nothing can hurt a ghost. Nothing can hurt a ghost.* But she recalled an earlier time when repeating a denial hadn't saved her from watching scavengers dismantle her corpse.

An icy pit formed in her nonexistent stomach. Keeping her eyes on Luna, she slid into the darkness next to the armoire. Only then did she allow herself to follow his gaze. With his eyes locked on the bed, he crept, still growling, one tentative step following another, to the nightstand then leapt, landing without a sound. His fur stood on end as he stared at the grime-encrusted covers.

Senka shifted position, straining to see what Luna sensed. She had a clear view of the bed. Nothing stirred.

A hand at her throat, Senka stepped out of the shadows. She stood beside the bed, illuminated now by a hint of the setting moon, the growling cat at her elbow. "Hush," she told Luna, resting her palm on his back, though whose nerves she was trying to steady she wasn't sure. Although his growl faded, his fixed gaze never wavered. She stared at the covers, tensed for a monster's attack.

Nothing happened. Willing herself to keep panic in check, she inched back the covers.

A coating of greasy ash stained the yellowed pillowcase. Her hand went to her mouth, stifling an exclamation. Gathering her courage, she pulled the sheet farther down, slowly, so as not to roil the unctuous debris. By increments, she revealed the shape of a torso drawn in ash.

"Oh, dear," she whispered. "This explains a lot."

A nine-inch long chunk of wood, sharpened at the end, lay amid the pile of ashes.

Whoever this used to be, someone had staked him. Or her.

Silas returned from his hunt to find Senka and Luna in the library, sitting together in one of the wingback chairs. He looked ruddier, more energetic.

"This looks cozy," he remarked as he sat in the chair opposite them. He smiled, but a look of doubt clouded his features. He glanced between Senka and Luna. "What is it?" he asked.

"We went exploring." Senka regarded him with concern.

"Yes?"

"And we found something upstairs."

Silas's eyes widened. "Yes?" he said again. He leaned forward, his elbows resting on his knees.

"I think it's the, uh, former resident," she said. Silas jumped up, the color draining from his cheeks. Senka sat forward, reaching for him and spilling Luna from her lap. "Whoever it is, they're dead! Someone staked them."

His relief was obvious and immediate. He sank back into the chair. Luna, wanting to reassure him, hopped onto his lap and stretched himself along one leg, purring.

"Who do you think did it? The staking?" Senka asked.

Silas shrugged. "People everywhere hunt my kind. And many of us deserve it. I have no doubt she did."

"Will they come back? Are you in danger?"

"Not from humans. And I don't believe my Maker would think to search for me here, especially if he is aware she no longer resides here."

Senka could no longer resist asking, "Who was she?"

Silas slumped in the chair. With one hand, he absently stroked Luna. "It is not an easy story for me to tell. It is complicated." He paused.

"Start anywhere." Senka drew her feet beneath her and settled back into the oversized wingback.

"The simplest place to begin is to say she was my sister," he said at last. Senka let out an exclamation of sympathy, but Silas raised a hand. "We were not close any longer," he said. "To be honest, I've rarely thought of her in years. The last time I saw her, a century ago … it ended badly. I visited her here, thinking she would keep me safe, at least for a season, but I hadn't realized her loyalties had changed. Although I managed to escape in time, I lost Luna." He looked down at the ginger cat now fast asleep in his lap. "The Luna of that period."

"Oh, I'm so sorry!" Senka thought of the pain that betrayal and loss must have caused him.

Silas smiled, his eyes warm. "I like to imagine his descendants populate the farms for miles around. I hope so anyway. My Maker would have had no interest in killing him."

"Your Maker attacked you here? How did he find you?"

"Tara. My sister. She sent word to him that I was here. "

"Did she know he wanted to end you?"

Silas nodded. "As I said, her loyalties had changed." For a moment, he watched Luna, snoozing on his lap. "We had been close once. As children, certainly, and, yes, after we were made. But over the centuries, we lost touch and drifted apart." He met Senka's eyes. It sounded like a confession when he said, "The same Maker created us, you see. And while he came to revile me, he worshiped her."

Silas stopped and looked toward the tall library window. Senka became aware the shadows in the room had melted into the soft pearl-gray of predawn.

At the same time, Senka asked, "Do you need to rest?" and Silas asked, "Do you sleep?" They laughed at the synchrony, and Senka felt a warmth of companionship she hadn't experienced in a long time.

"I don't know what's legend and what's fact about vampires."

"Nor I about ghosts."

"Well, I don't sleep."

Silas grunted his understanding. "Nor I. And certainly not in a coffin. The tales about sunlight are true, but as long as I keep away from windows, I'm safe."

"Will you go on with your story then?"

Silas looked down at the sleeping cat and nodded.

He began to talk.

Finn has been so quiet tonight, not asking questions, but he's been paying close attention. I can see it in his eyes, in the way he reacts to the story.

"Silas's tale will have to wait till tomorrow night," I tell him.

"I figured." He looks at me then seems to make a decision. "I wish my cat could stay here with me." I recognize the trust it took to show such vulnerability.

"What's your cat's name?"

"Bob. You know, like Bob Cat? Don't judge. I was six when I named him." We smile at each other. "He can't come here. My immune system."

"Chemo can work a number on immune systems, huh?"

"Mm-hmm." He's matter-of-fact about it. I find his lack of self-pity impressive.

"You're brave," I say, trying not to make a big deal of it. "What's on the schedule for tomorrow?"

"More dripping."

"Dripping?"

He purses his lips and uses them to point at a bag of medication on the pole beside him.

"Oh, I get it."

"Once I'm done that, I earn a gold star."

I raise an eyebrow in question.

"I get to sit in the garden for an hour. As long as there's shade. Chemo turns you into a vampire. No sun."

"The fresh air will feel good," I say with a laugh.

"I'll tell you about it when you come back."

I'm glad he's counting on my return. "I'd like that. See you at the usual time."

He regards me with a half smile as I stand. "Yep." He closes his eyes. The smile lingers. I wish nothing could ever rob him of it.

CHAPTER THREE

Evening three and I walk by a small knot of people in the hall—a worried mother and father, a charge nurse, a physician. I glance through the door across from where they're clustered and see a little girl, no more than four years old. These parents will be lucky; she'll make it.

Finn is lying down, reading. He looks up as I come in.

"What's the book?"

He holds it up. *Moneyball* by Michael Lewis. "I saw the movie."

"Do you play baseball?"

"I did. Before all this." His gesture encompasses the hospital bed, the medications, the monitors. "First base."

"Do you miss it?"

He shrugs and changes the subject. "I went outside this afternoon."

"In the hospital garden. How was it?"

"Fresh air smelled excellent."

"I bet."

He glances at his book then back at me. "You know the Luna Silas lost at the mansion?"

"Yes?"

"I was thinking of the symbolism—like you said, the allegory. Do you think Silas was right? That Luna had lots of descendants?"

This makes me smile. Although he hasn't come around to believing the story altogether, at least he's thinking about it between visits. "In the farms around the manor house, you mean? I think so."

"But you don't know for sure." He seems to be weighing something heavier than symbolism.

"No. But I don't know for sure he didn't. Sometimes, when there's no way to know without a doubt, I choose to believe the positive outcome. I think it's very, very likely the great-great-great-grandchildren of that Luna are the cat rulers of the whole district."

His eyes crinkle. "I'd like to believe that too. I don't want to think of him dying."

Ah, so that's where the weight is coming from. "Everyone dies." I watch closely to gauge his reaction.

"Yeah." It's a straightforward statement but not without a hint of trepidation.

"What matters is what we leave behind."

"Like grandkids?" From his tone, it's clear Finn isn't thinking about having children, let alone grandchildren.

"Well, for some people, sure. But also things we create, memories people have of us, the love we've shared with others. We leave lots of echoes behind."

"According to your story, there are people who stick around."

I'm not quite sure where he's going, but he's not wrong. "In a way."

"Like Senka stayed."

"Yes, she did."

"And Silas didn't die."

"No, he paid a different price."

"Like what?"

"Silas's story is centuries long, but I'll begin it tonight." It's better to talk about death in small doses. Time to get back to the story. "Are you ready?"

He rests his book on his bedside table and slides down beneath the covers. "All set."

"Okay, so the last time we saw Silas and Senka the sun was rising …"

Birds stirred in the garden outside the library window. Senka heard the squawk of a rowdy blue jay claiming his territory, the high-pitched *chip-chip* of hummingbirds battling over nectar, the fluid trill of wrens advertising for mates. The familiar sounds gave her a sense of peace in this strange, new place. Silas began his story, one hand resting on the arm of the chair, the other stretched, as if in protection, across the flank of the dozing ginger cat.

"My sister was exquisitely beautiful. She bore the features of my mother's people: long, straight black hair; soft brown skin; high cheekbones. Black eyes that missed nothing. Once she reached marriage age, many men wanted her for a wife, but Tara had no interest in any of them. She did not care to emulate our mother, in marriage and children, in scratching out a bleak existence, as so many women did in those days."

"When are we talking about?" Senka interrupted.

"This was the early part of the eighteenth century. We did not know our birth years. Our father neglected to record them." He paused in reflection. "I have chosen 1720 as mine, though age has little meaning to me now."

"I can imagine," Senka said with a wry smile. "Were you born in this country?"

"I was born in what is now called the Santa Cruz Mountains in the state of California. In fact, my father first cut down the trees and made your clearing."

"Oh!" Senka exclaimed. "Born there and made there?"

"Yes. Born there and made there," Silas echoed, a shade of sadness creeping into his tone. He was far away, his eyes unfocused.

Senka watched him, wondering what pain he was reliving. She called him back to the moment saying, "My sense of history is so bad. I didn't realize White people were living in the Santa Cruz mountains then."

Silas looked up at her, his eyes focusing again. He replied, "They weren't. My father was the sole White person I ever saw. At least until my Maker arrived."

Of course, Senka thought, the dark hair and eyes, the refined high cheekbones.

As if in answer, Silas added, "My mother belonged to the Awaswas, one of the Ohlone peoples. But that story is for another time."

"Why was your father there? This was too early for the Gold Rush, right?" She found herself intrigued to hear the history from Silas, who had lived it. Or was it just pleasant to watch his face shift and move through his emotions and memories?

"Yes, long before the Gold Rush. My father was … not a good man." His expression hardened. "That is far too kind. His violence toward my mother, my siblings, and me was only one part of his wickedness. My mother escaped into herself from my earliest memories. It was as though she were dead but going through the motions. I believe that is the phrase." Silas paused but didn't look at Senka. "Although Tara and I were desperate to escape him, we had no idea where to run."

Questions crowded Senka's mind, but looking at Silas's face, she realized he was deep in his memories and didn't want to pull him away from them again; she sensed he'd never related this story before.

After a minute or two, he went on. "One night, not long after sunset, I escaped into the forest to think. As I sat on a fallen tree, I realized the woods had become silent and still. Moments before, birds twittered as they settled down for the night, nocturnal animals rustled in the underbrush as they roused themselves. Now, all of nature held its breath. My heart raced so, I thought it would fail. An iron band tightened around my ribs. I was suffocating; my vision narrowed into a tunnel. My fevered imagination screamed if I should topple to the ground, I would disappear into the fallen leaves and be lost forever." He paused. One hand had risen to his throat as if his breath, stopped for hundreds of years, was once again constricted by panic. "Suddenly, a face appeared before me. In all the silence of the woods, I hadn't heard him coming."

"It was your Maker!" Senka whispered.

"Yes."

"Did it happen then?"

"My Making? No." Silas grimaced, his face like a clenched fist. "It isn't his way to take a human by force. He persuades his victims to ask for it. Some, even to beg."

"So what happened?"

"He helped me back to the house. His presence brought on a fear more intense than any I had ever known, yet he shepherded me home like a loving uncle. He was searching for a place to camp for the night, he said, when he stumbled across me 'having some fashion of fit.'

"When my vision cleared at last, what I saw disgusted me. The expression on my father's face as he looked at the stranger was that of a hungry wolf with a lamb in its sight. In the stranger, with his elegant clothing and his exotic accent, he saw an easy mark."

Luna, awakened by the jostling of Silas's gestures, yawned hugely, stood, stretched, circled, and lay down again. Watching him, Silas relaxed. His expression, twisted with disgust, softened. With one hand he rubbed at his face then swept his hair back. "My father was a greedy, wicked man," he said with a touch of regret. "But I no longer harbor hatred for him. None of us knew what chaos the stranger had brought with him. How could we?"

"What was your Maker like?" she asked, then amended: "What *is* he like?"

"Charming. Ruthless." He winced, squeezing his eyes closed. "In Paris once I saw him lure a child, all frills and ringlets and delicate innocence, away from her governess's side, seduce her into freely offering her neck, drain her of blood, and cast her into a fountain. When I asked him why, he said her purity offended him." Silas shook his head as if to dislodge the memory. "Humans are foolish about appearances. They let themselves be duped into believing a handsome form and face are indicators of virtue."

Senka laughed, shaking her head. "Oh, yeah. Don't I know it." Silas looked at her, a question in his eyes. "It's a story for another time, as you say," she responded. "So he's good-looking?"

Silas nodded. "Like a Viking god. Blond, blue-eyed, tall, athletic."

"Cleft chin? Like a superhero?"

"Exactly so."

"Sounds dangerous."

"You cannot imagine. My father was a fool to think him tame." He stroked Luna's head, preparing himself for the next chapter of his story. "He readily allowed the stranger to camp in our woods, to 'keep the man close' he said. We didn't see 'the man' all the next day, so late in the afternoon my father sent Tara to find him. Unchaperoned. I could guess what he planned."

Senka thought of the period plays, films, television series she'd seen in which manipulative fathers used their innocent daughters to entrap the unsuspecting stranger. "At some point, he'd pretend to discover them together, her 'virtue compromised.'" Her lip curled.

"Yes. Then he would affect moral outrage, play the wronged father. If this ruse didn't succeed, he would force her to say the stranger had assaulted her. In either case, he would be in a position to demand payment. If the man had been anyone other than my Maker, it might have worked. Tara didn't return until long after sundown. The stranger presented her as if she were a princess returning to court. He suggested my father was careless to allow her to roam the woods unescorted. Why, she might come to harm!" Silas chuckled, then clamped his lips together. "With all I know now, you would think he could not amuse me."

"What did your father do?"

"He could barely remain civil. Once we were alone, I asked my sister why she was gone so long. She said she and the stranger had talked, though she couldn't remember what they had discussed."

"What did your Maker do, wipe her memory?" Senka thought of her initial meeting with Silas. "In the cabin, when you first spoke, I felt something—like a current of power had passed by me. You were trying to compel me to step out of the shadows, weren't you?"

"You were aware of that?" He raised an eyebrow. "It's unusual for my power to fail. Clearly, it does not work on the dead."

"I felt it," Senka admitted. "But I could let it pass by me. Can you compel anyone living then?"

"It works on most. The talent to compel others is one of the many gifts one acquires in one's Making."

A doubt crept into Senka's awareness. "Did your Maker compel Tara to spend time with him?"

Silas waggled his head. "I don't believe so. I think he fascinated her. She had never met someone so urbane, so worldly. However, I am convinced he blurred her memories, made them harder to access."

"Another vampire gift?"

"Yes." Silas stood, scooping Luna up and depositing him on the chair. Vampire and cat both stretched, then Luna curled up in the corner of the chair and went back to sleep. Silas walked the length of the room and returned to stand behind the chair occupied by the sleeping cat, resting his forearms on the back.

Senka prompted: "So Tara couldn't tell you what she and the stranger had talked about?"

"No. Each day she disappeared, returning later and later. I was worried for her, and I wanted to ensure whatever was happening was not against her will. One day when she slipped away, I followed her. I hid in the undergrowth, near enough to see them, though I couldn't hear what they were saying. They sat close together, leaning against a large tree whose leaves and branches cast a wide circle of shadow. In a moment, Tara pulled up the long sleeves of her dress. I gasped, nearly retched! The insides of her arms were covered in livid bruises. She extended one arm to the stranger who lowered his lips as if he were kissing it. She moaned, then leaned in until their heads were touching. I don't know how long they stayed like that, but when at length the stranger looked up, he stared directly into my eyes. He had known all along I was there, watching them. I turned and bolted through the forest, terrified he was following me."

A question had been nagging Senka. "Silas, I'm sorry to interrupt, but this was all in the daytime, right?"

"Yes."

"How could he pull that off? Don't vampires burst into flames during the day?"

"Ah, no. That is a common misconception, thanks to certain authors," he said with a hint of a smile. "In the direct sunlight, yes, we burn. Not as humans sunburn; we instantly and violently turn to ash. However, where there is shade, as in the forest where my Maker camped, or where we are in indirect light, as in this room, we are not affected."

"And vampires' powers aren't lessened in the daytime?"

"No. Day or night, our powers remain the same."

As Senka contemplated this new information, she watched the light play across Silas's face. The more she got to know his features, his voice, his Silas-ness, the more she felt being with him was like coming home. She enjoyed not just his physical beauty, though she had to admit there was a lot to like in that department. Even more, she appreciated how direct, straightforward, *secure* he was.

But a voice in her head cautioned her: *you hardly know him. You've been fooled before.*

Luna woke, yawned, stretched, and jumped from his chair to find a sunbeam to bathe in. Silas observed him, a tenderness in his eyes. "At least *he* benefits from sunlight."

They watched him for a moment until Senka turned back to Silas. "I'm getting the idea things are about to get hairier."

Silas's expression clouded. He sat again and briefly stared at the floor before picking up his story. "It was late when Tara returned. She led me from the cabin to the fallen tree on which I had been sitting when the stranger had first appeared. Here she sat and gestured for me to join her. The first sentence she spoke was, 'Don't be afraid of him.' All I could do in response was pull up the sleeve of her dress, exposing the bruises. 'It doesn't hurt,' she insisted, but added, 'At least, I enjoy it.' She covered her arm. 'Silas! Listen to me. He could be our savior!' Having no idea what she meant, I shook my head.

"She told me he was hundreds of years old, powerful, that he had traveled the lengths of the world. And that he would take us with him. She spoke of his kindness, his gentleness, his brilliance. She was enraptured by him. And I? I found her enthusiasm contagious." He shook his head, an echo of the gesture made centuries before. "She told me he had admitted he was able to create others like him. She had pleaded with him, finally convinced him to turn her. And she persuaded him to turn me as well."

Silas laughed, but his eyes showed no humor. He got up and paced the length of the room again. "You see how he works?" He pounded his fist against his thigh. "Tara was an innocent. She thought everyone was as honest as she. At least, as she was then. That devil saw what our father was like, and he knew she was desperate to get away from him. He made her beg because he knew she would. He glorified his existence. Oh, he was exotic and unparalleled! And I bought every word of the story too. I was as gullible as she." He shook his head in disbelief at himself and sat across from Senka.

"Well, of course you were!" she said, more sharply than she'd intended. Silas lifted his head, hurt. She went on, her tone softer. "You and Tara were two innocents facing the world's most polished con man. You'd never left your little clearing, and he'd had centuries to perfect his schtick. What do you expect? Have a little compassion for your younger selves! You've had decades to become more worldly and sophisticated. Don't judge yourself then by yourself now."

Silas nodded. "You're right. The vision of hindsight is perfect."

"Yes, it is." She gave him a moment, then asked, "What happened next?"

Silas closed his eyes. "We went together the next day and asked him to change us both. Of course he agreed. Tara was first. He cradled her against him as if she were fragile porcelain. She raised her bare arm to him, and he bit. As he drank, he stopped now and then to ask if she was comfortable. She grew weak, and he sliced his own neck with his fingernail and held her mouth to the blood. At first, she licked at it with revulsion. But within seconds, she drank greedily, clutching him to her, blood smeared across her lips and face. When he pulled her away, she gazed at him, triumphant, radiant. Her bruises vanished. The desperation and fear always haunting her were gone. I longed to be turned more passionately than I had ever dared to want anything. Tara asked me if I was ready, and I nodded with such hope.

"He was on me in one ferocious leap. He grabbed a fistful of hair and bent my head backward. I thought he would break my spine. Then he ripped my shirt open and plunged his teeth into my neck, ripping away the flesh. The pain was a stab of lightning searing through my body. My sister screamed. I tried to fight him off, but his arms were like iron bands. I clawed at them, at his face as he sucked more and more blood from me. My head swam. Darkness flickered at the edges of my eyes. I lost consciousness.

"I came to with the taste of blood in my mouth. The stranger, my Maker, was pressing his wrist to my lips, his blood flowing over my tongue. The need to drink burned in me like a living fire demon.

Long before I had drunk enough to satisfy me, he jerked his arm away. I was in an agony of hunger. My sister pleaded for me, but he refused. 'He has had enough of *my* blood,' he told her.

"I lay on the ground, huddled against the pain. My Maker crouched next to me and rested his hand on my head. It was the first gesture of kindness he had shown me, and I felt so grateful I cried. I appalled myself but was too weak to stop. He whispered in my ear, 'You know it is not my blood you want now. You cannot be satisfied save with his.'"

"Holy shit," whispered Senka. "That asshole sent you after your father."

"And I was in no condition to resist." Silas shook his head. "No. I need to be honest. I was alive with power. And the idea of terrifying the monster who had terrified me all my life! It thrilled me. What my Maker knew that I didn't, what I had no way of knowing was what the first taste of human blood would do to me."

He lapsed into silence, a frown pinching the bridge of his nose. Senka gave him some time to dwell on his memories, then reached her hand toward him, palm up. He started. She suspected he'd forgotten she was there, but he looked at her as if her face held the hope he needed. He reached out his own hand and placed it in hers. Although Senka hadn't been sure there was enough shadow to make her solid, she wrapped her fingers around his cold ones and gave them a little squeeze. *What's done cannot be undone.* "What happened?" she asked.

Holding her hand tightly, he said, "My sister and I started back to our cabin. While we had been with our Maker, the sun had sunk behind the hills. The family was at supper when we burst into the cabin.

"Can you imagine how we looked? My sister with sprays of blood covering her dress. My shirt drenched with my own blood. Our Maker's blood smeared across our faces. The scene is fixed in my memory. Our brothers sat paralyzed, staring at us in horror. My mother, passionless as always, stood at the kitchen stove, a ladle in her hand, regarding us with no expression. I believe now she knew what the stranger was from the moment he arrived.

"My father sneered and said, 'Is that your blood, girl? Have you bedded that man at last?' He turned to me. 'And you. What fucking mess have you made this time?' His words, his tone, the contempt on his face enraged me. I grabbed him by the shirt front and dragged him from the house." He stopped.

Senka gave his hand a squeeze. "Go on, Silas."

He glanced at her, then away. He closed his eyes. "I meant only to scare him. I threw him to the ground and pinned his chest with my knee. I made sure he was watching and bared my teeth. For the first time, I felt the canines grow. I saw terror in his eyes. Triumphant, I sank my teeth into his neck." Silas stopped again. With his free hand, he covered his eyes, but he held onto Senka's hand as if it were a lifeline. "I swear I meant to drink only enough to weaken him." His voice cracked as tears rolled down his cheeks.

With all the understanding she could put in her tone, she asked again, "What happened, Silas?"

"I ripped his throat out." The words came in a snarl. "I drank every drop of blood that didn't soak into the earth. I couldn't stop; I was helpless against the urge. And he knew what the fever would be. My Maker *knew*. If Tara hadn't stopped me, I believe I would have killed them all. Our brothers screamed and screamed. But our mother—she stood in the doorway of the cabin, observing the chaos as if she had expected it. I have come to think she was hoping my father would die before the stranger was gone."

He paused again, deep in thought. As he went on, his voice carried a tinge of shame. "I ran into the woods, back to my Maker. I wept and he comforted me." Silas's usually kind eyes hardened with bitterness. "I was grateful to him." He shook his head. "Sometime later, Tara returned. She told me she had buried our father and quieted our brothers. She said our mother looked calm and strong. That night, we left those woods with our Maker. Other than Tara, I never again saw my family."

Silas leaned back and closed his eyes. Senka let go of his hand, rose from her chair, and knelt in front of him. "Thank you for telling me," she said.

"I have never …" He trailed off.

"I know. I'm glad you told me."

"You're not … disgusted by me?" He opened his eyes and looked into hers.

She shook her head. "Of course not." Then it occurred to her she should ask the question that had been in the back of her mind. "I mean," she began in as light a tone as possible, "do you still rip humans' throats out?"

His expression showed the truth of his words as he said, "No! I haven't fed on humans in over a hundred years! I prefer cervine blood. It is ubiquitous. Though leporidae are quite good in a pinch."

"Cervine. That's deer, right? What's leporidae?"

"Rabbits and hares."

"Well, good. That's kind of a relief." She gave him a half smile. "But no, Silas. I'm not disgusted by you—and I don't blame you. That would be like, I don't know, like blaming a lioness for attacking a gazelle. That's its nature. Here you were, newly made, manipulated into being half starved. And as I said before, you owe your younger self a little compassion."

Silas regarded her. Senka knew he was wondering if she were sincere, so she met his gaze, trying to show her wholehearted belief in her words. At last, a weight lifted from his shoulders and he smiled. "Thank you," he said. "I believe," he added, his hands on his thighs, "I'd like to go upstairs and pay my respects to my sister."

"You know there's not much left. Just ashes."

"Yes." His tone was matter-of-fact. He stood and started for the door.

Senka rose. "You still haven't told me about your falling out with her and your Maker."

Silas leaned against the doorjamb, his shoulders sagging. "I do not have the energy for that story right now."

"We can save it. Seems like we're going to have plenty of time together, doesn't it?" She saw her words register. He heard the unspoken promise, and she sensed, like her, he was grateful to think his seasons of loneliness might be behind him.

"Yes," he said again, his hand on the doorknob. "There's time for other stories later." He left the room, closing the door behind him, and Senka drifted over to take a seat on the floor next to Luna.

We sit in silence for several minutes until Finn says, "They're lucky they have so much time together, Senka and Silas." His expression is thoughtful, somber.

He doesn't refer to them as characters, but I'm not so inexperienced as to imagine he believes yet. "You look kind of sad about it."

"Not about them," he says. "I wish I could have that kind of time with one of my friends. And my mom."

I marvel at his unselfconscious honesty. "It's hard, being aware of the limitations of time," I say.

Finn grunts. We sit without talking until he says, "What's going to happen next?"

"In the story?" Or might this be a more metaphysical conversation?

He casts his eyes sideways to look at me without turning his head. "Yeah, the story."

"Tomorrow night the adventure really begins."

He chuckles drowsily, his eyelids drooping. "That's cool."

"Sleep well."

He nods and closes his eyes.

I slip out. The hall is empty now. I peek into the little girl's room. Her mom is asleep on the guest couch beneath the window. The child is awake, her eyes open. She doesn't see me and I move on. It's time to go home.

CHAPTER FOUR

It's a foggy night as I head back to the hospital, one of those nights that turn the streetlights into halos and make the world look like a setting for a gothic novel. I have company as I head toward the entrance. His footsteps grate and crackle across the pavement.

"How far have you gotten in the story?" he asks me.

"The manor house."

"Ah. And the young man? Finn?"

"Charming. Smart. Inquisitive. He's something else."

"It sounds as though you are happy to have chosen him."

"I am. What'll you do while I'm gone?"

"I plan to research the case I told you about."

I nod. "Good. See you at home?"

"Yes. I won't be late."

We separate and I go up to Finn's room. He looks like he's been watching for me tonight. I see he's set aside the pudding from his dinner tray. When a boy his age doesn't eat dessert, there's a reason for it. He looks tired, but at least the dark circles that were under his eyes yesterday aren't as pronounced.

"Hey!" I say taking a seat.

He nods with an upward jerk of his head, and the corners of his mouth quirk. "Hey, Storyteller."

"How are you this evening?"

"Tired. Long day."

"How come?"

"Tests," he says but doesn't elaborate. He changes the subject. "You know this story really well, huh?"

"Yep, I do."

"Have you told it to a lot of people?"

"A few."

"Were they all in the hospital too?"

"Most of them. One or two were in care facilities."

"For old people."

"Yes." I'm not sure what he's leading up to, but a long time ago I promised myself to be truthful with the people who hear this story. I wait for his next question, and it surprises me.

"Have any of them met each other?"

The idea makes me laugh. "I don't think so. What made you think of that?"

He shrugs. "I dunno. It'd be cool, like being in a club."

"What other clubs do you belong to?"

He looks away from me and fiddles with his hospital wristband. "I'm still an honorary member of the baseball team, The Crickets. Not a very threatening name, I know. And I started a club at school for people who eventually want to be doctors. My friend Adio runs it now."

It's remarkable to me when people who spend as much time as Finn has in hospitals plan to become doctors. "What kind of doctor do you want to be?"

"I'm not sure. I want to work for Doctors Without Borders, so, whatever they need most." That makes sense. Before I can respond, Finn says, "In a way the people who've heard this story *are* in a club, even if we don't know each other."

"True. There are a few things you share in common."

"Like being sick?"

"Yes, for one." I'm not prepared for him to ask what else they share. "Should I go on with the story?"

He nods. "We ended with Silas going up to see his sister."

"Yes. So then."

Senka and Luna sat next to each other on the library floor, shifting their positions to stay in a patch of sunlight as long as possible. Luna's rumbling purr provided a bass accompaniment to the twitters of the birds outside. When the sun had descended enough to cast its beams across the room rather than the floor, he curled up in her lap. Senka told him her reactions to Silas's story and commented on the expansiveness of the gardens beyond the windows. He didn't respond, but he was a good listener.

Silas's descriptions of his father and mother brought back memories of Senka's own parents, her own childhood, so different from Silas's, and not just because of the chasm of cultures between the early eighteenth and late-twentieth centuries.

Her mind leapt to one of her favorite memories of her mother. Sarah had been four or five, and for some reason—the nanny had been sick, maybe—her mother had brought her on a photo shoot. The company sent a driver, and she snuggled up to her mom, who draped an arm around her and narrated the view through the window.

"Do you see the big white house on the hill, sweet pea? That's where the dragon who played Toothless lives."

"For real?" Her eyes must have been Christmas morning wide.

"Oh, yes. Daddy and I met him at a party last month. He's delightful in person. Well, in dragon."

She giggled, tickled at the idea of the dragon holding a glass with one enormous claw and snagging an hors d'oeuvre from a roving waiter with another.

When they reached the location, a cavernous warehouse of a studio, little Sarah watched her mother go through hair, makeup, and wardrobe to become a bejeweled goddess ready to sell perfume. She observed the team—from the makeup woman to the photographer to the company representative—fawning over her mom, gushing at her beauty, her grace, her renown.

On the way home after the shoot, she turned to her mother and said, "I want to be just like you when I grow up."

"Oh, sweet pea," her mother answered, "don't be taken in. I'm not all I'm cracked up to be."

She hadn't known what her mother meant, but it had been the first time she'd noticed how sad her mother looked.

Memories of her parents inevitably led to the last one. She was two years out of high school, at the start of her career and still living with them. The doorbell rang one night as she was alone watching *The Late Show*. Her parents' lawyer stood at the door with a woman she didn't recognize, the sound of an audience laughing on the TV. The lawyer saying those incomprehensible words, so absurd she laughed before she realized he wasn't joking.

"Sarah, your parents were killed in a car accident tonight. I've brought your mother's therapist to help us process it all."

Like she could process becoming an instant orphan in one evening.

Thanks to a drunken reveler on the 405, Hollywood lost their favorite model and every starlet's go-to plastic surgeon in one fiery crash.

And who had been there to help her pick up the pieces? Who had descended in a flurry of flapping Birkenstocks? Who had thrown all his fierce love and incomparable efficiency into making her whole again?

Oh, Stan, she thought for the thousandth time. *What would I have done without you? I wish I could talk to you now, tell you how much I love you. That you were right about Kenny. Oh, I wish …*

She leaned down to Luna and whispered, "I wish you'd gotten to know him. Stanley. He's a great man. The best director, the best friend, the best confidant anyone could want. Remember his name, okay, little one? It's Stanley." She kissed the top of Luna's head to seal the name in place.

He blinked at her and purred his understanding.

The clouds were electric with pinks and golds by the time Silas returned to the library. "Well," he said as he entered, "my sister has certainly looked better in her time!"

"Silas!" Senka exclaimed. "That's terrible!" But she laughed despite herself.

He clapped his hands. "Look at that sky! I do not tire of sunsets. Each one is unique."

Senka laughed again, happy to see his enthusiasm. Telling his story and sitting with what remained of his sister, perhaps mourning her, had been therapeutic. A saying Stanley often repeated came back to her: *A burden shared is a burden halved.* She smiled, remembering. "Sarella," he would say, "spill it! A burden shared—"

"When I was upstairs," Silas interrupted her thought, "I was thinking of our conversation regarding your relative safety from my Maker and the creatures he sends after me."

"Do you think he ended your sister? Or ordered someone to?"

Silas shook his head. "It is a mystery I am not able to solve at the moment. If he did, it would mean a significant change in their relationship. I believe it is far more likely she encountered a vampire hunter, whether professional or amateur."

"There are professional vampire hunters? In the twenty-first century?"

"Oh, yes. They are not only for television shows and flawed novels."

Senka would have blushed if she'd had blood, though she suspected Silas didn't know she'd once been famous for staking vampires on TV. She covered her embarrassment by asking a question that had come up earlier, when she was chatting to Luna. "Silas, if vampires don't need to sleep, why was Tara in bed when she was staked?"

Silas raised an eyebrow. "There are more uses for a bed than sleeping, are there not?"

Senka's jaw dropped. "Vampires have sex?"

"We are very sensual creatures."

"I know, but … I always thought they got off on biting people. But they have actual sex, huh?" She was intrigued, trying to imagine the mechanics. "Even without blood flow?"

"I wish I could explain vampire anatomy, but unfortunately we have not been studied. Biologists, scientists in general, take no heed of us. All I can tell you is, yes, vampires have sex, and my sister was particularly fond of the activity. It is entirely possible a vampire hunter posed as a paramour and took her unaware, undefended. But"—he swept his hair from his face—"we are drifting from the point: your safety."

"Oh, right. What are you thinking?" Senka stroked Luna's side, and he stretched with a squeak then turned his head upside down to watch Silas.

"We have noted you are insubstantial in the light but visible."

"Mm-hmm."

"You gain solidity in the dark, from the shadows, and are virtually imperceivable, unless one knows what to look for. I, for example, was unable to see you in the shadows of the cabin, yet now I have no trouble finding you in the dark."

She was surprised to feel a prickle of pleasure at the thought. She nodded for him to go on.

"Do you have any idea what other qualities you possess?"

Senka shrugged. "The cabin didn't give me much of a playground for experimenting. Ghosts in folklore or novels and such, they walk through walls and maybe fly, right? Ring bells, turn on radios, make things go bump in the night? Once I discovered I couldn't leave the cabin, the *one-room* cabin, that ruled out trying to walk through walls. No bells, no radios, but I tried to levitate."

"How did you progress?"

"I'm very good at hopping," she said. Silas snorted. "I'd like to try again."

"You have more scope to experiment here. Walking through walls and flying would be useful, as would becoming insubstantial or solid at will, no matter the time of day or state of the light."

"Plus it would be cool. I mean, I'd love to have abilities like that."

"Would you be amenable to experimenting now?" Silas offered her a hand up from the floor.

"No time like the present, right?" She stood without taking his hand. *No point getting interested in a vampire,* she told herself. *This partnership is about getting rid of his Maker, then taking care of Kenny.*

Luna watched them curiously. Senka looked around the room. "I think I'll start small." She pointed to a patch of wall still caught in the last faint glow of the setting sun. "Maybe if I'm in the light, it'll be easier to go through a wall."

"Good thinking."

With a nervous flutter where her stomach had been, she went to the wall and reached out to touch it. Warmth lingered from the day's sunlight. "Can you see me?"

"Quite well."

She applied a little pressure and a little more, and, "Oh!" she said. Her arm had gone through the wall up to her elbow. Eyes wide, she turned to Silas.

"I knew you would succeed at once." He beamed at her.

She pushed a bit more, this time knowing what sensation to expect: a fizzy, springy feeling, like pushing herself into warm, carbonated Jell-O. When her whole arm and part of her shoulder slipped into the wall, she laughed with pleasure at the new sensation. "I can feel the cooler air in the other room!" Not knowing if the material inside the wall would cling to her, she squeezed her eyes shut, plugged her nose with her free hand, and took the plunge, thrusting her body into the music room. She felt a pop and opened her eyes to confirm she had, yes, passed through the wall. She felt as proud of herself as she had the night she'd won the People's Choice Award. "That. Is. Awesome!" Her voice rose to a shout on the final word.

She was about to go back through the wall to share her excitement with Silas but realized there were no illuminated spots on this side. She jogged to the door, flung it open, and, reveling in performing again, entered the library as if she wore a crown of laurels. Silas applauded and Senka offered him her most dramatic bow.

"You made it appear easy. Was it?"

"Pretty much."

"See how it feels over there." Silas pointed to a more shadowy patch on the same wall.

Senka went to it and placed her palm on part of the shadow. "It feels firmer. Or I feel firmer, I'm not sure which." She focused, at first unsure what to do. Remembering her previous success, she imagined softening her form. Her fingers tingled and sank into the plaster. She pictured herself as cotton candy, as smoke, as stardust. Closing her eyes again, she stepped forward and passed through the wall. She threw her arms over her head and performed a little victory wiggle.

Once again, she trotted back into the library. "I did it!" she exclaimed.

Silas stood, hands on his hips, and looked at her, grinning. "I could see you figuring out the process. So well done! Do you think you could repeat it where the wall is darker?"

"This is like a video game where they keep upping the difficulty every time you win a level."

"Do you mean, yes, you would like to try it?"

"Yes. I'd like to try it."

"Good!" Silas rubbed his hands together like a cartoon stereotype of eager anticipation. "Do you mind if I leave you to work on your own for a time? I feel like I have been on a chameleon's diet, and I need to change that."

Senka cocked her head at him. "I have no idea what that means."

"Ah, sorry. It was a popular saying in my vampiric infancy. It means I'm still catching up from missing a few meals. "

Senka smiled at his lighthearted tone. "I'll be fine. You go eat."

He faced Luna and made a little bow. "Would you care to join me in the hunt this evening?"

Luna yawned, showing his tiny, razor-sharp teeth and pink tongue, then rose and stalked toward Silas. Looking up into his face, he said, "Woh-ow!"

"We won't be long." Silas strode to the door followed by a ginger shadow. The two swept through, leaving the door ajar behind them.

The full moon was already low in the western sky, giving Senka splashes of illumination to work with even after sunset. She started again with the brighter areas, becoming familiar with the sensations that preceded her push through the wall, then moving to increasingly dimmer patches. At each spot, she closed her eyes and focused all her attention on her hand where it rested on the plaster. She felt her own insubstantiality, pushed her arm through, and pulled it back out once, twice, three times.

At length, she moved to the corner of the room between two towering bookcases where the light had struggled to penetrate in the daytime. Now the shadows were thick. There had been a time when shadows like this had been her only friends. She wondered if they would be allies or antagonists tonight. She squeezed into the narrow gap and held her hand to the wall. Again she closed her eyes and imagined herself as insubstantial, as stardust. She pressed against the plaster. When her hand remained on the surface, she offered herself a whispered encouragement: "You've got this. The wall is fizzy Jell-O." Her hand tingled and she pressed again. All of her remained in the library. "Pull your socks up, girl," she murmured. "Let's try it again."

From the other side of the wall, she heard a rending crack. *Silas? He's back sooner than I expected.* Without thinking, she stuck her head through the wall to look.

In the same moment, she felt the elation of success and the most chilling horror she had ever known. The door to the music room sagged on broken hinges. Glowing in a shaft of moonlight was a tall, pale, blond, athletic-looking superhero. Or maybe a Viking god. Instantly, she knew who he was.

Fear ripped through her. Even the moment of her death hadn't terrified her as this being did. Trying not to stir the air, she pulled her face back through the wall.

"I heard you, you know." His voice was light and faintly accented. *French? Swedish?* Silas had said he sounded exotic to them at first. *Is French exotic?* She realized in her terror she was clinging to pointless details. "You were talking to yourself," he went on. Hearing footsteps move through the music room, she sank deeper into the shadows. The space between the bookcases was so small she had to wedge herself in. He had stopped walking. "You are uncommonly quiet. There's something different about you. Ah! I know. How lovely! No heartbeat." He sounded satisfied with himself for having solved the little mystery. The footsteps started again. "You're not one of us, though, I think. Isn't that right? I can always smell a vampire." He had reached the doorway to the library and paused there for a moment. The door creaked open. He stood, unmoving, and scanned the room.

From her hiding place, Senka had an unobstructed view of him. He was breathtaking: elegant, dressed in an impeccably tailored light-grey suit with a sheen that spoke to its origins in a silk farm. His hands, one resting on the door, were the refined, sensitive hands of a pianist.

His hair, grown to his shoulders, was pulled back in a tidy ponytail, not a hair out of place. What surprised her was how sweet-faced he was.

I wouldn't cast him as a god, she thought. *I'd cast him as the young Spider-Man or Mr. Bingley or Westley in* The Princess Bride. *I'll have to tell Silas when he gets back.*

Oh, god! Silas! Fear ripped through her again. This creature had been hunting him for a century or more. How could she warn him?

Silas's Maker stepped into the room, alert, scanning the shadows. "How curious," he said with a happy laugh. "I heard you as I stood in the hallway, but I do not see you. How is that?" He looked around again. "There is no other exit and you could not have passed me." He laughed again, delighted. "I am surprised! Do you know how long it has been since anyone surprised me? How refreshing!"

Watching him, Senka wondered if Silas had misunderstood the situation. Could this happy-sounding creature, this kind-faced man really be hunting him? Why would he? Wasn't Silas like a son to him? He must have changed. He couldn't be as vicious as Silas thought. Not moving from her shadows, Senka asked, "How did you find us here?"

"Ah! She speaks!" His eyes searched the end of the room from which her voice had come, but Senka could tell he hadn't spotted her. "My dear, come out of the shadows. Come. Join me." Graceful as a leopard, he sat in the nearest wingback chair, crossed his legs, and smoothed the pleats in his trousers.

He would take command of any room he walked into. Senka became aware of her permanent costume of hiking shorts, T-shirt, and well-worn boots and immediately felt self-conscious about her appearance in a way she didn't with Silas. *Oh, for crying out loud, you're dead. Who cares how you're dressed?*

Even so, she hoped she could slip from between the bookcases without calling his attention to her. She was bound to look ungainly as she squeezed through the narrow opening. It occurred to her she could drift through books and bookcases as well as through walls, but since she hadn't mastered the technique, she opted for the squeeze.

She expected him to catch sight of her when she moved, but if he did, he showed no sign. She watched him, waiting to see what he would do next.

"Hello?" He sang the word in a clear tenor voice, then turned it into another song, "*'Waitin' on a woman. Honey, take your time, 'cause I don't mind. Waitin' on a woman.'*"

"I wouldn't have pegged you for a Brad Paisley fan."

He scanned the shadows, recognizing she had moved but unable to find her. "Of course!" he responded. "I love many kinds of music and I have known many musicians. The young Mozart, the always lovely Patsy Cline, Kurt Cobain before he was lost to heroin. More than I can name. Oof! I could tell you some exciting stories, you know!"

In the moonlight, Senka saw his eyes twinkle with amusement. *Silas got it wrong.* She stepped from the depths of the shadows into a shaft of moonlight. His eyes locked onto her.

"Ah!" He smiled with satisfaction. She sat in the chair she had occupied as she'd listened to Silas's story. Fascinated, he watched her every move. "You are, what? You are a being of shadows, is that it?"

"Something like that."

"I'm so glad you have chosen to join me."

"You haven't answered my question."

He raised his eyebrows. "Forgive me. I have forgotten the question you asked." He laughed like water burbling in a mountain stream.

"How did you know we were here?"

"Ah, well. To answer you, I'd first have to say I did not know there was a 'we.' Have you been traveling with Silas?"

Something about the tone of his response struck Senka as familiar, but she couldn't place it. "Not long. We met two nights ago."

"Ah." He raised his eyebrows again and nodded. "The ax-wielder. Now I understand."

"You found the monster then. I thought he would have burned."

"He did." He sounded apologetic. "But they leave an afterimage we vampires can detect. So you came here." He gestured to indicate the house. "I'm surprised Silas returned so soon."

"It's been a hundred years, he said."

"Yes, that's what I mean. I would think he'd have been scared off for centuries."

"His sister is dead. Did you know?"

The Maker's lips turned down in an exaggerated pout. "I did know. Did Silas?"

"He does now."

"So sad. It looks like someone has taken everything valuable, doesn't it? Taken or destroyed. Did you see the empty frame in the entry hall? It was a Whistler. Priceless."

With a flash of memory, Senka saw what he was doing. "Goats!" she spat. "It's the goddamn goats again." She wanted to kick herself for being conned by the same tactic of avoidance Kenny had used.

"Goats?" said the Maker, confused. "No, it was a seascape."

"A pretty face and a little deflection. You'd think I'd know better after all this time. Such an idiot!"

In the other room, Silas exclaimed, "What have you done to the door?"

The ancient vampire's eyes took on the piercing look of a master predator. He smiled and licked his lips. Senka would have laughed if this had been some campy movie. Faced with the reality, however, she found it terrifying.

The Maker rose from his chair, graceful, deadly. Silas appeared in the doorway and froze. "Ah," whispered the Maker, "at last."

As if his brain were misfiring, Silas looked between his adversary and Senka. The Maker's body tensed like a wildcat ready to pounce on its prey.

A yowl erupted from the hallway and both Silas and the Maker started. The unearthly sound of Luna and his belated alarm broke the spell. Senka screamed with all her might, "Silas, go! I'm okay! *Go!*"

As if he had been jolted by an electric shock, Silas sprang from the doorway and pelted into the hall. Senka heard Luna's yowl cut off in mid-screech as Silas plucked him from the floor without a pause. The sound of Silas running echoed through the entry hall. The Maker leapt, the superhuman predator in his element.

Let Silas have gotten away, Senka pleaded, though she wasn't sure to whom. *Oh, let him and Luna be safe. I can't bear to be alone again.*

She berated herself for her idiocy, doubting Silas's assessment of his Maker, but knew her first priority was her own dilemma. What should she do when the Maker returned? Should she stay in the light, visible but insubstantial? That way he could see her but not harm her. Maybe she should go back to the shadows, hidden but more solid? She wasn't sure whether her solidity would make her vulnerable to harm, even if he couldn't make her deader than she already was. She stood in the center of the room unable to commit.

The Maker's steps echoed in the hallway. Reacting from instinct, Senka flung herself into the shadows by the fireplace. He was back, no longer the languid, chatty sophisticate he had been moments before. Now, his pale eyes burned with fury. His canines, fully extended, dripped saliva. He glanced around the room and hissed. With an act of will, he pulled himself together. His teeth retracted; his body relaxed. But he still was a panther ready to spring.

"Back into hiding, is it?" He peered into the shadows where she had been earlier. "No, you wouldn't have gone back to the same hiding place, would you? You're too smart for that." He walked around the room, entering each shadow he came to. "He has changed, you know, our Silas. At least, since the last time I saw him. He is more daring." He dragged a hand across one shelf of books. "Is that because of you? Hmm? No answer? You're not going to talk to me now? Ah, my dear, I don't think I like you." He grabbed a bookcase shelf and with the screech of rending wood, ripped it from its place. Books scattered across the floor. He tossed the heavy shelf away as if it were a child's bath toy.

Senka shrank deeper into the shadows, confident he couldn't see her. He turned a full circle in the middle of the room. "You are wasting my time," he growled. "Come out!" As she had in the cabin, Senka felt the power whisper around her, but whereas Silas's had been like a breeze, this was a gale. She hung onto the mantel to stop herself from obeying.

He broadcast that to the whole room. If he figures out where I am and targets this wall, I'm not sure I can withstand him.

"Well, well, well!" he crooned. "You are an interesting problem. Living and undead alike, they all can be compelled. But you, not so. What to do?" He plucked a book from a shelf. Almost too quickly to see, he flung it into the corner where she had stood earlier. It struck with a force that rattled the windows and dented the plaster, then flopped to the floor like a broken bird. "Not there." He plucked another. It shattered one of the tall windows and sailed through, scattering glass in the bushes outside. "Not there." The third slammed into the bookcase not three feet from Senka, cracking a shelf. Books tumbled to the floor.

If one of those hits me, invisible-but-solid won't help. He reached for another book; she slipped from her hiding place and into the shaft of moonlight streaming through the west-facing window. He saw her and hurled the book at her head. Though she suspected it would pass through her, she didn't want him to know. She ducked, feeling the wind of its passing in her hair. It hit the far wall and exploded in a flurry of paper and leather.

"There she is. Our little hiker." He yanked another book from the shelf. Senka prepared to duck, but he only leafed through it as if he had become interested in a little light reading.

"You a big fan of romance novels?" Senka asked, gesturing to the lurid cover. "Danielle Steel a friend of yours too?"

"You mock me." Although his tone sounded nonchalant, his jaw clenched. He gestured in the direction Silas had fled. "It doesn't seem romance has been a friend of yours."

"Pal, you have no idea."

He dropped the book and prowled around her in a slow circle. As he did, she kept her eyes on him. "Silas never was much of a romantic, you know," he said. "You may have chosen the wrong vampire as your lover."

"He's not my lover!" She instantly regretted allowing him to goad her into a response. He was trying to pry information out of her, about their relationship, about Silas.

"Ah, no? Just a 'friend'?" His tone put the word in quotation marks, and his mouth turned down in an exaggerated, fake expression of sympathy. "It is unfortunate, no? Your friend doesn't care about you enough to stay and defend you."

"Hmm, yeah, sorry. That's not going to work on me. Try another."

"Again you mock me!" he hissed, nothing sweet-faced about him now.

Senka realized with a shiver that his circles had been getting smaller. He was now less than a foot from her. How could she have let her focus slip? She was counting on Silas's belief that the old vampire would be unable to harm her, that if he did attack, he'd pass through her, but she wasn't confident. She'd never dealt with a vampire this powerful before. Hell, this was only the second real vampire she'd ever encountered.

He stopped circling; she needed to get him moving again. "I'm sorry," she said, holding up her hands in apology. "I didn't mean to mock you. I know Silas respects you. Well, he fears you, and I think that shows a certain kind of respect, don't you?"

He made no reply, but his face shifted from snarl to sneer, and he began to circle her again. Senka went on. "He said you cared a lot for Tara. I'm sorry for your—" The ancient vampire's back was to the library door. Senka had a clear view to the music room. Her mouth dropped in horror. "Silas! What are you doing?"

The Maker whirled to face his creation. Senka knew her cue: she sprinted straight for the west-facing window, one desperate thought playing through her mind: *Please, please, please let me through the outside wall.* Before the vampire could register she had tricked him— that the doorway was empty—she reached the window wall, flung up her arms, and closed her eyes to protect against the impact.

In the next instant she felt grass under her feet and a breeze on her bare skin. She opened her eyes and, without a pause, hurdled a low bush and raced to the overgrown hedge maze she had seen that afternoon. She was pretty sure she could pass through a hedge if she could pass through a wall. There was no way she was capable of outrunning a vampire as powerful as the Maker, but she hoped she might avoid him within the maze, at least until he had to retreat from the rising sun.

A roar of anger—wild and ferocious—erupted from the house. Pure terror made her stumble. A dozen panes of glass shattered behind her. Another roar ripped the darkness. The air itself seemed to tremble. Birds rose, screaming and cawing, shaken from their roosts by the force of the ancient vampire's supernatural anger.

Senka reached the hedge maze and flung herself through the interwoven branches. She careened through two or three lanes before she stopped, trembling, listening hard. The old vampire screamed in fury and frustration. The squawking, cawing, chittering birds fell silent as if by a signal. The crickets and frogs quit their songs. Even the wind died. All of nature held its breath, helping her to hear her adversary's movements. She strained her ears. The outer hedge rustled and creaked, the branches rubbing together. She became aware of muttering. "Stupid bitch! I'm going to rip your throat out. Grind your bones to dust and suck on the marrow." She heard the sound of tearing foliage and snapping twigs. Was he ripping the hedge from the ground? He was strong enough. *Shit!* She hadn't planned for that. She thought he'd go around, work his way through the maze. If he did, she could stay at least a hedge away from him. Maybe it didn't matter; wafting through a hedge was faster than ripping it out of the ground. At least until he'd made a hole in every one. How long would that take? Till sunrise? She doubted it.

He let out a growl that rose to a roar, and the sound of shredding roots played counterpoint. Senka backed up to the next hedge, her eyes glued to the one in front of her. He was in the outer lane. Another growl, another chunk of hedge ripped from the ground. He was in the second lane. Senka slipped through the hedge behind her.

"Little fugitive," he sang, "I'm getting closer. You can't hide, and you can't outrun me." A piece of hedge flew over her head. Third lane. She passed through the next hedge and found herself in the center of the maze.

An image of Stanley flashed into her mind, an argument they'd had as they wrote the last season of *Blood Moon*. She had wanted a fight in a maze, but he had insisted mazes were a gross cliché. "I should die rather than putting a *farkakte* maze in my show," had been his exact words. *Yet here I am. I win, Stan.* She pressed her hand to her mouth to stifle a snort. Stanley had always said her greatest asset was her ability to see the humor in any situation. Or had he said it was the trait most likely to get her killed? *Too late for that.* She giggled.

Silence on the other side of the hedge, then an explosion of vampiric rage. "You dare laugh at me!" It was the sound of a thunderclap ripping the skies overhead. But for Senka, the terror it would have provoked moments before failed to materialize. Her laughter had broken his spell. Silas was right; someone who could waft through hedges couldn't be killed. For that, you had to be alive. Or at least not dead.

The ripping noises started again, but there in the center of the maze Senka was unconcerned. Until she felt a pressure against her ankle. She peered down to see Luna looking up at her, his eyes, as big as half dollars, glowing in the moonlight, and his hair standing on end. He looked terrified. "What are you doing here?" she hissed.

His tail raised like a flag for her to follow, he squeezed through a small gap between the ground and the lowest branch of the hedge. He poked his face through to see if she was coming. She trailed him until they were out of the maze, where someone else stood waiting for them.

"Silas! You need to get out of here," she whispered.

"I've come to get you."

"How did you find me?"

He gestured toward the maze and whispered, "I followed the noise." He held out his arm to her.

Relief and gratitude flooded her. She tucked her hand into the crook of his elbow, ready to flee this place.

Her fingers slid through his arm like mist.

"I'm not solid enough," she said, fear rising. "The moon is too bright." The concern in his eyes perversely pleased her. She'd have to think about that later. Now horror constricted her chest. She had to make Silas go and take Luna with him. "You've got to get out of here. You're the one who could be hurt. You and Luna."

"I can't leave you here alone."

"Go, Silas. I'm serious. I couldn't stand it if he hurt either of you. Meet me after dawn in the—"

The words died as she realized the sounds of destruction from inside the maze had stopped. From the other side of the nearest hedge came a voice: "But how charming! He has returned for his boon companion, but she only wants his safety. Go where you want, Silas, but know, after I am done with her, I will find you wherever you hide and I will end you."

Senka mouthed, "*Go!*" She tried to push him, but her hands went through his shoulders and poked out his back. Silas plucked Luna from the ground, gave her a final pained look—and was gone.

In the same moment, the Maker tore the last section of hedge straight from the ground and tossed it over his shoulder. He and Senka stood face-to-face. For a moment he paused, immobile, staring at her. Then he swung his fist like a mighty club straight at her head.

The fist swept through her. The vampire's momentum carried him forward and he had to catch himself on the tattered remnants of the hedge. Senka wanted to laugh but thought better of it. *No need to poke the bear.* Instead she said, "I'm guessing you haven't had much experience with ghosts."

The Maker said nothing, only reached out a finger and poked it through her stomach. His arms fell to his sides.

"Silas didn't know much about us either."

The Maker didn't speak. He glanced around as if searching for something, then backed away from Senka, folded his arms, and leaned against the hedge, watching her. She didn't trust his apparent calm. Whatever he was doing, he hadn't resigned the fight. She considered walking away but suspected he'd follow her, and she'd end up leading him right to Silas. "Hey," she began, "how'd you find us anyway?"

With icy calm, he replied, "Did it not occur to either of you I would have spies keeping watch on Tara's house?"

"We should have thought of that, yeah."

"*We?* You are so protective of him, yet you met but a short time ago. You mean *he* should have thought of that. He is the one who knows me after all."

Senka refused to be drawn into a Blame Silas game. "Why do you hate him so much? I'd think turning someone would make you feel closer to him, like a parent-child relationship."

"I'm guessing you haven't had much experience with vampires," he replied, echoing her earlier jibe.

"Only on TV, and I'm starting to think we didn't know our asses from our elbows. Come on, tell me. What did he do to you?"

"He hasn't told you? No? Hardly surprising. Well, fine." He looked off into the distance. What he saw there seemed to pain him. "We were inseparable once, he, Tara, and I. We traveled together across the world, throughout society. I showed them what they had been missing stuck in their dreary forest. But then, in London, we met a lonely little boy, helpless and starving, perhaps five or six. I longed to help him."

"You mean turn him."

"No, no! That wasn't what I meant at all. I do not turn my companions against their will." It was getting harder to see him, but Senka caught the fervent glimmer of his eyes. "I planned to see him fed, clothed, and warm. But Silas! Good god! He was so jealous. He hated the attention I gave the poor little thing. He was cruel to him, mocking him, hitting him. One night, I went with Tara to the opera, leaving Silas to care for the child—and Silas *murdered* him."

"He what?"

"When we came home, the little body was arranged grotesquely in Silas's favorite chair. He was utterly drained of blood. Silas stood nearby, gloating. I attacked him. I wanted to rip his limbs from his hideous body. But Tara interceded and he fled. I swore on the child's life I would end Silas, and I will never stop trying."

Senka felt cold and sick. "I don't understand. He killed the child out of jealousy?"

The Maker nodded. "It is not only the Maker who becomes attached to those he turns. Silas wanted all of my attention for himself. He was jealous even of his sister. It is why they became estranged."

Something didn't sit right with Senka. "That doesn't sound like him," she began. But then, it hadn't sounded like Kenny to murder her, either. The light was dim, and she could only just discern the old vampire's expression. In that moment, she registered her danger. The moon had set and no light shone on them. She didn't have a chance to flinch before the full force of the Maker's blow landed on her stomach. It lifted her off her feet and sent her flying through the air. She hit the grassy lawn and slid. If she'd had breath, it would have been knocked out of her. His blow caused no damage and left no mark; still, it hurt like hell. Before Senka could get her mind around the pain, he was on her again. He stood over her, gloating, and kicked her hard in the back. Fire shot up her phantom spine.

Rage hauled her to her feet, pain be damned! No one—*no one*—had hit her in life, and she'd be goddamned if she'd take it now. She'd been a vampire fighter on television; she'd be a vampire fighter in reality.

Teeth gritted, snarling, Senka dropped into a battle stance, blessing every fight choreographer she knew. A momentary look of doubt crossed the ancient vampire's face and was gone, banished by his confidence in his own superiority.

This time when he struck, she was ready for him and dodged his blow. Taking advantage of his loss of balance, she walloped him with a roundhouse kick to his thigh, hoping to see his knee buckle, but it was like kicking a granite wall; it had no effect on him, but her whole leg exploded with pain. She stumbled away from him. His fist connected with her side, sending her through the air and into the trunk of an oak tree.

Rage overcame the pain once again, and Senka clawed herself back to her feet, raising her fists and snarling. He *laughed*. Fury narrowed her focus to a pinpoint. She couldn't fight him; he was too strong. All she could do was dodge him.

A realization struck her. In the house she had passed through a wall even in the deepest shadow. She hadn't been able to control it, but if there was a time to learn, it was now. She dropped her arms to her sides as she felt the vampire rush at her. She imagined herself as moonlight, as stardust. His fist struck her gut and again she was lifted off her feet to slam into the garden wall. She stood. Moonlight, stardust. Another blow. *Stay focused, you can do this!*

She lost count of the blows. She lost count of the number of times she picked herself up. She closed her eyes and refused to look at the vampire. His violence mounted with her passivity.

I can't go back to the emptiness of the hours and days. The crushing loneliness. I can't lose Silas.

There had been no blow for—*How long has it been?* She opened her eyes to the sight of a fist inches from her face.

It passed through her.

Her tormentor was no longer the elegant being who had entered the library, so calm, so urbane. Instead, his once neatly coiffed hair had come loose of its tie and hung about his face like a disheveled mop. His suitcoat was gone, and his shirt and trousers looked like they'd been through a reaper. They stared at each other. Without a word, the vampire backed away from Senka then disappeared.

For a long time, she didn't move. She felt no sense of victory. He would never relent; it was only a matter of time before he returned. The familiar ache of loneliness clung to her.

A bird twittered in a nearby tree. Others responded. The chorus rose. The watery light of predawn revealed the garden around her.

I'm not alone, she fought to reassure herself. *Silas will be waiting for me to find him.* She looked up. Trotting toward her from a distant stand of trees, Luna. Warmth flooded her. She smiled in greeting and walked toward him.

"Mrrrrp?" he asked her.

She stooped and swept him into her arms, burying her face in his fragrant fur. "I'm fine," she said. "Don't worry, little one." His rumbling purr banished every pain, every ache of the long and brutal night. He squirmed in her arms, turning himself so he could see her face, then rubbed his cheek across her chin. "Your whiskers are pokey, dude."

She carried him all the way to the copse, and he let her. Silas waited within the trees. They stood for a moment, appreciating being together. Senka tucked her hand into Silas's. "Is it too light out to travel?"

"Not yet."

"Then let's get out of here."

They did.

As Finn fiddles with the tape on the inside of his arm, smoothing it down around the cannula where it enters his vein, I wonder if he'll ask me about what's troubling him.

"You're so quiet. You usually have something to say at the end of a chapter."

"Can I ask you a question?" He looks up at me with a frown.

"Of course."

"Are you—" He stops.

"What?"

He stares at me, making a decision. I stay silent. After a moment, the frown leaves his face, and he says, "Did Silas really kill the little kid?"

I don't believe that's what he was going to ask, but I'll go with it. "That's hard to hear."

"Yeah."

"It was for me too, when I first heard it."

"Did he?" His tone is urgent.

"I'm going to ask a favor."

He groans. "Wait for the story to tell itself in its own way?"

"Yes."

He frowns again. "I'd prefer not to."

"Let me ask you this. What's your guess? Do you think he murdered the boy?"

"The Maker said he did," he counters.

"Yes." I wait.

"But Senka didn't believe it."

"No, she didn't."

He watches me for a moment, brows knit. "Do you believe he didn't?"

I smile. "I'm guessing you know the answer."

"Yeah, I guess I do." I'm relieved he answers my smile with one of his own. "Can I ask another question?"

"Of course."

"Senka learns to fade in shadows because she remembers what it felt like to be so lonely, like no one remembers her, right?"

"Yes. I'm glad you picked up on that."

"So, then, all the time of being lonely, it … it was, like, awful, but … like … it helped her in the fight."

"I've found sometimes, not all the time, a hard experience can teach us important lessons."

He nods, thinking. "Yeah, that's true. At least in my experience." He glances up at me but turns his attention to the fringe on his blanket. "It gets tough in here sometimes."

"I can imagine."

"Maybe I'll try to look for the lesson."

I feel a lump in my throat. "Good, but don't get discouraged if you don't find it right away."

"I know. I feel better thinking about hard times that way."

"Me too."

Finn nods and looks at me from under his thinning bangs. "This is kinda embarrassing, but would you … could you do me a favor?"

"Anything in my power." I'd say the same thing to anybody I told this story to, but somehow, I mean it more when I say it to Finn.

"Would you mind hanging out for a while?"

"If you want me to."

"Thanks."

"Are you going to try to sleep?"

"Yeah."

"Goodnight, Finn."

"Goodnight." He pauses, and adds, "Storyteller."

CHAPTER FIVE

The next night, Finn's smile lacks a few kilowatts, but at least he's sitting up.

"You okay?" I take my usual seat by his bed. "Tough day?"

"I mean, yes and no." He traces the logo of one of the ball teams on his blanket. "My mother was here. She's the night manager at a hotel, so she can't spend as much time with me as she wants." He's quiet. I think it must be hard for a sixteen-year-old boy to share his emotions with a virtual stranger. Still, maybe after these last few days, I'm less of a stranger, even if I don't yet rank as a friend. He looks up and says, "She has a lot to deal with, and like, I hate that she has to worry about me too."

I nod my understanding. "May I tell you something I've learned about worry?"

He studies my face. "Sure."

"To worry about things—money, the future—is a waste of time because our worry won't change anything. To worry about a being—someone like you—is a privilege. That kind of worry comes from love, and to kindle love in someone is to give them something precious."

He considers my words. "I never thought about it like that." He sighs. "I just wish—" I let the silence extend while he decides whether to trust me with a new confidence. "I wish the doctors would tell me what they tell her. I'm not a kid—I'm sixteen. They talk to her, and I see she's worried, but I don't feel like I can ask questions because I'm afraid it would be harder for her. And maybe it's better for her to think I don't know how sick I am."

"I wonder if it would be easier for you if you didn't know. But you prefer the truth, don't you?"

He shrugs. "Probably." He looks up at the bag dispensing medication into his arm. "We should have enough time before the nurse comes in to change that," he says, indicating the bag with his chin. I wish he weren't an expert in the subject. He nudges me, "When you stopped, Silas had just used vampire travel to get him, Senka, and Luna away from the estate. What happens next?"

"Well, I'll tell you."

"I have so many questions," Senka said, not bothering to take in their new location. She ticked each one off on her fingers. "Where are we? Are we safe here for more than a couple of hours? And, Silas, honestly, what the hell happened between you two?"

Silas set Luna on a nearby table. "Which one do you want to start with? Or could we start with making sure you're all right? Did he harm you?"

Some of her tension softened at his concern. "How much did you see?"

"Nearly all of it."

The cat hadn't taken his eyes off Senka, and now he said, "Meow-wow!" Senka held a finger out to him. He touched it lightly with his nose, then rubbed a cheek against it. Senka smiled. "Thank you, Luna. I love you too." Luna gave her a slow blink. She continued, "It was rough, but I'm okay. I'm relieved you two weren't hurt."

"That I was powerless to help you galls me." Silas pushed his hair back, frustrated.

"I know." Her voice warmed with her appreciation for the sentiment. "But we were right! Now we know for sure he can't destroy me. I need to practice being insubstantial, though."

"How did you do it?" Silas asked, grasping her elbow. "I saw your attempts. It appeared as though the … the right combination came to you."

Senka wasn't ready to relive the nightmare of loneliness it took to achieve her feat of intangibility. She said, "The right combination is as good a description as any. Tell me this, though: why did your

Maker rip up the hedges? Why didn't he … tesseract or whatever you call it when we travel together?"

"Tesseract?" Silas seemed to be tasting the word, but shrugged, accepting it. "That is only for longer distances, not simply a few feet."

"Okay, then why didn't he—I don't know—turn into a bat and fly over them?" Silas's eyebrows shot up. He pressed his lips together, trying to suppress a smile. "What?" Senka asked. "He would have gotten to me much faster."

Silas patted her arm. "Although Bram Stoker was a gift to the Victorian gothic novel, what he knew about the reality of vampires would have fit in a thimble."

"So you don't turn into bats?" Senka's face fell, but she tried to mask her disappointment.

"No. And we don't need to sleep in coffins in order to cross water." He cocked his head to the side and smirked, "In one thing he was correct: we can be very sexy."

Senka snorted. "Is that so?"

"Oh, yes. Speaking in all modesty, of course, we are far more charming than your lycanthrope or your reanimated man."

Her jaw dropped. "Those exist too?"

He shrugged and, lips quirking, said, "I have no idea. But if they do, vampires are superior in all ways."

"No doubt," she said, laughing.

Silas sobered. "Truly, though, Senka. I am sorry you had to face my Maker alone, and I am more relieved than I can say that you are unhurt."

They stood close together in the little room. She looked up into his eyes and words abandoned her for a moment. Then she dropped her gaze and took a step back. "Are we safe here?" she asked.

"Perfectly." Silas turned away from her, crossing his arms and resting one hip on the table next to Luna.

The room couldn't have been more different from the estate they had left moments before. It was a compact, overstuffed sitting room. Filtered sun slipped through sheer curtains, permitting light to enter but no lethal rays. A worn rug, dotted with a faded pattern of pink roses, covered most of the wide-plank wooden floor. Two inviting rocking chairs snuggled side by side facing a loveseat well-suited for bustle-clad women. All three sidled up to a shallow fireplace. Under the window, two padded chairs crowded around a tea table on which stood a whale oil lantern. The room smelled of history and furniture polish. The entire effect was simultaneously cozy and claustrophobic.

"Where are we?" Senka asked, perplexed.

"The Monterey Peninsula. Pacific Grove."

"California? What year is it?"

"Not even Stoker says vampires are capable of time travel. This is a museum. Well, it's a display of what the keeper's cottage would have looked like in the heyday of the lighthouse."

Alarm shot through Senka. "And we're safe here how? Won't there be tourists and docents trooping in and out?"

"Only for a few hours on the weekends." Silas lounged in one of the rocking chairs, his long legs stretched in front of him. "It's closed during the week. On weekends, I will retire to the attic, and you can be the resident ghost." He sounded like he was suggesting it would be a vacation for both of them.

Senka wasn't reassured. "I don't know a ton about being a ghost. If all the books about vampires have gotten it wrong, what's to say all the books about ghosts haven't too?"

"We will need to experiment, true." Seeing her doubtful expression, he added, "Some *very cautious* experimentation. I'm fairly certain you can't be seen by living humans. Until we know for sure, you can join me in the attic, if you'd like."

She recognized it must feel very different for Silas, who had traveled in the company of a cat for who knew how many years, to suddenly have a ghostly companion to think about. "I'm sure this place will be fine," she said. Yet, she needed reassurance there wouldn't soon be a repeat of the night before. "What about your Maker?"

Silas stopped rocking, his apparent serenity lessening a few degrees. "There are a handful of locations where I've been safe for a prolonged period. This is one of them. He never found me here."

"So why did you leave?" Senka asked, sinking into the other rocking chair.

Silas cleared his throat. "I ... um ... I became overly familiar with one of the residents and stayed too long."

"You mean you fell in love?" She had no idea why an unaccustomed flutter started in her heartless chest.

Silas avoided looking at her. He clucked at Luna, trying to lure him off the table and onto his lap. "I cared for her. I trusted her. It may have been love." He gave up on the cat, who ignored him. "Whether it was or not, I stayed long enough to attract attention." He shrugged. "I didn't age, of course. Her family—living people, as was she—became suspicious. And there was the other challenge with my appearance." He pointed to his face and sleek black hair. "This was in the mid-1800s. Thousands of indigenous peoples were killed in California during that time. I was fortunate to have the luxury of leaving." He shifted in his chair. "However, more to the point, I'm ashamed of my carelessness, thinking Tara's house would be safe for us. But I promise you, this is a better location. My Maker has no reason to watch the lighthouse; as far as I'm aware, he doesn't know I've been here before. Across the road is a golf course with large herds of deer. If a few become mildly anemic, no one will notice. Can you be comfortable here?"

"I think so. Thank you." She was silent until one of last night's painful memories came back to her. "Silas," she began. He looked at her, aware of the change in her tone. "You have to tell me why your Maker hates you so much. I think I deserve to know the truth. What did you—" She stopped herself, not wanting to sound accusatory. "What happened between you two?"

Silas rested his head against the back of the rocking chair and closed his eyes. His skin looked chalky and drawn. He sighed. "You're right." He opened his eyes. "You deserve to know." He gathered his strength and faced her. "Please understand, this happened long ago. Two hundred years or more. I am different now, and I'd like to think I would act more quickly. In those days, I had been a vampire for mere decades, and I remained under his sway."

Luna appeared in Silas's lap, startling both vampire and ghost, picked his way across the two adjacent rocking chair arms, then stepped onto Senka's lap where he curled up, purring. "I am nothing but a thoroughfare." Silas smiled as he said it.

Senka shifted her position without disturbing Luna, so she could look at Silas. "Tell me the story," she prompted.

Silas leaned back and closed his eyes again. "Do you remember I told you—was that only yesterday?—about my Maker and the little girl in Paris?"

"I remember." The story turned her stomach still.

"That was not a single occurrence. In the years we were together, my Maker murdered dozens of children. So many I lost count." He looked at Senka with a pained expression. "Please, please believe me. I did not condone it—in fact, I wanted to stop him. Tara did as well, but we felt powerless. He gave us the education we had always longed for. He taught us languages; opened our eyes to the arts, to the beauty of the human creative spirit." Silas shrugged. "We were a family, in some warped manner, and we felt prized as we never had before." Silas squeezed his eyes closed, as if he couldn't bear to see Senka's expression. "We tried to convince ourselves that his predilection for children was nothing but an eccentricity of our kind. We told ourselves a child here, a ... an infant there didn't amount to anything important." His hand covered his eyes as he remembered.

Senka felt sick thinking of it; the monster that had attacked her the night before had lured children to suffer the full force of his savagery.

Silas went on. "One evening—this was in London—we came across a little boy, an orphan, ragged and starving, sprawled against the wall of a pub. He wore no shoes, no coat on a cold October night. My Maker crouched and whispered to him. The child was so trusting, so innocent, despite all he must have endured in his short life. We took him back to our flat, fed him, bathed him, clothed him. For weeks our Maker coddled the boy—little Jude—gave him trinkets, sweets, and encouraged his affection. We knew he was toying with the child, and at any moment he would change and Jude would be dead, discarded."

Realizing she was clutching Luna's paw, Senka forced herself to let it go, afraid she'd hurt him, though he hadn't complained.

"I don't know why we dared to defy him at last. Perhaps this boy reminded us of Will, our youngest brother, undoubtedly dead for many years by that time." Silas rubbed the back of his neck before going on. "One night, the three of us planned to leave the child at home as we attended the opera, the London premiere of *Lucia di Lammermoor*. At the last moment, I acted the rascal and refused to go. Tara pretended to be angry with me and climbed into the carriage, insisting they be on time, that she hated all the fashionable ninnies who arrived late. Our Maker believed we were engaged in a sibling spat. He laughed and drove off with my sister, leaving me with Jude." Silas paused again. "I wrapped him up in a wool coat and blanket and whisked him as far away as I could, to Scotland. I knew a childless shepherd and his wife. Although I gave them a great deal of money to look after the boy, they took him in out of love and generosity. I visited him every few years throughout his life. He grew up to be a kind, compassionate man."

They sat in silence for a time, Silas with his eyes closed; Senka, patient, waiting for him to be able to go on. At length, Silas grimaced. "I went back to our flat, hoping when my Maker returned from the opera, we would convince him to stop preying on children." Silas laughed without warmth. "That didn't happen. He raged. He cursed. He accused me of betraying him more profoundly than he had ever been betrayed. Tara stayed quiet, as we had planned. I saw no reason to endanger her, and our Maker did not suspect she was involved. But he attacked me in a diabolical fury, and as I could not fight him, he would have ended me if Tara had not intervened. She could not fight him either, of course, but she could pull him off me long enough so I could escape. He has never forgiven me since; it is not in his nature to forgive. He will hunt me until he ends me. The only question is, when will he succeed?" He rubbed his forehead then let his hand rest there, covering his eyes.

Senka watched him. She had no doubt the story was true. What she couldn't get her mind around was—"So all his fury and hatred is because you didn't let him kill one child?"

"It wasn't only the child; it was the disloyalty." Silas let his hand drop and met her eyes. "I had taken a decision on my own and acted against him. To any Maker, such behavior shows growing independence that bodes conflict. One finds the same thing in nature: lions, gorillas, elephant seals ... others. Most Makers choose either to subjugate the rebel or cast him from the family. My Maker has always favored a more ... permanent course."

Senka nodded, biting her lip. "You should know he told me you killed the child."

"What?" Silas's nostrils flared, and he sat forward.

She rested a hand on his arm. "I knew he was lying. I think he was trying to drive a wedge between us."

"I could never harm a child!"

"I know."

"*Never!* Even then, before I foreswore human blood. I will never, never forgive myself for allowing him to kill all of the children he did. I am repelled by my weakness." Silas's hands clenched, and Senka wrapped her fingers around his.

This vampire is one of the kindest, most ethical beings I've ever met, she thought, aware of the irony. *I know more about his history and his character in a couple days than I knew about Kenny in over a year.* "Silas," she said. "You shouldn't beat yourself up about this. You rescued that boy at a pretty sizable cost to yourself. At the same time, that evil creature ... it's likely he's still killing kids." She leaned toward him. "I think there's only one path forward."

"Which is?"

"We turn the tables on him. End him before he can end you."

Silas loosened his fist and turned his hand over to slide his fingers between Senka's, and she let him. He brought her hand up to his lips and kissed it with such tenderness that tears prickled her eyes. "I am grateful," he said, "to have existed long enough to meet you." They smiled at each other, ghost and vampire. "Your courage is inspiring."

"It's easy to be courageous if you're already dead," she said, laughing.

"Nonetheless."

Though Luna had fallen asleep, he began to purr; his little body vibrated with the rumblings.

Silas sat in thought for several moments. Senka watched him, waiting for the objections she knew were coming. "I have longed for many years," he said, "to find a way to free myself from my Maker. My inability to harm him isn't a choice, it's one of the conditions of being a vampire. It means I wouldn't be able to help—you would be on your own—and I can't allow you to do that."

Senka took her hand back. "Yeah, see, that's not the way it works. You, me, and Luna, we're a team. I like you both. I'm not about to tell either of you what you are or aren't 'allowed' to do, and I'd appreciate the same respect from both of you. I value your advice, well, yours more than Luna's. You have a lot more experience on the planet than both of us combined. But, my friend, you don't get to give or withhold permission."

"But—"

"Uh-uh. No. Sorry. Besides, there are ways to help me that don't include fighting the evil one. If this turning-the-tables thing is going to work, we have planning to do." Excitement rose within her with the prospect of action. "Where do we find him? How is he vulnerable? I underestimated him last night. I won't make the same mistake again. How do I prepare to take him on?"

Silas shook his head. "I know I should try to stop you, but I can't help feeling ..."

"Excited?"

He laughed. "Yes. I haven't felt this hopeful in ... perhaps ever."

They gazed at each other like the two enthusiastic co-conspirators they were.

Senka broke the spell. "Right! Let's brainstorm. We'll make a list of questions we have to consider about your Maker." She stopped. "You know, I am sick of calling him 'your Maker' all the time. It gives him too much power. What's his name?"

Silas looked doubtful for a moment, as if he were afraid to say it aloud. "This is truly breaking protocol." He swallowed. "Harou de Bellême."

"De Bellême. Was he nobility?"

"No. That's where he was from. An ancient town in Normandy. His ancestors were Viking raiders."

"Of course they were. Okay, so, list. First, what do we need to think about in regard to Harou? Next, how do I need to train? Third, what's our plan?"

They brainstormed, Silas taking notes on their ideas and future tasks. He answered Senka's questions regarding the old vampire, though he found it difficult to call him by his name. Senka delighted in saying it, once even howling, "Har-ooooooo," and though Silas winced, he didn't protest. Luna woke up and helped by batting at Silas's pen, sitting on their papers, and chasing a fly that had bumbled in through an open window.

"Are you confident you can become insubstantial at will?" Silas asked.

Senka clicked her tongue. "I wouldn't bet my … um … comfort on it. I'll need to practice." She didn't admit she wasn't looking forward to practicing that skill, nor that it took an emotional toll to plunge into the darkness of her years of loneliness.

Tapping the pen against his teeth, Silas asked, "How about the reverse? Do you think you could make yourself solid in the light?"

"That would be useful. That's kind of ghost manifestation stuff. With all the talk of ghostly visitations, you'd think it has to be possible, right? Put it on the list under 'Things for Senka to Practice.'"

As night fell, Luna reminded Silas it was time to hunt with a loud "Mer-ow!"

"Do you think …" Senka began, but felt uncharacteristically shy. She tried again. "Do you think … I could go outside? I mean, not to hunt with you or anything. Just to take a walk."

Silas grinned, delighted. "It appears you are now free to go outside any time you choose. Why don't you take a stroll while we hunt? Then I'll find you and we can explore the town together."

A date? Senka thought. She wasn't sure how she felt about the idea, though she was aware of an undeniable flutter where her heart used to be.

Silas held the door open for her. She watched as he and Luna trotted into the darkness.

The first newness that struck her was the rich smell of the sea air.

It had been so long—years—since she had been back on the coast where she'd spent the greatest part of her life. She stood, taking in the scent of the air for several minutes. She became aware of the surf—its crashing rhythm, the hiss and boom recalling dim memories of running beside the waves, playing a one-sided game of chicken, daring the water to flow up the sand and drench her. She remembered lying on a beach towel under an umbrella, gossiping with her girlfriends long before she had become famous; both gossiping and fame were silly concepts to her now. She thought of Kenny and the time they had walked along a beach at sunset holding hands. In those days, she imagined her life would be one long romantic movie. For the first time since her death, she found herself thinking of Kenny not with anger but with sadness. She hugged herself and thought, *It would have been idyllic if he hadn't turned out to be a murderer.* The incongruity struck her, and she laughed.

She set off along the lighthouse path. Seagulls squawked overhead, playing in the updrafts. They flashed white in the light of streetlamps. Bats swooped in and out of the shadows under cypress trees. She watched their acrobatics and whispered to them, "Not *one* of you is a vampire." When she had put some distance between herself and the lighthouse, she turned back to get a good look at it. It was a squat building, not at all like the majestic lighthouses farther up the coast. The light flared out at its designated intervals, ceremonially protecting ships whose GPS made it irrelevant. There was something touching in that. Its days of usefulness were over, yet people still cared enough to preserve it, so the beacon carried on, protecting the fishermen and sailors who didn't need it.

Continuing along the path away from the ocean and crossing a deserted street, Senka found herself in a cemetery. In life, she had felt cemeteries were wasteful places, co-opting greenspace for nothing more than warehousing used bones. Now, she found this one cozy. There was comfort in the idea of people's remains being contained in one spot, not scattered around a forest in the dens of various carnivores.

The gravestones were set into the ground in tidy rows, and Senka wandered among them. The first graves she came to were of infants.

Baby Howe, September 15, 1953.
One day. Not much of a life.
Douglas Driver, Our Little One, 1955.
Our Bug-Bug, July 10–September 9, 1954.
How does anyone grieve a loss that huge? I guess they create a memorial. For some people, that's a grave, where they can visit and leave flowers or toys and keep it tidy.

As she thought this, she spotted a pinwheel on the ground next to a gravestone. Lucy, August 28, 1998. "You need to be catching the wind," she told the pinwheel. "You're not much fun lying there." She picked it up and pushed the stake into the ground. The multicolored wheel gave a couple of half-hearted turns, then found the breeze and spun in earnest.

"How kind of you," said a voice behind Senka. She turned, startled, and saw a tiny Asian woman smiling up at her. She wore an elegant green brocade dress—something off a 1950s *Vogue* magazine cover—and her bright eyes twinkled with good humor and intelligence out of a face that looked like an apple forgotten for years in a refrigerator's back corner. She reached out her soft, papery hands and took one of Senka's, patting it. "The teenagers come, you see. They're just having fun. They don't know any better and why should they?" She laughed. "They're full of life, and we love seeing them. But they do make a mess of the presents sometimes. And don't get me started on the deer!" She waved a hand to forestall any questions about the cervine residents of the graveyard and laughed again.

Senka realized she was grinning back. She asked, "Are you buried here?"

Without releasing Senka's hand, the petite ghost turned and pointed toward a low stone wall. "Over there," she said, "near the older part of the cemetery." She pulled Senka toward her and whispered confidentially, "I was one hundred and one when I died, you know!" Her twinkly eyes beamed, and she laughed with delight. She took a step back and surveyed Senka from head to toe. "I don't think I've seen you here before. Are you new?"

Senka shook her head. "I'm not buried here."

"That's unusual. I've never heard of someone visiting from a different graveyard. I had no idea it was possible."

"I'm not from a different graveyard," Senka said, shaking her head again. "I'm not officially buried at all."

The other woman's eyes clouded. "Oh, dear. That doesn't sound good." She peered up at her taller companion. "And you were quite young when you died, weren't you? I'm so sorry, my dear."

"Thank you." Senka smiled down at her. "That's nice of you. No one's ever said that before."

"Now," the old ghost said, turning businesslike, "you must tell me how you got here."

They walked to the stone wall and sat side by side as Senka said, "Well, I died in a cabin in the woods, but it ended up burning down, and afterward, I could leave." She found herself wary of talking about Silas, even with this kind fellow ghost; she didn't want to accidentally give away his location. To change the subject, she said, "How many of us are there here?"

"Not many. Let's see. I'd say four or five, though they don't all come out regularly."

"Out of all the people buried here, there are only four or five ghosts?"

"Oh, yes. Not all the dead are interested in being ghosts, you know."

"Wait—you mean it's a choice?"

The old woman looked at her, surprised. "Of course! We have to have a reason to stay."

"What's your reason?" Senka asked, then felt embarrassed. "I'm sorry if that's a rude question. You don't need to answer."

The resident ghost smiled at her and patted her hand again. "Don't worry—I'm not offended. I stay because there's so much to experience! I love the sound the wind makes as it blows through the treetops, or the birds chippering and twittering. Sometimes a heron sits at the very top of the tallest pine over there; it glows pink in the setting sun. Or the silly geese strutting about like staff sergeants on patrol." She smiled, and her eyes disappeared into a cascade of wrinkles. They looked beautiful on her. "And the golfers on the course next to us"—she waved toward the far edge of the cemetery—"make me laugh with their grumpy muttering after they miss a shot. Oh, and the families who come to visit. So precious. Of course, there are my own great-great-great-grandchildren. My oldest great-great-great-granddaughter is pregnant, you know, and I can't wait to meet the little one. Oh, my dear, there's so much more to stay for." Still holding Senka's hand, she looked around at the night with evident contentment. "Why do you stay?"

"Well …" Senka drawled the word, gaining time. "To be honest, I didn't know it was a choice till now. I don't know much about being a ghost."

"No one does, dear. There are a few things I learned from my predecessors here, but there's no user's manual. Very much like life, I would say."

They sat in companionable silence for a moment, until Senka said out loud the truth she hadn't dared to consider before. "I stayed because I wanted revenge on the guy who killed me, but that's changed lately. I mean, it's not totally gone, but it's less burning, I guess you could say. Now I'm staying because I'm happy. There are these two beings I've met. I think I care about them, maybe a lot. We need each other. I'm useful. Does that make sense?"

"Eminent sense, my dear."

Senka caught a movement out of the corner of her eye and turned to see Luna strutting toward her along the top of the wall, his tail held up like a flag announcing the presence of royalty. As he reached her, he said, "Wer-ow!"

"And who is this?" asked the new friend.

"Luna. He's come to tell me our companion is done … with his business." Luna hopped down from the wall and twined around the old ghost's ankles. "He likes you."

"And I him," she said, smiling.

"Would it be okay … " Senka began, again wondering about protocol. "May I ask your name?"

"Of course, dear! It is Wang Ai-Xiu. Oh! You see, I may be born, bred, and buried in California, but I still give my name in the traditional way. A habit from my parents."

"Call me Senka. Thank you, Mrs. Wang. It was a pleasure meeting you."

"And you, dear. Please visit any time."

On an impulse, Senka leaned down and kissed one wrinkled cheek. Mrs. Wang, charmed, smiled up at her. Luna strutted off, tail raised in the 'follow me!' gesture, and Senka complied. She turned back to wave to Mrs. Wang, then trotted after the confident cat.

Silas waited for them where the cemetery abutted the golf course. As soon as she saw him, Senka called out, "I just met a ghost! She says there are four or five of them in this graveyard!"

Silas grinned. "How curious I'd not met any before you! I'm so pleased you have a cohort."

"She was really nice. And Luna liked her too!" She felt like a kid reporting on her first day at a new school. "Okay!" She bounced on her toes. "Show me the town."

Silas guided them up the length of the golf course. A chill rose from the grass beneath their feet. The moon, a day past full, hung low in the sky, its face obscured by a dense fog. As it floated in from the ocean, the fog twined through the trees. It haloed the streetlamps and porch lights and softened the edges of the world. They walked through quiet streets past sleeping houses. The incessant barking of sea lions led them to the water's edge where they strolled along the path that hugged the bay.

As they passed a couple walking in the opposite direction, Senka flinched. It had been a long, long time since she'd been in the presence of living people, and there was so much she didn't know about potential interactions with them. When the couple passed without acknowledging them, she was relieved. But as they walked on, there were more and more indications of an active nightlife in full swing. She heard music in the distance and the loud voices of revelers. She glanced at Silas out of the corner of her eye; he seemed unperturbed, composed.

A group of twenty-somethings skipped down a staircase and into their path. One young woman cried out to her friends, "Look at the kitty!" They all stopped and turned to Luna. Senka wasn't sure if they could see only him, or if she and Silas were visible too. The question was clarified by a male voice. "Hey, mister! Is that your cat?" With a composure that spoke to his far greater experience with the human world, Silas answered, "Yes. He's my little companion." There was a general ooh-ing and ah-ing, and three of the group crouched down to pet Luna. After a couple of minutes, they moved on, thanking Silas.

Luna walked over and sat on Silas's foot. He gazed up the length of the vampire's body to his face and said, "Meoooow!"

Silas looked down at him. "Are you tired? Do you want to ride?"

"Mrowp!"

Silas picked him up and placed him on his shoulder. "Are you comfortable?" Luna rubbed a cheek against Silas's ear. "I'll take that as a yes." He turned to Senka. "I do not believe they saw you. Did you feel the same?"

Senka considered no one in the group had glanced at her and they had spoken only to Silas. "I don't think they did."

"Let's try an experiment. There's a bar up that way a block or two. It's always crowded. Are you game?"

Senka felt her nerves kick in, but she was also curious. "Let's give it a try."

As they walked, the sounds of a live rock band grew louder, and they passed more people. Most never glanced their way, though a few pointed to Luna, who rode on Silas's shoulder.

As they approached a middle-aged couple, Silas stopped them. "I beg your pardon," he said. "I've lost my friend. Have you seen a woman, early thirties, quite beautiful, long auburn hair in a ponytail? She's wearing hiking shorts and a T-shirt."

"No, I'm so sorry," replied the wife. "Sure sounds like I'd have noticed her, but I haven't seen anyone like you describe. Have you, honey?" She turned to her husband.

He shook his head. "Nope, sorry. If we see her, where should we tell her you and the fur buddy are headed?"

"We're going back to the hotel. I appreciate your help. Thank you so much."

As the couple continued down the sidewalk, Silas turned to Senka. "Based on that encounter, I'd say humans can't see you." He pointed to the streetlight above them. "Even in the light." Senka looked at him, a smile on her face. "What?" he asked.

"You think I'm beautiful." The unfamiliar school girl feeling returned, even as she laughed at herself for her giddiness.

"Of course," Silas said, his tone light. "I'm undead, I'm not blind."

With only a little hesitation, Senka slipped her hand into his, and they walked another block until they stood outside the bar. The air pulsed with the noise of the band inside as customers flowed in and out. A group leaned against the outside wall, smoking. Again, a few people looked at Luna and smiled, but no one paid the least attention to Senka.

A laughing couple, arms wrapped around each other, stumbled out of the door and collided with Silas. Luna dug his claws into Silas's shoulder to keep from being knocked from his perch. Still linked with his girlfriend, the man spun around. "Nice cat, Cap'n Jack," he said with a sneer, and gave Silas a mock salute. The woman dissolved into laughter, and they stumbled down the street.

Silas looked after them, more amused than annoyed. "There's a May–September romance for you." When he turned back to Senka, she was staring at their retreating backs, frozen with shock.

As if she'd been stung by a wasp, she lunged after the retreating couple. "You fucking asshole!" she shrieked. "Come back here and face me!"

Neither turned around. They didn't even glance back.

Of course they can't hear me. They can't even see me.

She watched them weave and stumble across the street, then disappear up the hill toward a parking garage.

Silas put a hand on her arm. "Are you all right?" he asked, sounding alarmed.

Senka grabbed his hand, hard. "That was fucking Kenny. The guy who killed me."

Finn's jaw drops. "What?" he exclaims. "They ran into Kenny?"

"Yep."

"That's so random," he protests.

"Not entirely. When he and Sarah were married, he talked about buying a second house in Monterey."

"Jesus. Senka must have been creeped out to see him."

"She was," I say, thinking he sounds awfully close to talking about her like a real person, not a character in a story.

"How am I supposed to sleep now? I want to know what happens next." He looks so outraged I can't help smile.

"I bet as soon as you've closed your eyes, you'll be out like a light."

He flops back in bed with mock exasperation. I can see him thinking: there's a little crease between his eyebrows. He turns on his side so he faces me. "Can I ask you a question?"

"Always."

"How come some ghosts decide to stay? I mean, in the story."

Since I want to answer with details I know will help him, I take a moment before I begin. "Well, in my experience, it's as Mrs. Wang explained. For her, it's enough she enjoys seeing her great-grands. I know one woman who's waiting for her wife to join her; then they'll decide together whether they'll stay or go. Once, I met a man who worked for NASA; he's waiting to see if humankind finds extraterrestrial life."

He looks at me through squinted eyes. "You know these ghosts personally?" It's a question, not a blank denial. We may be getting somewhere.

"Of course," I say, as if it's the most natural thing in the world. Which, of course, it is. It's time to introduce a more challenging topic. "What about you? Would you stay or go?"

He thinks, his eyes cast up to the ceiling. "I don't know. There are things to stay for. People. But I'm not sure what I'd choose."

"It's good you don't have to decide now."

He sighs and lets it go. "Yeah." He yawns. "Are you gonna hang out again till I'm asleep?"

"Of course."

"Thanks." He smiles. "Tomorrow's going to be good. My main day nurse, Joe, said he'd have time to play Slapjack with me. Do you know that game? I'm a master at it. And I ordered tapioca pudding for dessert for lunch and dinner." He looks as excited as a ten-year-old.

"Sounds like a good day."

"Then you'll come back when it gets dark and tell me the next part of the story." I like that it's not a question.

"Yes, I will. Lots happens in the next part."

"With Kenny?"

"Yes, and Senka. And others."

"Others? Ooo, mysterious." His eyes sparkle with amusement. He doesn't press for details.

He's beginning to understand the way of stories.

CHAPTER SIX

Tonight I have to wait in the hall while a nurse finishes adjusting one of Finn's monitors. I hear her narrating all of her actions for his benefit. Although she has a grandmotherly tone, she's talking to him like someone who knows how smart he is. She uses technical terms and explains why she's making the adjustments. I smile at her as she passes by. She's at least a head shorter than me—and I'm not tall. A petite Filipina woman, no longer young, in scrubs decorated with images of SpongeBob. It can't be easy working in the pediatric oncology ward, but that doesn't stop her from committing herself to her charges.

As I look at Finn, I realize how much his once-wild mop of hair has thinned. Seeing him every day, I haven't noticed the change before. He seems unfazed; he's all peppiness tonight. I'm barely through the door when he says, "Oh, good, you're here."

"I'm here," I agree. "How was your day? Did you win at cards?"

"I won a game and Joe won a game. He's faster than I thought he'd be."

"Sounds like a good match-up. How was the tapioca?"

"That stuff never gets old. What did you do today?"

His question takes me by surprise, and I'm not sure how much detail I'm ready to share. "The usual," I hedge, knowing the words are inadequate.

"What does that mean?"

"I hung out with friends. I read a little bit." General but honest.

"Oh."

He's not satisfied, even a little disappointed. He knows I'm hedging. I wish he weren't quite so astute. Deflection time. "Are you ready to hear the next part of the story?"

"Yeah!"

"Okay. Remember where we were?"

"Outside the bar on Cannery Row."

"You know the place?"

"Of course. Senka was upset because she'd just seen Kenny." He snuggles into his covers and turns so he can watch me.

"Okay, then. Here we go."

Senka, Silas, and Luna stared at the spot where Kenny had disappeared. "Let's go," Senka said, pulling Silas by the hand.

"Where?"

"After them!"

They ran across the street, Luna bobbing without complaint on Silas's shoulder, and jogged up the little hill to the parking garage. They were in time to glimpse the girl's back as the door to the first level closed behind her. They followed, Silas hanging back in the shadows as Senka strode forward.

The couple stopped behind a fancy little sports car. *A McLaren,* Senka thought, rolling her eyes at the ostentatiousness of it. "Get in the car, babe," Kenny ordered, and gave the woman a smack on the rear.

"Ow!" she yelped. "That really hurt!"

He scoffed and said, "Don't be a baby!"

"I mean it. Don't hit so hard. I told you before."

"Jesus, get in the fucking car."

Her answer was lost to the roar of the engine. She climbed in, and the roof folded down. Senka heard her say, "It's too cold to put the top down. I'll freeze."

"Why didn't you wear a coat?"

Before Senka could register he had moved, Silas stood beside Kenny's door, looking down at him.

Kenny's fists gripped the steering wheel as his head snapped in Silas's direction. When he registered who it was, he laughed and his muscles relaxed. "Hey, it's Cap'n Jack the cat boy," he said as his girlfriend giggled once more.

Silas stood unmoving, gazing at Kenny with the intensity of a tiger eyeing its prey. Kenny gazed back, a smirk on his face. The girlfriend prodded Kenny's arm. "Let's go," she said. "This guy gives me the creeps."

With a screech of tires, Kenny backed the car out of the parking space. He turned back to Silas. "Just kidding, pal. No hard feelings, right?" Not waiting for a response, he sped toward the exit.

Senka stepped beside Silas and reached for Luna. The three of them looked after the little sports car. As the sound of its screeching tires faded away, Senka muttered, "Asshole."

"Do you think," Silas asked, "the girlfriend is in any danger?"

Senka considered it. "Given what I know," she admitted at last, "I can't promise she's safe."

"Yes. That is what I thought as well." He looked down at her and held out his arm. "Shall we go?"

Silas transported the three of them back to the lighthouse. Senka sat in the rocking chair, brooding as Silas paced the compact living room. Luna perched on the loveseat, his pupils dilated with tension as he looked from one to the other.

Silas spoke first. "He's older than I thought he'd be."

"Time hasn't improved him."

"He's also … what's the word people use? Entitled."

"Yeah. He wasn't like that when we were together. Not openly anyway. He was, I don't know, confident. Assertive."

Silas took a seat across from Senka. "What are you thinking?"

For the first time since she had seen Kenny, Senka met Silas's eyes. She reached a hand out to him and Silas took it. His steadiness made her realize she was shaking. "I don't know. My thoughts are jumbled. For years, the thing, the consideration or obsession, maybe, that's been keeping me going is revenge. I guess I hoped—and I didn't even know this was how I was thinking, you know?—I hoped maybe he'd been found out and arrested and he was in prison. Then maybe

I could let that be enough. But I'm not sure it would have been, you know. Seeing him, I wanted to slug his self-satisfied mug. No, that's not true." She shook her head so hard her ponytail whipped back and forth. "I wished he were dead. I mean, he murdered me. We're not talking an accident here. But then I start thinking … well … I just … I don't …"

In one effortless movement, Silas pulled Senka from her chair and sat her next to him on the loveseat. "If you were alive," he said, holding her hands, "I'd tell you to take a breath. Remember what that felt like? Taking a deep breath could be so calming. Hold my hands. Focus on our connection."

Senka clung to him, needing his rootedness. What she wanted to do was wrap her arms around his waist and press her face into the crook of his neck, but she couldn't; she wouldn't allow herself to. Yes, Silas struck her as good, ethical, kind. But she'd misjudged Kenny. *Misjudged?* That was the century's great understatement. She wouldn't make the same mistake again.

After watching them for a moment, Luna leapt from the table to the loveseat, forced himself between them, and began to purr. Senka used the moment to reclaim her hands and settle against the loveseat's arm. Luna squeaked with disapproval, but Senka ignored him. "I'm better," she said. "Calmer. I want to know a few things. First of all, what has Kenny been doing for the last decade and a half? Did he face any questioning after I disappeared? What did people do? What did he say? What is he doing now? Who's the girl we saw him with? Does she know the truth about him? That's more than enough for starters."

"How do we find the answers?"

"We go to the library and google him. You'll have to do the actual typing so I don't freak out the other patrons."

"Perhaps it is time we purchased a laptop. We can't be dependent on library hours to know what's going on around us."

"I wouldn't have thought of getting a laptop. Have you had one before?"

"Several, but I always have to abandon them when my Ma … when Harou finds me."

Senka looked at him, acknowledging he made a point of saying the Maker's name, then added, "I hadn't thought of you using a laptop, but you are a very hip vampire." She elbowed him lightly in the ribs.

Silas smiled. "Your capacity to be upbeat in difficult situations is one of your most delightful qualities."

"So I've been told," she laughed. "I always feel better having an action plan."

Senka and Silas spent the daylight hours practicing and planning. With the sunrise, there had been few shadows in the little keeper's cottage, and anyway, Senka wasn't ready to draw out the searing loneliness that allowed her to be insubstantial in darkness. Instead she thought it best to focus on intangibility. As a warm-up, she practiced passing through the walls—first interior, then exterior. The skill was easy in daylight. Feeling confident about her progress, she turned her attention to becoming solid in light.

She considered the martial arts practitioners who could make themselves so heavy the strongest person couldn't lift them. Standing in the light from the window, she pictured herself as an anvil, a sequoia, Denali. When she felt she had gained substance, she told Silas, "Okay, give me a try." He set down his book on the history of the lighthouse and reached out to touch her. His hand passed through her torso.

"Damn," she said, dropping her rigid pose. "Back to the drawing board."

"I was thinking …" Silas ventured. "Would you learn to hover?"

"Hover?"

"Yes, as the spirits do in Dickens. They float through the air. Marley and the host outside Scrooge's window."

"I can give it a try. Why?"

"I'm considering skills that might prove useful."

"Add it to the list of what I need to work on."

She went back to her practice, trying a dozen other approaches. If it wasn't heaviness that led to density, perhaps it was imagining the elimination of space between her atoms. Next, she thought if loneliness made her insubstantial, perhaps companionship made her tangible. But if that were true, she should have been tangible from the moment she joined Silas and Luna. Maybe another emotion. She fell back on her actor's exercises, conjuring joy, anger, laughter, and, in desperation, jealousy. None worked. Seeing she was becoming frustrated, Silas suggested a break. Although she wanted to press on, she knew he was right. "I think I'll take a walk. Hopefully an idea will come to me outside."

"You'll be safe? You won't—I don't know—blow away in the wind?"

She laughed. "I don't think so." Realizing that Silas wasn't joking, she added, "I won't go far, just where I can see the ocean."

Luna looked up as she left but didn't follow her.

It felt strange and exhilarating to be outside in the daytime. The marine layer had kept the lighthouse muffled in fog all day, yet she sensed the warmth of the sun's rays. The lighthouse was set surprisingly far back on a level spit of the peninsula and was surrounded by the green grass of the neighboring golf course. Senka floated through a quaint split-rail fence and stood feeling the breeze flow into and out of her, enjoying the vibrancy of the ocean, wrapped around her on three sides. The ever-present seagulls sang their wild cries.

She gazed as far out into the bay as she could, as far as the fog would allow, and let her mind wander where it chose. She found herself thinking about shadows, how, alone in the cabin, she had loved them. They were friends. They were safety and comfort. She looked around; even now, in the fog, there they were, muted but present. The shadow of a tree, off to her right. The shadow cast by the fence behind her. Subtle arcs within the sand traps. She remembered the feeling of drawing the shadows around her like a security blanket whenever she was lonely or frightened. She reached out with her imagination to the fence shadow and drew it toward her. Then she reached out to the silhouette of the tree. Extending herself, she reached for the dark smudge in the closest sand trap. She drew them all around her, wrapping herself from head to toe as if she were enfolding herself in a cozy comforter. She felt calm, centered. Careful not to disturb the shadows wrapped around her, she walked back to the fence she had passed through. Her hand met the splintery wood of the top rail and rested there. She turned her back and leaned against it.

The feeling of the pressure of this fence against her back transported her to a time when she was alive. She had been twenty or so, learning to ride for a western she and Stan had written. She'd been leaning against a fence then too, watching her trainer canter a beautiful bay mare in circles, shouting instructions as he modeled what he wanted her to do. "See my seat?" he called. "It doesn't leave the saddle. I'm digging into her gait to propel her along."

When I was alive, she thought, *it never occurred to me—I never once thought about how amazing it is to have a body. To feel a horse under me. Or the good ache the day after an intense workout. Or being snuggled up with someone.*

Her mind went to Silas. She pushed herself away from the fence and imagined releasing the shadows and leaving them behind her. She turned and walked through the fence once again.

As she entered the keeper's cottage, Silas was chatting to Luna but broke off as soon as he saw her. She stood in front of the curtained window in the brightest part of the room. "Can you come over here?" she asked Silas. She looked around the room for the closest shadows. One under the nearby table, one under each of the chairs, a good-size one in the corner where the weak sun couldn't penetrate. She repeated the process she'd used outside, gathering the shadows and wrapping them around her. "I'm pretty sure I'm tangible."

Silas went to her and laid a hand on her arm. "You are," he said. "This is excellent." His other hand rested at her waist.

She looked up at him. He was standing very close. "This fog is … is good," she stammered. "No sun rays to burn you." *Seventy-five percent of me wants to run away. Seventy-five percent wants to kiss him. That's fifty percent more than I contain. I'm going to explode.*

"The curtains help," he responded, gazing at her.

"Yeah." More words were nowhere to be found. She could perceive only the depth of his eyes, the feeling of his hands resting on her, his smell like a pristine pine forest.

She took a step backward, putting distance between them. He let his hands drop and cleared his throat. "Marvelous work," he said.

"Thank you. I think I'll practice being intangible in shadow." As she said it, the ache of the abject loneliness she needed for the skill crept into her heart. *Nonexistent heart*, she reminded herself. "Or maybe I'll alternate, practice them both."

"A beneficial plan." Silas's lips quirked. "Please let me know if I can help." He returned to his seat next to Luna and picked up his book.

The fog persisted into the late afternoon, so when the sun hung low in the sky, Silas left for the computer store. While he was gone, Senka took the short stroll to the cemetery and sat on the low wall by Mrs. Wang's grave. Before long, she wasn't alone.

"Hello, dear. I'm so glad you've come back. How's your young man?"

Senka debated whether to explain he wasn't all that young and he wasn't exactly a man, and besides, she couldn't really call him hers, but decided to let it go and take Mrs. Wang's question in the way it was intended. "He's well, thank you."

"I'm so glad. And Luna?"

"Also well. Taking a nap."

"Ah, yes. As they do." Mrs. Wang patted her hand, turning to look out over the expanse of the cemetery toward the bay.

"Mrs. Wang, may I ask you a question?" Senka shifted her position on the wall to better see the other ghost. Mrs. Wang smiled and tilted her head toward Senka. "Can ghosts hover in the air?"

"Oh, my, yes. I choose not to myself. I prefer to have my feet on the ground." She tapped her feet against the grassy lawn for emphasis. "But yes, I have done it, and I've known many residents who enjoy flitting around in the treetops of an evening." She laughed delightedly.

"How? I mean, how does it work? I'm learning to make myself solid in light and insubstantial in shadow. I haven't figured out how to hover, though."

"You've made some impressive progress, haven't you? Well done, dear! Now, let me see. How does it work? Hmm. Think happy thoughts."

"Think happy thoughts? Really?"

Mrs. Wang laughed again. "No, not really. My granddaughter was in a production of *Peter Pan* eons ago. I've always liked the idea that with fairy dust and happy thoughts we can fly. Being a ghost is a bit like fairy dust, don't you think?"

Senka took in the crinkles of laugh lines and the bright, shining, intelligent eyes and answered, "No! Not at all." The two of them hooted with laughter.

"*Che succede?*" asked a voice in the growing darkness. "*Qual é lo scherzo?*"

Stifling her laughter, Mrs. Wang whispered to Senka, "That will be Signore Peluso. His grave is in the next row, five over. He seems very sweet, but I honestly don't know. I don't speak Italian!" She and Senka dissolved into laughter again, though Senka was pretty sure she was laughing more at Mrs. Wang's laughter than at anything about the situation. Controlling herself, Mrs. Wang called out, "Good evening, Signore Peluso. Won't you join us?" Turning back to Senka, she whispered, "He doesn't speak English, but he understands the gist. And as I say, I am woefully inept at Italian, I'm afraid."

A small bear of a man wearing a chef's toque and jacket limped into view. He lowered himself onto the wall next to Mrs. Wang. Senka caught herself staring, mouth agape, and snapped it closed. Still, she couldn't tear her eyes away from the massive salt-and-pepper beard and the forest of hair forcing its way above the partially unsnapped jacket. The only feature visible on the man's face was his nose. The rest of him was covered by hair.

"Signore," her companion was saying, "may I introduce you to my new friend, Senka? Senka, this is Signore Riccardo Peluso. He was a chef, you know."

Senka rallied from her fascination enough to respond, "Pleased to meet you."

"*Buona sera, signorina.*" He stood and bowed, then sat on the wall again, turning, like Mrs. Wang, to look out toward the bay.

Mrs. Wang inclined her head toward the newcomer and with accompanying gestures said, "We were talking about flying. Can you fly, signore?"

"*Sì, Sì, certo!*"

Senka leaned forward, eager to learn. "How? *Come?*" It was one of the few Italian words she knew.

"*Facile. Salta e non cadere.*" He mimed leaping, one foot off the ground, one on, and held the position.

"Jump and don't …" Senka looked helplessly at Mrs. Wang, who shrugged.

"*Cadere. Cadere!*" said the former chef.

"Hot?" Senka asked.

"*Non il calore. Cadere.*" He tumbled off the wall and sprawled on the ground, then sat up with a flourish of his hands. "*Vedi? Cadere.*"

"Fall down!" cried Mrs. Wang in triumph. Signore Peluso nodded vigorously.

"Jump and don't fall down?" Senka asked. She looked at the prostrate man, wondering if that could be right. The two old ghosts burst into laughter, and Senka joined them.

"*Guarda. Ti mostrerò.*" He scrambled to his feet, crouched exaggeratedly, then sprang into the air. He hovered. His two observers applauded. He beckoned to Senka. "*Vieni,*" he said, adding in heavily accented English, "You come. You try."

Senka cast a dubious glance at Mrs. Wang but stood. Recalling what Signore Peluso had done, she crouched and sprang into the air. It was a respectable jump but nothing more. She landed back where she had started.

"*No, no. Non cadere!*"

"Right. Don't fall. Got it." She tried again. Same result. "Shoot! What am I doing wrong?"

Signore Peluso lit on the ground next to her. "*Dubiti troppo di te,*" he said, patting her shoulder. "*Non dubitare di te.*" He shrugged as if he'd explained everything.

"I'm so sorry, Signore. I don't understand."

"I believe he's saying," Mrs. Wang chimed in with great

tenderness, "you doubt yourself too much." She smiled up at Senka. "Don't get discouraged. Keep trying, and any moment it will click."

Senka tried again, crouching, leaping, landing back on the ground. Refusing to be discouraged, she kept at it. All at once, she noticed a teenager standing a few feet away, watching her. He wore baggy jeans, red Chuck Taylors, and a Guns N' Roses T-shirt faded to gray. His blond hair hung limply beneath a backward baseball cap.

"Dude, you're terrible at this." His tone was so frank Senka couldn't help laughing. "Here," he said. "Lemme help. I'll take one hand and, Signore, you take her other one." He grabbed Senka by the wrist and held her free hand out, indicating to Signore Peluso he should grab it. "On the count of three, we all jump. Signore, me and you will pull her up then hold on till she's got the hang of it. Got it?" Senka and Signore Peluso nodded. The kid counted, and on three they leapt.

Senka's arms felt like they were yanked out of their sockets. She dangled like a toddler between them. She looked down and saw Mrs. Wang gazing up at her, a smile splitting her wizened face. Signore Peluso said, "*Buona, ora* no fall. *Facile, no?*"

Senka looked up at her wingmen. "Do I need to think about anything? Imagine anything?"

"Dude, you're trying too hard. You don't gotta do anything. Senka, right? Thought I heard that. I'm Bink, by the way. Senka, you're still thinking like a living person, all gravity bound and like that. The laws of physics don't apply to you anymore."

Senka, who had been looking at the ground with concern, looked up into the trees. She saw the fog tendrils weaving through the branches like exhalations of the nighttime. She thought, *Maybe I have been thinking of myself as living. Or at least as corporeal enough to be bound by gravity. Just don't fall. Simple.*

"Dude! You're doing it!"

"Don't let go!" Senka cried. "I'm not sure I've got it."

"You do," Bink said. "Signore, hold one finger, like this." He demonstrated by grasping Senka's index finger; she stayed aloft.

"Well done, dear!" called Mrs. Wang from below.

"We're gonna hold just your hair now. That cool?" asked Bink.

"It's cool," Senka replied.

Each took hold of a lock of her hair. Senka hung in the foggy air. Looking down at the smiling Mrs. Wang, she felt elated. "Okay, you can let go now."

Bink laughed, "We already did."

Senka turned in place and saw her two teachers grinning at her from across an expanse of several feet. Signore Peluso's great beard waggled and he spread his arms, crying, "*Brava! L'hai fatta. Sei così brava!*"

Senka whooped and, following the hints and guidance of her coaches, did a victory lap around the cemetery. She landed in front of Mrs. Wang. "That is so much fun!" She high-fived Bink. Turning to Signore Peluso, she hugged his bearlike figure. "*Grazie, Signore,*" she said. His teeth appeared within his beard as he beamed at her. After stooping to give Mrs. Wang a kiss on the cheek, she said, "I'd better get back home. I hadn't planned to be out so long, and I don't want Silas to worry."

Mrs. Wang took her hand and patted it. "It's been such fun tonight, dear. Do come back, won't you?"

"Of course." With a wave to the other two, Senka leapt into the air and soared back in the direction of the lighthouse, feeling freedom in the sea breeze. She landed in front of the cottage and, because she could, walked through the outer wall.

Silas was sitting at the kitchen table, peering into the illuminated screen of a laptop. Standing behind him, Senka rested her hands on his shoulders.

He smiled up at her. "How is Mrs. Wang?"

"She's good. I met a couple of other residents, too. I learned some things that I'll show you later. How'd it go for you?"

"Well, I think. We are set up here, and I have begun to look for some answers to your questions. To begin with, look here." He pointed to a headline on the screen: "FANS HOUND DISBARRED LAWYER OVER STAR'S DEATH." Silas went on, "I've read a handful of articles. It seems Kenny returned from the cabin and faced a great deal of suspicion, which he somehow weathered."

"He wasn't charged?"

"Without a body, no one could prove you were dead. He insisted you had deserted him. He said he woke up on Saturday morning, and you and your bags were gone."

"Why didn't anyone search the cabin?"

"They did. Well, that is to say, they searched *a* cabin. He took them to a cabin near Fort Hunter Liggett."

"That's over a hundred miles from where we were." Senka sank into the padded chair next to Silas.

"He, or someone working with him, set up a separate cabin there, complete with all the expected tire tracks and footprints. Two sets, including one matching yours. You knew this, Senka, but yours was not a spur-of-the-moment murder."

"No. But I didn't think it was as thoroughly planned as it sounds like it was. So why was he disbarred if they couldn't prove anything?"

Silas shook his head. "The disbarment had nothing to do with your death."

"What do you mean?"

"The reason for the disbarment was associated with the cause of his termination from the firm months before. It was a bit of a scandal."

"He was fired? He couldn't have been. He went to work up until the day he murdered me."

"Well, no. It appears he was fired from his job and hadn't worked for eight or nine months before you died."

"But that would have been before we were married. We lived together. How did I not know about it?"

"He kept so much from you." Silas rested his hand on hers.

"Did any of the articles say why he was disbarred? Or why he was fired?"

"There isn't much detail. It appears he was caught in some kind of malpractice. The firm dismissed him, though they tried to keep it a secret, which is interesting. Reading between the lines, I would guess he committed fraud of some kind that greatly embarrassed them."

"So they tried to keep it secret, but he got disbarred anyway?"

"According to the articles, someone in the firm leaked the fact he'd been fired. I'm sure the leak was lucrative. Any number of outlets would have paid dearly for it around the time of your disappearance. The bar association followed up with an investigation and the eventual disbarment."

Senka rubbed her forehead with her free hand. "How could I have been so stupidly blind?"

"I don't think you were. I think Kenny was very good at deceiving people. Including the police. Several of the articles I read note, in a situation like yours, the husband is always the first suspect. As you can see from this headline, your fans thought he should be. As did someone named Stanley Hoffman. He and a Peter Guterman seem to have pressured the police for years, even after the case was designated a disappearance rather than a death. They were convinced Kenny did something nefarious. Do you know them?"

"Yes." Senka's chest ached. "Stan was my best friend. And my director." She shook her head. "Those are completely inadequate words to explain who he was. He ... where to start?" She looked away from Silas and out the window into the dark, remembering. "I was still in high school. I auditioned for this indie film, an adaptation of *Hamlet* that Stanley had written and was directing. He was already a name in Hollywood and I was a nobody. I mean, people knew my mom because she was this top model, but there was no reason for Stan to take a chance on me. But he did. Jesus, Silas. I look back on my breakout and it seems like a miracle. I mean, I was a Hollywood cliché."

"In my centuries of existence, I have learned to wonder at and to treasure those miracles, though I am no longer surprised by them."

"You mean they happen regularly?"

"One can discern a consistency when one has the time to observe."

"Well, I definitely treasure this miracle. That little indie film made my career. I was seventeen and agents were vying for me. I had film and TV offers coming out my ears. It was wild. But more than that, way more than any of that, I had Stan. I mean, we fell in love with each other." She waved her hand to forestall any misunderstanding. "I don't mean romantically. First of all, he's gay, and second of all, he's way older than me. He was my mentor, but we also confided in each other. He guided me, but we co-wrote a ton of scripts. Oh, it's so hard to ... he's like no one else I've ever known. Overflowing with love and creativity. Even when I was a shit to him, and that was a lot—I'm embarrassed to admit how often. I was so self-absorbed and so ... ugh, I hate to think about it. But despite all my assholery, he loved me." She was silent for a moment, and Silas waited, knowing there was more she needed to say. "A little more than a year after I graduated from high school—I had just turned nineteen—my parents were killed by a drunk driver who hit them head-on going a hundred miles an hour in the wrong direction on the freeway. I was an only child with no other family. Stan helped me through it all. Stan and Peter. The funeral, the estate, the lawyers, the press. Oh, god, the press! They were relentless."

"It must have been a challenging time. You were so young," Silas said, his voice full of quiet empathy.

Senka shook her head, staring into the past. "I was lost after they died. I wonder if they became ghosts to stick around for me. I don't know why I haven't thought of that before. I wasn't really close with my dad, but my mom was amazing." Senka looked up at Silas. "When all this is over, let's go down to Forest Lawn to check if they're there." He picked up her hand and held it with both of his to seal the plan. "Stanley did everything he could for me. Both he and Peter did. They set me on my feet and I went back to work. And then Stan and I got this crazy idea for a TV series. We loved it, but we weren't sure anyone else would. Then HBO greenlighted it, and the next thing you know, *Blood Moon: Huntress of the Shadows* is the number-one show. And Stan helped me keep my feet on the ground then too."

"*Huntress of the Shadows?*" Silas raised an eyebrow. "A provocative title. What was it about?"

She groaned. "I played a vampire hunter." Silas covered his mouth with a hand, but Senka caught the twinkle in his eyes. "Oh, go ahead and laugh," she said with a chuckle of her own.

"It is merely the irony. I promise, had I known, I would have been quaking in my boots."

"I was very good at the staking part."

"I have no doubt."

They sat in silence until Silas said, "I think I understand why he means so much to you."

"And to the last day I was a shit to him. He tried to warn me. He and Peter didn't trust Kenny. I wouldn't listen when Stan asked me not to go away with that slimebag. But he never gave up on me. They tried to get someone to pay attention. Oh, Silas, they must have been beside themselves." Tears filled her eyes. "They would've known I'd never disappear like that. I'd never do that to Stan. Oh, god, they tried to find me."

Silas reached out and tucked the lock of loose hair behind her ear. The gesture reminded her of the moment Kenny had done the same thing as she was dying. When Silas did it, though, the gesture and the way he looked at her were full of tenderness. The thought made her cry harder.

Silas gestured toward the laptop. "The article says they maintained pressure for years," he said. "In time, it became apparent the police were dropping the case, so they hired a private investigator. At last, when she was unable to find anything, they created an arts award dedicated to you. They held an annual gala, they rallied your fans, they kept your name alive."

She sat forward, frowning. "You're talking about them in the past tense. Are they dead?"

"I haven't researched that yet. Let's see what we can find." He reached for the computer.

"Google Stanley first, please," she said, wiping her eyes.

Silas typed into the search bar and pages of links popped up. Most had to do with Stan's career, many with the award he'd created. At the bottom of the second page, they found a link referring to Stanley but it was an obituary for Peter. "Oh, no, poor Stan," Senka whispered as they scanned the article. "This is three years ago," she added. They could find no reference to Stanley's death. Four pages in, they saw what they were looking for. A tiny footnote on a film trade site mentioned Stanley's assistant was holding an estate sale for him. He was moving from his Hollywood mansion to a posh assisted living facility. The blurb was dated one month ago.

"Oh, Silas!" Senka gripped his sleeve. "I need to go see him. Even if he can't see me, I need to see him. Can you ... will you take me?"

"Of course," he said without hesitation. "You wait here for Luna to return from hunting. I haven't eaten yet, but I'll go now and come back at once."

As she waited, she scrolled through three or four articles about Stan and the investigation into her death. She learned little more than Silas had already told her. When Luna trotted in, Senka explained the situation to him. He listened, unblinking and, once she had finished, settled down to a post-meal bath. The looming question was, where was Stan?

Senka returned to the laptop and typed in "posh LA assisted living facilities." She thought of what Stan would want and added to the search bar "for movie people." It felt strange to be using a computer again; it was not something her living self would have pictured a ghost doing. An article popped up at the top of the list: "Hollywood Takes Care of Its Retirees." Skimming the article, she immediately knew this was the right place and mapped the location, ready to show Silas as soon as he returned. She didn't have long to wait.

As he walked through the door looking refreshed, his first question was, "Where are we going?"

"Here's what I found." Senka showed him the map. He studied it and examined an image of the facility.

"I believe I have a sense of it." He held his arm out to Luna, who settled into his usual traveling spot in the crook of Silas's elbow. Senka wrapped her hand around the other arm, clutching his sweater, and felt the icy coldness of vampire travel.

They stood in front of a graceful building with a roof like a bird in flight. The sound of a waterfall reached them, and the scent of roses hung in the night air. The warmth of the Los Angeles evening was a shock after the cool fog of Pacific Grove.

"It's lovely here," Silas said. Senka gave his arm a squeeze. They went inside.

As soon as the doors opened, a stunning young woman of model proportions looked up. "Good evening, sir," she said. "I'm so sorry, but visiting hours are over. In fact, I'm surprised the guard let you through the gates."

"I understand perfectly," Silas replied. He, Senka, and Luna continued undeterred to the reception desk. He smiled at the young woman. "How do you manage to get enough sleep if you're here all night and auditioning all day?"

"How did you know?"

Silas smiled. "I have a very good sense for these things. Are you sure you won't let us in?"

"I'm sorry, I can't. I need to keep this job. Anyway, we'd have to get preapproval from the administrator for your cat."

"I understand," Silas said again. "I wonder, would you be allowed to tell us where we might find our friend when we come back?"

"I guess I could do that. What's your friend's name?"

"Stanley Hoffman." He glanced down at Senka and offered her a reassuring smile.

The receptionist turned to her terminal and tapped the keyboard. "Oh!" she said, peering at the screen. She looked up. "I'm so sorry."

Senka's fingers dug into Silas's arm. *We're too late.*

The receptionist went on, "He's in our end-of-life unit." Seeing the look on Silas's face, she added, "You didn't know?"

"We haven't seen him in a long time," he replied. "Can you tell us where to find the end-of-life unit?"

She did, adding, "I think it's sweet you include your cat like that. You know, saying 'we' and all."

Once outside, they followed the young woman's directions, walking along a path teeming with colorful, fragrant vines and flowering hedges and ending in front of a sweeping 1930s-era three-story house. Inside, they were stopped again, this time by a nurse. "I'm sorry," he began, "you can't—"

"You will let us pass." Being on the sending side of the power Silas projected with those words was like standing in the sand as a wave rushed out all around her feet. The effect on the night nurse was immediate.

"I will let you pass," he said, and went back to his work.

They climbed the steps to the top floor and scanned the room numbers until they found the right one. At the door, Silas and Luna hung back while Senka hurried to the bed.

By the dim light of the room, she saw a scarecrow of a man. She could have circled his wrist with her thumb and forefinger as it lay on the blanket. His sunken cheeks were peppered with stubble. An oxygen tube ran under his nose. Other tubes and cables extended to a pole overcrowded with plastic bags of varying sizes. A monitor showed his heart rate, oxygen saturation, pulse, and assorted other numbers and graphs. Senka sat on the edge of the bed and brushed his graying curls back from his face.

Stanley opened his eyes and looked around the room as if trying to find the source of the touch. Then he focused.

"Sarah?" he said and began to weep. "Sarah? Is that you?"

"So he sees her? Stanley sees her?" Finn asks. There's an intensity to his tone.

"Yes."

"How?"

"That's part of tomorrow's story."

"Because he loves her?" Finn wants an answer.

"That's part of it."

"Because he's dying." It's not a question.

I hesitate but remind myself I've sworn to be honest. "Yes," I say. "That's the main reason."

He gazes at the ceiling. When he speaks, it's not what I expect. "My mom taught me to ride a bike like that. Holding my hair, then surprising me when she let go and I was riding on my own."

I have a flash of memory. "That's how my mom taught me too." I had forgotten.

He sighs. "I should sleep now."

"I'm sure you're tired. It was a full day today."

"I think I'll need all my energy tomorrow."

"How come?"

"They're starting a different treatment. It'll be three different drugs. And I won't have any days off." Suddenly his face looks five years older.

"I'm sorry, Finn. Would it help if I came early tomorrow?"

"Can you do that?" His forehead wrinkles in surprise.

"Yes."

"Oh. I thought you could only come after—in the evening."

The change of direction to his sentence makes me hopeful his doubts are eroding. "No. I can come during the day."

"Oh." He thinks about it for a moment, then answers, "No, it's okay. There are too many people in and out all day. I can start the new meds on my own."

"Will you tell me about it when I come?"

"Sure." He manages a smile.

"Shall I stay for a while?"

"Yeah. Please."

I lean back in my chair and he stares at the ceiling until, at last, his eyes drift closed.

CHAPTER SEVEN

I'm at Finn's bedside before he notices me. "How are you feeling this evening?"

"Okay." His smile is tired.

It's always like this. People call it a fight, a long battle. The words are misleading; they suggest action and movement. They don't describe the daily tenacity, the moment-to-moment stubborn insistence on continuing to survive, despite hourly invitations to succumb. They don't convey what it takes to lie in bed, more alone than you've ever been, while poison goes into your arm in a wildly hopeful attempt to kill the disease before either the disease or the poison can kill you.

"You can be honest with me." I rest my hand on his arm, and he turns his head, assessing my sincerity before he speaks.

"Not good. The new meds make me nauseated. They've tried, like, fifteen other things to make me not nauseated, but none of them are working."

"I'm sorry to hear that."

"My mom was here all day."

"Oh, yeah?"

"She's going to be here all day from now on. I just wish she wouldn't worry." He pauses, then says, "She brought me salted caramel ice cream." This makes him smile, which makes me smile. "I couldn't eat it, though." There is no self-pity; it's a statement of fact.

"No. That's understandable."

His expression clouds. "I *think* she understood."

"I'm sure she did." It occurs to me that anyone who has raised a young man as kind as Finn would more than understand he couldn't eat the ice cream she'd brought him.

Finn says, "I've been thinking about Stanley. You know, being sick in the hospital like me."

"Have you?"

"About what it would feel like to see Sarah again."

Oh, my god, this kid. "It would be something else, wouldn't it?"

"I'd be happy to see her, someone I loved so much, but angry too, you know? Like, I wouldn't know right away she was a ghost because, like, who would think that first thing?"

"Yes." The wording of his question isn't lost on me. Whether he has decided to believe in the truth of my story or is just willingly suspending his disbelief, I don't know.

"Then maybe I'd realize and I'd be grateful for the magic or whatever that let her come to see me, but sad she was dead after all. Does that make sense?"

"It does." We sit with our separate thoughts for a moment. When Finn doesn't go on, I ask him, "Would you like to hear how Stan reacted?"

He nods. "Yeah."

Stanley focused on Senka and said, "Sarah? Sarah, is that you?" He began to cry. Tears traced the path of the wrinkles around his eyes, both the laugh lines Senka remembered and new lines of pain that had developed since she'd last seen him.

She smiled down at him, stroking his hair. "It's me, Stan."

"Where have you been?" He grabbed her hand and pressed it to his chest. "We looked for you. How could you do that to us?" His joy at seeing her was turning to outrage. The heart monitor's steady peaks and valleys juddered and became erratic.

"I know you did. Thank you. I know." She shook her head. "It sounds so feeble to say thank you for something … I don't know how to say it. I can't begin to describe how important it is you looked for me, you tried to get some kind of justice."

"We did!" He was crying again. "I was sure that paskudnyak Kenny had done something. But now here you are." His voice, at first a whispering rattle, gained strength with his anger and his pale cheeks reddened.

"Stanley." She reached her free hand to wipe his face. "Stanley, look at me. You knew me better than anyone. You saw every mood, every thought. Look at me. You know I'd never have left you voluntarily."

He fought past his emotion and focused on her face, scrutinizing her features. With a shake of his head, he closed his eyes. "I'm dreaming again. Should've known. You and Peter. I dream about you two all the time."

"No, you're not dreaming," she said, brushing his hair away from his face. Stanley opened his eyes and looked at her again. "You remember our first project together? Your *Hamlet* adaptation? You let me play Ophelia, remember? We'd sit around after rehearsal, get smashed, and talk about why the Elizabethans were so comfortable with the supernatural."

Stanley's lips curled in a shadow of a smile. "It's when I first knew I loved you."

"You were always more loving than my own dad even."

"We talked and talked about Will and the ghost of Hamnet. Son ghost versus dad ghost."

"That's right." Senka met his eyes, trusting his imagination would connect the dots. It did.

"Ghosts … are real?" He looked doubtful, as if he were afraid she'd laugh at him.

She nodded. "Ghosts are real."

"And you … you're a ghost?" His eyes filled with tears again even as he breathed a laugh. "I sound meshugana, even to myself."

"It's been pretty crazy all right."

The tears spilled over. "Sarella. It was him, wasn't it? Kenny." He spat the name. "I knew it—*we* knew it! What did he do?"

"I'm sorry I didn't listen to you," she said, wiping his eyes and nose with a corner of the sheet. "You tried to warn me."

"Water under the bridge. Not important. You … *you're* what's important."

She took both of his hands in hers. "It was poison. Not the painful type. I just kind of went to sleep. But you and Peter hired a PI."

"She didn't find anything." He shrugged dismissively.

"No. But that's because he misdirected everyone. He set up a dummy cabin somehow. But we went way farther north. The Santa Cruz Mountains."

"The cops, Artie, they tried to track your cell phone. After LA, no pings to any tower."

With a flash of memory, Senka said, "He made me turn my phone off before we left the city."

"That fucking Kenny."

"How did he do it, Stan? Do you know? The cabin, footprints, all of it."

"Oy, sweetheart!" He extricated a hand and adjusted the oxygen cannula under his nose, then took her hand again.

"Is this too much?" Senka asked, concerned. "I don't want to wear you out. Should we go?"

"We? Who's we?" Stan peered around the room and spotted Silas. "Who's this?"

Senka turned and beckoned Silas and Luna over. Luna hopped onto the bed and picked his way up to Stanley's stomach, where he sat gazing at the old man, head cocked to one side. "I think you might be a bit heavier than Stan needs right now," Senka commented as she shifted Luna onto the sheet next to Stanley. The cat pressed against the old man's hip and tucked his paws in, purring. "That's Luna. And this is Silas."

Silas carefully took the ailing man's hand. "It is a pleasure to meet you."

Senka leaned close to Stan's ear and whispered, "Ghosts aren't the only things that are real. He's a vampire."

"Of course he is," said Stanley, as if he heard such things every day. "I knew we were right all along."

"Well," Senka responded, "at least we weren't entirely wrong."

Stanley patted Silas's hand, a complacent smile accentuating the laugh lines around his lips. He studied the vampire's face for a moment as the machinery prolonging his life clicked and whirred around him. At length, having satisfied himself about Silas, he nodded and returned to the subject. "So, Kenny, may his name be erased. We couldn't prove anything, the PI, Peter, and me. And let me tell you, he should have won an Emmy for the performance he put on. Grieving husband, abandoned by his wife, why would she do this, blah, blah, blah. The police ended up being taken in one hundred percent. Well, that and the cabin."

Silas sat on the end of the hospital bed. "The cabin, yes," he said. "We read about it. Did you find out how he was able to arrange all of that?"

"Your Kenny," Stanley began, wagging a finger at Senka. "He was mixed up with some very bad people. Again, we couldn't prove this, at least not enough to satisfy the police. Artie—the PI—she was convinced. Peter and I were convinced. But we didn't have enough hard evidence. These people, they were good at covering their tracks."

"Who were they?" Senka was reeling again at how much she didn't know about the man she had married.

"Did you know he'd been fired from his firm?" Stanley asked, sidestepping her question.

"Not until a couple of hours ago."

"Ah. I win. Peter and I had a bet. I was sure you'd have told me if you'd known. He thought maybe not. So, Artie sweet-talked one of the associates there, at the firm, and he spilled the tea. The word there was Kenny's major client was some Russian oligarch."

"Can you be fired for representing someone like that? They may be unsavory, but everyone has the right to representation." Senka looked from Stan to Silas.

"No, you can't be fired for that," Stan said. "You can, however, be fired, and disbarred, for embezzling from your law firm."

"He embezzled from the firm? Why?"

Silas laid his hand on Senka's arm. "Let him tell the story in his own way," he said.

"Thank you. She always did this." He gave Senka's hand a squeeze. "Where was I—yes, embezzling. You've heard of kompromat?

Compromising information, right? Well, it turns out this oligarch, to keep Kenny in line, introduced him to gambling. Or, maybe not introduced, but enabled him. It's the old story."

Senka groaned. "The old story? It's a goddamn cliché."

"That may be so, but Kenny liked to stand out, didn't he? TV star wife, fancy car, bespoke suits—this was Kenny. So we're not talking the nickel slots, here, bubbala. We're talking high-stakes gambling. Poker, baccarat, what else I don't know. What I do know is this oligarch got him into some fancy games, and Kenny lost big. The oligarch bailed him out, so now he owes the oligarch. He lawyers for free in return.

"And gambling isn't his only bill, not by a long shot. So he embezzles from the firm. He was not slick, this Kenny, so it wasn't long before a senior partner caught wind of it. He fires Kenny, who's disbarred for flagrant misconduct or some such, and now he's useless to his bankrolling oligarch. At least as a lawyer. We couldn't find out every kind of nastiness he did to extricate himself, but it looks like he was sinking in debt. So." He spread his hands to indicate the inevitability of the rest of the story.

"Are you telling me," Senka said with disgust, "I got murdered for my money? Of all the ridiculous, tawdry—"

"As if there's a good reason for your husband to murder you?" Stanley cut in.

"Anyway, it explains some things."

"Like what?" Silas asked.

"Well, for one, he told me a 'business associate' owned the cabin," Senka said. "Now we know who it was. Did you ever see anyone else there before I came, Silas?"

"No, but that doesn't mean much. I wasn't often there."

Stanley raised an eyebrow. "There's a story here, I think. But one mystery at a time. I agree it explains you dying in a cabin no one ever stumbled across. Out-of-the-way places of death seem to be this Kossack's specialty. It also explains Kenny having the chutzpah to set up a red-herring cabin."

"But it doesn't explain how he did it so convincingly," Senka offered.

"True, but we can guess he had help. And it explains, however much we hate this plot point, why he killed the most beautiful, most talented, kindest—" His voice broke, and he went silent, patting Senka's hand. He cleared his throat. "So now *you* talk. I'm worn out. I'm a dying man here, you know. I only lived this long because I quit smoking after you disappeared."

"Well, if that's what it took, it was worth it."

"You're not funny. Besides, now I've outlived Peter, and for this I'm not grateful. So talk. Tell me everything. I'm going to rest my eyes and breathe."

"Before we tell you everything, Stan, this should have been the first thing I said. I'm so sorry for the many, many times I was selfish and self-absorbed. When I treated you badly and—"

"Stop." Stanley held up a gnarled hand. "That wasn't important to me. Could you be a little bratty sometimes? Sure. Was I annoyed with you sometimes? Of course. If it helps you, you're forgiven. Good? Can we move on? I want to know what's happening with you."

Senka leaned forward and kissed his whiskered cheek.

For the next hour or so, Stanley lay, speaking little, now and then asking questions or remarking on a detail, as Senka and Silas filled him in. Once they finished, he asked, "Your goal is to end this Harou and kill Kenny, is that it?"

"Yes," Silas answered without hesitation.

"In that order. Harou first, then Kenny," Senka said.

"Why is that?" Stan squinted his eyes, assessing her.

"It's what I want," she said. Seeing he wasn't satisfied, she went on. "If it takes a while to get to Kenny, what are the consequences? But if Harou gets to us before we get to him, that could be the end of Silas."

Stanley grunted, bushy eyebrows raised.

"It's not as selfless as it sounds." Senka looked away from the trio whose eyes studied her.

"I see," Stanley said. He patted her hand again. "It's important, bubbala, vital, maybe, to go through life with someone."

Senka didn't correct his choice of the word.

"The *right* someone," Silas added, his eyes, as he looked at Senka, telling Stanley everything he needed to know.

Stanley offered a tired smile. "I am liking this one. Who knew a vampire could turn out to be more of a mensch than a living person?"

Senka snuck a peek at Silas, allowing herself to admit that Stan had always been a good judge of character.

"Now, kids," Stanley went on. "I have some advice for you, so listen." He took both their hands. "Season three, episode eight. Farshteyst?"

Silas looked blank, but Senka, after a moment, understood. "Oh, I see. Stan, that's good." She turned to face Silas. "In the story arc of season three, we'd been chasing this one vampire. In episode eight we decided to stop chasing and lure her to us. We set up an elaborate scheme in a drippy old cellar, very atmospheric. We had decoys and ruses to make her think she'd taken us by surprise and we were weaker than we really were. Of course, it's not a fleshed-out plan, but it's a good start." She paused and watched, waiting for Silas's reaction.

He looked between them. "You're proposing, as I understand it, we lure Harou to some location—"

"It doesn't have to be a cellar," Senka added quickly.

"Not necessarily a cellar," Silas continued, "and ambush him."

"Bingo," Stanley said as Senka nodded.

For a moment, Silas stared at them. Bemused, he said, "Senka, you've seen him. To defeat Harou ..." He trailed off as words failed him.

"I know," Senka replied. "There are so many details to fill in, but I think bringing him to us, to a place we know so much better than he does, it's a start, right? And we'd have the element of surprise. He doesn't know how much we've learned. And we could enlist Mrs. Wang and the others at the graveyard. I know they'd help us."

"Do you believe this might work?"

"I do."

Silas sat, thinking. "All right. If you believe there's a chance to end him, I am ready to try. If the plan fails, it fails, but either way, I will be free of fear."

Finn startles me by saying, "Can I ask a question?"

It's not that I forgot he was there, but I will admit I was caught up in the story. I recover and answer, "Yes."

"If a vampire is ended, does he become a ghost?"

"No. Only living people have the chance to be ghosts when they die."

"So if Silas is ended, he's gone. He and Senka can't be together anymore."

"Yes, that's the danger." That was the danger, for sure.

He considers this for a moment, then says, "Can I ask another question?"

"Of course."

"Last night you said Stan can see her because he's dying." He looks at me, so earnest.

"Yes. People who are … face-to-face with death, I guess we could say, are more aware of the afterlife. Not all people who see ghosts die, though."

"There are cultures that have celebrations for their ancestors. They make a point of remembering them."

"Yes." He's quiet for so long I ask, "Are you okay?"

"Just thinking."

"Thinking or worrying?" I wonder, of course, if he's contemplating his own mortality.

"Thinking." He stops me from asking any more questions by adding, "I'm ready to go on with the story if you are."

After Silas said he was ready to try to end Harou, Stanley was impressed. "You are a brave man, my friend," he said. "Or being, vampire, whatever." He waved his hand to indicate he had no time for the nuances of terms. "I'm glad in *Blood Moon* we didn't paint all vampires as bad guys." Stanley shifted his position and winced with pain.

"Stan! Are you hurting? Do you need some meds?" Senka stood and peered up at the many bags hanging from the IV pole.

"No, no. They make me foggy and I want to be clear. I'll take some in a while maybe. Right now we have some planning to do. What do you want to chew on first?"

Senka looked at Silas and Luna, still purring next to Stan. "Harou."

"Right. Nu. Step one, lure this Harou to you. How?" Stanley closed his eyes, a hand resting on Luna's side, and waited for them to plan.

Silas spoke first. "I am aware …" He hesitated, clearing his throat unnecessarily. "He monitors news sites for signs of me."

"How do you mean?" Senka asked.

"I am not sure, but I have suspected for some time he finds me when I behave carelessly and a story appears in the news, one a knowledgeable observer would associate with vampire activity."

Stanley opened one eye. "Please tell me you're not talking about frail damsels drained of blood."

Silas's pale face turned even chalkier. "No! Deer!"

"Ah! Good. Go on." Stan closed the open eye.

"My habit is to take what I need from several deer, spreading out the effect on a whole herd. The deer recover quickly, no animal dies, no one notices. There were times in the past, however"—he cleared his throat again—"when I was less measured, and my activities drew attention. Local media ascribed the animal deaths to coyotes, wolves, whatever was in the area. Harou always knows the truth, of course, and it doesn't take long for them to find me."

"Silas?" Senka began. "That made me think of something." She glanced at Stanley. "We read, when we were doing our show … In a couple of episodes, if I killed a vampire, all the vampires they'd made died too." She left her question unspoken.

Silas shook his head, "We are not connected in that way. The plot you describe was the invention of an author who struggled with his dénoument." Stan gave him a ghost of a smile, and Senka felt a wave of relief. Silas continued, "I believe if I let my presence be known, Harou will notice."

Senka felt the first stirrings of hope. "There are tons of deer in the cemetery. It would be perfect to draw him there."

"Then we take him unaware—"

"And we stake him!" Senka finished with conviction.

"My darlings …" Stanley's eyes were open again. "You have a start. It's a very rough start, but it's a start nonetheless. Sarah was always good with plots. Between the two of you, you'll come up with a doozy. And now," he reached out to both of them again, and his tone became serious. "Now I have an important question to ask you." He turned his focus to Silas. "Do you have a way—a not-so-bloody-way ideally—to take a human life?"

Silas's eyes narrowed. "Whose life did you have in mind? Kenny's?"

"No. Mine."

"Stan, no!" Senka exclaimed. "What are you talking about?"

"Bubbala, please try not to be upset." He took Senka's hand and held it between his own. "Darling, I'm sick. The ticker is done for. If I die today or a week from today, what's the difference? I'll tell you. A week of pain. I've had such a good life, and now that I've seen you again, I'm ready."

"Stan!" Senka exclaimed with new energy. "You could come with us! When you die, you can choose to stay, you know, as a ghost. You could—"

"Sweetheart. Thank you. I love that you would want that. But you see, Peter moved on. At least I assume he moved on since you haven't mentioned seeing him floating around here somewhere."

"No," Senka admitted.

"No. I thought you might have mentioned it. So Peter moved on and I'll move on too. Who knows? Maybe I'll get to see him. Maybe not. I'd like to take my chances." He reached up and patted Senka's cheek. "I love you, darling. And as much as spending time with you again is a blessing, Peter was the love of my life. I'm ready to go."

"I understand," Senka said, though she couldn't keep her voice from breaking. "I'll stay with you. I want your last sight to be the face of someone who loves you."

"Thank you, sweetheart." He turned to Silas. "So what do you say?"

Silas had been gazing at Senka, his face a picture of tenderness and compassion, but now he turned to Stanley and, with simple directness, said, "We have a way to pacify our prey if we choose. Prolonged application would stop the heart. It seems to be quite painless, but if at any time it becomes uncomfortable, you could tell me to stop."

"Thank you." Stan turned to Senka. "Every performer's dream, no? I get to play my own death scene. What do you think my last words should be? Not that you can do much to spread them to the waiting world."

"How about 'Either that wallpaper goes or I do'?"

Stanley chuckled wheezily. "Already been used, as you know very well. Here's a good one, 'I haven't had champagne for a long time.' It's true too."

"That is a good one. I kind of doubt Chekhov said it, though, don't you? Not the sentiment, the dying words."

"That's the problem with last words. Some poor schlemiel might say, 'I hate the cat'—you should pardon the example, Luna—and lapse into a coma. Then when he dies fifteen years later, somebody publishes those were his last words."

"How about, 'You are wonderful.'"

"Who said that?"

"I did. And Arthur Conan Doyle."

"Oh, Sarah. You are wonderful. I was a genius to cast you as Ophelia all those years ago, even though you were greener than crème de menthe."

"I was, wasn't I?"

"Oh, boy, were you ever. Cute as a button, though. Silas, you should have seen her. So smart, so sassy. She would have knocked your socks off."

Silas smiled at Stanley. "She already has."

Senka's phantom heart skipped a beat.

"Well, good." He clapped his hands. "Okay, kids, I'm happy. Sarella, give me a kiss."

Senka leaned over and pressed her cheek to his. She whispered in his ear, "I love you forever, Stan. Say hi to Peter for me when you see him." She kissed his paper-thin cheek, feeling the scratchy stubble. Sitting back, she met his eyes.

"Goodbye, bubbala."

"Goodbye, Stan."

"Silas, my friend, thank you. I'm ready."

The vampire nodded, then turned to the poles crowded with monitors and disabled the alarms. As Senka kept her eyes on Stanley's, Silas laid a hand on the great director's neck. She watched as the light in her friend's eyes dimmed. At last, with a faint smile, he heaved a final, contented sigh, and the light went out for good.

It wasn't until then Senka let herself cry, though not for Stan's death. She wept for the years she had lost with him; she wept because he was no longer part of the world; she wept with gratitude that she had been given the gift of saying goodbye. Silas wrapped an arm around her as she cried, saying nothing. What good were words? From time to time, he murmured soft sounds and stroked her hair or rubbed her back. He was there, solid, patient, loving. Luna insinuated himself between them in a space much too small for him and, knowing the therapeutic qualities of a good purr, geared his engine to high and cocooned them all in a resonant rumble.

After a time, Senka reached forward, closed Stanley's eyes, and kissed his cheek. Picking Luna up, she cradled him in her arms and turned to face Silas. "Let's go home," she said. "We have planning to do."

We're silent together, as usual, until Finn says, "Stanley was lucky."

That's what a lot of people feel when I tell this part of the story, though for different reasons. "In what way?"

"He got to see Sarah again. And he got to choose when he died."

"Yes." As Stan would have said, We should all be so lucky.

Finn takes a deep breath and lets it out. His eyes meet mine. "He got to have her with him, so he knew it wouldn't be scary."

"That was important to Senka too."

He looks at me for a moment longer. I think he'll say more about this, but then he lets go of a held tension and changes the subject. "I get why he didn't stick around."

"Do you?"

"Yeah. Senka has Silas." He smirks and adds, "if she ever gets over being scared of committing. Stanley wanted to be with Peter again, if he could. Do you think he found him?"

"I wish I knew, Finn."

He's quiet, thinking, then, "It would've been weird for him. To stay with Senka and Silas. My mom always wants me to get to know the guys she dates. I want her to be happy with someone, but it's awkward the whole time. I feel like a third wheel."

"And you think that's how Stan would have felt?"

"Maybe."

"Maybe he would have." *The men his mother dates.* "Is your dad in the picture, Finn?"

"No." He shakes his head. "I've never met him. It's just Mom and me." He sounds completely unconcerned. "Hey!" he adds with a sardonic smile. "I haven't puked this whole time."

"There's a plus."

"No kidding." He sighs. "I'm ready to sleep now. You'll stay?"

"Of course."

"Just checking."

I watch him drift off, thinking about his mother. And my own.

CHAPTER EIGHT

The next day, I arrive at the hospital a little earlier than usual and find a trio of nurses working around Finn. I watch as one helps him put on his pajama top, another changes a bag of meds, and the third, the Filipina woman I saw the other day, enters information into the computer that extends on an arm from the wall. They move in a practiced dance, working around and with one another. There's something beautiful about it. The two working with Finn talk to him, kind and reassuring. He looks pale and listless. The last wisps of his hair have fallen out as the stronger medication attacks the new cell growth.

I slip out of the room to give him time and privacy. I walk the hallways. I'm far more familiar with other wards, the adult oncology floor, the cardiology center, the ICU, and of course the hospice care house.

The walls are bright with cheerful images of teddy bears, toy blocks, and balloon animals in multiple hues. I come across a playroom furnished with cozy chairs and couches in primary colors. I can imagine a parent and child cuddling up here to read *Goodnight Moon* or *Cat in the Hat*. Paintings and drawings cover the walls of the art area. Most are wild finger paintings, many exuberant, a few a somber black.

Three exquisitely rendered drawings appear to be from the same artist, judging by the style: a tender portrait of a sleeping woman, the mother? Two of a teenage girl. In one, her long flowing hair catches the wind from off the ocean and streams behind her like a flag of victory. In the second, the same girl wears a cap that clings to her hairless scalp. She looks at the viewer, pulling us into her confidence. She is further proof, if I needed it, that each person's cancer is unique.

I head back to Finn's room. He's asleep when I get there. I don't mind waiting. I have time.

"How are you this evening, Finn?" I ask as he opens his eyes.

He whispers his response. "Not feeling too good."

"Did I wake you?"

"No. Glad you're here."

"Is it the nausea?"

He nods. "Can't keep anything down."

"I see a new bag of fluids." It's large, bloated with an opaque liquid.

"IV nutrition. Can't throw it up."

"Got it." I watch him for a moment. "You look like a ninja warrior without your hair."

"Or an alien." His eyes smile. "I like it, though." With some effort he turns toward me, one hand resting under his cheek. "If a person decides to become a ghost when they die—" He breaks off and swallows around a throat made raw by nausea.

"Yes?"

"They're stuck wearing whatever they die in, right?"

"That's what I've seen."

"I'd be in pajamas. Forever." He raises an arm to show me the set he's wearing.

"Pickle Rick," I say, the image making me grin.

It's good to see his eyes crinkle. "You know *Rick and Morty*?"

"Of course!"

"My favorites, just in case. Got another pair I like. I'll rotate."

I rest my hand on the bed rail, my chin on my hand. "Sounds like you're planning carefully."

He shrugs with one shoulder. "Can't hurt."

"No. I think it helps to have an action plan when there's a lot of uncertainty."

"Thought so too."

He looks so tired, though I can see he's trying to rally. "Finn, do you want me to just sit with you this evening?"

"Not tell the story?"

"Yeah."

"I'd like to hear the story, if it's okay with you."

"Of course, if you feel well enough."

"I want to know how it turns out."

"We still have a lot of story to go before you'll know how it ends."

"Better not skip a day." The hint of a smile appears around his eyes.

"You're right." I nod. "Senka, Silas, and Luna were about to leave Stan's room."

"Senka's grieving."

"Yes."

Dawn broke as they arrived at the lighthouse. Senka felt a weariness she hadn't experienced since she was alive. "I don't get it," she remarked to Silas. "I don't have a body, but I feel like my heart is breaking. My bones hurt. My eyes are throbbing."

Silas opened his arms, offering comfort. She hesitated, then thought, *He passed Stan's vibe check.* It felt like one last gift from her constant champion. She stepped close to Silas. He wrapped his arms around her, his presence a balm, like the scent of the redwoods on a warm breeze.

With his cheek resting against the top of her head, he said, "When we are alive, we give our experiences corporeal descriptions. We say, 'There's a hole in my heart' or 'I'm walking on a cloud.' The truth is it's our spirit that is wounded or gladdened. Without a body, without a heartbeat, our spirits still respond. We still feel grief. We still feel love."

Senka looked up at him. "You must have seen so many deaths in all your years. I mean, the deaths of people you cared about, loved even."

"Yes, many."

"Does it get easier?"

"To lose someone you love? No. But over time, the immediacy of the pain turns to the tenderness of a bruise; we're conscious of it only when it's pressed."

"Wouldn't it be easier not to love someone who's going to die?"

"If emptiness is easier, then perhaps. For me, the cost of loving someone mortal has been less than the price of a cold, barren existence."

Senka resettled her cheek against Silas's chest. "Yes, I see that. I'm glad I loved Stan. I'm glad he was part of my life. Life would have been a lot less interesting without him."

Silas held her for a moment longer, then stepped back. "I'm afraid we need to think about the day. Our cottage is open for tours."

"Oh, shoot," Senka groaned. "I don't have it in me to play the friendly neighborhood ghost right now."

"No. I suggest we both slip up to the attic until the place is quiet again."

"Sounds much better."

He turned to Luna. "Would you like to come with us or would you prefer to spend the day outside?"

"Mrr-owp! Meow-row," Luna responded.

"I'll take that as a preference for the latter."

Luna jumped down from the table on which Senka had deposited him and trotted toward the open door. "Be careful!" Senka called after him. "The road is busy during the day." Luna flicked his tail as he rounded the corner into the hallway and out of sight.

"Senka." Silas reached out and touched her arm. "I think what you need is rest. 'Sleep that knits up the raveled sleeve of care.'"

"The Scottish play," Senka said reflexively. "Do you think I *can* sleep? I've never needed to."

"I think it is worth a try."

Senka nodded. Silas picked up the laptop and its cable, and together they climbed up to the top of the cottage. In the parlor, the sun had begun to shine through the filtering curtains, but here the light was dim. The room smelled of dust and aged wooden beams. The roof slanted low enough Silas had to stoop to avoid hitting his head. In the corner farthest away from the small dormer windows, deep in the shadows, lay a thin, bare mattress.

"Will you ... would you mind lying here with me?" Senka asked.

With an alacrity that confirmed his willingness, Silas folded himself onto the mattress, and the two arranged themselves to fit together on the patch of foam rubber.

"You know my favorite thing about this cottage?" Senka whispered.

"What?"

"No freakin' mice." She felt, rather than heard, Silas laugh. He wrapped an arm around her, and she closed her eyes. She didn't think she could fall asleep, but some instinct took over, and when she opened her eyes again, the angle of the light had softened and she was alone on the mattress. She lay unmoving, trying to retain the fading remnants of a dream.

She'd been standing on the bank of the Hudson, far upriver from Manhattan. All around her, the trees were radiant with fall foliage. A mist rose from the river, softening the outlines of the hills in front of her, paling the sunlight of the fall day. Out on the river, a rowboat cut its way toward her. As she watched, she saw two people side by side on the stern seat, while a third—his back to her—ferried them from the bow. As the boat came nearer, she recognized the two passengers as Stan and Peter, and she flung her arms above her head, waving, laughing, and calling to them. They spotted her and waved so enthusiastically they almost tipped the boat. Stan beckoned her toward them. She took a step into the river, noticing she didn't sink but stayed on top of the water. She was about to run to them when she felt a pull from the bank. She stepped back onto dry land. The boat turned parallel to the shore. Stan and Peter watched her. Before they disappeared into the mist, they raised their arms to wave goodbye. Senka brought both hands to her lips, then flung them outward, blowing her friends a mighty kiss at the same time she wept for her loss.

Even as Senka replayed it in her mind, the dream's images began to fade. She turned over on the mattress and saw Silas sitting against the opposite wall, deep in contemplation. He looked up when she stirred and smiled at her. She smiled back and sat up. "Are the tours over?"

"Not quite but soon, I think." He got up and returned to the little mattress, sitting with his back tucked against the outside wall. Senka shifted her position and joined him. "How are you feeling?" he asked, bumping her arm with his.

"It's bizarre to have slept after all these years. But you were right; I feel more at peace. Like I can think a little straighter." She turned to him and scrutinized his face. "You looked like you were deep in thought."

"I was." He paused. "This plan—"

A pang of guilt stabbed Senka. "Silas, wait. Before you say anything else, I was pretty cavalier about insisting on this one idea. If you think it's too dangerous, we'll come up with something better."

"I was about to say I think it could work."

"You were?"

"With a few more details besides lure him, surprise him, stake him, yes. For one thing, we will need help. Would your new friends in the graveyard be willing to lend us a hand?"

"I don't want to assume, but I'm pretty sure they would." She laughed. "I bet Mrs. Wang will think it's all great fun."

"Senka, it *won't* be great fun. If Harou rises to our bait, which I believe is assured, I cannot predict what he will do. Please do not underestimate him. Do not allow your friends to underestimate him. Remember we are speaking of Harou: he's ancient, wily, powerful, and unimaginably cruel."

"I understand. I'll lay it out when I ask them tonight." Senka frowned and picked at a ragged hole in the foam rubber. "I wish you would stay away, though. Why do you have to face him at all? You can't fight him, and he'll do everything he can to end you. It's so dangerous."

"It is. But even you, yes, with your friends at your back, are not a match for him alone. I cannot fight, but I can distract. I'm starting to believe that together we have a chance where neither of us would succeed alone."

With effort, she pulled a few more bricks from her protective wall. "I don't want you to get hurt."

He took her hand in his. "I have been hurt before. I'll be hurt again; it's inevitable. We cannot guarantee each other's safety." He leaned forward and rested his forehead against hers. "Thank you for wanting to try, but we'll have to risk this together."

"I don't like it, but I get it. What else do we need?"

"Something to stake him with."

"Good thought." Senka looked around the empty attic. "Does it have to be made of anything in particular?"

"Only something sharp at one end."

"So the whole wooden stake thing …" She waved her hand in a gesture of dismissal.

"A fable. Though wooden stakes are often plentiful in the countryside, so it's understandable how that superstition came about." Silas rose and pulled the attic door open a crack, listening for a moment. "It sounds like we are alone. Do you want to check so I do not startle the docent?"

Senka made herself insubstantial and floated down into the main cottage. Finding it empty, she called up to Silas with the all-clear. "So a stake," she said as Silas entered the room. They scanned the parlor, noting and dismissing the fireplace poker as too cumbersome. It didn't take them long to search the rest of the little cottage and come up empty-handed. "Who doesn't have a nice pointy object lying around their museum?" Senka exclaimed. "We'll have to look someplace else."

They sat in the parlor discussing their plan. The question of when to set it in motion provoked the most discussion. Silas preferred to start at once, that night, though Senka thought it wiser to wait until they'd nailed down the details.

The sun settled toward the horizon, lengthening the shadows in the room. As its disk dipped into the Pacific, Luna interrupted the debate, padding in and announcing his return with a high-pitched "Mew!"

"There you are!" Senka chided as Luna hopped onto her lap and started to knead her thigh. "I was getting worried about you." He regarded her for a moment, then yawned hugely, showing his tiny teeth and making a noise like "Kheck." With an ungainly flop, he turned onto his back and stretched his arms long over his head, exposing his full belly. His back toes pressed against Silas and a mighty purring rumbled from deep within him. He closed his eyes, and his head drifted backward until it rested on the loveseat. "How can you sleep in that position?" Senka asked him.

"I should also find something to eat," Silas said, rising.

"Well, I obviously can't go anywhere." Senka gestured at Luna stretched across her lap. "I'm a cat bed. I'll think about our staking problem while you're out."

For a time after Silas left, Senka watched Luna sleep. She stroked his elongated body from the pointy chin to the fluffy fur of his tummy. He was warm and solid and vibrant. Once or twice, his paws twitched as he dreamed of running or hunting or climbing or whatever the cat companion of a vampire might dream about. Senka relished the peace of having no other responsibility than to cradle him as he slept.

Far sooner than she would have liked, Luna woke and gathered himself into an upright position. He stretched, yawned, then settled down again, making a perfect circle in a corner of the loveseat. "Ah, well," Senka said, "all things must pass." She stood and started to dust the cat hair off herself but paused. Instead she made herself insubstantial and watched as the hairs drifted through her to the ground. With a satisfied grin, she left the cottage.

The wind off the ocean blew cool and clean, carrying with it tumbling, swirling wisps of fog. The lighthouse beam illuminated a sweeping tunnel of gray as it reflected off the minuscule droplets of vapor that hung in the air. Senka rose, joining the fog. It flowed through and around her—cold, wet, and cleansing. An eddy of fog caught her eye and she spiraled with it, somersaulting and swooping low over the keeper's cottage. She spun a circuit around the lighthouse and chased the yellow beam out towards the bay. A startled seagull did a double take as she overtook it, then opened its beak and squawked at her before veering away to join its pals. Feeling free and wild, a part of the wind and the fog, Senka joined a squadron of pelicans, their wingtips skimming the crests of the waves. Wind-borne spray beaded on the great birds' wings and passed through Senka as they would a cloud. She broke away from the long skein of pelicans and flew back over the line of sand, over the lighthouse, and into the cemetery, coming to rest in a treetop, and draping herself across its branches as the fog did, crowning it with a silky silver gauze. The flight left her exhilarated, renewed. She felt a part of everything around her. After so many seasons of loneliness, she belonged to this place and to the beings inhabiting it.

She allowed herself to sink through the tree's branches until her feet found the earth. Over by the old part of the cemetery, a glimmering figure reflected the moonlight, and Senka made her way toward it. As she came closer, she saw it was Mrs. Wang dancing to the accompaniment of her own humming. "Hello, Mrs. Wang," she called out.

"Hello, dear!" Mrs. Wang cried, spreading her arms in welcome. "Do you know how to foxtrot?"

"Of course! Any self-respecting actor knows how." She bowed low and swept into position. "I'll lead, okay?"

They moved into the dance, Mrs. Wang singing, "Fly me to the moon and let me play among the stars. Let me see what spring is like on Jupiter and Mars." Senka twirled the old ghost, who laughed with her usual delight. As the song ended, Senka dipped her with a flourish.

"Oh, my dear! That was such fun," she said when Senka had righted her. "My husband and I used to go out dancing most Saturday nights for, oh my goodness, it must have been until Ai-Bao was in his eighties." She leaned into Senka, "I've always loved the foxtrot best, you know, though his favorite was the tango. Too much drama for me." She laughed again. "Oh, my, it's a lovely night, isn't it?" She sat on her wall and patted the stone next to her.

Senka joined her. "It is," she answered. "I was flying out over the ocean. The wind and the fog feel so alive."

"You've taken to flying like a fish to water. Like a flying fish to water." She laughed at her own joke, which made Senka smile. "There was a funeral here today," she said in a gossipy tone. "In the newer part of the cemetery." She turned and pointed behind them toward an open, grassy area. "It was very nice. Just the family. Very intimate, you know. But then ..." she giggled. "But then, someone on the fairway along there ..." She pointed beyond where she had indicated before. "They must have hooked their ball because it came flying over and landed—thunk!—right on the coffin. It made a terrific noise. It bounced off and fell into the grave!" Mrs. Wang dissolved in a fit of giggles.

Her laughter was always contagious, and Senka couldn't help

joining in, though she exclaimed, "Mrs. Wang! That's awful! Were the family upset?"

"I thought they took it very well," Mrs. Wang responded, collecting herself. "One of the workmen came over and fished the ball out of the grave." She leaned into Senka and, in a tone suggesting she was scandalized, said, "Frankly I think the golfer was lazy. If it had been me, I would have insisted he play it where it lay." She looked at Senka, her eyes bright, and the two burst into giggles all over again.

Pulling herself together once more, Senka said, "Your jokes are pretty edgy, Mrs. Wang."

"I take that as a compliment, dear." She smiled and patted Senka's hand.

They sat in contented silence for several minutes, gazing out toward the bay. At last, Senka said, "My best friend died last night."

Mrs. Wang turned, her serious eyes alight in the moonshine. "How terribly hard, dear. I'm so sorry."

"I'd never been with someone as they died before."

"How did it feel?"

"Like it was the most important thing I've ever done."

"Yes. I can understand that."

"I miss him."

"You always will, dear. Someone who is precious to us doesn't stop being precious simply because they've died. But the pain will lessen with time."

"That's what Silas said too." They sat in silence again, watching the fog make rings around the moon. "Mrs. Wang? May I ask for your help again?"

"Of course. I can't promise I'll give it, but you can ask." She smiled and winked.

"Fair enough. You see, my 'young man' as you call him, well, he's ... he's a vampire."

"Ah," said Mrs. Wang, "I thought as much."

"You did?"

"Well, you know, I've seen him with the deer."

"Oh! I see."

"He and your Luna often come through the cemetery. He's very good-looking, isn't he?"

"I think so."

"Yes." Mrs. Wang patted Senka's hand. "He's quite kind with them. He treats them with such respect." Fascinated, Senka realized she hadn't imagined what Silas was like as he hunted. She waited for Mrs. Wang to go on. "He gathers them around himself in a circle and thanks each of them." She paused, her head cocked to the side like a bird's.

"What does he do then?"

"Oh, well, bites their throats, dear. He takes a few sips from each one, so as not to weaken them, I suppose. Then he thanks them again and releases them. Such a gentleman. He reminds me a bit of my husband. If Ai-Bao had been a vampire, of course." She sounded wistful. It was the first time Senka had seen Mrs. Wang look sad. She wrapped an arm around the older ghost's shoulders. Mrs. Wang offered her a rueful smile. "Thank you, dear. Just a moment of melancholy. Now tell me what you need from me. Of course I want to help you and your lovely young ... lovely vampire."

"Thank you, Mrs. Wang. I appreciate that. Well, you see, every vampire has a Maker."

Mrs. Wang nodded. "That makes sense."

"Yes. And there's a certain connection between them that's part familial, part twisted subservience. Silas didn't like what Harou, his Maker, was doing—this was, like, two hundred years ago—so he objected."

"What was this Maker doing?"

"He was killing children."

"Oh, that's horrific." Mrs. Wang glanced in the direction of the children's cemetery. "And Silas stopped him?"

"Well, he stopped him from killing one child. That made his Maker furious and since then he's been trying to end Silas."

"We certainly don't want him to do that, do we?" She looked fired up for such a good-humored ghost.

"No, we don't. And the only way to stop him is to end him before he can end Silas."

"And how will we succeed?"

Senka warmed at her friend's use of the word *we*. "The plan is for Silas and me to lure him here, a place we know better than he does, take him unaware, and stake him. It would help a lot if you and the others could keep an eye out for him and let us know when he comes, probably sometime in the next week. The thing is, I can't promise it would be safe for everyone. Harou is powerful and unpredictable. We wouldn't want any of you to fight, just keep an eye out for him. Would you be willing to do that?"

"Of course I would, dear. Honestly I would have helped you right off the bat. Anyone who would foxtrot with an old biddy like me deserves all the help I can give." She patted Senka's arm. "And besides," she added, frowning, "this Maker sounds like a bully, and I hate bullies. I always have."

"Thank you so much, Mrs. Wang. I can't tell you how grateful I am. Would you mind asking Signore Peluso and Bink to watch for Harou also? And let them know he's dangerous?"

Mrs. Wang slapped her thigh. "A team of co-conspirators! I'm sure they'll be agreeable."

"Um, there's one more thing you should know. To lure Harou here, Silas has to leave some evidence. Which means he's going to have to kill a deer or two. And it's going to have to be messy, brutal, as if a wild animal had killed them."

"I see." Mrs. Wang sat for a moment in silence. "It's a shame for the deer. And I have the sense it will be very hard for Silas, won't it?"

"He hasn't said anything about it, but I think it will. It's just, this is the one way he knows to attract Harou's attention."

"This Harou will be on the lookout for signs of vampire activity, is that it? Or at least what he expects vampire activity to look like."

"Exactly. Silas is pretty sure he monitors local news feeds. He thinks it'll take Harou a week or so to notice."

"Well, we'll be on patrol."

"Thank you again, Mrs. Wang. This would never work without your help." She said good night and walked back to the keeper's cottage, feeling hopeful and relishing the sensation of the springy grass beneath her feet.

Silas was back when she returned, peering at the laptop screen. Luna, on the table next to him, pretended to doze with his tail draped across the keyboard as if by accident. They both looked up as Senka came in. She enjoyed a moment of taking in the scene, the pleasure of seeing these two beings who had made her existence immeasurably more precious. She allowed herself to place a hand on Silas's shoulder. A look of uncomplicated happiness suffused his face. With a hint of wonder, Senka thought, *With everything going on, grief and danger and plots of revenge, right here there is peace.* "Mrs. Wang is with us," she said, "and she'll talk to the others."

"Excellent. Look what I've found." He swiped the laptop and Kenny's face filled the screen. "He is on Facebook and posts regularly. Considering his criminal activities, one would think he'd be more careful with his privacy settings." He scrolled down the page. Kenny in a variety of exotic locations. Kenny pointing to himself in front of an opulent house marked "Sold." Kenny at a restaurant cheek-to-cheek with the young woman they'd seen him with. Multiple tawdry memes.

"He's not making himself hard to track down, is he?" Senka commented. "Either he's still working for his Russian oligarch or he's settled his account somehow."

"I think it's the latter." Silas continued to scroll. "Look how often he posts. He doesn't have time to be working for the oligarch."

An image flashed by as Silas scrolled. "Wait, go back. Stop! That one." It was a selfie of Kenny and the young woman taken in what looked like a living room or a den. In the background, a framed poster hung on the wall: the image of Sarah Sommers, at the ready with a sharpened wooden stake. The text announced the air date of season eight, the season that had died with Sarah. "That fucking …" She couldn't think of a word bad enough to describe him. "He's using my so-called disappearance for pity points." Her rage, banked while she focused on Silas's problem, flared to bonfire intensity.

Silas stared at the photo, teeth clenched. "I'd say this answers one of your questions. The young woman he's with has no idea of the criminal he is."

"No. He's whitewashed himself." She sat next to Silas. "He has no remorse. It's like he's using that poster to flaunt the fact he killed me."

"Are you positive you want to wait? We don't know what he might do to the young woman. Perhaps he should be our first priority."

"We have to take the gamble, Silas." Senka shook her head. "Harou comes first."

"If I am ended, you will be on your own. I won't be here to be your second."

Silas's use of the dueling term sounded right in Senka's ears, though she hated the implication of the words. *If you're ended, I don't want to stay—* She stopped, taken aback. She hadn't realized she felt that deeply connected to him. The idea scared her, despite Stan's vote of confidence. *I'll think about that once Harou is dead,* she told herself. "Harou comes first," she said aloud. "That reminds me." She shut the laptop, happy to erase Kenny's smug face. "When I was at the cemetery I noticed a couple of flower vases by a headstone. They have long spikes on the bottom to hold them in the ground. I think they'd be effective as stakes. A little top-heavy maybe, but convenient; they're right there."

"Good. We have our scouts, we have our battle plan, and we have our weapons. The sooner we engage with Harou, the sooner we can turn our attention to Kenny." He slapped the table with conviction. "We need to start now, tonight."

"What?" Senka stood, alarmed. "Are we prepared enough? Shouldn't we do a few dry runs?"

"We'll have time to practice our plan as it will take several kills for the report to reach Harou." He rose from the table. "Ideally, I'll find a deer in the cemetery rather than having to hunt one up and carry it back there."

"Just so you know, Mrs. Wang thinks you're very kind to the deer."

Silas's eyes widened in surprise—or perhaps alarm. "She's seen me?"

"Yes, and I warned her you'll need to kill some."

"I really must pay more attention to my surroundings, now that I am aware of the presence of ghosts."

"For all you know, ghosts have been watching you from the shadows for the last three hundred years."

"That's terribly disconcerting."

Senka spent the first few minutes after Silas left trying not to think about the deer that was about to lose its life for their plan. But as much as she felt sure of her decision to face Harou before dealing with Kenny, she couldn't deny the lure of learning more about Kenny's life since he murdered her. She decided to distract herself by looking for anything that could tell her more about Kenny's disbarment. She shifted Luna off the laptop where he was lounging (he protested with an undignified squeak), opened it, and googled, "How to learn why a lawyer has been disbarred." A memory popped into her head. She and Kenny had been sitting at their kitchen island one morning when a bantering dispute had driven them to Google. She had typed, "What year was the movie *The Pink Panther* made?"

"Oh, my god, babe!" Kenny had said, trying to pretend he wasn't annoyed. "Google doesn't care about verbs and articles. Just say, '*Pink Panther*.' At the most '*Pink Panther* movie.'"

"But I like talking to it like a person," she'd said. "It feels like a conversation."

He had walked away, abandoning the discussion, and been distant and passive-aggressive for the rest of the day. Why hadn't she seen such immature behavior as a red flag?

Add that to the list of things I'll deal with later, she thought.

She refocused on the search results and was surprised how easy it was to find out if a lawyer had been disciplined and for what reason. She clicked over to the State Bar of California website and searched Kenneth Loche. The dark red entry glowed on the screen: "Disbarred for misappropriating funds, misrepresentations, issuance of non-sufficient funds checks, and other violations." It added Los Angeles County and the effective date, two months after he had murdered her.

"Kenny, you idiot," she said. "You really made a mess of things."

Clicking back to Facebook, she opened the search box for his page and typed in the year of her death. She had never paid attention to Kenny's social media accounts and was surprised to see her face come up over and over. He had shared every post her production company had made. Sometimes he'd added pictures of the two of them out somewhere, including dozens from magazines. He'd gone silent for a time after he murdered her; then his posts turned to her disappearance and his desperation to find her.

Senka stopped scrolling at one image, another selfie, this time taken at one of Stan and Peter's rallies. She could make out a tiny figure on a stage in the distance, arms raised, exhorting the crowd. Stanley. What interested her more were the two people behind Kenny. One, a man, stocky and thuggish, his square head turned away from the camera, looking at the stage. The other, a woman, her hand hooked in Squarehead's arm. She looked over Kenny's shoulder straight into the camera, wearing an enigmatic smile. She was the same build as Sarah Sommers. Same height, same weight, same coloring. She could have gotten work as Sarah's body double. Senka would have bet she was the same shoe size. "Is that how you did it?" she whispered to the picture of Kenny. "Is that how you made those footprints?" It would have been natural for someone seeing a woman in a car or at a distance to have mistaken her for Sarah.

Hearing Silas come through the back door, she closed the laptop. Rather than walking directly to the parlor, he went to the kitchen. She heard water running. When he entered the parlor, he was freshly scrubbed and his sweater was gone. He sat in one of the rockers.

"Watson," he said, a hint of mischief in his eyes, "the game's afoot." Senka felt a flutter of excitement mixed with fear.

"Where did you leave it?"

"In the corner near the golf course, there is a pile of wood chips."

"I've seen it."

"I left it there. I thought it would seem less obvious than somewhere more conspicuous."

"Smart. We have some time until sunrise," she said. "Let's go walk the cemetery and decide where this execution is gonna go down."

Silas smiled. "I read a review of *Blood Moon: Huntress of the Shadows*. The reviewer said you were 'badass.' I see what she meant."

The graveyard was empty when they arrived. Senka pointed out Mrs. Wang's and Signore Peluso's graves, realizing she didn't know where Bink was buried. She, Silas, and Luna walked up and down the tree-lined alleys that marked the oldest section, taking note of broken concrete to use as impromptu weapons, stands of trees that could be hiding places, and gravestones covered with lichen and weather-beaten from a century in sea air. Senka showed Silas the empty vases, spiked on the bottom.

"Let's practice pulling them out of the ground smoothly," Silas suggested.

Senka loosened both from the grip of the grass growing around them. She pulled up one, then the other. Easy, she thought. As a final test, she positioned herself three tall trees from her target, launched herself toward a vase, snatched it up, spun, and rammed it into a tree trunk. "I think it could work," she said, tugging it out of the tree and putting it back in place.

Not long before sunrise, she rose into the treetops and hovered with the fog. "Can you see me?" she called down.

"Not at all. I see nothing but mist. One moment!" With alarming speed, Silas clambered straight up the trunk of the Monterey Pine in which she hid. In seconds he was at her level. "I see you now," he said.

"How did you do that?" she gasped.

"Another vampire talent. Harou will be faster than I. What would you do if I were him?"

The first idea that came to Senka's mind was to get out of there as fast as possible, but she challenged herself to come up with other options. "I might be able to go solid, grab a branch, and stake him."

"You wouldn't get beyond going solid. He'd knock you out of the tree."

"I could force him to go higher until the branches wouldn't support his weight."

"Which might work, though it would only lead to a stalemate, I think. Yet there are occasions when gaining time in a battle is all one can hope for."

"Yeah. It was a pretty standard trick in the show for me to feign injury or defeat and then come back extra strong."

"When we have come through our adventures," Silas said, "I look forward to watching *Blood Moon: Huntress of the Shadows* from pilot to final episode."

Senka took him in, his hair shining almost blue in the moonlight, the strength and character in his face, the way he looked at her as if she were …

She leaned across the branch that separated them and met his cool lips with hers. It was only a brief touch—to kiss him she had to make herself more solid, and as soon as she did, she started to sink—and it left her wanting more. Silas caught her before she had sunk more than a branch and pulled her to him. She wrapped her arms around him, burying her fingers in his hair. They kissed like two beings who had been waiting an eternity for each other. Senka breathed in the cool, pine-forest fragrance of him. She abandoned herself to the feeling of his lips against hers, the strength of his arms pressing her to him, the warmth that flooded her.

Warmth. She opened her eyes. "The sun's about to rise. I can see the first rays. We'd better get back."

"Yes." He held her for a moment longer. "I am so pleased," he said, his lips brushing her cheek, "that you have learned to make yourself solid at will."

Laughing, Senka floated to the ground, Silas close behind as he scrambled head first down the trunk. They called to Luna, hunkered next to a gopher hole hoping for a snack. He turned and, tail uplifted, led the way home.

They spent the day drawing a map of the graveyard and discussing the pros and cons of fighting in each area. They found themselves sitting closer together than they had before or resting a hand on an arm or knee for emphasis. Once, they gave up the pretense and stopped for a lingering kiss. The sun had begun its descent before they'd completed a list of the tactics they wanted to rehearse during the coming nights. Senka particularly loved the idea of practicing a tricky stake handoff she'd used in season two, episode seven, though Silas discouraged anything complicated on the grounds that stage combat, however complex, didn't carry the same pressure as staking an in-the-flesh vampire. The idea sobered Senka, and they finished the list with practical, straightforward techniques to review.

The list done, Silas searched the web for reports about the deer. They were rewarded with a brief article on a local television news website.

MOUNTAIN LION ATTACK SUSPECTED

It's not often we have mountain lion attacks in the area, but when one is suspected, it's best to be on the alert. Wildlife specialist Kim Johnson called the station today to report that a deer found near the PG golf links was likely the victim of a mountain lion. "It may have been driven into a populated area due to the drought or to recent wildfires," Johnson said. "And of course, there's abundant food for it around here with our large deer population."

Be on the lookout if you are running or walking near the golf course and take evasive measures if you see a mountain lion.

"Do you think he'll notice such a small article?" Senka asked.

"Not the first one, no. But if reports like this continue, he will notice."

"We'll just have to make sure reports like that continue."

Silas nodded. "I'll kill another tonight. The hunting practices of vampires and mountain lions are nothing alike, but humans rarely notice. They don't allow themselves to imagine the unimaginable.

Where, for example, is the lost blood? Why did the mountain lion kill but not eat? They will develop any number of theories except the correct one."

"I get that. I was in a show about vampires, and it never crossed my mind they might be real."

They went back to planning, considering what Harou might do, practicing what they could in the small space of the cottage. When the sun had settled beneath the horizon, Silas stood. "I should have gone shopping for a change of clothes," he said. "After this hunt, I'll have to wash out what I'm wearing." He turned to Luna. "Are you coming?" The cat stood, stretched with a thoroughness that seemed unnecessary, then stalked to the door before turning to wait for Silas. "I'll return soon, then we can go to the cemetery together and practice techniques."

Left to herself, Senka worked on rapid transitions from solid to insubstantial. She practiced hovering, plunging to the ground, and somersaulting through the rocking chairs and loveseat. She began to feel confident; after all, she hadn't broken any of the furniture.

She was getting ready to try a more elaborate combination of moves when Bink plunged through the roof, shouting as he dropped to the floor. "Dude! You know the guy you wanted us to keep a lookout for?"

"Harou? The vampire?"

"Yeah, him. He's here. I just saw him on the golf course."

"That's impossible! He can't be here already. There's only been one news report."

"I don't know about reports, but he's here, dude. I saw him with my own eyes. He's hella scary looking. And, Senka, he's not alone. There's this other thing with him? I don't know *what* it is, but as soon as it saw Silas, it attacked him, man."

The night nurse, now in Tardis scrubs, comes in to check on Finn. It's good timing. He looks exhausted, and we should stop for tonight anyway. When we hear her coming, Finn pretends to be asleep and is pretty convincing. She checks the monitors, makes her notes, and tiptoes out.

As soon as she's gone, Finn whispers, "You're gonna stop now, aren't you? Is Silas okay? Where's Luna?"

"The story—"

"The story tells itself. I know." He sighs in resignation.

"You got it."

"They're okay." He watches me to see if I'll react, but I've always been a good poker player. It's gratifying to know he cares about their well-being.

"You didn't mind the romantic stuff? The kissing?"

He snorts. "You don't know much about teenage boys, do you?"

"Enough to fill a thimble."

His smile lingers for a heartbeat then fades. "Senka and Silas make a good team."

"I think so too."

"It helps," he says. I raise an eyebrow, not sure what he's referring to. "You know, to go through a tough time with someone you care about."

"Oh, I see. Yes, it does."

"I'm glad you've been here."

He's caught me by surprise. I'm so touched I don't know what to say. I manage, "Are you?" Totally inadequate.

"Yeah."

"Thank you." Tears prickle behind my eyes.

"Mm-hmm." It's a simple acknowledgment of his feelings and mine.

I pat his unencumbered arm. "Time to sleep?"

"Yeah." He sighs deeply and closes his eyes.

Chapter Nine

Finn is constantly on my mind, no matter what I'm doing throughout the day. I always experience a growing connection, but with him, it feels like something more. He looks better tonight. It happens like that sometimes, if the body acclimates a bit to the treatment. It's a relief to see a whisper of pink in his cheeks.

"I'm glad you came early tonight," he says as I enter the room.

"Oh, yeah? You want to find out what happens to Silas and Luna."

"Sure, but, you know, I'm glad to see you too." His expression is frank, open.

"Thank you. That makes me feel good." I blink a couple times to forestall the tears that threaten. "Have the nurses been in for your nighttime check?"

"Yeah. But they've been coming by more often. They'll probably interrupt."

"We can always pause."

"Yeah." He looks away from me then turns back. "Listen, I told my mom about you today. I hope that's okay."

"Of course it is." Though I have my doubts about her reaction. "What did she say?"

"She didn't believe me. She said she did, but I heard her talking to Joe, you know, my day nurse? She said I'm having hallucinations. Joe said it can happen with the new meds. I told her you've been coming since before the med change, but she doesn't believe the hospital would allow a storyteller after visiting hours." It's the most he's spoken in one go, and the monitors show an uptick in his heart rate and dip in his oxygen level.

"Well, she's right," I tell him. "I don't work for the hospital."

"I didn't think you did. I'm not gonna talk to her about you again. I wish she believed me, but it's not worth it. It just worries her. " He sighs. "She tries not to look scared, but she is."

"How about you?"

He turns to face me and puts his hand under his cheek. He looks so young. "No, I'm not scared. I mean, sure, there's stuff I'd like to do. Drive a car, have a girlfriend, go to college. But I'm scared for Mom if I die. She'd be so sad."

"It's hard for the people left behind when someone they love dies."

"Does the pain turn into a bruise? Like Silas told Senka?"

For a moment I'm silent, thinking how to put this. "The memory of someone we've loved very much is both a pain and, as Stanley would put it, a blessing. Or, say, a source of comfort. Your mother will always love you. If you were to die, she'd always grieve for you. But she'd also *always* feel lucky you were her child."

"I feel lucky she's my mom." He's quiet, thinking, his brow creased at the bridge of his nose, as usual. I watch him, waiting until he's sorted out whatever he needs to sort out this evening. I won't push him. His expression clears and he looks up at me. "Okay if we start the story?"

"Of course."

As soon as Senka heard Bink's words, she leapt, soaring out through the roof toward the cemetery, Bink close behind her. Images flashed through her mind: Silas fighting for his existence against a formless monster. Silas staked through the heart, turning to ash as his sister had. Harou baring his teeth as he bent toward Luna's neck. She rubbed her forehead as if she could force the gruesome images from her mind.

At the cemetery, she lingered above the treetops. From the first glance, she knew their plans were in tatters. Silas stood among the worn and mottled graves. In one hand he hefted a chunk of broken concrete. It wasn't Harou facing him, though. It was a dog the size of a grizzly bear, so black it absorbed the light around it, its eyes glowing red. Even from a distance, she heard its rumbling growls. Two glowing, ghostly figures, Mrs. Wang and Signore Peluso, moved this way and that, looking for a way to help Silas.

But where was Harou? She didn't see him anywhere. "Bink!" she cried. "Where's the other vampire?"

"Over there! See 'im?"

She looked where he pointed. "Goddamn it! What's he doing on the golf course?" She turned back to Bink. "I have to find out what he's up to. Can you stay here and try to help Silas?"

"Sure thing!"

Senka lingered only long enough to see Bink go into a dive and come down hard on the hell dog's back. Or that's what he tried to do. In reality, he sailed through the beast and hit the ground. She didn't know why, but this creature was impervious to ghosts; Silas was on his own.

Wrenching herself away, Senka flew to the top of a tree between the graveyard and golf course. She peered down at the ancient vampire, unable to figure out what he was up to. He strolled along the edge of the fairway as if it were Golden Gate Park on a rare balmy evening.

Movement at the edge of her vision caught her attention. An electric shock of understanding ripped through her.

In the middle of the fairway, a boy, no older than thirteen and slight as a damselfly, spun round and round with his hands flung up to the night sky. His hair, raven black, fluttered in the breeze. Despite the chill, his black hoodie was unzipped, revealing a T-shirt that read "Wears Black, Loves Cats, Avoids People." He seemed oblivious to his danger.

Harou stalked the boy.

Senka tumbled from her hiding place. "No!" she screamed with all her might. Harou stopped, turning to look at her with his infuriating smile. The boy turned too, dropping his arms, but appeared confused. He noticed Harou and jumped in surprise. It would have been comic in another setting. "Oh! Jeez, give me a heart attack. No one's usually here this time of night."

"I am so sorry I startled you," Harou said, suffusing his tone with avuncular warmth. "It was not my intention."

"It wasn't just you. I thought I heard something."

"I did too," Harou answered, exaggerating his accent for the charm appeal. "The wind in the trees, perhaps?"

"Sounded kinda shrieky." The boy's expression softened. "It was prob'ly a gull. They love to fly around at night. Anyway, g'night." He waved a hand and walked on.

Harou moved in his wake.

"Don't touch him!" Senka shouted. She ran toward Harou, pulling up within an arm's length of him. "I know you can hear me. He can't, fine, but you sure as hell can."

Harou laughed. Ignoring her, he called, "It's a lovely night for a walk."

The boy turned back. "Yeah, I guess. I was looking for bats." He started to move on.

"Don't go." Harou moved toward him.

"Leave him alone, Harou!"

The vampire spun to face her, his face twisted with rage. "You dare to call me by my name?"

"Holy shit!" The boy stumbled back a few paces. "Okay. Bye-bye." He continued walking backward, keeping an eye on this mercurial stranger.

Burying his anger, Harou turned his back on Senka. "What a shame." He stuck out his lower lip in mock sadness. "I had hoped to take my time with you, little boy, but the hiker spoiled my plans." He walked toward the child.

"Look. Um …" The boy held up his hands to forestall the stranger's advance. "I don't know what you're talking about. I'm … I'm just gonna go home."

"Son, you are not going home." In a child's heartbeat, Harou was behind the boy, gripping him so hard he couldn't struggle. Shock and fear swept over his innocent face.

"Don't. Please." Senka moved closer, having no idea what she could do or say to set the boy free. "I'm sorry if I offended you. Please let the kid go."

"What will you give me to spare him?"

The boy craned his neck, trying to see his captor. "S-spare who? I don't know what you're talking about."

"Shut up!" Harou commanded, giving the boy a vicious shake. "I am not talking to you." The boy's eyes stretched wider as he tried to see who else was there.

"What do you want? I don't have anything to give you." Senka edged closer.

"But you do; you have Silas. If my clever monster does not end Silas first, you can bring him to me. So simple."

Senka flashed with rage. "I will never, never let you end Silas."

"Ah, well, you have only yourself to blame." Harou bared his teeth, his fangs protruded, and he twisted the young boy's head to expose his neck. The boy cried out.

"Stop!" she begged. "Please stop."

"Why do you care if this child lives or dies? You do not even know his name." The kid shook in terror.

"He's just a child. He doesn't deserve this."

"Are you …" The boy struggled to produce a whisper. "Are you gonna kill me?"

"Ah, my boy, you are going to have a very special death. You are going to be killed by a vampire. How many of your friends can claim that, hm?"

A roar of anger and pain erupted from the cemetery. Senka and Harou both turned toward the noise, unable to tell which of the combatants had made it. Feeling the hold on him loosen, the boy tried to pull away, but Harou tightened his grip so hard the snapping sound of the boy's ribs breaking reached Senka. He shrieked with pain. Without thinking, Senka rushed Harou and drove a fist into his face. Harou's head snapped back, and he reflexively released the boy who staggered away from him, his arms wrapped around his rib cage.

"Run!" Senka shouted at him, forgetting the boy couldn't hear her. He didn't need prompting. He started to stumble-run across the fairway to the street.

Prepared for Harou's attack, Senka crouched in a fighting stance, but he stood motionless, looking at her, his face twisted into a snarl of utter hatred. Not taking his eyes off her, he reached into his coat pocket and pulled out a handful of—she couldn't tell what. Sparkling grains dribbled from his hand to the grass. With a snarl, he threw them at her.

The pain was instantaneous. Where the grains touched—her hands, arms, face, lips, eyes—boiled, blistered. Like acid. Senka screamed in agony, scrubbing to get them off, but only smearing them across herself. They ate into her. The pain blotted out all other sensations, all thoughts.

Until the image of falling cat hair came to her. She forced herself to concentrate, to will herself beyond the pain. She lost her solidity, became insubstantial. And watched as the grains fell to the ground, glittering there like new-fallen snow. The pain stopped. The nameless substance she was made of mended itself. She stood, sobbing, staring at the ground. *Salt*, she realized. *It's fucking salt.*

A terrified screech pulled her attention back to the boy. He hadn't gotten far. Harou held him, the fingers of one hand knotted into his hair, the other arm wrapped around his neck.

"Don't," she whimpered.

With a growl of hatred, looking directly into Senka's eyes, Harou gave the boy's head a vicious twist, breaking his neck.

"And there you have it," the vampire spat. "Congratulations. You could have given me Silas, but now, this boy is dead." He dropped the child to the ground and headed toward the cemetery.

Senka stumbled to the body and huddled next to it. "I'm so sorry," she whispered.

A milky white shadow grew around the inert form, sculpting an echo of the fragile body. It gleamed like marble in the moonlight. Senka gasped and reached to touch it. A hand emerged, bridging the gap to clasp hers. She drew the ghostly figure from the lifeless body. His eyes wide, he stared at Senka, taking her in. Without letting go of her hand, he looked down at what remained of his human existence.

"Oh, man. I'm dead?" he said, his tone wistful more than anything else. He returned his attention to Senka. "He was talking to you. Are you a ghost?"

"Yes." Senka refused to allow herself to look away from the child. This moment needed to be about him, not about her shame at failing to protect him.

He nodded. "And I guess I'm a ghost too?"

"Yes," she said again. "You're taking this awfully well."

He tipped his head to one side and contemplated her. "I'm glad you're here. I'd be totally freaked out without you."

He didn't blame her; instead her presence emboldened him. "I wish I could do more ... could have helped at all. I'm sorry I didn't stop him."

Before the child had a chance to reply, Bink was at her shoulder. "Aw, little dude," he groaned, looking from the body to the newly minted ghost. "What kind of asshole kills a kid?"

Senka recalled the danger with a shock of terror. How long had Harou been gone? Still holding the boy's hand, she stood and gripped Bink's arm. "Can you take this boy and his body to the cottage, Bink? I want to keep his remains safe."

He nodded. "Raccoons, yeah. I got him."

She turned back to the child. "What's your name?"

"Jeremy. Jeremy Maly."

"Okay, Jeremy. This is Bink." She glanced over her shoulder to indicate her friend. "He's going to look after you while I—" She stopped, not knowing how to explain what she needed to do.

"Are you going to kill the scary guy? The ... did he say he was a *vampire?*"

"Yeah," she said. "You're damn right I am."

"C'mon, little dude," Bink said, lifting the boy's body and nodding toward the cottage. "I'll show you."

Senka didn't wait to see them go. She leapt into the air and flew back to the cemetery.

The creature was no longer a dog. An enormous baboon, eyes blazing red, swatted Silas with a hand the size of a grand piano, sending him in an arc that ended when he smashed into a tree trunk, bark showering around him. The baboon advanced, teeth bared, its tail a twisting snake; its mouth was open, searching for prey to sink its fangs into. Broken branches, scarred trees, cracked and fallen gravestones spoke to the violence of the battle. The glowing figures of Signore Peluso and Mrs. Wang moved at the edges of the battleground. Unable to directly engage with the creature, they had resorted to shouting encouraging words or handing Silas stones or fallen branches to use as weapons. Now Mrs. Wang helped him to his feet.

Harou closed in on him.

Senka hesitated. *If I'm insubstantial, I can't do anything but distract him, which won't last long. But if I'm solid …*

The memory of searing pain stopped the thought before she could complete it.

Silas, blood dripping into his eyes from a gash on his forehead, undaunted by impossible odds, ran at the creature armed with nothing but a tree branch. The sight overwhelmed her with admiration. With love.

Fuck it. She dove at Harou. At the last minute, she drew the shadows around herself and became as dense as she could. She slammed into him, tumbling and somersaulting until she came to a stop in the grass. She had knocked him to the ground! His expression of surprise, visible for only a second before he hid it, was more gratifying than her Emmys.

"Ah, the little hiker has learned a trick or two since I last saw her."

"You don't know the half of it, asshole!"

"Brava, you knocked me down." He clapped, sneering, and started again toward Silas.

"Hey, Harou!" As she hoped, he turned back with a snarl. "How come you need your buddy there to do your fighting for you? Are you too weak and old to win your own battles?"

"Little hiker! You do not honestly think I have existed this long by falling for schoolyard taunts? No, no! Watching Silas fight my friend is exciting. One can see how our 'indigenous American' clings to his existence as he never did before. Is that because of you?" His eyes ravaged Senka. "Oh, that's delicious! It will make his destruction so much more satisfying."

"You won't end him. I won't let you." She leapt into the air and dove toward him again. He was ready for her this time. She saw him reach into his pocket to pull out another handful of salt, and her courage deserted her. She stopped her dive and hovered out of reach.

Harou looked up at her with a mocking smile. "You think you know all about being a ghost? You know nothing. A little sea salt. Torture, wasn't it? For centuries, witches have used it to rid the world of meddlesome spirits like you."

Fear fluttered in Senka's midsection, but the role she'd played in life came back to her. She forced her lips into a sneer. "And yet I'm still here. Makes you wonder, doesn't it?"

"Wonder? About what, my little hiker?"

"About how powerful you really are. How many times have we met now, Harou? And here I am, still fighting you."

He snarled. "You will call me my lord!"

"Why? You're no lord, no matter how fancy your name is. Harou de Bellême. Silas told me that's just where you're from."

It was the first time Senka had seen him astonished. Rattled even. She had meant to keep his attention, but what she'd done was something far more significant.

"He told you my full name?" He stared up at her, slack-jawed. She saw a transformation. No longer stunned, he was enraged. "He told you my full name?" This time he roared it. In a fit of fury, he flung a handful of salt. She had no time to dodge; it flew through her, stinging and burning as it went.

I can pull him away from Silas. She flitted toward the nearest tree. When she was sure he was watching her, she slipped into the branches of the towering Monterey Pine. "You think you know more than me about being a ghost," she called. "Maybe you do. But you're a coward." She had his attention. "Silas told me lots more than your full name. He had plenty of stories." He was at the base of the tree, peering up, trying to discern her in the shadows. "How you're so weak you can only feed on kids." His hands grasped the lowest branch. "How you took advantage of him and Tara and turned them against their will." Harou growled low in his throat. "How they made a total fool of you by rescuing that—" He sprang. As Silas had warned her, the powerful vampire rose up the tree like a hot flame through dry bark. As quickly as she soared up through the branches, he was at her heels. *He's got to reach a branch too thin to support him.* But he kept coming. She burst through the top of the tree, sending a flock of roosting crows cawing into the night. Only then, teetering on the smallest branches, did he stop.

How is he doing that?

His face twisting with hatred and malice, Harou spoke. "*Fantazmë, nuk je i kërkuar.*" Senka had no idea what language this was. "*Të fryjë era nga bota …*" he intoned.

Something odd happened. The cemetery around her, the dark green of the trees grew lighter, as if the color were being leached out. Or a white fog was moving in to obscure the scene. But she could see the glowing ghosts beneath her, the creature. Silas. As she looked down, the creature struck Silas, sending him reeling, yet she found the sight didn't trouble her as it had before.

Harou was still intoning. It was lovely. Like singing. "*… e të gjallëve …*"

A glowing streak, like a meteor, struck the old vampire and sent him spinning end over end from the treetop. Senka observed, calm and detached, as he smashed against the ground and lay unmoving. Bink appeared beside her, eyes wide, mouth stretched, more terrified than she would have thought him capable.

"Bink, I feel like I'm stoned. Everything's fuzzy."

"Senka!" His face was inches from hers. "You can't let him finish that. It's a spell. It'll send you away. Like, banish you from the world of the living."

"I thought that was our choice, when to go."

"The spell takes the choice away. It's old. Like, ancient. Older than he is. Don't let him finish it, no matter what. There are three phrases. Got it? Three phrases. Don't let him finish the third phrase, okay? Do whatever it takes." He peered at her, his face pinched with worry. "Are you cool?"

Senka felt unsteady, otherworldly, but the colors were coming back into the trees, the night sky. "Three phrases. Got it. I'm okay. I'll be okay."

He gave her a last look and was gone, back into Silas's battle.

From her perch in the treetop, Senka watched the powerful vampire pull his shattered bones back together.

Now is the time. He's weakened. Find something to stake him with.

With tremendous effort, Senka willed herself to refocus on the world. Blearily she peered at a treetop twig waving at her in the light breeze from the ocean and broke it off. *I'll stake him with this.* Clutching it, she descended until she stood beside him in the dewy grass.

The dead, those who had chosen to go on, were all around her, beneath her feet. She pulled strength from their moldering remains, as the trees in this graveyard took sustenance from the decaying bodies beneath them, reaching their roots deep into the caskets.

Senka raised her arm to drive the stake through Harou's chest and realized that what she held was a delicate frond of new pine growth, not strong enough to stake a blueberry muffin. The damp chill of defeat flooded her. She let her arm fall, the twig with it, and watched Harou rearrange the bones of his skull.

"We're opposites, you and I." She spoke without emotion. "You are a body without a spirit. I'm a spirit without a body. But neither of those things is inherently bad or good, is it? Silas is the most caring, most ethical being I've ever known. *You* are pure evil. Kenny, body and spirit intact, is a scumbag. I haven't met any wicked ghosts yet, but they must be out there. It stands to reason."

There was a sharp, popping crunch as Harou shoved the bones of his jaw back into place. "Sweetheart, you still don't know whom you are talking to." A leg crunched and returned to one piece. "When I was first made, the Savoys were new to the Château de Chillon." Crunch went the other leg. "I sat in a window with the little daughter of Count Humbert looking out on Lac Léman." He straightened his arms. "Oh, the pitiful count! He always believed the little girl had fallen into the lake and drowned." A series of pops came from his spine. "Do you know how old that makes me?"

A crash caught their attention. The creature had changed once more: a horse-size rat lumbered among the gravestones. Senka looked for Silas. He was pulling himself from the fragments of a stone ledger that, until moments before, had covered one of the oldest graves. Despite the distance, she could see he was covered in blood. She didn't think it was rat blood.

I have to help him somehow.

A blow hammered her head, and she fell to the ground. She hadn't realized she'd let herself become solid in the shadows of the trees. Harou stood over her. "I am nearly one thousand years old, you stupid whore."

His booted foot caught her in the stomach, lifted her from the ground, and sent her tumbling through the air. She landed hard in the grass then slid, coming to a stop against a bush. She opened her eyes and was face-to-face with Luna, hiding deep inside the foliage, his wide, terrified eyes glistening green in the moonlight. "Just stay there!" she whispered to him.

She dragged herself to her feet. *Think!* she commanded herself. She needed to end Harou. She needed to get to the old grave where she and Silas had practiced with the spiked vases. She couldn't just stroll over there without tipping him off.

She took a step toward him and, making sure he saw her, charged. He side-stepped and struck her in the back. She used the force of the blow to carry her where she needed to go.

The vases were gone. With rising panic, she scanned from grave to grave. Everything was gone: the dead flowers, the pinwheels, the ragged weeds, the overgrown grass. Of course the groundskeepers had chosen today to clean the place up. She clutched at a headstone, dizzy with hopelessness.

Gentle hands steadied her. Signore Peluso. The kindly bear of a man was looking at her, distress written in his eyes. A half-formed idea flashed through Senka's mind and she leaned into him. "Signore, is there anything sharp in the groundskeeper's shed?"

"*Che cosa?* What ees 'sharp'?"

"Oh, god. Um ... sharp ... *acuminatus? Acuto?* Like a knife!"

"Ah! Knife. *Sí. Affilato.* I look."

"Give it to Silas. You understand?"

"Silas. *Sí!*" He flew off.

Senka studied Harou. He was taking in the battle, the blood covering Silas, the creature—now a snarling jackal—with smug pleasure. She walked to him, her hands empty. *How the hell will we survive long enough to stake him if I can't find a stake?*

He turned toward her, careless, as if he were greeting a friend in the park. With a languid smile, he spoke. "*Fantazmë, nuk je i kërkuar.*" The incantation's effect was immediate, stronger than the first time. With the initial phrase, the colors seeped from the world. "*Të fryjë era nga bota e të gjallëve.*" It was music. Senka felt the stirrings of a breeze. Why fight it? Did it matter if she stayed or if she left? Harou began the third phrase. "*Të fryjë era—*"

Luna yowled. His screech tore the air, on and on, shrill and wild. Senka snapped into focus and stood swaying. "Whatever it takes," Bink had said. There was nothing left to do.

She stepped forward and merged with Harou.

He felt like a carcass, rotten and crawling with maggots. The twisting, turning, writhing of them poisoned her.

His outrage shrieked in her mind. No one, nothing had ever dared to do what she was doing now. He wanted to tear her from him. He grabbed at his chest with his claw-like nails and ripped. Blood sprang from eight savage slashes. He thrust his hand into his pocket, filling it with sea salt and grinding it into his wounds. Although she sensed the sting of it, it was nothing like the acid burn it had been before. Harou twisted and turned, trying to dislodge her. She clung to him.

The more she lodged herself within him, the more she became aware of his thoughts, his memories. The hatred he had for her, whom he could not control. For Silas, who had disobeyed him, betrayed him, made a fool of him. Disrespected him. Disrespected *him*, the mighty Harou de Bellême to whom kings and emperors had bowed in terror. The more Silas evaded him, the more of a fool others thought him to be. He was frantic with the desire to punish the younger vampire, his *creation*, to torture him, to rip his throat and drink his blood and end him. The twisting maggots of his rage made Senka sick.

His memories washed over her. A stone window opening onto a lake, no glass in the frame carved into the rock. A child prattled away, her blond hair gleaming in the sun reflected off the surface of the water. Her eyes regarded him with childish trust as she held up a roughly carved horse, her treasure. The room behind them empty, he took her tiny hand and pulled her wrist to his mouth. He bit. The blood was so sweet. He'd meant to sip, but she screamed. He clamped his hand over her mouth and sank his teeth into her throat. He couldn't stop. He drained her. Oh, the feeling of triumph. The thrill of the fresh blood pounding in his veins. He was already thirsty for the next child he would kill.

Senka retched and a gulping sound came from Harou's mouth. Revulsion weakened her, but she refused to release her grasp on him. She tried to become solid, perhaps to blast him apart from the inside, but something prevented her—physics or magic, she didn't know which. Harou whirled and tore at himself. His hatred, his anger, his lust for blood ate at her. She was losing her hold on him.

With a mighty wrench, he pulled free and staggered away from her.

Senka collapsed to the ground, groaning. If he cast salt on her now, she wouldn't have the strength to withstand it. As she sobbed in frustration and defeat, he turned toward Silas.

Mrs. Wang appeared in front of him. Harou stopped, nonplussed by the petite old ghost. Senka couldn't hear the words that passed between them—the creature fighting Silas snarled and roared—but she could see the perplexed expression on Harou's face. Mrs. Wang's was alight with a wide, kindly smile.

What is she doing? Senka wondered.

Signore Peluso appeared beside Senka. "I find." He made a slashing movement. "*L'ho dato a Silas.*"

At first Senka couldn't remember what he was talking about, but she heard Silas's name and looked for him. She spotted him standing near an obelisk-like monument. As she watched, he stepped clear of the monument and faced the monstrous jackal. In his hands was a machete as long as a broadsword. The creature howled once more, its red eyes burning. Then it crouched, ready to spring. Before it could, Silas bolted toward it, raising the machete as he ran. With a mighty swing, he buried the blade in the monster's neck. The jackal staggered but didn't fall. Blood sprayed from the wound, steaming where it hit the ground. Wrenching the blade free, Silas pulled it back and swung again with all his strength. It hit the beast's spine, severing it, and the weapon exploded into flying fragments of metal. The jackal fell at Silas's feet, its head hanging by a strip of skin. An eerie silence fell across the cemetery. The blood pooling around the dead jackal steamed, then the body itself began to boil. The skin seethed and as the bubbles burst, they let loose a noxious smell of pollution and putrefaction. The corpse liquified and oozed into the ground, and with a choking gurgle, it was gone.

Silence. Nothing stirred. Then Harou spoke.

"Ah, my son, you have fought well." His self-inflicted wounds already healed, he pushed Mrs. Wang out of his way as if she were a wisp of fog. He gazed at Silas, who sagged with fatigue. "You always were a great warrior. You and your sister, both of you. Ah, but she was a formidable vampire. You, on the other hand, so sad. You could not conquer your compassion."

Senka, beaten, watched from the ground. Harou was too close to Silas, too fast. She couldn't reach him before he reached Silas, and even if she could, she had no weapon. She dragged herself upright and limped toward her beautiful vampire. At least she could be near when his Maker ended him.

As spent as he was, Silas wasn't ready to give up. "Tara helped me, you know." His voice grated, his hatred for Harou clear in every syllable. "We plotted together to save little Jude. You never suspected, did you? She rescued others, too, over the years you were together. She wrote to me. She told me how you thought she loved you. She hated you as much as I, though she feared you more."

Harou's pretense of calm, his carefree confidence vanished. He snarled like a feral beast, revealing dripping fangs, and raised his hands, tipped once more with razor-sharp claws.

This was the end. She was about to lose Silas. Anguish gnawed at her heart.

At the edge of her vision, she saw an orange streak in the darkness. Before her conscious mind registered what it was, something deep within her knew. Silas must have seen it too, because at the same moment they both cried out, "Luna, no!" The cat didn't pause. He reached Harou and clawed up the vampire's leg to his back. Harou twisted and turned, trying to lay hold of his tormentor. Luna sank his teeth into his prey's neck, aiming to sever the spinal cord. It would have worked with a rat; it doubtless had on hundreds of occasions. But the ancient vampire reached back and grabbed Luna's head, yanking his teeth and claws from the flesh, and flung him hard against a gravestone. The brave cat hit with a sickening thud and lay still.

Senka howled. Grief, rage, and desperation robbed her of words. With no idea of her next move, she started toward Harou. Through the haze of roiling emotions, she heard Silas call her name. "Catch!" he shouted, and threw a dark object toward her. It turned end over end, now glinting in the moonlight, now dark as night. She snatched it from the air, glanced at it, and launched herself at Harou who grinned with the anticipation of ending them both for good. As Senka neared him, the evil creature reached into his pocket once more, pulled out an overflowing handful of sea salt, and flung it at her. Senka leapt and somersaulted over his head. The salt splayed out and hit her full in the face and chest. The pain was a white-hot poker. Her mind fixated on one thought: *You must stay solid or you'll drop your only weapon.*

Her feet struck the ground behind Harou. She forced her eyes to open to the burning salt. Half blind, she thrust out and drove the jagged handle of the machete through his back. There was a sound like the crunching of a thousand November leaves.

It was the most satisfying sound Senka had ever heard.

With a cry of agony, she let herself become insubstantial and felt the salt fall away.

Harou stood before her. Senka trembled, staring at the indestructible vampire, despair suffocating her.

Then he exploded in a cloud of ashes. They hung in the air for an instant until a gust of wind picked them up and carried them away.

Senka and Silas never could remember going to Luna. They were just there, cradling his body between them. He looked up at them and purred.

"Oh, little one, little cat," Senka whispered. A tear fell onto his fur, and she wiped it off.

Silas stroked his forehead in the spot Luna loved. "You are brave and valiant. Were it not for you, Harou—" His voice broke and he couldn't go on.

Senka finished for him: "Were it not for you, Harou, may his name be erased, would have ended us both." The vibrations of Luna's purr rumbled through the three of them. He blinked slowly. "Yes, little one," Senka answered. "We love you too."

Silas leaned down and kissed his head. Senka followed suit, savoring the smell of his fragrant fur. Luna sighed and his deep purrs went silent.

A light pressure against her leg made Senka look down. Twining around her ankles, then Silas's, was the shining figure of a once-ginger cat.

In the same moment, all the ghosts exclaimed, "Oh!"

"What is it?" Silas asked.

"It's Luna. The ghost of Luna," Senka told him. "Can't you see him?"

Silas searched the ground. "No." He managed a thin smile. "He is not for my vampire eyes."

"Oh, Silas. I'm so sorry. He's rubbing against our legs. He's beautiful. All silver and glowing."

Luna's ghost looked up the long expanse of Silas's body and uttered a tiny meow. With that, he turned and trotted off toward the trees, his tail waving like a flag. As he reached the dense undergrowth at the edge of the cemetery, he looked back once and flicked his tail in farewell. In a blink he was gone.

"Why didn't he stay with us?" Senka looked at Silas, the tears in her eyes reflecting his.

"Perhaps he thinks it best to make room for a living companion. Or perhaps he wants to explore the world. He was devoted, but cats value their independence precisely as we do. And, you know, my love, they need to know they are seen."

"It would have been hard for both of you that you couldn't see him. I get it."

The two of them, the ghost and the vampire, stood forehead to forehead, mourning their loss. At last, Mrs. Wang stood beside them, a hand on each of their backs. "I am sorry, my dears, so sorry your Luna won't be with you any longer. Weren't you fortunate to have had all the love he gave you!" She smiled up at them.

Silas cleared his throat. "Yes," he said, his voice thick with tears, "we were."

"Mrs. Wang?" Senka stopped and looked at Silas. "If you don't like this, tell me. But I thought ... Mrs. Wang, would you mind if we buried Luna here? With you?" She looked again at Silas, who nodded his agreement.

"I would be honored."

They borrowed tools from the groundskeeper's shed and dug a tiny grave then placed Luna's body into it on a bed of soft grass and fragrant pine needles. Mrs. Wang, Signore Peluso, Bink, Silas, and Senka shared a moment of silence. Then Silas filled in the dirt and replaced the turf, doing his best to hide the fact the earth had been disturbed.

They were finishing when a voice called out, "Excuse me! Sir?" They looked up to see a man picking his way toward them through the dew-damp grass, his slippers flapping and his robe sash fluttering in the breeze. "Hey, excuse me. Christ, it's cold out here! Hey, did you hear all that racket earlier? It sounded like a tree fell or something." He tried to peer into the darkness. "Christ, I can't see a goddamn thing. They really should add more lighting."

"It was a biker gang." Power rippled out from Silas, and the man reacted.

"It was a biker gang. Did you hear them?"

"You saw the whole thing." Another wave.

"I saw the whole thing. It was crazy."

"Go back to bed and call the police in the morning."

"I'm gonna go back to bed and call the police in the morning when it's not so dark. Thanks, man. G'night!" He flapped off back to his apartment, waving over his shoulder as he went.

"A biker gang?" Senka asked.

"I am not fond of them. They're too noisy."

They sat on Mrs. Wang's wall, more weary than they had ever been, the old ghost next to Senka, Signore Peluso next to Silas, Bink on the grass in front. High up in a Monterey Pine, a great horned owl called, helping to restore the battlefield to a place of natural beauty.

After a long period of companionable silence, Bink spoke. "You guys were hella awesome tonight. I mean, like, total samurai or some shit." He pumped a fist in the air. "Like, Senka, dude! The way you did that flip over the bad guy's head. That was gnarly! And Silas, holy shit, dude! You can take a lickin' and keep on tickin'! You guys had me scared a couple times, I'm not gonna lie. Like, Senka, you let him get awful close to finishing that incantation, dude. I wasn't sure you were gonna stop him."

I almost didn't, Senka thought. "What was he saying, Bink?" she asked. "What does it mean, do you know?"

"Oh, yeah. I think we all know." When he looked to Mrs. Wang and Signore Peluso for confirmation, they nodded. "It kinda gets passed down, I guess."

"So what does it mean?" Senka asked again.

"It feels kinda creepy to say it, but I guess it's safe in English."

"I don't believe the language matters so much as the intent," Mrs. Wang interjected. "Go ahead, Bink, dear. Tell her what it means."

"Okay, what I heard is it goes, 'Ghost, you are not wanted. May the wind blow you from the world of the living. May you disappear without a trace.'"

They all shivered a little.

"You must never let someone say the full incantation, Senka, dear. You must stop them somehow."

"I know," Senka replied. "Whatever it takes." An image came to her mind, and she asked, "Mrs. Wang? What did you say to him, to Harou?"

"Oh! I asked the same question my husband asked new acquaintances."

"Which was?"

"Whether he could dance the tango."

Senka glanced at Silas. She could see he understood Mrs. Wang's response no better than she did. "Why did he ask that?"

"Well, dear, my Edgar always said a man who could dance the tango had energy, passion, and didn't mind looking like a dag-blasted idiot. A man who couldn't dance the tango wasn't a man to be trusted."

"And you were trying to see if Harou could be trusted?"

"Oh, no! I was trying to distract him." Mrs. Wang folded her hands in her lap. "It's such a surprising question it's hard to ignore. And it worked," she added with a shrug.

Signore Peluso had been leaning out around Silas to see Mrs. Wang as she spoke. In a heavy accent, he said, "That was a good think." A wide smile parted his beard.

Mrs. Wang grinned, looking, for a moment, like the schoolgirl she must have been a hundred years ago. "I've been teaching Signore Peluso to speak English, you know."

"Aw, man." Bink shook himself like a wet dog. "That was a lot of excitement for one night. Silas, I'm hella glad you didn't get ended. Congrats on killing that dog-thing. Senka, you rock, my dude."

Silas stood. "Bink, thank you for your help tonight."

"No prob!" He waved a salute to the others. "Laters, all. I'm outta here."

"Mrs. Wang, Signore Peluso," Silas offered them a courtly bow. "I would not be here were it not for your help. Thank you. *Grazie per l'aiuto.*"

"*Tu parli Italiano?*"

"*Certo!*"

Signore Peluso clapped his hands with excitement. He was ready to launch into a prolonged conversation but stopped himself. Instead he said, "*Forse possiamo parlare domani.*"

"Yes," Silas replied, "tomorrow. I'd like that."

Signore Peluso and Mrs. Wang shared a look. She patted Senka on the shoulder, Silas on the hand, and then the two ghosts walked off, arm in arm.

Silas and Senka were alone. He sat next to her and she reached for his hand, their fingers entwining. For a long while, they simply appreciated being together, listening to the foghorn's mournful wail across the bay.

"For more than two hundred years," Silas said at last, "my existence has been unchanging. I have been hunted, lonely, rootless. My only true companions have been the Lunas, always gone too soon. In less than two weeks, I am free, I have a home, and I have met someone I would like to spend eternity with, if you are willing."

From an outdated sense of self-preservation, Senka started to pull away, but Stan's image appeared in her mind's eye. "I am liking this one," she remembered him saying. She felt her hesitation melt. She had known Silas for a matter of days, but in that time she had seen examples of his courage, kindness, strength … trustworthiness.

"I am willing." Senka leaned into him, enjoying the feeling of his arm pressed against hers, the pine-y smell of him, the tickle of his long hair as it fell forward and across her cheek. After a moment, she asked, "Will you tell me about your battle? I didn't see much. I liked the last part of it, though."

"I could say exactly the same to you."

"True." She thought about how to tell him, but her mind shied away from reliving all of it.

"Shall we say we will tell each other in time, but not just now? Is that all right with you?"

"Yes," she said, relieved. She looked at the debris around them. "Do we need to do something about all this? The broken gravestones. And the trees."

"There is little we can do. I have no power to mend stone or wood. If any broken gravestones belong to our friends, I think they have forgiven us. The rest, I'm afraid, is up to the groundskeepers."

"I'm sure they've forgiven us; it was the monster's fault."

"It was a transmogrifier."

"I don't know what that is."

"Some cultures call it a shapeshifter."

"Aren't shapeshifters human?"

"It may have been, at one point. Before it met Harou."

"What an awful thought."

"Yes. I feared it would take on its human form as it died. The cowardly part of me didn't want to face that."

Senka sat up. "You are not a coward, Silas. Anything but. Your compassion doesn't make you weak. It doesn't make you a bad vampire any more than it made you a bad human. It's much easier to cast judgment than to find compassion. Harou didn't know what he was talking about."

Silas smiled at her passionate tone. "I would wager all I have that you know how to dance the tango."

"You better believe it, buddy!" She leaned in to kiss him, but pulled back to look him up and down. "Oh, wow! You're a mess! All I've been registering is you're still here, he didn't end you. Are you hurt?"

"I was, but the wounds have healed. I need to rest and eat. And bathe. And change my clothes. And you? The salt? The horrible incantation?"

"I'm fine." She waved a hand to forestall his concern. "Speaking of eating, though, how did he find us here so fast? You thought it would take at least a week for him to hear about the dead deer."

"I am embarrassed to say I neglected to calculate the speed of internet news alerts. It was nearly a fatal miscalculation. For both of us."

"But we're here, and he's not. The sky is lightening. Want to go back to the cottage?" A realization hit her in the pit of the stomach. "It'll feel so empty without Luna."

"Yes, it will. He was a very brave cat."

"Luna the twenty-third. As Stan would say, 'May his memory be a blessing.'" They stood and, hand in hand, headed out of the cemetery.

Senka froze, a horrified look on her face. "Oh, shit," she said.

Silas snapped into a fighting stance and scanned the graveyard, ready for battle. "What is it?"

"Oh, Silas." She turned to him and grasped his hands. "Something bad happened."

"I know."

"Something else. Harou—when I first got here tonight—he ... he killed a boy, like twelve or thirteen years old. I tried to stop him, but I couldn't."

Silas looked stricken. "Oh, no. Oh, Senka."

"I asked Bink to take him to the cottage. He's ... Silas, he must be waiting there for us."

"Oh, good heavens." He looked toward the cottage and back at Senka. "He's a ghost?"

"Yeah, but his body's there too. I didn't want something getting at it. There isn't a tour today, is there?"

"No. At least that's a positive. But what will we do with his remains? He can't simply disappear. His family will be beside themselves."

"I know. I have kind of an idea, but I need to get his input. Let's go back to the cottage."

The door to Finn's room opens, and a nurse's aide comes in. Finn has no time to pretend he's asleep.

"Oh!" she exclaims. "Can't you sleep?"

I move out of her way.

"I'm listening to a story," Finn answers her.

"That's nice." She's all efficiency, there to check his monitors, and doesn't give him another glance. She finishes her task and says, "I'll turn off the observation light, okay? That should make it easier to sleep."

"Thanks," Finn says. She leaves, closing the door behind her, and he turns back to me. "I'm really sorry Luna died."

"Me too." It's one of the hardest parts of the story to tell.

"But his memory is a blessing, like you said before."

"It sure is."

He blows air through his lips like a horse. "This whole death thing is complicated. I mean, not just what it's like to die, but what it's like to love someone who dies. Or even to hear about someone who's died." He shakes his head. "One of my favorite baseball players died a couple years ago. I was really sad."

"I get it." The characteristic crease forms between his eyebrows. "Hey," I say before he can get too deep into his new thought. "We're not going to solve death's questions tonight. Are you ready to get some sleep?"

He nods, then remembers something. "I meant to say ..." His eyes show how earnest he is. "Senka was really brave. I'm not a fan of being hurt, but she let herself be, like, tortured in order to stake Harou."

"She couldn't have done any of it without the beings around her."

"Yeah, but she's super brave too."

I can only smile.

I sit by his bedside. It's not long before his breathing is steady and even. I watch the monitors for a time. The blips of his heartbeat spike rhythmically. Blood pressure and oxygen levels are stable. I think about his mother again. What is it like to have brought this young man into the world and see him as he is now? I wish I could talk to her and tell her it will be all right.

Eventually.

CHAPTER TEN

The dark circles under Finn's eyes are back.

"Did you watch the baseball game?" I'd heard earlier that Finn's team, the Oakland A's, played this afternoon.

"It was on." His response is listless, though he musters a smile as he turns to me.

"It didn't hold your interest?"

"Not so much. What happened to the kid?"

It takes me a beat to catch up to the subject change. "You mean Jeremy, the boy on the golf course?" He gives me a slight nod. "He was very generous. Silas and Senka couldn't have taken the next step without him."

"How did he know he could choose to stay? I wouldn't have known if you hadn't told me."

The answer is that you just do, but I want to give Finn more. "Have you ever gone hiking?"

He answers with a nod again. His eyes stay on me; he trusts I'm getting to a point.

"You're on a hike, and there's a rushing stream across your path. Something tells you whether you can jump it or not. Your intuition, I guess."

"Same with bouldering," he says.

"Yes, like that. When you know you can make the jump from one boulder to the next even if you've never climbed on boulders before."

He mulls this over. "If you stay, you can choose to go later, when you're ready." He watches me, waiting for confirmation.

"Right. There's an important thing to know, though." I lean forward with my arm over the bed rail. "For those who decide to stay, it can be hard because the people they love don't know they're there."

"Unless they're dying too, like Stanley?" As if it's the most natural thing in the world, he takes my hand. I can't talk for a moment.

"Yes," I say at last, "that's right."

He clears his throat, a watery sound, but takes a breath and goes on. "Mrs. Wang couldn't tell her grandkids she was proud of them."

"Exactly." I nod.

"You hear stories. People seeing ghosts. Broken radios turning on." The conversation seems to be tiring him, but his drive to have clarity isn't new to me.

"That does happen, yes. Ghosts have tried to call attention to themselves throughout history. But you know how living people react."

He looks disappointed but nods. "Scared, mostly."

"Yeah." I wrinkle my face in shared disappointment, and he smiles. We sit in silence until I ask, "Anything else you want to know?"

He shakes his head. "I'm good."

"Should I go on with the story?"

"Yeah. Please." He squeezes my hand and releases it.

The sun was rising over the golf course as Silas and Senka returned to the keeper's cottage. The first thing they saw was Jeremy's body. He was sitting in the larger rocking chair, hands folded in his lap, head lolling from his broken neck.

"Jesus, Bink!" Senka muttered, but realized putting him in the rocking chair didn't, in reality, disrespect his body. Besides, she couldn't think of a better place to have left him. The boy's ghost, she noticed, was nowhere to be found in the tiny cottage. "Jeremy?" she called.

"There." Silas pointed at the window overlooking the lawn that stretched toward the ocean.

Senka parted the sheer curtains and saw, his face pressed to the glass like a Dickensian orphan, the pale ghost of the slight boy peering in at them. She hurried to open the door and called him inside. "What happened?" she asked when he was safely in the cozy sitting room.

"I was looking out the window," he answered, unable to meet her eyes, "and suddenly I was outside. I tried to get back in, but I couldn't."

Senka sat on the loveseat and patted the cushion, inviting him to sit next to her. "That kind of thing used to happen to me too. Don't worry—we'll teach you. The ghosts in the graveyard and me. When you first die, it can be confusing."

Silas, who had slipped away to wash the gore off himself, returned and sat in the unoccupied rocking chair across from the boy. "I am sorry Harou took your life. I wish I could have ended him years ago, but Senka has performed that service for us now."

Jeremy looked up at her with open admiration. "You got the bad guy?"

His tone made her smile. "*We* got the bad guy. I didn't do it alone."

Silas leaned forward, hands on his knees. "It is a bit unreal to think he's gone after so many centuries. I can't quite fathom the freedom of it."

"I believe it." Senka shifted to face Jeremy. "Listen," she began, then wasn't sure how to go on. She tried again. "I'm sure I speak for Silas and me both when I tell you that we're going to take care of you. I mean, when you need us, okay?"

"Yeah. You and the ghosts will teach me, you said."

"Right."

The sound of voices shouting interrupted her.

"Is that noise coming from the cemetery?" Silas asked. He went to the window facing the street and the graveyard beyond. "Ah, our bathrobed friend of last night must have alerted the police," he commented with satisfaction.

Senka and Jeremy joined him. "Looks like half the squad room turned up," she said. They watched for a moment longer as the officers fanned out, calling to each other as they did. "I'm going to slip out and see what's going on. Jeremy, stay here with Silas. I'll be right back."

Emergency vehicles lined the cemetery's drive, and uniformed police were already cordoning off a large area with yellow Do Not

Cross tape. Senka noticed Mrs. Wang standing by her grave and went over to her. "I'm so sorry about all this hubbub, Mrs. Wang."

"Don't be silly, dear. I always loved police procedurals. Now I'm right in the middle of one."

"Was anyone upset their grave got damaged?" Senka scanned the cordoned-off area for any ghosts who might have been roused by the activity.

"Oh, no." Mrs. Wang waved a dismissive hand. "The residents there are long gone."

"I need to get back to the cottage. Will you let me know what happens with all this?"

"Of course! And if you and Silas want help with any more adventures, do let me know, won't you? I haven't had so much fun in decades." Even in daylight, Senka could see her eyes twinkling.

When Senka returned to the cottage, she said to Silas, "Mrs. Wang turns out to be a *Law & Order* devotee. She's hoping we'll involve her in our future adventures."

"Oh, goodness!" He pushed his hair back from his face. "And here I am hoping not to have many more adventures. At least, not that involve my imminent end."

"Yes, let's keep those to a minimum." She looked at Jeremy and guilt washed through her. She sat next to him. "How are you doing?"

"Okay, I guess." He shrugged. "I mean, it's kind of dope to be a ghost. I just ... I'm worried about my parents."

Senka wondered if it was hard for a boy his age to admit that. "You can go see them, you know."

"I can?"

"Of course." Senka's brow furrowed. "But you have to remember they won't be able to see you."

"I know. Like *Our Town*. My brother's high school put that on last year. He played George." He shrugged. "I never saw ghosts, but I always knew they were there. My mom and dad have this little shrine set up in our living room for the ancestors. They put pictures up and burn incense. So even if they can't see me, they'll know I'm nearby."

Silas cleared his throat. "Jeremy, did your parents know you were outside so late? What were you doing?"

The boy looked away from them. "I wanted to see bats."

"And you snuck out to see them?" Senka said, keeping her tone neutral.

He nodded. "Do you think they'll be mad at me?"

"No. No, they won't be mad." She considered him for a moment. "Jeremy, why did you stay? Why did you choose to become a ghost?"

As if a switch had been flipped, his face transformed from somber to shining with excitement. "I want to do more stuff!"

Silas covered a smile. "What kind of 'stuff' do you want to do?"

"Adventures," he proclaimed. "Like in *The Mysterious Benedict Society* or *The Umbrella Academy* or *The Buried Bones Mystery* or—"

"Wow!" Senka said, stopping the flood. "You've read a lot."

"*Umbrella Academy* is a TV series," Jeremy said, sounding like the stuffiest of professors.

"Of course. Silly me." Senka sat back and studied the boy. "Can I ask you a difficult question? One I want you to think about carefully?"

Jeremy's mood changed in an instant; he regarded her somberly. "I'm ready."

Mercurial boy, Senka thought. She bit her lip, hesitating, then leapt into the void. "You mentioned *The Buried Bones Mystery*. How would you feel if Silas and I borrowed your body?"

Jeremy looked from Senka to Silas to his body, still propped in the rocking chair, and frowned. "Why?" he asked with nothing in his tone but curiosity.

Senka bit her lip again. Her insides squirmed with doubt. She needed to discuss her thinking with Silas, make sure she wasn't blinded by her obsessions. But she also wanted to try her plan. How to explain this to Jeremy? "I have an idea that it could help us make another bad guy pay for doing, well, something bad."

Jeremy looked at her like a pup who'd just smelled a steak. "Yeah, I want to help you take down a bad guy."

"Think carefully, okay?" Senka said, holding her hand out to slow him down. "We need to consider all the angles."

He nodded. "What did the bad guy do?"

Keep it simple, she thought, then said, "He murdered someone."

"Like I was murdered?"

"In some ways, yes."

Jeremy gazed at his body, thinking. "You're not going to carve the bones out and bury them in a box, are you?"

"No! Good god, what made you think that?" Senka's hand had gone to her throat at the question.

"*The Buried Bones Mystery*. They find a box of bones." He went on without giving her a chance to respond. "Here's what I want. You can use my body, but I want my parents to be able to have it back. I don't think they'll be any more sad if you use it first. And I'll feel better. It's my first adventure, and I get to help you catch a bad guy."

Tears gathered behind Senka's eyes. She glanced at Silas, who met her look with a raised eyebrow. "Thank you, Jeremy. I promise to keep your parents in mind."

The boy nodded. "Can I go outside now? I want to see what's up in the graveyard."

Senka hesitated, unsure whether it would be the responsible thing to let him wander around unsupervised. He cut through her doubt with a snort.

"What's going to happen? I'll get hit by a car? I'll get in the policemen's way?"

Hearing him sound like a sassy teen made her smile. "I guess you have a point. See if you can find Bink. He'll show you around."

Without another word, Jeremy dashed out of the cottage toward the cemetery.

Senka tucked herself into the corner of the loveseat. Silas shifted to sit next to her. "Am I terrible?" she asked him.

"To use his body in a scheme to entrap Kenny?"

"Yes. Is it morally reprehensible?"

Silas knit his brow and answered her with a question of his own. "Is there a kinder option we can undertake for his family?"

Senka leaned forward. "I'm not married to the idea of using Jeremy's body. My biggest concern is, whatever we do, we need to act fast. I can't imagine the pain of not knowing what's happened to your child."

They sat quietly for a moment, thinking. A flicker of movement in Senka's peripheral vision caught her eye. A tuft of cat fur, its end lodged in the back of the love seat, fluttered in the room's air currents. She plucked it from the fabric and held it up for Silas to see. It glowed a soft orange in the light filtering through the curtains. She turned it this way and that, watching as it caught the light and shone. She held the tuft to her nose, hoping to catch Luna's scent. "Nothing," she told Silas. It was Luna, not his fur alone, that exuded the warm and spicy smell.

Silas took the tuft of fur from Senka's fingers and held it up to the light, then placed it on the mantel. "We'll take it with us when we move," he said.

"Yes." Senka dragged her thoughts back to their dilemma. She gestured to Jeremy's body. "Would it be easier on his parents if we carried him back to the golf course and left him under a tree or something?"

"As if he was climbing and fell? It's a possibility."

"I'd want us to keep watch over him. We can't have raccoons or whatever bothering him."

"There's a problem with that idea. We're not thinking about lividity."

"What?"

"Bruising, blood pooling. The blood in a corpse obeys the law of gravity."

"That is a problem." She looked over at the body, sitting upright in the rocking chair. "It would be tough to explain why his blood pooled in his rear end if he fell out of a tree."

"Exactly." Silas stood and paced the little room. "It is hard to make the situation any better for his family, is it not?"

"However we get his body back to them, he'll still be dead."

"He seems to have taken it in stride."

"We'll see." She shook her head. "It takes a while for it to sink in, that you're not going back to the world of the living." Senka's mind returned to the cabin, to the feeling of being trapped. The years of loneliness.

As if reading her mind, Silas wrapped his arms around her. "I wish I'd been able to help you then," he said, his cheek resting against the top of her head.

She relished his closeness for a moment but knew they had a decision to make. She pulled away from him. "I didn't mean to make this about me. The bottom line, I think, is this: will it matter to the family if he's found on the golf course where he actually died or if he's found in a stranger's yard?"

"It's impossible to know." He brushed the hair from his face.

"It's going to be unspeakably painful for his parents either way."

"Given that, I propose a perfectly moral option is to use an appalling tragedy to further the course of justice."

"I'm not an ethicist and I'm far from neutral, but I agree with that argument. Plus, Jeremy said it's okay. Let's go for it."

Silas slapped his thighs, sealing the deal. "Right. Well, based on our track record so far, I'd say planning hasn't been a great deal of use to us. Nonetheless, we should think through the process carefully."

"But quickly."

"First question: how do we keep Kenny from throwing blame for the child onto the young woman, his girlfriend?"

"Or whatever she is." She rubbed her temples. "He's slippery enough for something like that. I think the first thing we need to do is find out where he lives and scope the place out."

They moved to the table and opened the laptop. Silas typed Kenny's name into the search box and followed it with the words, "find address." The first option was the White Pages; he clicked on the link. The listing read Kenneth Loche, age: forty-two. Next to that, they saw "Pebble Beach." Underneath was the line, "Used to live in: Beverly Hills."

"Pebble Beach, huh?" Senka raised an eyebrow. "We know he's not hurting for money anyway."

Silas clicked on the blue button: "Unlock the Full Report." The screen changed and presented them with the option of seeing Kenny's address, contact information, and criminal and public records, all for a mere $9.99. They exchanged a look and grinned. Silas clicked "Select," and entered his credit card information.

"Do all vampires have credit cards?" Senka asked.

"Of course. How else do you shop online? Credit cards, bank accounts, automatic bill pay. It's so much easier now than it used to be when one had to go into a bank to withdraw cash. Very few banks remained open after dark."

"I guess you have to switch banks pretty often, huh? Otherwise, people might get suspicious because you don't age."

"Every few decades. Here's our report." He double-clicked the PDF icon. The first information they saw was the address of Kenny's house in Pebble Beach, followed by the purchase date and price.

Senka snorted. "I guess we know he didn't use all my money to pay off oligarchs and lawyers."

"Goodness, staking vampires on television must have been a lucrative profession."

"I would've done *Blood Moon* for the fun of it, but the paycheck didn't hurt." They continued to scroll. "Christ, look at this. He buys a huge house for cash, but look how many times he's been sued for not paying his creditors. Everybody from the contractor who did his remodel to—look at this, Silas—to the salon where he gets his hair cut. How do you rack up a twenty-five thousand dollar bill at a salon?"

"He's settled all of them. It's not that he doesn't have the money. I see no record of him filing for bankruptcy."

"No, it's a power trip. He wants to see what he can get away with. What an asshole."

"There are no indications he has been investigated for another murder."

"So either I'm the only lucky one or he's very good at getting away with it. With or without his oligarch coaching him." Senka stood and made a circuit of the room. "Silas, I don't think Jeremy is going to be enough. There's nothing to tie him to Kenny. Here's a guy who, sure, he's kited a few checks, but not for a long time. He's had some gambling problems, but nothing looks recent. He's a jerk about paying his bills. None of that points to his being a murderer. Isn't it likely the police will decide someone planted the body or something? We have to make it impossible for them to look elsewhere."

"Perhaps it's time to bring in a specialist." Silas cocked an eyebrow. The addition of a slight smile made him look like the evil conspirator in a comedy.

Senka stared at him for a moment, not understanding. The penny dropped, and she guffawed. "I'll be right back."

She returned minutes later, Mrs. Wang in tow. "Oh, heavens!" the old ghost exclaimed, seeing Jeremy's body. "I'm glad you warned me, Senka, dear. He and Bink seem to be enjoying themselves following the investigators about."

Using broad strokes, Senka and Silas filled her in on Kenny, Senka's death, and their ideas so far. Mrs. Wang was matter-of-fact about it all. When they were done, she sat back and tapped her lips, thinking. "Let me see. Planting a body. I believe I recall a *Diagnosis: Murder* with something like this. Or it might have been a *Columbo*." She squinted and considered. "It seems to me your first task is to make sure there's something in this Kenny's house that ties the boy to him. DNA, you know. Pieces of his hair perhaps. Then, of course, you'll want to use his tools to bury the body. If he has any. Have you checked?" Senka and Silas shook their heads. "That'll be important. Then it might be fun—" She broke off and turned to face Senka. "Is it possible, do you think, to find any of your remains?"

"I don't know. It was a long time ago, and they were dragged off by different animals. I wouldn't know where to look."

Silas cleared his throat. "If it's important, Mrs. Wang, I might be able to track some down."

"Well, it's up to you, you know." She grinned, causing her multitude of wrinkles to develop wrinkles. "But it might be fun to plant some of Senka's remains in his house. You know, for the police to find. That could eliminate the stumbling block of no priors. And wouldn't it be lovely for him to finally be called to pay with the remains of his true victim?"

Senka and Silas exchanged another look. "Mrs. Wang," Senka said, "I wish we'd had you on our team when I was doing television."

Mrs. Wang smiled modestly but with obvious pleasure.

"Right!" Silas clapped his hands with a burst of energy. "What is our order of operations? We need to investigate Kenny's house—"

"Case it," Mrs. Wang threw in.

"Case his house." Silas smiled as he corrected himself.

"I can do that today, during the day." Senka felt a thrill of excitement to be taking action against her murderer at last.

"Good," Silas agreed. "We also need to locate at least some of your remains, Senka. That's my task. It will have to wait for tonight, of course."

"How are you going to do that?"

"Vampires have an extraordinary sense of smell, especially for, well, human, uh ... body parts, to put it bluntly." He swept the hair back from his face in a nervous gesture.

"In all my years of existence, there is so much I haven't learned," Mrs. Wang said with a delighted chuckle. "Now don't forget the DNA from the young man."

"Right. That's important. Senka, we will need to accomplish that task together, I think."

"I'll check for a shovel today. But yes, it'll be quicker if we move the body together tonight."

"I can't quite picture how we will do all of this without Kenny seeing us," Silas said.

"There's bound to be some improvisation. But I'll find out everything I can when I get there." The three of them looked at one another for a moment. "Okay, well, no time like the present, right?"

"Be careful," Silas requested. "Whatever that means for a ghost."

"Good luck, Senka, dear," Mrs. Wang said, enthusiasm warming her tone.

Senka left the cottage and flew high enough to get her bearings. The bay was behind her, the open ocean to her right and straight ahead. She took off across the peninsula. She was nervous at first. The fog had burned off with the warmth of the day. She associated flying with fog and nighttime and wondered for a moment if she'd have the power in the daytime to make it the full six miles, but soon the cozy updrafts rising from the warm ground below and the sound of the tumbling surf gave her confidence.

It was different flying during the day than at night. Seagulls wheeled around her now as then, but there were crows and jays as well as the occasional hawk, its tail feathers gleaming red, that came closer to investigate her. She skimmed the tops of trees, their scents wafting to her in the breezes.

Even without the line-up of cars waiting to go through the Pebble Beach security gates, she would have known the moment she crossed into the luxury neighborhood. Houses and lots first doubled, then tripled in size. Elegant, sweeping golf courses hugged the coastline.

Although Senka had studied the satellite view of Kenny's house on Google Maps, it took her a couple of passes over the neighborhood before she found it, perched on a rise that overlooked the Pacific. It wouldn't have appealed to her, fronting, as it did, on the famous and heavily touristed 17-Mile Drive, but she understood why it appealed to Kenny. It was another example of his hunger to be noticed, as Stanley had said. She shook her head; the privacy hedge, ostensibly screening the house from the road, had been trimmed low to allow passing tourists an unobstructed view of the mansion.

The house itself wasn't as large as Tara's mansion, but it was hardly a cottage, either. And there was plenty of land for burying a stray body, though most of it was on a hillside. She drifted around to the side of the house that faced the ocean and landed on the large concrete patio. This side was all glass on both stories. She slipped through the first massive pane and found herself in an open, modern living room made up of white walls and hard surfaces. She listened for a long moment but heard nothing. As she glanced around the room, she was struck by how impersonal everything felt; it looked staged by an interior designer. This was a room to impress, not to live in.

Senka moved through an archway into the dining room. Here, too, the glass wall overlooked trees and ocean. It was a narrow room with an exotic-wood table long enough to seat ten. Had Kenny changed so much he was having dinner parties now? Senka doubted it but admitted to herself she didn't know.

A swinging door led to a galley kitchen, so narrow it felt claustrophobic. It didn't look like much cooking took place here. The counters were empty except for a butcher's block knife set and a fancy coffee maker. Out of curiosity, she opened the refrigerator. One carton of low-fat milk, a growler of beer from the local hipster microbrewery, and a bottle of Skinny Girl Spicy Lime Margaritas. "Spicy lime," Senka whispered to herself, thinking of the young woman she had seen with Kenny. She closed the refrigerator and moved on. A nook, no doubt described in realtor's language as "unpretentious," held a kitchen table and two chairs. One side of the table was set with a placemat. A half dozen unopened boxes commandeered the other. Larger cartons, opened and spilling their paper and bubble wrap guts, huddled around the chair legs. *The young woman might drink here,* Senka thought, *but there's no room for her to eat here.*

Two doors led off the kitchen. Senka poked her head through one to find a utility room, the washer and dryer, water heater, and the like. She retreated from that door and tried the other. It led into an entrance hall where a polished wood staircase spiraled up to a second floor. As Senka contemplated whether to go up or finish exploring the downstairs first, she heard a noise above her. Someone had turned on a vacuum cleaner. Never for one moment of his life had Kenny willingly done a chore. Whatever changes he may have gone through, Senka couldn't believe he would pick up a vacuum. She climbed the steps and peeked over the landing. A tiny, round woman in a pink tracksuit ran the vacuum brush back and forth over the hardwood hallway. As Senka watched, she burst loudly and tunefully into an upbeat song that must have been blaring through her earbuds. "*Tengo, tengo la camisa negra,*" she sang, doing a little two-step and wiggling her butt before returning to her vacuuming.

She's either more comfortable with her employer than you'd expect, or she knows she's alone, Senka thought. *I'm gonna gamble on the latter.*

She went back down the stairs, passed through the entry hall, through a closed door, and into a den. This room reflected the Kenny she knew. A flat-screen TV occupied most of one wall, faced by a shabby, much-used leather club chair, its back to the ubiquitous windows and the view. Beside it was a newer overstuffed Chesterfield chair with a matching ottoman. It was upholstered in a startling shade of yellow guaranteed to make anyone sitting in it look sickly. Kenny's girlfriend had no taste at all. Or he had gotten it dirt cheap in a clearance sale.

Senka couldn't figure out the depth of their relationship. The signs conflicted. Yes, her preferred beverage occupied the fridge, but she had no place at the table. Unless they ate in front of the TV? Yes, she gets her own chair in a room clearly dedicated to himself, but is he making a concession with that chair, or is he passive-aggressively indicating she's not worth the money for something nice?

As she turned to take in the whole room, she felt a shock of recognition. Here was the poster she had spotted on Kenny's Facebook feed. Sarah Sommers, battle ready for the final season of *Blood Moon: Huntress of the Shadows*. She walked up to it, taking it in. It was odd to see herself like this, alive, vibrant, wearing something other than hiking shorts and a T-shirt. The separation between Sarah Sommers and Senka felt keener, clearer than ever.

On a hunch, she grasped the bottom corner of the frame and gave it a little tug. *Kenny, you are so predictable*, she thought as the hinged frame swung away from the wall. Behind it was the safe she'd expected. She tried the handle, not surprised to find it unyielding. "Ah, but you cannot stop a ghost," she whispered. She eased her face through the cold steel of the safe door and stopped. It was pitch dark. Not a flicker of light penetrated. She pulled her face free and plunged her hands in instead.

The first objects under her fingertips were stacks of rectangular paper held together with a strap. *Currency*, she thought, *with bank bands*. But what denomination? Next, she felt a square booklet with a stiff cover. A passport, she was sure. Her fingers encountered cold metal. A second's worth of exploration left her with no doubt: it was a handgun. She wondered if this last was a post-her purchase or one more thing she hadn't known about Kenny. On the next shelf, she felt a letter-size piece of paper. There was no way to discern what it was. By itself on the top shelf sat a small, flat box, the kind a jewelry store would use for a necklace. Senka tried to open it but found she couldn't simultaneously be insubstantial enough to go through walls and solid enough to grasp the box. She let her hands drift through the lid. Sure enough, a necklace. Plus two rings. *Presents for the young woman?*

She withdrew, made a mental note of the papers and the box for further investigation, if they had the chance, swung the frame back into place, and continued her search of the room.

Against the opposite wall stood a desk, positioned for an unobstructed view of Sarah's poster. In stark contrast, on the wall behind the desk hung a life-size painting of a nude woman posed in the same position as Ingres's *Grande Odalisque*, except the front of Ingres's model faced a wall as she looked over her shoulder toward the painter. This painting was reversed, with the front of the subject's body facing the viewer, her head turned toward the wall. Senka had only seen Kenny's girlfriend with her clothes on, but she was pretty sure she recognized the back of her head. There was nothing artistic or beautiful about this painting. Senka couldn't even describe it as high-priced pornography. It erased this woman's individuality and made her interchangeable with any other woman.

"If I had flesh," Senka whispered, "it would be crawling right now." She turned back to the poster of Sarah Sommers. It and the painting faced each other.

There's something twisted about that, she thought.

She headed to the desk and tried the drawers, disappointed to discover none of them were locked. The lap drawer held the usual collection of pencils and pens, some scratch paper, the charging cable for a laptop. Nothing interesting. In one of the large drawers, she found file folders relating to Kenny's multiple nonpayment disputes. A binder-style checkbook caught her attention, and she leafed through it. The ledger noted payments to investment accounts, lawyers, the usual utility companies, the housekeeper who continued to boogie upstairs. There was nothing unusual here, except he paid by check and not online bill pay. Another drawer was dedicated to financial statements. They had been thrown in willy-nilly, but a cursory inspection showed Kenny was making sure he'd never again be broke. Every statement reported a healthy balance.

Senka glanced at the desk clock and saw she had been in the house for over an hour. She didn't know how long Kenny would be out, but she wanted to be gone before he got back; she didn't relish running into him. She left the den and returned to the entry hall. The last door opened into a four-car garage. At the far end, utility shelves arrayed in rows like library stacks held dozens of storage boxes, and fully occupied two of the four car spaces. The other two spaces were empty.

Senka chose a shelving unit at random and grabbed the first box she saw. She pulled off the lid. A beaded silver evening gown winked at her in the dim light of the dusty windows. With a nauseating jolt, she recognized it. She had worn it to the Emmys the year before she died. Resting on top of the dress was a piece of scratch paper. It read, "Appraised at $300,000. Post."

Post? she thought. *Post what? Post my 'disappearance'? Post to eBay? Maybe Post is the name of the appraiser?*

Balancing the box on her knee, she lifted the dress and saw another beneath it. It was a diaphanous emerald green number she'd worn to the Golden Globes that same year. This one had an associated piece of scratch paper too. She almost dropped the box trying to pull it out. "App @ $250,000. Hold." Everything about Sarah was reduced to a dollar amount. Feeling ill, she replaced the box on the shelf and left the garage.

Back in the entrance hall, she climbed the stairs to the second floor. The hall was empty now, and she stepped into the first room. It was furnished as a guest room but looked like no one had ever occupied it. This house was all flash, no substance. *Just like Kenny,* she mused.

She slipped through the door and back into the hallway. The recollection of a similar search flashed into her mind. A brave orange cat had been her companion on the adventure then. The grief that washed over her left her weak, and she grabbed hold of the banister. She missed Luna and Stanley so fiercely the feeling erased all other thoughts. She stood for some minutes, trying to get her bearings. At length, she looked up. Through a window cut into the wall above the stairway, she saw the tops of tall pines, the blue sky. She thought of Silas, waiting for her in the keeper's cottage, of another time when he had said, "Remember how calming it used to be to take a deep breath."

Feeling stronger, she turned her back to the stairs and moved into the second bedroom, relieved to find it was Kenny's; she was ready to be done with this search.

The room was long and narrow, but French doors opened onto an upper stone deck overlooking the ocean, giving the room a sense of openness. The enormous bed, so large it had to have been custom-made, occupied half of the room. She rummaged through the bureau, poked into the closets, and came away with two conclusions. Kenny hadn't lost his taste for bespoke suits, and his girlfriend didn't live with him. He had cleared one drawer and a quarter of a closet for her. Senka's hunch was confirmed in the bathroom where she found a crowded medicine cabinet on one side of the sink bench and a toothbrush, razor, and single lipstick tube on the other. Kenny's cabinet and drawers held nothing unusual.

"At least he doesn't have a drug habit," Senka whispered, then admitted, *As far as I can tell.*

She was about to leave when an idea flashed into her mind. She opened the half-filled drawer and pulled out the tube of lipstick. It was well used and had lost its pointed tip, but she leaned toward the mirror and began to write, "It's ti-."

A gasp froze her hand in mid-stroke.

The housekeeper had come into the bathroom. As Senka watched, unsure what to do, the pink-clad woman crossed herself and backed out of the room, her face ashen.

"Oh, great," Senka muttered. "I scared the shit out of an innocent person."

She wondered what the woman had seen. At the very least, a hovering tube of lipstick magically writing on the mirror. She contemplated leaving the message unfinished, but thought, *What the hell, the damage is already done.* "I may regret this," she whispered, and finished scrawling the words on the mirror: "It's time to pay."

She'd slipped out of the bedroom and was halfway down the steps when the entry door opened. She doubled down on her insubstantiality.

Kenny stood in the doorway. In the daylight, the signs of aging were more evident. The past decade had etched deep lines around his eyes and the creases on either side of his mouth gave him a permanent expression of discontent. His eyes were still a startling shade of blue, but Senka saw in them an iciness she hadn't noticed in life. She'd also never before seen him in a polo shirt complete with the signature Burberry plaid collar. She rolled her eyes at the pretentious display.

Kenny sniffed like a dog on the scent of a rabbit. "Smells like a hospital in here," he said. He called over his shoulder, "Open the windows, would ya, babe. The fumes from all those cleaning products will kill you."

A far-off voice shouted back, "You open 'em!"

"I can't," Kenny called back. "I've gotta get changed. I've got that golf thing in half an hour."

To Senka's horror, he bounded up the steps two at a time. She half submerged herself into the wall to avoid contact with him. Kenny's girlfriend came in and closed the front door. With a weary sigh, she dropped her handbag on the entry table and disappeared into the den. Senka heard the whoosh of a sliding glass door being opened. The young woman crossed the entryway and went into the kitchen, where she opened a couple more windows, then reappeared and plodded up the steps.

Senka studied her, curious. Up close, she looked younger than Senka had thought, at most twenty-two or twenty-three. Was this a relationship of convenience? Kenny had his arm candy; the girl had her sugar daddy?

She stood, undecided, torn between her eagerness to get out of this unsettling house and the temptation to eavesdrop. The choice was made for her by the woman saying, "What the fuck is on the mirror?" Senka flitted up the stairs and into the bedroom. The shower was running.

"What?" Kenny's voice echoed from the shower stall.

"I said," the woman responded, raising her volume, "what the fuck is on the mirror?"

"What are you talking about?"

"Your cleaning lady is fooling around with my stuff."

"How?"

"She's ruined my lipstick! She wrote on the mirror with it."

The water went off. "What did she write?"

"You've been paying her on time, right? You ... you're not doing, like, one of your power moves, are you?"

"What did she write?" His voice was harder this time.

"It says, 'It's time to pay.'"

There was momentary silence. The water went back on again. Kenny said, "Babe, how do you know it was her?"

"Who else would it be?" The girl's voice rose in pitch.

"I don't know, but you can't just go accusing the only person of color who comes in here."

"I'm not! Where the hell did that come from? Ken, that's not fair!" Senka's eyebrows went up: *Ken?* The girl was still talking. "It's got nothing to do with her skin color. Who else could it have been?"

The water went off again, and Senka heard the shower door open. Kenny's voice: "Brit, you're really overreacting. It's just lipstick. Hand me my towel, would you?"

"I'm not bugged by the lipstick. It's the fact she's using it." The earlier confidence in her voice was gone. She sounded younger, smaller.

"Oh, so you don't want the brown woman using your lipstick? That's pretty bigoted, babe."

"That's not what I meant!" Her voice quavered.

"Brittany, hand me my towel, please. I'm freezing here." There was a rustle, and he went on. "I don't see why you're getting so upset over this. I'll buy you another lipstick."

"It's not ... oh, never mind."

"What? Now you don't want new lipstick?"

"No, that's not what I meant—"

"Okay, problem solved. We'll go shopping tomorrow. You can pick out your ten favorite colors. All better?" Brittany wandered out into the bedroom; Kenny's voice followed her. "What, no 'Thank you'?"

"Thank you," she said in a defeated tone. *Jesus*, Senka thought. *Did he gaslight me like this? Wouldn't I have noticed?* She wanted to put her arm around this Brittany and tell her to walk out the door and not look back.

Brittany sat on the edge of the bed, staring at the floor. Kenny came in and Senka closed her eyes. The sight of Kenny naked turned her stomach. Though, judging by the brief glimpse she got of him, he hadn't stopped working out. She opened them again when she heard the snap of an elastic waistband. As Kenny put on a fresh polo shirt, lemon yellow with a tiny alligator, and a pair of lime-green pants, Brittany looked up.

"Can I come with you?" Her tone was babyish.

Kenny laughed. "To play golf? It's a foursome, Brit. Two per cart. What are you gonna do? Ride on the roof?"

"Well, maybe just to meet you for a late lunch."

Kenny stood in front of her, placed his hand under her chin, and tilted her head up. "You are the cutest thing," he said, and kissed her perfunctorily. "I'm gonna be late." He headed out the door and down the steps, Brittany trailing after him. "You'd hate it. It'll be a bunch of guys talking guy talk. Sports, finances, a bunch of stuff you wouldn't understand."

"Well, what am I going to do here?"

He had grabbed his keys and was standing in the open doorway. "You're a big girl—figure something out." He turned and strode toward his McLaren.

That McLaren, Senka thought. *If Stanley could see that.*

Brittany followed him to the edge of the patio. "Ken, I'm hungry. There's nothing to eat here."

He stopped and turned back to her, tilting his head to one side. Self-conscious, she pulled her sweater around herself, hiding her objectively perfect figure.

Kenny laughed, as if he were indulging a child. "You sure can put it away, Brit. You're an animal. Go ahead and get something delivered. See you in a few hours." He turned back again. "Hey, you know what? If it'll make you happy, I'll get rid of her. There're plenty of other housekeepers." He flashed her his famous Kenny grin, climbed into his ostentatious sports car, and roared out of the drive.

Brittany stood for a moment, watching him go. In a small voice, she said, "I just wanted you to talk to her, not fire her." She turned back into the house with a resigned sigh. Senka followed as she wandered into the kitchen. She opened the freezer and, finding it empty, closed it and opened the refrigerator. She stared into it for a moment. With another sigh, she pulled out the Skinny Girl Spicy Lime, took a tumbler from the cabinet, emptied the bottle into it, downed a quarter of the liquid, and moseyed out of the kitchen, Senka right behind her.

In the entry hall, she hesitated, undecided where to go, then opted for the den. There, she stood in the center of the room and looked between her portrait and the poster of Sarah Sommers. She took another swig of her drink. "Fuck you," she said to the poster, and laughed. "Well, fuck you both." She raised her glass to her own portrait and the picture of Sarah. "But fuck you most." She pointed at the poster, following her gesture until she was face-to-face with the television vampire hunter. She sipped her drink as she studied Sarah's face. "You're skinnier than I am. You're smarter. You're fitter. You're goddamn perfect. Of course, he never mentions you got paid to work out with some Norwegian trainer for, like, sixty hours a week."

Well, seven hours a week, Senka thought, *and she was Brazilian, but you've got a point.*

Brittany took another hefty drink. "Where are you?" Her eyes narrowed, and she looked like she wanted to take a bite out of the poster. "I wish you'd just turn up dead so he could get over you and marry me."

Senka had heard enough. She felt dirty witnessing the abuse this girl was going through at Kenny's hands. It was clear he felt no remorse for killing Sarah. He used her so-called disappearance for pity points, for financial gain, and now to string Brittany along. If a byproduct of taking care of Kenny was getting him away from this girl, so much the better.

She rose through the house and headed back to Silas.

The alarm goes off on Finn's monitor. I can't see anything amiss, but we wait for the nurse to come. It's the same Filipina woman I've seen a couple times before. She enters his room with an air of efficiency and kindness. She looks at Finn and, seeing he's awake, pats his arm and laughs. "Do you know what time it is?" Her accent is light and warm.

"Late?" He smiles back at her.

"Way late! Can't you sleep?" She hits the mute button on the alarm and fusses with the various plastic pouches and lines.

"I'm not ready to sleep yet. Soon."

"What are you doing? It's not good to lie here and worry, you know, sweetheart."

"I'm not worrying." He watches as she pulls an empty medicine pouch off the pole and untangles the line that feeds from it.

"You promise?"

"I promise."

"Okay, then. That's good. So what are you thinking about?"

Finn hesitates and glances at me. I've moved to the sleeper couch under the window to make room for the nurse. "Diwata, what would you say if I told you someone came here every night to tell me a really good story?"

She looks down at him under her arm as she attaches the new bag of medicine. "I'd say you're very lucky, Finn." Her tone is soft and kind.

"You wouldn't think I'm crazy?"

"No, sweetie. I'd think you were blessed by a good friend." She turns back to the dosage monitor, snapping it closed and hitting buttons to set it for the next few hours.

A voice crackles through her communication device. "Location, Diwata?"

"I'm in Finn's room," she replies, raising her volume.

"Can you check in on Erin? She needs to use the restroom," the disembodied voice tells her.

Diwata makes a face at Finn and mouths, "Sorry," then says, "Be right there." The communication device bleeps off. "Sorry, honey. Wish I could stay. You need anything?"

"No, I'm okay."

"Try to go to sleep, okay?" Blowing him a kiss, she heads out the door.

I go back to my chair and sit. "She seems like a good nurse," I say.

"Yeah. I like her."

"She's right too. It's time for some sleep."

"I hate how Kenny was gaslighting Brittany," he says. I guess it's *not* time for sleep. "What will you do when you finish telling me the story?"

The change of subject takes me by surprise. "How do you mean?"

"Where will you go next?"

"Oh, I see. I don't know yet."

"Is there a kid on this ward to tell it to?"

"Not right now."

"There's always someone, though, right?"

"Yes, there's always someone."

"I'm glad you chose me."

"Me, too. When I started, I didn't know how smart and wise you'd be. I'm glad to have gotten to know you."

"Me too. To know you, I mean."

We sit in companionable silence, until I say, "Do you think you're ready to sleep now?"

"What did Silas say about it again? Sleep?"

"'Sleep that knits up the raveled sleeve of care.' It's a line from Shakespeare."

"I like the way that sounds."

"Me, too."

He closes his eyes. "Okay, I'm going to put it to the test."

"I'll be here."

Chapter Eleven

It's a rainy, blustery evening, a rare occurrence in our part of the world, even in springtime. The floors on the ward are extra-squeaky from the dampness brought in by people's shoes all day, and yellow plastic tent signs warn of the danger of slipping.

A tall blond woman is talking in a low voice with Diwata outside Finn's room. I'm not sure if they're about to go in or are coming out, so I lean against the Fall-Free Zone poster and watch them. Finn's mom looks so much like him. Or I guess I should say he looks like her. She's lanky and athletic-looking, too. And she has the same little crease between her eyebrows as she concentrates on what Diwata is telling her.

"We'll see how he does with the second line. In the next day or two, Dr. Pran will let us know if he thinks a central line would be better."

"Okay." She rubs her eyes. "Diwata, I trust you. What do you make of the results from today?"

"Well, they do show the cancer isn't progressing as rapidly as it was."

"But it's still progressing."

"Yes. It's still progressing."

"What does that mean?"

"Moira." She takes the tall woman's hands in hers. "Can you arrange with your work to take some time off? Will they let you?"

"Oh, God." Finn's mom begins to cry. "I'll ask. It won't be paid time off, and I just don't know what I'll do. My savings are shot." She stops herself. "I'm sorry. This isn't your problem."

"Don't be silly. You have nothing to be sorry for."

"Jesus, cancer sucks."

"Yes. It does." Diwata stands on her tiptoes to give Finn's mom a hug. "Go on. I know you have to get to work. I've got him for tonight."

Moira nods and heads toward the exit sign. Diwata watches her go, sighs, and moves down the corridor to a room across the hall.

Finn should be alone long enough for the next part of the story.

I walk into his room and see what they were referring to. A new pole has been set up next to the original one, the lines from it converging at a port that has been inserted into Finn's other arm. His eyes are closed. I read the labels on the various pouches. Three separate chemo medications and a pump for a pain med hang from the original pole. The new one contains a nausea drug, a large bag of saline, and IV nutrition.

I look down at Finn and see his eyes are open. He's watching me. "That's a lot to keep track of," I say, pulling my chair up to his bed and taking a seat.

He musters a smile. "Would it be okay if we just did the story today? I want to know what happens, but ... I don't have much energy."

"Of course. Do you remember where we stopped? Senka left Kenny's house?"

"Yeah."

His eyes stay on me as I begin tonight's chapter.

When Senka returned to the lighthouse keeper's cottage, she sat for several minutes next to Silas, her legs draped over his, her face pressed into the crook of his neck. For so long she had resisted this closeness, distrusted it, but now it felt more natural, more right than any choice she had made in life.

He said nothing, only wrapped his arms around her. At length he murmured, "Have I mentioned recently how happy I am you learned to make yourself solid at will?" She snorted into his neck, and he pulled away. "That tickles." He tilted his head to see her face. "Are you ready to tell me about it?"

She filled him in on all she had seen and learned. "I can't believe I didn't see how awful he is," she said at last. "I mean, you know, before he murdered me. But Silas, I feel terrible I lost the housekeeper her job. I didn't think about who would be blamed when I wrote on the mirror."

"Then let's make sure she isn't fired. Or at least, she has a very tidy severance package."

"I like it! Okay, so what have you been up to?" She disentangled herself and curled up in her usual corner of the loveseat.

"First, there is something I need to talk with you about. From last night." He turned so he was facing her. It made for a strange tableau: the two of them immersed in their conversation on the loveseat with Jeremy's body as an insensible spectator. "There's no point in talking about the fight," Silas went on. "They are always the same: one gives blows, one takes blows. You are wounded and you inflict wounds. They are a hateful way to settle a dispute." Silas swept his hair back from his face, leaving his hand on top of his head as if to hold his skull in place. "There was a moment I doubted I could defeat the transmogrifier. I *knew* either it or Harou would end me. And I felt an urge to let it happen." An icy chill permeated Senka. Silas sat back against the arm of the loveseat. "I have been battling him in one way or another for well over two hundred years. It seemed like enough. But then I remembered you telling me I owed you my existence. I remembered that you ... you love me, I believe." He looked at her for confirmation. Without hesitation, she nodded. "And I love you." Tears welled in her eyes, and she had to blink to focus on Silas. "At that moment, Signore Peluso appeared beside me like a messenger from you. He handed me the machete and pointed at you. Immediately I felt a surge of hope and strength. Without the slightest doubt, I knew that together we would defeat them." She saw his eyes, too, swimming with tears. They looked at each other and laughed at their shared emotion.

"Thank you," Senka said, wiping her eyes. "Thank you for fighting to stay with me." She chuckled. "Your debt is paid. To be honest, I'd forgotten I said that. I'm glad you didn't."

Silas leaned forward and took her hand in his. Turning her palm up, he kissed it. "And now," he said, "my report. Our friend here"—

he gestured to the corpse in the rocking chair—"has completed his journey through rigor mortis, which is lucky because it will make him easier to transport and to bury. I found some duct tape under the kitchen sink. We can take that with us in case there's none at Kenny's."

"Good idea. From what I could see, Kenny doesn't do anything for himself. I didn't see a single tool in the garage, and there weren't any sheds or outbuildings."

"So we will need to find a shovel. I performed a street view search of his house. There are neighbors on both sides who could conceivably see him burying a body."

"Which means they could conceivably see *you* burying a body."

"Yes."

"Silas." Senka paused, gathering her thoughts. "What do you think ... I mean, anyone looking is going to see a man burying a body, right? You're going out to buy clothes anyway; why not pick up something Kenny-ish, too? That way, if someone does see you, they're likely to think it was Kenny. From what I could tell, he wears polo shirts and khakis. That's what he was wearing before he changed into his hideous golfing pants."

"I like that idea." He scrubbed at his face with his palms. "It is going to be a busy night."

The time until Silas could leave for the mountain clearing passed slowly. They kept busy by brainstorming solutions to pitfalls and snags that might arise during the night. Senka suggested they wrap the body's wrists in duct tape right away rather than wait until they reached Kenny's. Although they knew any lingering marks would clearly have been made postmortem, they decided the longer the tape was on, the greater the likelihood it would affect the skin.

After what felt like days, Silas straightened and glanced out the window. "It's dark enough," he said. "What will you do while I'm gone?"

"Chew my fingernails, if I can."

"I will be back as quickly as possible." He kissed Senka and glanced around the living room.

"What are you looking for?"

Silas's gaze returned to her face. "Luna. I was going to take him with me. I forgot for a moment."

"Oh, Silas. I'm so sorry."

His smile was strained, but he kissed her again, held her close for a moment, and was gone.

Senka stood in the center of the room, wondering what to do with herself. Opting for research, she opened the laptop. With a few clicks, she was at a local television station's website. It was the top story.

INFORMATION SOUGHT ON MISSING TEEN

Police are seeking information regarding the disappearance of 13-year-old Jeremy Maly. Maly was last seen yesterday at around 10 p.m. at his home near the Pacific Grove Golf Links. His disappearance coincides with a later disturbance at the nearby El Carmelo Cemetery. The child was wearing black athletic pants and a black hoodie. Anyone with information is encouraged to call the police hotline.

Senka made a note of the telephone number. They would need it later. Turning in her seat, she studied the corpse slumped in its rocking chair. In a way that she never had in life, she recognized this body of flesh and blood, like Stanley's, like Luna's, was an empty shell. What made it Jeremy Maly had gone. Jeremy was across the street, learning to fly with his bats.

She refocused her attention on the problem of Kenny. *Calling the hotline is out, but I can type.* She created an anonymous email account, tapped "Compose," and pasted in the tipline address. In the subject box, she added, "Suspicious Activity on Golf Links," then paused for a moment, thinking. She typed, "I live near the PG golf links. I couldn't sleep last night, and I was standing on my balcony when I saw the boy in the description. He was walking along by himself. I saw someone, an adult male, approach him. They talked for a minute, but the boy tried to walk away. The man followed him. Then I saw the man grab him and drag him to a car on the road that runs parallel. The boy didn't yell or anything, so I thought maybe the man was his father taking him home because it was late, like 2 a.m. That's why I didn't report this earlier. Plus, I was distracted by the racket from the cemetery. But then I saw the report and thought I'd better contact you. The boy was dressed like it says, dark pants and hoodie. The man was blond"—Senka stopped to think about the light last night, backspaced, and replaced that with, "The man's hair looked blond or maybe gray. He was wearing ..." She pictured what she'd seen in Kenny's closet, "a tan jacket like golfers wear on cool days. He had on light gray or white pants. I hope this helps you find the child." She clicked on the paper airplane and the email whooshed off.

Buoyed by a sense of satisfaction, Senka considered what other mischief she could get up to. *Kenny's girlfriend.* Senka hadn't been active on social media—her publicist had taken care of posting for her—but she opened Silas's Facebook account and went to Kenny's page. He didn't mention his relationship status—*no surprise there*—but she clicked on one of his photos of himself with Brittany, and hovered the cursor over her image. It was tagged. Brittany Ricci. The girl had commented on the photo too: "We had so much fun that day!" Senka clicked on her name.

Scrolling down the page, she noticed Brittany posted to Facebook far less often than Kenny. She had a rudimentary presence including, unlike Kenny's, her relationship status. She listed her current occupation as "Model," though she didn't mention any representation and noted she had once been named Miss Teen Bakersfield. High school: Bakersfield High. No college. Undoubtedly, Kenny had met this child somewhere and promised her connections and fame. Senka paused. Brittany was in her early twenties, not a child. Not chronologically anyway. Still, she was naive if not innocent. *Whatever happens,* Senka thought, *we can't let Kenny implicate her.*

She figured there was a different social media platform Brittany used but had no idea what it might be. Just before she died, there was a new one starting to get big, but she couldn't remember the name. In frustration, she closed the laptop and looked around for something else to keep her busy. She considered going to see how Jeremy was faring, but before she could act on the idea, Silas reappeared.

"I didn't expect you back yet!" she exclaimed. "Did you find any bones?" She noticed a bag in his hand. "Wait a minute. Did you get clothes too?"

Silas smirked, delighted to show off his efficiency. "I did. To both of your questions. What do you want to see first?"

"What do you think?"

"Right. Clothing."

"Silas!"

He laughed. "All right, just a moment." He reached into his pants pockets and pulled out several small pieces of bone. Shoving the laptop aside, he scattered them on the small table.

Senka bent down to peer at them. "They don't look like much. What are they?"

As Silas spoke, he separated each from the little pile. "This is a bone of the thumb. These"—he pulled out seven small bones, all with visible tooth marks—"are also digital bones. I think these are from the right hand."

"You mean finger bones, right?"

"Yes." He pushed those aside and picked out two that were somewhat larger. "These—"

"Are vertebrae. I recognize those."

"Right." He added them to the pile of identified bones.

"And you're sure these are all human bones?"

"Oh, yes. Not only human but yours."

"How can you tell they're mine?"

Silas looked uncomfortable. "It is hard to explain without being somewhat off-putting."

"Please tell me. I'm interested. And I promise not to be put off."

He looked skeptical but said, "You know dogs have the ability to detect thousands of smells, faint smells even, that humans are oblivious to."

"Yes, but, Silas, you never smelled me, my body."

"That was merely an example. You know, also, mantis shrimp can see a range of color humans can barely conceive of."

"I didn't, but I believe you."

"They're a breathtaking part of nature."

"Okay." Senka crossed her arms and leaned against the edge of the table in a 'get on with it' posture.

"Right. Well, vampires are able to detect each particular human's essence. If I had tasted your blood, my ability to do so would be a great deal stronger, but even without that, since the moment I first encountered you, I would know any room you'd entered in life or in death. I would know any article of clothing you'd ever worn. And I certainly know your bones."

"I'm not put off. I think it's kind of ... sexy. I didn't know I had an essence."

"Oh, yes. It's quite distinct. I find it particularly enticing."

They stood close now, and Senka reached up, drawing his face toward hers to kiss him. "You've got a mighty fine essence too, mister." She forced herself to return to the task at hand. "Want to show me your clothes now?"

"Not yet," Silas said, though he stretched his hand out for the shopping bag nonetheless. "I have one or two more treasures from the woods." He reached into the bag and pulled out a long bone. "Left femur." He reached in again. "Two ribs. Parietal bone. And, very important, mandible, though this one is a bit mangled, I'm afraid." All the bones bore the marks of animal gnawing, but the jawbone looked like it had been in a tug-of-war.

Senka regarded the bones with mixed feelings. She was impressed Silas had found them in such a short time, and she was excited to have so much material to plant in Kenny's house. On the other hand, she was acutely aware she was looking at her own remains, and the surreal quality of the moment left her feeling unmoored. She recognized the feeling as the same sense of otherness that had prompted her to let go of the name Sarah and adopt Senka, woman of the shadows. These bones were no more her than Jeremy's body was him. With that thought, she felt stronger again, ready for action. "Time to put all this stuff to use, don't you think?"

Silas took the folded clothes out of his shopping bag. As he changed into a revoltingly Kenny-like lemon-yellow polo shirt, khakis, and a windbreaker, Senka transferred the bones into the now-empty bag. "Finishing touch," Silas said, and tucked his long, dark hair into a knit cap. He presented himself for inspection. "What do you think? Will I pass for Kenny?"

Despite the costume, Silas bore no resemblance to Kenny. The difference wasn't only his copper skin or his deep brown eyes. *Silas has a—well, an essence about him that is nothing like Kenny's,* she thought. "You look good enough to be mistaken for him at a distance."

"We need one more tool. Wait here a moment." He left the cottage and was back in a few minutes carrying a shovel. "Lighthouse maintenance shed," he explained. He handed it to Senka and hoisted Jeremy's seated body from its chair as if it weighed nothing.

Senka held the shopping bag and the shovel in one hand and grasped Silas's arm with the other.

They stood in a grove of cypress trees at the property line of Kenny's house, which was dark, though a line of light showed at the bottom of the ground floor windows.

"He has his shades drawn," Senka said. "I'd better have a look inside so we don't walk in on him. I'll be back as soon as I can."

She flew up to the house and wafted through the den window and the heavy blackout shade covering it. The room was ablaze with light. Kenny sat alone in front of the TV watching a football game.

Senka knew little about football. Her self-absorption in life had made her immune to Kenny's obsession with it. One of the things she was sure of, though, was it wasn't a summer sport. Either he was watching a rerun or a game he'd recorded. Whichever the case, she couldn't guarantee the game holding his interest till the end.

She flitted through the rest of the house. Brittany was nowhere to be found. Did Kenny take her home, or did she muster enough self-respect to call an Uber and reclaim her life? Senka hoped for the latter but suspected it was the former. She zipped back through the den, checking that Kenny was where she'd seen him last, then returned to Silas.

"Blackout shades are covering all the big windows. He's watching TV in the den. I think we can get into the garage without him seeing us, but I can't be sure he'll stay there. If he did see you, you could always 'persuade' him he hadn't, couldn't you?"

"It might become complicated if he calls the police instead of confronting me."

"Okay if we gamble on him staying put?"

Silas nodded his agreement, and they carried their various burdens to the front door. While Silas waited, Senka passed through the door and unlocked it, opening it wide for him to carry Jeremy's body through, then hurried to get the door into the garage.

They skirted Kenny's McLaren and made their way to the farthest corner, hidden by a bank of shelving. Silas set Jeremy's body on the concrete floor and propped him against a shelf, then duct taped his arms to one of the supports. With an apology to the Jeremy back at the cemetery, Senka pulled a dozen or more hairs from his head and sprinkled them on one of the shelves and on the floor.

They left him there and moved to the unit Senka had explored earlier. She pointed out the box where she'd found her dresses. "Let's see if there are other boxes with my stuff. I'm hoping we can find one that would lend itself to bone storage better than mixing them with evening gowns."

Silas started at one end of the shelving unit, Senka at the other, examining the contents of each box. They found more gowns, Sarah's two Emmy awards shrouded in bubble wrap, autographed publicity photos each in its own protective sleeve. Every object was accompanied by a note of its appraised value. There was nothing personal or sentimental, nothing that couldn't be used as currency.

"There is no jewelry in these cartons. Don't all Hollywood stars have masses of diamonds and sapphires? Do you think he's sold it all?" Silas asked when they met in the middle of the shelving unit.

"I didn't go in for all that. Except my engagement ring. You know, *there's* something. Wouldn't it have raised questions if he had that? The police would've asked why I didn't take it with me. I suppose he could have taken it apart and sold the diamonds."

"It does seem like a reasonable question."

"I guess. Anyway, we'll have to shift some contents around to make an empty box. It doesn't make sense to mix the bones with any of the existing contents."

They combined two cartons of gowns and placed the bones in the newly empty box—they had to tilt the femur at an angle to make it fit—then slid it back onto the shelf, lining it up with the others.

That done, they went back to the body. Silas pulled off the tape holding the corpse's arms to the supports and stuffed it into his pocket. A trace amount of tape residue remained on the shelf. He freed the drooping wrists from the duct tape they had applied that afternoon, shoving it under the shelving unit as though Kenny had forgotten to get rid of it.

"On to the next chapter?" he asked, and lifted the body while Senka grabbed the roll of tape, the bag, and the shovel. She opened the door to the entryway and peeked out. The television still blasted football action. Silence from the rest of the house. They slipped out the front door, keeping to the shadows as they skirted around to the ocean side of the house.

As Senka had hoped, the brush-covered hillside here served to shield them from the house yet afforded a view by the neighbors. They chose a spot for the body's temporary grave, and Silas rested it on the ground.

"We'll have to pay attention. If Kenny looked out an upper window, he'd probably be able to see us."

"I would feel more confident," Silas said, "if you were to watch Kenny while I did the digging."

Although Senka didn't like the idea of leaving him, she saw the logic in his suggestion. "Okay. I'll be back soon." She flew up the hill and back to the house.

Kenny hadn't moved from where she'd left him. Looking at him, she found herself at once fascinated and disgusted, as if she were inspecting a specimen in an entomology display. The memory of him watching her as she died—so emotionless, so calculating—returned to her. She recalled the terror she'd felt that night as if it had happened to someone else.

An unexpected thought presented itself to her. *That person, the person I was ... she doesn't need revenge. She needs justice.*

The idea froze her in place. *Can that be true? The whole reason I stayed, the reason I'm here is because I want revenge.* But something had changed. She wasn't sure what; she only knew it had. And she suspected it had to do with the being standing on a hillside, digging a shallow grave. But she'd have to contemplate all that later.

She shook herself from her reverie and started to pace the room. She passed by the nude portrait of Brittany and pushed the edge of the frame so it hung askew. She walked over to her own picture and, glancing back over her shoulder to confirm Kenny was watching the game, tugged on the corner and swung the poster back, revealing the safe.

For the first time since she had died, she wondered exactly how much she could interact with a living person who wasn't on the edge of death, as Stanley had been. She returned to Kenny and rested her elbows on the back of his club chair. He didn't appear to notice. She leaned toward his ear and whispered, "Kenny?" Nothing. She raised her voice. "Kenny?" No reaction. She bellowed, "Kenny!" He reached up and scratched his ear.

The TV remote was tucked into a little pouch attached to his chair, the top half sticking out. She pressed the power button. The television went off. Kenny sat up. She pressed it again and the TV popped on. "Fucking Japanese television," Kenny said, sitting back. She turned the TV off once more. "Goddamn it," Kenny growled, getting up.

Oh, shit! Senka thought. The last thing she wanted was for him to leave the room. She turned the TV back on again. He paused and glanced back as the game resumed but continued toward the door at the far end of the room. Senka hadn't looked in there during her previous visit. When Kenny opened the door, she was relieved to glimpse a sink and toilet. He left the door open as he raised the toilet lid and let out a copious stream, flushed, and returned to the den.

I always knew you didn't wash your hands, Senka thought.

Noticing the poster hanging open, he went to it and swung it closed, pulled on it and closed it again to test the mechanism. He looked at it for a moment, shook his head, and started back to his chair. Instead of sitting, he plucked the remote from its holder and hit the pause button, then headed for the door that led to the rest of the house.

Shit, shit, shit! Wait. He only paused the TV, so he's got to be coming back. She followed him past the staircase and into the kitchen where he filled a glass from his growler of hipster ale.

Her relief was short-lived. Beer in hand, Kenny turned toward the sliding glass door between the kitchen and the patio overlooking the ocean and hill where Silas dug. Senka stood in horror as he pushed a button next to the door and the privacy shade began to roll up.

Snapping out of her panicked freeze, she sprang through the moving shade and the glass door and gripped the outside handle, holding the door closed with all her strength. She craned her neck to see over her shoulder. Silas, his back to the house, kept digging. He hadn't noticed the change as light from the kitchen streamed through the door and across the yard.

Senka felt the door jiggle. All her attention went to keeping Kenny inside and unaware of Silas. He looked confused, clicking the lock back and forth, pulling on the door. He set his beer on the counter and used both hands to try to open it. Senka fought to keep it closed. Her face took on a snarl of determination and effort.

Suddenly she heard a high-pitched noise on the other side of the door. She looked up. Kenny stared at her, his face a mask of shock and terror. He backed away from the door and pressed against the refrigerator. She realized in her effort to keep the door closed, she had made herself more solid than she had ever been. Solid enough that he had seen her.

She almost laughed. Her snarl must have been something to behold. She regarded him for a moment longer, then let herself fade.

Breathing heavily, Kenny continued to stare at the door. He was so pale Senka thought he might pass out.

After several minutes, his hands shaking, he picked up his beer and drained the glass. He flicked the lock on the door and poked the button to make the shade descend. Senka slipped in and watched him refill his glass and carry it unsteadily back to the den. He sat in his chair, gazing at the floor, his beer forgotten in his hands. After some time, he glanced at the poster. Shaking his head again, he turned back to the frozen image on his television.

"You are fucking loony toons," he told himself. "You weirded yourself out with your own reflection." He laughed. "Fucking Brittany and all her questions tonight. And Dolores writing on the mirror. What the fuck was that about?" He raised his glass and took a sizable swallow. Senka noticed his hand was steady now. "I'm firing her tomorrow," he said, and hit "play" on the remote.

Senka stayed with him for another fifteen minutes, judging by the clock on his desk, chastising herself for giving in to the temptation to mess with him. Once she felt sure he wasn't going anywhere, she left to check on Silas's progress.

He was replacing the ground cover that had been disturbed by his digging and looked up as she arrived. "Does it look believable to you?" he asked in a whisper as he dusted his hands on his pants.

"It's perfect. It has a believable balance of effort to hide it and indications of disturbed earth. Where should we leave the shovel?"

Without a word, Silas tossed it down the hill. It disappeared into some brush.

"What about your fingerprints?" Senka asked, alarmed.

"Vampires do not leave fingerprints. If we did, they would be all over the boxes in the garage."

"Oh, I should have thought about that."

"No need. We are a team. Shall we go make a phone call?"

She placed her hand in his and they were gone.

Finn, who has been lying with his blanket pulled up so high only his eyes show above it, chuckles. "Call the tip line. Pretend they're neighbors."

"Yep. Well, Silas did because Senka can't be heard on a phone."

He studies my face for a moment. "Hey, Senka?"

Butterflies take wing in my non-existent stomach. "How long have you known?"

"A long time," he says with a shrug.

"What gave me away?"

He rolls his eyes and looks at me as if to say, *You must be kidding,* then holds up his index finger. "No one can see you but me." His middle finger joins the index "Auburn hair in a ponytail, hiker shorts, T-shirt."

"Of course you caught that."

"Well, yeah."

"It doesn't scare you? Sitting with a ghost?"

"Considering that before you came, I thought only babies believed in ghosts, no. But you know what you said about the body not being what makes a person who they are? You're what is, right? So what are you? The soul?"

The world is full of questions that are hard to answer. "I guess some people would call it a soul."

"Not everyone, though?"

"No, not everyone. There are lots of names for it."

"Like what?"

"Atman, pneuma, jiva, spirit, energy. Silas would say essence. There are many more."

He nods. "It doesn't really matter what it's called, does it? I mean, you're it. You're here. That's good enough." He shifts his slight form and winces.

"How are you feeling?"

"Nausea med is working."

"Well, there's a plus. You ready to sleep?"

"Wish I didn't have to. I'd rather talk to you. Or if you couldn't stay, read a book till my mom comes."

"I get it," I say, wishing there was more to do than just acknowledge his feelings. I've seen this many times, the awareness of all that remains undone.

He sighs and a couple of the lines on his monitor jump. "Okay," he says with resignation. He pulls one arm free from the blanket and extends it over the bedrail toward me. "Good night, Senka."

I take his hand and squeeze it, trying to communicate emotions I can't put into words. "Good night, Finn."

He tucks his arm back under the covers, taking care not to bump the IV. He watches as I lean back in the chair and swing my legs up onto his bed, then closes his eyes.

The lines on the monitor hold steady in their rhythms.

CHAPTER TWELVE

It's easier now that Finn has confessed he knows who I am. I don't have to keep up the pretense. Tonight, I skip the door and slide through his window instead. He's alone. His mother must not have been able to arrange for time off yet, poor woman.

He's asleep, his face relaxed, and for the first time I notice how sunken his cheeks have become. When he's awake, his animated face reflects his thoughts and feelings, disguising the effects of his illness.

The knit cap he wears for warmth has come askew in his sleep. I settle it back into place. I let my hand linger on his forehead, trying to give him what comfort I can.

"That feels nice." He startles me; he hasn't opened his eyes.

"How are you today?"

"Tired."

"Was it a busy day?"

"Trying to be peppy for Mom. She's afraid."

"It's natural she's afraid of losing you. I'm not sure you can change that."

He opens his eyes and looks at me, serious. "I've decided to stay if I die. I wish I could tell her she can still talk to me when she wants."

"Finn," I say, sitting down. He turns to face me, and I lower the bed rail so we're not looking through it. "I'm here so you'll know what's possible. You may not be able to help your mom. Sometimes we can't help, no matter how much we want to. No matter how much we love someone."

"I wish it weren't that way."

"I get it."

He studies my face. He knows I no longer have human family in the world of the living. My family is in the world of the undead and the living feline. But he also knows I do what I can. He smiles a tired smile and says, "You've helped me. I'm not afraid like I was before you came."

"I'm so glad."

"Senka?" He pauses, weighing the question. "The story's almost over, isn't it?"

He's not asking only about the story of Silas and me, of how we created an existence worth prolonging. "Yes, it is."

"How much longer, do you think?"

"A few more nights."

He nods. I see no fear or sadness in his face; instead I see acceptance. He says, "You can start if you're ready."

It was harder than I would have guessed to find a phone we could use. When I died, public phones weren't as common as they'd once been, but you could find one every few blocks. Now there weren't any. We checked in five or six locations before we ended up on Cannery Row and stopped a tired chef plodding home after his shift. Silas invented a story about losing his phone, and the man handed his over with a grunt of understanding, then leaned against a nearby wall, taking drags on his cigarette.

Adopting the voice of a captain of industry expecting to be obeyed, Silas spoke as soon as he heard the beep. "I live in Pebble Beach. I have just seen my neighbor acting very suspiciously. He dug a rectangular hole and deposited something into it, something the size and apparent weight of a body. I could tell the body wore dark clothing, and I remembered the missing boy from the golf course. I thought it odd he was digging on the edge of a hillside in the middle of the night. Odd *and* suspicious. You need to get someone over there as soon as possible." Silas gave Kenny's address and hung up. He handed the phone back, thanked the chef, and for insurance, added, "You will forget this interaction." The tired man looked at the phone in his hand with some confusion, then pocketed it and walked on.

"What now, Obi-Wan?" I asked. Silas glanced at me with a smirk, but before he could respond, I said. "I guess nothing's going to happen before daylight. Or do you think they're monitoring the tip line all the time?"

"I'm afraid I know no more than you do."

"How long is it until sunrise?"

"Nearly two hours."

"That gives us time to see how the folks in the graveyard are doing. Let's go there before we head home, okay? Afterward, we can decide what to do next."

"Perhaps Mrs. Wang will have some fresh plot ideas for us," Silas said, the corners of his mouth quirking.

We arrived at the cemetery to find Mrs. Wang and Signore Peluso engaged in an English lesson, though both teacher and student were pleased to see us.

"*Buona sera*," Mrs. Wang greeted us in American-accented Italian. "*Come siete?*" She turned to Signore Peluso. "*È corretto?*"

"*Completamente corretto!*" Signore Peluso responded, beaming.

"We're teaching each other, you know," Mrs. Wang confided, patting the stone wall next to her. I sat as Silas and Signore Peluso chatted in rapid Italian.

"That's wonderful, Mrs. Wang." I kissed her cheek.

"Yes, though he's a much better student than I am. Thank heavens he's a kind and patient teacher." She put her arm through mine and leaned in. "How have you and Silas progressed?"

I filled her in, then asked, "What's been going on here?"

"Oh, my dear, it's the most excitement we've had. Of course, not for the groundskeepers. But for Riccardo, Bink, and me—and dear Jeremy—it's been a treat. Bink has taken Jeremy under his wing, and the two of them were over there all day"—she waved in the direction of the houses near the golf course—"following the police as they did their door-to-door questioning."

"I didn't know they did that here."

"Oh, my, yes. Everywhere. On *SVU*, they always have the uniforms conduct door-to-doors. They ask the residents if they saw anything unusual."

"Did they? See anything?"

"No. Bink reported everyone was asleep."

"Mrs. Wang, what do your shows say about hotlines and tip lines? How fast are tips acted on?"

"It depends on how many come in, but Olivia Benson always follows up as soon as the uniforms give her a credible tip. And Janet Scott and Rachel Bailey insist they be told about any call of the slightest interest. Then they either delegate or follow up themselves."

I wasn't sure who these people were, but Mrs. Wang sounded so confident I was inclined to believe her. "So they'd follow up quickly. And are the lines monitored all the time?"

"Oh, my, yes. The first forty-eight hours are crucial. They want to chase down every lead as soon as they possibly can."

"Good." I stood. "Thank you, Mrs. Wang. That helps." I looked at Silas, who caught my signal and rose, patting the chef on the back.

"Before I return to the cottage," he said, "I think I will find something to eat."

"Of course! You must be, what was it? Gut foundered?"

"Exactly!" Silas smiled at me.

We said goodbye to our friends and Silas went in search of deer while I walked through the damp grass back to the keeper's cottage. The empty rocking chair reminded me I was alone. No Jeremy. No Luna. The cottage didn't feel so homey anymore. *When this is settled,* I thought, *we'll find someplace that belongs to us.*

As I waited for Silas to return, I opened my email. I added the tip line email address, typed "More Info" into the subject box, and began to write. "I sent you an email earlier tonight about seeing a man with the young boy who is missing. I saw him again! He was dressed in a white polo shirt and lime green pants. I saw him get into his car, and I noticed there was a Pebble Beach resident's badge on the front. I hope this helps." I pressed "send" and hoped for the best.

When Silas returned, looking refreshed, I was reading an online government publication on what to expect if one's child goes missing. It reiterated what Mrs. Wang had said: the first forty-eight hours are the most crucial.

"I just keep thinking how frantic Jeremy's parents are feeling right now," I said as he kissed the top of my head. "Their lives have been irrevocably changed, but they don't know it yet."

"I can't imagine what it would be like to lose one's child, especially to violence."

I shook my head. All I could manage to say was, "No."

We sat, isolated in the misery of our thoughts. At last, Silas said, "The sun is rising."

I looked out the window. "No fog. It's going to be a warm day."

"And the cottage is open for tours today."

"Silas, couldn't you transport yourself to Kenny's garage or something? Somewhere not in the light? Then you could be there, hide somewhere, I guess, and know what's going on."

Silas shook his head. "When vampires travel, or when you travel with me, we are not jumping from point A to point B with nothing in-between. We are moving extraordinarily fast, at the speed of thought, but we are still moving through space. From here to Kenny's garage, I would be exposed to direct sunlight. In filtered light, I am safe for a handful of minutes, as you know. In fact, even if the light is coming through clear glass, I can last for a short time, a minute or two. I cannot withstand an instant in direct sunlight."

"I see. If the fog drifts in, would you be able to come?"

"If it's thick enough, I will come." He pulled me from my chair and wrapped his arms around me, resting his chin on top of my head. Tension I hadn't known I was harboring melted. I leaned into him and hugged him to me. He said, "You will be fine, my love. If something unexpected arises, you will think of a way to respond. Remember the crises we have been in—you have risen to each. It's you who has cleverly seen us through."

"I feel braver when you're there," I answered, inwardly acknowledging how little I sounded like a badass vampire hunter.

"The man who murdered you cannot harm you now, no matter how foul he is."

"I'm not afraid for me." I looked up into Silas's face. "I feel responsible to Jeremy and his family. I'm afraid the police won't find him. I'm afraid Kenny will somehow weasel out of it all and keep being horrible to Brittany. I'm afraid I've left the housekeeper—Dolores, I think—without a job, and who knows what her story is?"

"I see. Yes. Perhaps three hundred years of existence have caused me to forget there are many levels of pain. You are so kind, you want to protect everyone."

"I didn't used to be kind. When I was alive, I mean." I disengaged from him and sat in my corner of the loveseat. "I was too self-absorbed to think much beyond what I wanted. If I'd looked past the tip of my nose, I would have noticed all the red flags Kenny raised. Hell, flags he was waving around. It wasn't until I had over a decade of involuntary monastic solitude that I started to think about others. And then I met you and Luna, and—" I paused, gathering the courage to say it. "And I fell in love."

The words sent a shock of nerves through me, and I jumped up from my seat. "This isn't the time to talk about all this. Maybe self-recrimination is another form of self-absorption. I should see what's going on at Kenny's, even if it's unlikely the police have gotten there yet." Silas's expression, half confusion, half amusement, softened my fears. "What will you do while I'm gone?"

"I will hide in the attic as I monitor the news, look for real estate, and read a novel," he said without a pause.

"I see you've been thinking about this already." I laughed. I hadn't laughed for hours. It felt good, lifting my spirits and my confidence.

The trip to Kenny's house passed in minutes. As it always did, the sea air left me feeling cleansed and refreshed. I was a bit disappointed, though unsurprised, not to see police swarming the property. The blackout curtains were still drawn throughout the house, and I found Kenny sprawled in his giant bed, snoring softly. I watched him for a moment. Disgusted, I made my way downstairs to the den. The first thing I noted was he hadn't straightened Brittany's portrait since I'd knocked it askew the night before. I wondered if he hadn't bothered or he hadn't noticed.

Glancing down, I saw a laptop charging on the desk. I sat in the desk chair and opened the computer. Password protected. *Of course, I thought.* I looked around the desk, under the laptop, and in the drawers but found no convenient scrap of paper noting the password. I leaned back in the chair and considered what Kenny would use. I thought about the growler of beer and tried variations on the name of the hipster brewery. No luck. I typed in names of football teams, cursing my inattention to his obsession during my life. After a dozen tries, the computer locked me out for an hour. I flipped the lid closed, irritated, and made a restless circuit of the room.

Light. That's what I need.

I punched the buttons next to each panel of blackout shade and watched as they rolled up into their valences, revealing the sunny day, the sweeping view of the ocean, and the hillside where Jeremy lay buried, waiting to be found.

A noise in the entryway drew my attention. I flitted across the den and through the door. The housekeeper, laden with shopping bags, was just closing the front door. Once again, she was dressed head to toe in pink. I followed her as she headed into the kitchen and set down her load. She pulled one bag aside and began to unpack it. A votive candle, a bouquet of flowers, a handful of mini candy bars, and a glass jar of a milky white liquid.

The bag unloaded, Dolores produced a simple glass vase from her copious purse, filled it with water, and popped the flowers in. In her light, tuneful voice, she sang, "*Recuérdame! No llores por favor. Te llevo en mi corazón …*" She lapsed into humming as she positioned the vase on the counter, placed the tall votive next to it, and lit the candle. She added the jar of liquid and arranged the tiny chocolate bars around the trio.

As understanding dawned on me, my eyes prickled with tears. *This is a gift for me! Maybe I startled her yesterday, but she wants me to feel welcome.* I peered at the liquid in the jar and saw tiny specks of floating cinnamon. *It's horchata!* I realized. *Oh, my gosh! I used to love that stuff.* Dolores was busy pulling out a plate and coffee cup. Before the pink-clad woman could turn around, I tugged a daisy out of the vase and balanced it on top of the jar of horchata. I waited with anticipation as Dolores set the plate and cup on a tray and turned back to her shopping bags. She spotted the daisy and froze. A surge of pleasure coursed through me as a beaming smile brightened the woman's face. Dolores broke into a torrent of Spanish too fast for me to follow, though she was clearly thrilled her gift had been acknowledged and appreciated.

Still chattering to her ghost, Dolores finished her preparations—arranging coffee and a pre-made breakfast sandwich on the tray—picked up the load, and bustled out of the kitchen. I followed her upstairs and into Kenny's bedroom. Balancing the tray, Dolores tapped the buttons to raise the blackout shades.

"Mr. Kenny," she sang out with a heavy accent. "Good morning. *Buenas días.* Breakfast." Kenny groaned but didn't move. She set the tray on one side of the large bed and exited the room.

Kenny groped for his phone and peered at the time. With a sigh of resignation, he scrubbed at his face, gaping a yawn. He sat up and scratched his head, as if he were washing his hair. That done, he hiked himself back against his pillows and pulled the tray close. Reaching for his phone with one hand, he used the other to shove half the breakfast sandwich into his mouth, scrolling through the phone as he chewed.

Though I was eager to know what he was looking at, I couldn't bear the idea of being in bed with him, so I tucked myself inside the headboard and the wall behind it, my face poking out so I could read over his shoulder. A dozen or more texts from Brittany. Without answering any, he moved on to Facebook and scrolled through his feed. He flipped over to Instagram—that was the name of the app I'd been trying to remember!—and watched a couple of dog videos.

I guess even assholes like Kenny get a kick out of dog videos, I thought.

At last, he put the phone and the coffee cup down and crawled out of bed. He wasn't wearing pajamas, and this time, I allowed myself to take him in. As much as I hated to admit it, he still looked good. *And wasn't that what drew me to him?* I thought. *He looked good on the red carpet.*

I lingered as he showered, shaved, and dressed for the day. Seeing he was putting on light-colored khakis and a burnt-orange polo shirt,

I couldn't help smiling. It was close enough to my description of him in the emails that I hoped it would catch the attention of the police. He was sliding into his shoes when the doorbell chimed. He paused.

"Fuuuuck!" he groaned.

I heard the door open, then a man's deep voice and Dolores's lighter one muffled by distance, then silence. Seconds later, there was a quick tap on the bedroom door.

"What?" Kenny called.

The door opened and Dolores poked her head in. "Mr. Kenny," she hissed, her face creased with concern. "It's the police."

I felt a shock of excitement, nerves, anticipation all rolled into one. I tried to read Kenny's expression, but he kept his face neutral.

"What do they want?" he asked, sounding unruffled.

"They want to talk to you. That's all they say."

"All right. Take them into the living room. I'll be down in a minute." Dolores started to leave, but Kenny called her back. "Ask them if they want some coffee." The housekeeper nodded and closed the door. I heard her patter down the stairs.

However much Kenny was trying to appear unruffled, he wasn't as collected as he seemed. He sat for a moment, staring at the shoe in his hand. With effort, he shook his head as if dislodging a pesky thought and finished putting his shoes on. I slipped through the wall and down the stairs to the showy living room.

Two plainclothes police occupied the angular armchairs. The man, looking like a *GQ* model on a budget, rested one ankle on a knee and spread his arms wide, his hands draped over the armrests and tapping the outside of the chair restlessly. The woman, a stork in a power suit, looked around the room with obvious interest.

"I feel like I'm in an upscale doctor's office," she muttered to her partner. He snorted and glanced around.

Before he could answer, Dolores swooped in with two mugs of coffee on a tray. "Here you go, Detectives," she sang, handing out the coffee with a sunny smile. "Let me know if you need anything else." As she left through the dining room, Kenny entered through the main archway, striding in with his best lord-of-the-manor attitude.

"Officers!" His tone was all warmth and hearty welcome, though he must have known he was addressing detectives, not beat cops. "How can I help you?"

Both detectives rose, but it was the woman who spoke. "I'm Detective Stacey Washington, this is my partner, Detective Henry Velasquez."

"Please sit." Kenny waved them back into their seats but stayed in place, gazing down at them.

Detective Washington continued. "We're looking into the disappearance of a juvenile. Perhaps you've read about the case?"

The shift in Kenny was so subtle I doubted the detectives noticed. He relaxed just a bit. After all, what did this have to do with him? He walked to the snow-white couch across from them and sat. His aging good looks, his golfer's tan, even the electric color of his polo shirt were set off by the starkness of the white cushions. If I didn't know him, I'd think he was gorgeous.

"I heard about it," Kenny answered, adopting a grave tone. "I'm not sure how I can help, though. I understand he lives in Pacific Grove." He spread his hands, indicating their surroundings. "I don't get over there very often."

Detective Washington went on. "Of course. I doubt you can contribute anything useful, but my partner and I have to track down every lead we get." If she had intended to needle Kenny with her dismissal, her ploy fell flat.

"Surely only the substantive leads." He smiled, but his eyes were cool.

The detectives, I judged, were too experienced to be rattled either by the opulence of their surroundings or by a rich guy's condescension.

Detective Washington returned his smile. "You're so right," she said. "You must have some experience with this kind of thing." She waved her hand to include their conversation, the situation, law in general. I saw the implication wasn't lost on Kenny; his smile became a little icier.

"If you're suggesting I'm used to being questioned by the police, you're mistaken. However, I am familiar with the law. I'm a lawyer."

Washington said nothing, just tilted her head to the side. It was Detective Velasquez who said, "You mean you *were* a lawyer. You were disbarred, weren't you?"

Kenny stopped breathing, and this time I wasn't the only one to notice. He hadn't imagined they'd looked into him before coming over. His pressing question must be, Why?

He cleared his throat. "I still hold a Juris Doctor." There was a defensive edge to his tone. "Perhaps you can tell me why you think I could possibly help with your case."

Detective Washington reached for her bag and pulled a photograph from it. "This is a photo of the missing child. Have you ever seen him before?"

Kenny took a look at the photo. "No."

"May we ask your housekeeper if she has?"

"Sure." Kenny raised his voice. "Dolores!"

The sweet-faced woman appeared so promptly I was convinced she'd been lingering around the corner, listening to the conversation. "Yes, Mr. Kenny?"

"Take a look at the photo these detectives have. Do you know this boy?"

Detective Washington held the photo up. "Have you ever seen him before?" she asked, correcting Kenny's phrasing.

Dolores took the picture and studied it. She looked up at Detective Washington, a frown creasing her forehead. "This is the missing boy?" she asked. Washington nodded. Dolores scanned the photo again, but shook her head. "No, I have never seen him." She handed the photo back and looked from one detective to the other, eager for their next question.

"Thank you," Detective Washington told her. "That's all we need for now."

"Oh, one thing." Detective Velasquez stopped her before she could leave. "*Habla bien inglés.*"

"*Gracias,*" Dolores responded, her cheeks coloring to match her outfit.

"*¿Vive usted aquí? ¿En esta casa?*"

"*¡Claro que no!*" She laughed. "I go home at four in the afternoon." She frowned. "Usually."

"*¿Preferirías hablar inglés?*"

"*Sí. El no habla español.*" She indicated Kenny with a subtle twitch of her head.

"*Supuse que no.*"

"Ah!" Dolores responded, eyebrows raised.

I was impressed by the detective's moxie, questioning Dolores in front of Kenny, assuming Kenny wouldn't understand Spanish. He went on. "You said you usually go home at four. Did you yesterday?"

"No. I ..." She hesitated and shot Kenny an embarrassed look. "I left a little early yesterday."

"*¿Porqué?*"

"Something ... something happened. It scared me at first."

Kenny, who'd been looking out the window with feigned lack of interest, whipped to face Dolores so fast I thought his neck would crack. Both detectives perked up.

"Can you tell us what happened?" Detective Washington asked.

"I saw ... I was thinking I saw ... a ghost."

The detectives' shoulders slumped in disappointment. Kenny glowered at her. "What are you talking about?"

"I finish cleaning, but I remember I didn't empty the trash in your bathroom, Mr. Kenny. I come back there, but when I go in, I see ... I see writing appear on the mirror."

"There was writing on the mirror?" Detective Washington asked.

"No, no." She looked at Detective Velasquez for help. "*La escritura aparecía en el espejo mientras miraba.*" She studied his expression to see if he understood the distinction.

"The writing was appearing on the mirror as you watched. Is that right?"

"*Sí, sí,*" she answered, excited now. "The words were coming as I watched."

Kenny snorted. "Oh, for fuck's sake."

Detective Washington shot him a quelling look and turned back to Dolores. "What did this ghost write?"

"I only see the first letters. I make a noise and she stopped. She wrote, 'It's ti-.'"

The room went silent.

Velasquez asked, "You said, 'She wrote.' Why do you think it was a female ghost?"

Kenny sat forward with a snarl. "Are you actually believing this shit? She obviously wrote on the mirror herself, and now she's trying to blame it on the fucking spirit world!"

"Sir, you need to calm down," Washington said, her tone sharp. "We're trying to understand what Ms.—?"

"Sanchez. Dolores Sanchez," the housekeeper slipped in.

"Thank you. What Ms. Sanchez experienced."

Kenny sat back with a look of disgust. "I'm perfectly calm."

Detective Velasquez asked again, "So why do you think it was a female ghost, Ms. Sanchez?"

"Because she was writing with lipstick. Men ghosts don't write in lipstick."

"I see." He snuck a peek at his partner, who picked up the questioning.

"Ms. Sanchez," she said, "is it possible someone, I mean a living person, got into the house and wrote that?"

As if speaking to a child, Dolores said, "I was watching while she wrote."

"I see," Washington said, echoing her partner. She turned to Kenny. "Sir, you suggested Ms. Sanchez wrote on the mirror herself. Did you see what was written?"

A look passed across Kenny's face, one I'd seen in life. For the first time, I recognized what it meant. He was choosing whether or not to lie. He seemed to decide telling the truth couldn't harm him. "I did. It said, 'It's time to pay.'"

The detectives made notes in their pads. "What did that mean to you?" Velasquez asked him.

"I have no idea. I pay Dolores punctually."

I glanced at Dolores in time to catch her rolling her eyes, but she said nothing and the detectives appeared not to notice.

"You haven't always paid your creditors punctually, though, have you, sir?" Detective Washington asked.

Kenny stiffened. "Those matters have been settled through the legal system and have no bearing on this conversation."

"They do, sir, if someone is threatening you," Washington said, unimpressed by Kenny's haughtiness.

"Or trying to connect you to the disappearance of a teenager," Velasquez added.

It appeared Kenny had forgotten the original reason for their visit. He paled but recovered. "I fail to see how the two are linked."

Velasquez and Washington shared a look. The handsome detective turned to Dolores. "Ms. Sanchez, thank you. We'll contact you if we need to speak again. We appreciate your honesty."

Kenny snorted again, and Dolores left the room with a purposeful step, shoulders squared.

"Where were you last night, sir, from, say, eight p.m. onwards?" Detective Velasquez continued.

Kenny, who'd been glaring at Dolores as she exited, snapped his attention back to the two detectives. "Uh, let's see … I was here. In the den. Watching football."

"Football? At this time of year?"

"I keep some of my favorite games on the DVR so I can watch them again."

"I see. Were you alone?"

"No," he said, lying so smoothly even I couldn't see a tell. "My girlfriend was here."

"Was she watching with you?"

"No. She was in here. Reading."

Detective Washington glanced around the room. I'd have bet she knew no one lolled around reading in this pristine space. Velasquez was speaking, "And you didn't leave the den all evening?"

"No, I left to—" Kenny stopped cold. His eyes widened, and it looked as if he had stopped breathing. I laughed out loud knowing he'd remembered seeing me.

Washington looked at her partner, her eyebrows raised, then back at Kenny. "Sir? You all right?"

Kenny forced his features back into their neutral expression. "Yes, sorry, fine." He shook his head and laughed weakly. "Just Dolores's ghost story, I guess. Uh, I went to the kitchen to get a beer. That's the only time I left the den."

Doubt was written across the detectives' faces. Velasquez asked, "And your girlfriend could corroborate that?"

"I would think so."

"But you didn't, say, get her a beer too."

"No." Kenny faked a carefree laugh. "I guess it would have been polite, huh?"

The detectives didn't laugh with him.

Washington asked, "Is your girlfriend here now, sir?"

"No." He bit the word but added, "She went home this morning."

"She's an early riser."

"Yes," Kenny said and left it at that.

"We'll check in with her later." The detectives stood. Kenny rose with them.

Velasquez pulled a card from his pocket and offered it to Kenny, saying, "Thanks for your time. If you think of anything that might help us in our search for Jeremy Maly, the missing juvenile, please give us a call."

That's it? What about the tip? The digging? I thought. I wasn't sure what to do, but I knew I couldn't let them leave.

Kenny closed the door after them and returned to the living room, watching them through the glass. I slipped out and hovered near the detectives. They walked to the car in silence before Washington said, "It's a beautiful day, isn't it? It's not every day you get to take in a view like this."

Velasquez looked at her, confused. The penny dropped. "Right!" he said with a little too much cheer. "Let's go take a closer look, huh? Like from the hill there."

My spirits lifted as I followed them to the edge of the slope. I glanced back and saw Kenny watching them. Velasquez stretched and inhaled, patting his chest. The detectives surreptitiously scanned the slope for signs of digging.

"See anything?" Washington murmured.

"Hard to tell. How about you?"

"Maybe. Ten o'clock?"

"Yes!" I shouted, not caring they couldn't hear me.

Velasquez tried not to appear to be looking but cast his eyes sideways to see where Washington had indicated. "Yeah. It's possible. It looks like the ground has been disturbed fairly recently. Hard to tell unless we can get closer."

"Try it. Act like you're just wandering in that direction."

Detective Velasquez stretched again and swung his arms from side to side as if he were loosening a stiff back. As he did, he moved a few yards to his left and stopped again.

"Can I help you with something else?" The sound of Kenny's voice made them turn around.

"Just admiring the view," Velasquez called. The detectives sauntered back to their car as Kenny headed toward the front of the house.

"See anything?" Washington muttered.

"Definitely disturbed."

"Enough for a warrant?"

"Could be."

They were too close to Kenny to continue the conversation. Dolores stood by the front door, her curiosity spurring her from the house. The detectives reached their car, parked in front of the large garage doors. Velasquez waved, whether to Dolores or Kenny, I couldn't tell. "Thanks again," he said.

"No, no, no!" I cried. "You can't leave now! You have to find Jeremy!" The detectives reached for the door handles. I tore through the garage door, along the rows of shelving until I found the box. I shoved it. It flew from its shelf and tumbled to the floor with a clatter as the top sprang open and the contents tumbled out.

Dolores let out a little scream as Kenny exclaimed, "What the hell was that?"

I hurried back through the big garage door.

"Is anyone else in the house?" Washington demanded, all business.

"No, no one!" Dolores's hands were clasped to her heart. "Except the ghost."

Kenny looked at her with irritation. "I'm sure it's nothing."

Velasquez glanced at Washington but spoke to Kenny, "Given the circumstances, sir, we need to check this out."

"What circumstances?" Kenny demanded.

"The writing. The calls we received on our hotline." Without waiting for a go-ahead, the detectives brushed past Kenny and Dolores into the house, me just behind them. They eased open the door to the garage and peered into its gloom. Both drew their service weapons. With utmost caution, they split up and walked around the McLaren blocking their way.

"Clear," Washington said from her end.

"Clear," Velasquez responded from his. He looked back at Dolores and Kenny standing in the doorway. "Would you give us some light, please?" Dolores flipped the switch.

A banker's box lay on the ground at the foot of one of the shelving units. Strewn about it were various-sized objects. Washington and Velasquez, guns still drawn, crossed the garage floor to get a closer look. They peered down at the objects, then looked at each other in surprise.

Washington turned to Kenny. "Sir, why do you have human bones stored in your garage?"

With an instinct for cliffhanger endings, Diwata bustles into the room. Finn groans.

"Do you have pain, sweetheart?" she asks him, frowning.

He looks at me and chuckles. It's a joy to hear. "No," he says. "I'm okay."

Diwata looks at the chair where I'm sitting and turns back to Finn. She cocks her head to the side. "It must be a really good story."

Finn's jaw drops, and I know my expression is a mirror of his. "How do you know?" he asks her.

"You told me the other night. A friend comes to tell you stories."

"You believe she's here?"

"I told you I did."

We exchange another look.

"Cool!" he says to both of us. We both laugh.

"I'm almost done here, then you can get back to it," Diwata says as she inspects Finn's skin where the IVs go into his arms.

"Naw," he says, already resigned. "She"ll want me to sleep now."

Diwata nods. "I like her."

I'm nervous because I've never done this before. I say, "Finn, if it won't wear you out, would you please tell her I like her too? I like the way she always looks at you as soon as she comes in, and she tells you what she's doing. And I like how compassionate she is with your mom."

"Diwata?" he begins. "Senka—that's her name, Senka—says she likes you too. You look at me when you come in. That's true. And tell me why you've come in, which I like too. And … and she says you're compassionate to my mom. Thank you for that. I don't know what she'd do without you and Joe."

Diwata has been listening, her hand pressed to her chest. I think she has forgotten to breathe. She glances at the chair, then back again to Finn. She has tears in her eyes, but she smiles down at him. "Please tell her thank you."

"She can hear you." He smiles up at her.

Diwata nods. She bends down and kisses Finn's knit cap. "You are amazing," she says with a sniffle. "Sleep tight." She gathers her things and leaves, closing the door behind her.

"That was fun," he says, grinning at me. It's the happiest I've seen him in a few days.

"Yes, it was! And you were right. It's time to sleep now."

He starts to settle in but stops and says, "I like how Dolores accepted you were there. Like Diwata."

"Yeah. Me too."

He pulls the covers up, and I turn off the last of the lights. "Senka, when you leave here, do you go home?"

"I do."

"Is Silas there?"

"Yes."

"Good." Could this young man be any more thoughtful? "See you tomorrow," he adds.

I go back to my usual spot on the chair and watch until he's asleep. I stay a little longer, hoping his dreams are sweet ones.

CHAPTER THIRTEEN

I find myself restless, unable to settle down and focus on much of anything. The sun hasn't set, but I head to the hospital early. I'm hoping Moira, Finn's mom, will be there, but when I enter his room, he's alone and awake, a pillow wedged under his back to keep him on his side. The nurses are concerned about bedsores. He hasn't had the strength to get out of bed for a couple of days.

He's seen me come in through the window, and his eyes are wide with amazement. "Cool!" he whispers.

I smile at him. "It kind of is, isn't it? I thought I'd come a little earlier than usual today."

"Good."

"Finn," I say, taking my usual seat and lowering the bed rail. "You said your mom is the night manager at a hotel, right?"

"Yeah." He grimaces. "She's coming back tonight. One way or the other, she's taking a leave."

"One way or the other?"

"Either they'll give her time off or she'll quit."

I'm relieved she'll be able to spend more time with him, but Finn is worried about her. "Silas and I can help with her expenses. Anonymous transfers, that kind of thing."

"You'd do that?" It's the first time I've seen his eyes mist over.

"Of course. I've already talked to him about it. We don't have many expenses, and Silas is a pretty keen investor." I cock an eyebrow at him, hoping to get a smile.

"Thank you," he says with such sincere gratitude that now we both have misty eyes.

Trying to keep my voice steady, I say, "Ready for the next part of the story?"

He nods and offers a whisper of a smile. "What did that *paskudnyak* Kenny do when you shoved your bones off the shelf?"

"I'm impressed you remembered Stan's name for him. So, Detective Washington had just asked Kenny why he had human bones in his garage, right?"

"Right."

For a moment, Kenny stared at the detectives. Then Dolores gasped and pressed her hands to her heart. "That's why the ghost is here."

"Shut up," Kenny snarled. To Washington and Velasquez he said, "What are you talking about?" He started toward them, walking around the car.

"Stay back, sir!" Washington ordered.

"I don't have any bones. Are you sure they're human?" Kenny seemed unable to settle on a line of defense.

Washington ignored him. "Check the area," she told Velasquez. "We still don't know why these fell."

Velasquez nodded and, gun pointing toward the floor, made his way along the shelving units to the back corner of the garage. Kenny and Dolores watched with varying degrees of fascination. "Clear," he said, holstering his gun. Washington holstered hers as well.

"I told you," Dolores said, looking smug. "It's the ghost. I bet those are her bones. *Pobrecita*."

"It's not against the law in California to possess human bones," Kenny insisted from his place near the car.

Without responding, Velasquez returned to his partner. Washington, looking like a grasshopper about to jump, had squatted to study the bones. She gestured to Velasquez and used a pen to point out some tooth marks.

"Rodents?" he muttered.

"Something like that," she whispered in reply. "I'd say these bones spent time outdoors."

"Somebody dusted them off then. There's no dirt. Looks like the neighbor's tip was worthwhile. We're gonna need to look around, don't you think?"

"Yeah." Washington rose and looked at Kenny. "Sir, we're going to need to search your property."

"You'll have to get a warrant," Kenny said, reflexively. "It's not illegal to possess human bones," he repeated.

"Mr. Kenny?" Dolores's face was wrinkled with concern. "Why you have this ghost woman's bones?"

"I don't!" Kenny stuttered. "They're not mine. It's not illegal."

"That depends on whose bones they are, sir," Velasquez said. "And what's been gnawing on them."

Dolores looked shocked and a little nauseated.

Washington took over. "To be clear, we're going to get the warrant, and I'll require you to keep out of the way while we search your premises. You can stay or go, whichever you prefer, but I expect you to keep us apprised of your whereabouts."

"Oh, I'm not going anywhere, except to call my lawyer." Kenny shoved past Dolores and stalked off toward the den.

"Fine by me," Velasquez muttered, and pulled his cell phone out of his pocket.

The detectives waited in the kitchen for the search warrant to come through. I had no idea how long it would take for a judge to issue it. I wanted to update Silas but was loath to miss any part of the search. Worry nagged at me: so far, neither detective had mentioned my disappearance, and I wasn't even sure they'd heard of it; they would have been teenagers when I went missing. Knowing about it might provide the impetus they needed to have the bones tested right away.

My decision whether to stay or go was made for me; Velasquez went out to the driveway, leaving his phone behind on the counter. Before the screen could go blank, locking me out, I opened his Google app and typed in my name, being careful not to shift the phone on the counter. The first hit was headlined, "Was Husband Involved in Star's Disappearance? Fast Friend Thinks So." I clicked on the link and grinned. The picture splashed across the top of the article was of Kenny and me on the red carpet at some awards ceremony.

"Any word from Dickinson?" Velasquez asked as he reentered the kitchen.

"Nothing. He said he'll text as soon as the judge signs the warrant."

"Were you using my phone?" Velasquez asked, staring at the screen with a puzzled expression.

"Of course not."

"Huh," he said, scrolling.

"Why?" Washington watched him as he read. "What's up?"

He looked at her. "I'm starting to believe there really is a ghost here," he said, bemused. "Look what was on my phone when I opened it up." He handed the phone to Washington. She read and looked up at him, slack-jawed.

"'Was Husband Involved in Star's Disappearance?'" she muttered, reading the headline aloud. "Holy shit."

"Are you thinkin' what I'm thinkin'?" He took the phone back.

"Unless you're thinking ghosts are real, yeah. But how did this—"

"Doesn't matter. You think those bones are hers? And what? He goes back and finds them after he's sure a bunch of animals took care of the body? How would he know where to look? I mean, they'd be bound to drag them all over the place. To their dens or whatever. Wouldn't they?"

"That's not my area of specialization," she said, and reached a long arm out to the coffee pot.

"Okay, but we're gonna have to get a DNA test on them."

"Ain't that a fact."

I let loose a mini victory dance.

As Washington sipped her coffee, she and Velasquez searched both Google and police databases for anything they could find on the disappearance of the former television star Sarah Sommers.

"Here's the picture that was circulated after she disappeared." Washington held her phone out for her partner to see. "Apparently our guy snapped it at a rest stop on their way to Cleveland National Forest."

"Could be anywhere," he replied. "They were going to a cabin down there, I read."

"That's what it says here."

"Okay, so in this picture, I see her in a T-shirt and those cargo shorts hikers like to wear."

"Yeah?"

"Ponytail."

"Yeah?"

"Only a movie star would wear a necklace like that to spend the weekend in a cabin in the woods."

"TV star," Washington corrected.

I looked at the picture. I'd forgotten that necklace. It was a sunflower about the size of a quarter, made of diamonds and yellow sapphires. "In my defense," I said aloud to the detectives, "it was a gift from Kenny. But I take your point."

They were interrupted by the arrival of the warrant. The forensics team wasn't far behind. Washington directed them to the garage and the hillside. "Get those bones to the lab for priority testing," she told the garage team. "Then see what else you can turn up in there."

I found myself torn in three directions. I wanted to be sure the team in the garage didn't miss the wad of duct tape Silas and I had planted. I wanted to stand vigil as the hillside team found Jeremy's body. I wanted to follow the detectives to the den where Kenny had retreated. I opted for the last.

They found him sitting at his desk under the nude painting of Brittany, which was still askew. His lawyer, the embodiment of a linebacker gone to seed, sat opposite him in a chair dragged in from the dining room. They looked up as the detectives entered. The other chairs in the room faced the television, so each detective perched on an arm, facing Kenny. From their seats, they had a clear view of the hillside. The forensics team was getting their tools laid out. I hovered by my poster, where I had a good view of all the players.

"This is my attorney, William R. Sullivan from Sullivan, Schwartz, and Miller." Kenny dripped with noblesse oblige.

The detectives nodded to the lawyer, who nodded back. Washington began. "Have you remembered anything about the bones that you'd like to share with us?"

I enjoyed the diplomacy of the phrasing.

"As I've already told you, I've never seen them before." Sullivan's presence seemed to have bolstered Kenny's confidence; his commanding tone had returned.

"Sir, I wonder if you could tell us about your wife's disappearance."

Sullivan inserted himself before Kenny could answer. "That's ancient history, Detective. It was a painful time for my client, and I don't see why he needs to answer questions about it now."

"It's not that long ago in the big scheme of things, Bill," Washington snapped. "And given the sudden appearance of those bones, I think your client might find it helpful to answer questions about it."

Kenny's eyes narrowed with distrust. "You know each other?"

The lawyer waved a hand as if tamping down Kenny's concern. "It's a small town," he said. He turned back to Washington. "Why would my client find it helpful?"

"I think it's possible your client is the object of a smear campaign."

Sullivan's wooly-caterpillar eyebrows rose. "Oh?" He glanced at Kenny, whose face remained neutral. To Washington, he said, "How so?"

She folded her arms across her chest, her elbows sticking out like knobby twigs. "Threatening writing on an upstairs mirror, a hotline tip suggesting he has something to do with the disappearance of the male juvenile in Pacific Grove, and now the possible planting of bones in his garage."

I felt a stab of panic. Did Washington actually think Kenny was innocent or was she pretending in order to get him talking?

"And you think, what?" the lawyer probed. "Someone is trying to frame him for the juvenile?"

"We think it's possible." Washington looked at Velasquez for corroboration.

"Definitely possible." He nodded, his expression somber.

"No, it's not!" I exclaimed. "I mean, yeah, that's exactly what's happening, but the bones are mine."

"What do you think, Ken?" Sullivan turned to his client. "Are you willing to answer some questions about Sarah's disappearance?"

Kenny sighed. "I guess. Whatever I can do to help."

I almost gagged.

"We appreciate that, sir," Velasquez said. "This happened down south, so we're not real familiar with the case. Could you sketch it out for us?"

With a wistful expression, Kenny looked across the room at the poster of Sarah. The others followed his gaze and regarded the poster as well. Standing next to it, I found myself in the line of sight of four people and suddenly felt self-conscious. *They can't see you*, I reminded myself.

"Sarah worked hard," Kenny said at length. "She was dedicated to that show. It never would have been popular without her. Every chance I could, I'd take her away someplace to relax. The weekend she disappeared, we planned to go down to a little cabin I found on Airbnb. It was totally off the grid, so she wouldn't be bothered by texts or emails or calls from her director. She could relax. We planned to hike, laze around reading—just, you know, just be. We stopped for dinner on the road, so we got there after dark, and I surprised her with some special scotch. As we sipped it, we got into a stupid squabble, you know, like people have in any relationship. I was afraid she was working too hard. I told her I didn't think her director had her best interests at heart. That made her pretty upset because they were close. She got emotional—actors can be like that—and she slammed down her glass and stomped over to her sleeping bag. My mom always told me you should never go to bed mad, so I tried to get her to talk to me, but she wouldn't. Finally I climbed into my sleeping bag and went to sleep. It'd been a long day, you know? When I woke up the next morning, she was gone. I figured she went for a walk because the car was there, you know? So I made breakfast and waited for her to come back. But she didn't." He shrugged as if he couldn't find words for the rest of the story, but added, gazing again at the poster, "I miss her every day. I can't stop blaming myself. I shouldn't have tried to get her to take it easy." His voice cracked, and he turned away from his audience.

Wow, I thought, *that was quite a performance.* I studied the detectives' faces, trying to get a read on how much they believed, but I couldn't tell.

"Disappearances like this are always hard, sir," Washington said in a compassionate tone. "Those left behind tend to blame themselves, even when they shouldn't."

"It can be especially tough to move on when a spouse goes missing." Velasquez, too, had softened his tone.

"I haven't been able to move on. I keep thinking she's out there somewhere, and she'll come back to me someday."

I was so appalled I spoke aloud. "That's the biggest pile of horseshit I've ever heard. You guys cannot believe this."

Velasquez nodded at the poster. "She looks pretty fierce there."

Kenny laughed. "She was," he said with a tone of mixed love and pride.

"I used to watch *Blood Moon* on reruns," Washington added. "I thought she was the biggest badass in creation."

"Is that her too?" Velasquez asked, pointing at the life-size nude on the opposite wall.

Kenny looked over his shoulder and seemed surprised to find it there. I snorted. Had he forgotten about Brittany?

"Uh ... no," Kenny said. "That's my girlfriend."

"The one who was here last night?" Washington prompted.

"Yes."

"Left early this morning. That the one?"

"I only have one."

"Back to your wife." Velasquez took up the questioning again. "When she left the cabin, did she take her belongings with her?"

"Yes, everything."

"Her suitcase, her purse, cell phone. The sleeping bag too?"

"She left the sleeping bag, but she took everything else."

"You didn't hear her leave?"

"I was a sound sleeper in those days. But I think if she had moved the sleeping bag, I would have woken up."

"How do you think she got out of such a remote area?"

Kenny sighed, oh so weary. "The police at the time found

footprints they attributed to her. They were able to track them out to the main road. Their theory was she got a ride from there. I've always believed them."

Washington stepped in. "But no driver ever came forward to say they'd picked her up?"

"No."

Velasquez took the reins back. "I'm sorry to have to take you through this difficult time again, sir, and we appreciate your help with filling us in."

"No problem." He rested his hands on the arms of his chair as if he were about to get up.

Velasquez stopped him. "I was reading a little about the case earlier, sir. Sounds like Ms. Sommers's director believed for the rest of his life that you were involved in her disappearance."

Sullivan chimed in. "Is there a question in there, Henry?"

"Excuse me, yes." Velasquez ducked his head, looking chagrined. "I meant to ask what you thought about that."

"Stanley lost a lot when Sarah ran away." He pointed to the poster. "He couldn't finish that season and took a major financial hit. Frankly, I believe he couldn't stand to think he'd worked her to the breaking point. He had to blame someone, so he blamed me."

Oh, hell, no! I thought. *You are not trash-talking Stan and getting away with it. Let's find out what you're hiding.* I leaned forward and unlatched the poster from the wall. The other three, who had been looking at Kenny, saw his expression change and turned to look. They watched in absolute silence as the poster swung away from the wall, as if on its own, to reveal a safe. I held the poster open and looked at the group in front of me. Kenny wore a horrified expression, Sullivan frowned, and the detectives glanced at each other, struggling to keep their expressions neutral.

"I wonder if you'd mind opening that for us," Washington said, breaking the silence.

Kenny looked like a cornered animal. He snarled, "No!"

Sullivan turned to him in surprise. "They have a warrant, Ken. It gives them blanket access to the house and grounds."

"Not that." Kenny sounded like a recalcitrant child.

"Sir," Washington said in a tone suggesting she'd dealt with this kind of situation before, "you can either open it, or we can have someone in here with a drill in two minutes."

"The law's on their side, Ken." The lawyer regarded him with concern.

The tension drained from Kenny's body. He was going to try to play this off. "Sorry," he said. "Of course I'll open it. Just a couple sentimental things in there. Oh, and a gun, just to warn you." He crossed to the safe. To open it, he had to stand very close to me. Seeing the beads of sweat on his temples, I smiled with grim enjoyment. Kenny keyed in the six-digit code and pulled the safe open. Before I could react, he stepped aside and directly into me. For the second time in my existence, I blended with someone. It was so much worse without my permission. The Maker had felt like roiling maggots. Kenny felt like a cold, dark basement crawling with rats. I jerked away from him.

"You all right, Ken?" Sullivan asked.

"Yes, fine." Kenny shivered and wiped his sweaty brow. "I felt ... I thought ... Never mind." He moved away from the safe, his arms stiff at his sides as if he didn't know what to do with his hands.

Velasquez started to pull objects from the safe, narrating for Washington and the lawyer, who were both taking notes. "One Glock .45 caliber semiautomatic. Can we see your permit for this, sir?"

As if he were beyond fighting, Kenny shrugged. "I don't have one." The scribes made notes.

"One, two, three, four, five $10,000 bundles of hundred-dollar bills. Do you agree, sir, that there is $50,000 in cash here?"

"Yes."

Again, the scribes made notes.

"A velvet jewelry box containing ..." He opened the box. Though his expression didn't change, I could tell he was surprised by what he saw. He cleared his throat. "Containing a necklace: gold chain, jeweled sunflower pendant. And a diamond ring." He looked up at Washington, who had stopped writing and was staring back at him.

Oh my god, oh my god, I repeated to myself. *Is this it?*

Sullivan looked up from his notes, wondering why the recitation of objects had stopped. "Is that it?"

Washington spoke. "Sir, I'd like to show you a picture." She took her phone from her pocket and found the photo of me that had been circulated after my death. She showed it to Kenny, then to the lawyer. "Sir, can you tell me if this is the photograph of your wife that was used by law enforcement following her disappearance?"

"Yes."

"Can you tell me when this photograph was taken?"

"I took it at a rest stop on our way to the cabin the day Sarah disappeared."

"Sir, is the necklace she was wearing the same one in this box?"

I could see Kenny had already concocted a story. He sighed, the misunderstood hero in a melodrama. "Yes. It's the same necklace. That's why I didn't want to open the safe. That's what I meant when I said I had some sentimental objects in there."

"Sir, you told us earlier your wife took all of her belongings with her when she left. You specifically said she left only her sleeping bag."

"I know." Kenny sat in his club chair looking deflated and pitiful. "That's what I've always said. But she left her wedding ring and that necklace. I'd given it to her on the last birthday we spent together."

"Why didn't you tell us that? Or, for that matter, the investigators back when she disappeared?" Washington sounded more perplexed than anything.

"I was ashamed," he said, his voice cracking.

Oh, shit, I thought, *he's going to talk his way out of it.*

Kenny went on. "She left them behind. Like, right on top of her sleeping bag." He looked up at the detectives with tears in his eyes. "You can't imagine what it feels like to know your wife is gone, and she left behind the symbols of your love. I didn't want to believe she'd abandoned me. I thought if I showed these to the police, they'd stop searching. I had to find her, to apologize. To beg her to come back to me."

I was impressed despite myself. If I hadn't known the truth, I might have believed him. I finally understood why he'd gotten away with it all those years ago.

"Ken," Sullivan said, as if talking to a child, "you withheld material evidence."

"I know. I'm so sorry!" He fought to contain his tears. "I loved her so much!"

I could almost hear Stanley telling him not to overplay the moment.

Kenny sniffled, and Sullivan heaved his bulk from the chair to hand him his handkerchief. He lingered, patting his client awkwardly on the shoulder.

"Henry, what else is in the safe?" Washington prompted.

"Passport. Some papers." He pulled the stack out. "Will, life insurance policy." He paused again. "Sir, who is Brittany Ricci?"

"My girlfriend."

Velasquez shared a look with Washington. "Life insurance policy in the name of Brittany Ricci," he went on with his catalogue of the contents. "A list of names, addresses, and phone numbers."

"Is that it?" asked Detective Washington.

"That's it." Movement outside the window caught Detective Velasquez's attention. He looked at his partner and pointed with his chin. She turned, took in the activity, and nodded to him. "Excuse me," he said to Kenny and his lawyer. "I'll be back in a moment."

With a jolt of excitement, I leapt from my place and flew across the room, out the window, and to the hillside.

My excitement was replaced by sadness. I was looking at Jeremy's exposed body. White-suited forensic technicians clustered around him, performing various tasks. Detective Velasquez appeared at the crest of the hill. "What have you got?" he called.

"Barring some bizarre coincidence," a tech called back, "we've got your missing male juvenile."

Velasquez nodded and turned back to the house. He didn't look surprised. I followed him as he returned to the front door. Instead of going toward the den, he went to the garage. Standing at the door, he called, "Jen." Another white-suited tech looked up. "Anything?"

"We found some duct tape under this shelving unit. Gotta test it, but looks like there's hair stuck to it. Stray hairs around this shelf. Eyeballing, looks like the hairs are similar, but gotta test 'em. Also residue from the tape on the front corner strut. You know the drill. Oh, and Henry? There's a bunch of boxes with women's stuff and, like, a couple Emmy awards? They look like the real thing. Everything has an appraisal value attached to it. I mean, like a piece of paper with the value literally written on it. It's weird."

Velasquez nodded again, turned on his heel, and headed back to the den. He stopped at the door. "Stacey," he said. When his partner looked up, he beckoned. She joined him in the entryway, closing the door to the den behind her. He said, "Looks like they found the kid. Jeremy."

"Aw, shit." She slumped against the wall.

"Yeah."

"I was still hoping he'd turn up at a friend's house, you know?"

"I know. What do you want to do?"

"Honestly? I want to go back in there and break his jaw."

"Probably not wise."

"No." She closed her eyes, took a deep breath, and let it out slowly. That done, she said, "What else is there to do? We arrest him."

"For one or both?"

She looked at him with a grim expression. "You think he killed his wife?"

"Let's just say I don't buy the tears. But suspicions aren't enough to convict the guy."

"No," she said again, sounding resigned. "We need to talk to the girlfriend."

"About the alibi for last night?"

"Yeah. And we haven't asked him about the night Jeremy disappeared."

"No. We got distracted by a box full of human bones." He rolled his eyes.

She nodded, grim. "Let's go."

They went back into the den, and I followed at their heels. I glanced out the wall of windows and saw the forensic team was still working below the sightline of the room. Kenny wouldn't know the body had been found. He had moved back to sit behind his desk. Behind him, the large nude still hung askew.

Will no one straighten that stupid painting? I thought. I felt a little pang of sympathy for Brittany. There she was, exposed for all to see, but no one seemed to pay her any attention.

The detectives stood together facing Kenny and his lawyer. Washington spoke. "Sir, I need to inform you that the body of a juvenile male has been found buried in a shallow grave on your property."

Kenny sprang from his chair as the lawyer rested his face in his hand. "That's impossible!" Kenny shouted. "Let me see it. You must have planted it there!"

"Ken, stop talking," Sullivan commanded.

Kenny whirled on him. "They did. They obviously smuggled it in while we were talking!"

"Ken, shut up," the lawyer said, a bit louder.

"Asking me about Sarah. Insinuating I killed her. Nosing into my safe—"

"Ken! Shut the fuck up!" William R. Sullivan heaved his impossible bulk out of the chair, making even Washington look short by comparison. Kenny stopped talking and gawked up at him. The lawyer pointed to the desk chair. "Sit down and stop talking," he said, his tone flat. Kenny obeyed. The dining room chair creaked as the lawyer lowered himself back into it.

"Sir," Washington began, "I am arresting you on suspicion of the kidnapping and murder of Jeremy Maly. You have the right to remain silent ..."

I thought I'd feel triumphant, but I was too aware of all the ways Kenny could avoid answering for my murder. The detective finished reading him his Miranda rights, and Velasquez asked a question.

"Sir, it would help us to clear you if you could tell us your whereabouts last night and the night before. We can save this conversation for when we get down to the station, but since your attorney is already here, I thought you might want to take care of that as soon as possible."

Sullivan squinted at Velasquez but nodded a go-ahead to Kenny.

"I told you." He was shaking but worked to keep his voice steady. "Last night I was here watching a game I'd previously recorded."

"Right. And your girlfriend …" He consulted his notes, "Brittany Ricci was in the house and can corroborate that, correct?"

"Yes!" To my ears, Kenny sounded a bit too forceful.

"And the night before? Between the hours of ten p.m. and five a.m.?"

I gritted my teeth in suspense. This was something Silas and I hadn't prepared for. If he'd been out in public, drinking late, say, we were sunk.

Movement outside the window caught my eye. The others saw it, too, as they all turned to look. A gurney had been brought up to the edge of the hillside, and part of the white-coveralled team was moving a body bag onto it. Sullivan puffed out his cheeks and released a stream of air. The blood drained from Kenny's face, leaving him ashen. There was silence in the room as two technicians wheeled the gurney over the bumpy lawn and toward the waiting transport van.

Velasquez cleared his throat. "Can you tell us, sir, where you were two nights ago between the hours of ten p.m. and five a.m.?"

"I … um … I was at home. Brittany and I went to dinner, and we … we got home about ten-thirty. Then we watched something on TV and went to bed around one a.m. I slept until nine the next morning. Yesterday morning."

"And Brittany Ricci was with you the entire time."

"Yes."

I hoped that wasn't true. I tried to think of ways Silas and I could undermine his alibi if it turned out Brittany could corroborate it for the night Jeremy died.

My thoughts were interrupted by the door to the den slamming against the inner wall. Brittany flew in like a tempest.

A noise in the hall catches our attention. It's Diwata exclaiming happily.

We hear a murmur of voices.

"That's my mom," Finn says.

"Oh, I'm glad she's here and you guys can be together!"

"Me too, but what about the story?"

"It'll wait till tomorrow."

"How will you tell it if my mom's here?"

I straighten his cap again. "We'll figure it out," I say. It won't be the first time I've told the story with a caregiver in the room. I raise the bed rail into place.

"Senka?" Finn's face looks pinched.

"Yes?"

"Will you stay? Even though my mom is here?"

"Of course."

"I love my mom. But I like having you here too."

The door opens, and Moira comes in. I get up to leave the chair open for her, but I stay close by, lingering in the shadows where Finn can see me.

CHAPTER FOURTEEN

I stayed late last night, watching Finn and his mom. He loved having both of us in the room together. Tonight, when I arrive early, his smile transforms his battle-weary face.

I've been waiting for our window of opportunity. Thanks to encouragement from Diwata, Moira leaves to get dinner. The door closes behind her, and I say, "Your mom is a lovely person, Finn."

Suddenly, his eyes have a light in them; he looks happy. "Yeah, she is." He glances at the door.

"Should we get right to the story?"

"Yes, please. Don't know how long she'll be gone."

"Remember, Brittany had just come slamming into the room? She started yelling as soon as she walked in. Honestly, I was glad to hear her get mad and fight back a bit."

"What the hell is going on, Ken?" Brittany shrieked. "Dolores told me the police found a woman's bones in your garage? And some other shit about a ghost that I couldn't even follow. And then I see a body bag getting loaded into some creepy van. What's the deal?"

"What are you doing here, Brit?" Kenny asked, trying unsuccessfully to conceal his alarm.

"What am I doing here? I'm your girlfriend, for Chrissake."

Detective Washington rose and pulled herself up to her full height. She looked more imposing than I would have thought she could. "Ms. Ricci, would you sit down, please?"

"Who are you?" Brittany looked the detective up and down with the insolence of someone inexperienced with the police.

Washington introduced herself and Velasquez, who nodded as he manhandled the Chesterfield to incorporate it into their little grouping. Brittany sat, proving my assumption that the color of the chair would do nothing for her complexion.

Washington went on. "Ms. Ricci, can you tell us where you were last night?"

"I'm not in any trouble, am I? I have nothing to do with whatever he's been getting up to."

"Jesus, Brit," Kenny said through gritted teeth.

Washington didn't allow him to continue. "No, you're not in any trouble. So can you tell us where you were?"

"Yes." She sighed. "Last night, we—Kenny and me—we got into a fight, and he drove me home."

Velasquez pulled out his notebook and made a note. Washington asked, "What time was that?"

"Not long after he got home from his golf game." She said the last two words in a tone that oozed disdain. "About five, I guess."

"I see. So you weren't here in the evening and you didn't spend the night?"

"No."

"Officers," Kenny interrupted. "You need to understand she doesn't have the best memory. She gets drunk and blacks out."

"Fuck you, Ken."

"I'm sorry, babe, but it's true. You know it is."

Brittany turned to the detectives. "He does this kind of shit to me all the time—gaslighting me. I remember better than he thinks I do. I remember a lot more than he thinks I do."

As if the interruption hadn't happened, Washington continued her questioning. "What did you two argue about?"

"Her!" Brittany pointed over her shoulder at the poster.

"Sarah Sommers?"

"Yeah!" Brittany turned in her chair to look at the poster, stopping cold when she saw it had swung away from the wall to reveal a safe. "What the heck is that?" She looked back at Kenny and for the first time noticed her portrait. "Why's that crooked?" She looked around the room. "Are you kidding me?" She slumped back in defeat. "Nobody noticed. Why do I bother? You all have a life-size nude hanging in your faces, but not one of you notices it's crooked." She laughed bitterly. "You were all over that, though." She jerked her thumb in the direction of the poster again.

Washington didn't spare the painting a glance. "Where were you two nights ago?"

"Here."

A wave of disappointment overtook me. I saw Washington and Velasquez echo my emotion, though their expressions were subtle.

"You were here throughout the evening and night?" Washington clarified.

"Well, kind of. We went out to dinner. I drank a little too much. We got back here about ten thirty, I guess, and Kenny made us a nightcap. Or two. I don't remember much after that. I kind of passed out." She sat up straighter. "But it's not like he said. I don't do that a lot. It was just that night. I remember I went home last night. Anyway, yesterday I woke up around five or six in my chair here, got up to pee and get a drink of water, and went back to sleep. I don't know what time I got up for real. It was light out, and I called an Uber to take me home 'cause Ken wasn't downstairs yet."

Kenny sank into his chair, his head pressed against the back. Sullivan rested his chin on his fist and regarded Brittany with a baleful expression.

"Thank you, Ms. Ricci. You've been very helpful."

"No problem. You know, for the last two years, he's been telling me he can't marry me because his wife might come back. If it turns out those are her bones in the garage—"

Before she could finish her sentence, Kenny leapt from his chair, his face red with fury. "Shut up, you stupid—"

The lawyer was on his feet again. He moved faster than I thought him capable. He slammed his fist on the desk almost cracking the top. His face inches from Kenny's, he roared, "Sit down and don't say another word!"

Kenny sank into his chair, stunned. Silence blanketed the room.

The lawyer turned back to the two detectives. "Let's get my client booked, shall we?" he asked, his voice steady and calm. He looked again at Kenny. "Go with them. Don't open your mouth. I'll call Salazar. You'll be out in two hours."

"Who's Salazar?" I asked, but no one heard me. I saw the detectives share a look. Velasquez gave an almost imperceptible shake of his head and rolled his eyes.

As I rose up through the roof of the house, the sun was setting. I hadn't realized so much time had passed. At the cottage, tours were long over, and Silas sat on the loveseat, paperback in hand, reading Dorothy Sayers's *Busman's Honeymoon*. He looked up with pleasure as I alighted in front of him. Setting the book aside, he stood and wrapped his arms around me, holding me close. I buried my face in his shirt and took in his ever-present pine forest scent.

"I can't wait any longer," Silas said. "Tell me everything."

I started at the beginning with Dolores's daisies-and-horchata tribute then recounted the day in detail, ending with Brittany's statement revealing she couldn't supply a reliable alibi for Kenny. "Then the lawyer said he'd call Salazar, and Kenny would be out in two hours. Who do you think that is?"

Silas reached for his laptop and quickly found an answer. "Ignacio E. Salazar, Monterey County Superior Court." He opened Facebook, went to Kenny's page, and searched *Friends*. Salazar's name was the first to appear. Kenny had tagged him in a picture with two other men, the four of them making an asterisk with their golf clubs, the wind ruffling their hair as they stood on a green at the edge of the ocean.

"Is that how it works?" I asked. "His golfing buddy gets him out?"

"If he isn't setting bail, he can call the judge who is and put in a good word. That would be persuasive enough, I think."

"We can't let it happen, Silas."

"I don't know that we have a choice, my love."

"I've got to go back to his house." I jumped up. "I have to be ready for him if he ends up back there."

"And do what?"

I shrugged. "I don't know. I'll figure that out if I need to. I'll improvise, like you said before."

Silas rose and smiled down at me. "Of course you will. Shall I come with you, now that it's dark?"

"I'd love you to." I wrapped my arms around him and he held me close. "But I'm not sure what to expect at the house. It would be complicated if you appeared in front of a bunch of forensic techs sifting through the rooms." I looked up at him. "I'll be back by midnight. If he's not home by then, he won't be coming back tonight." I kissed him and set off on the now familiar route to Kenny's house.

The driveway lay empty of vehicles, the techs gone. In the garage, the shelves were bare, though the McLaren still blocked the door into the entryway. I went through and stopped to listen. Silence from the house. I flitted through all the rooms to make sure no one remained. Gambling on Kenny coming home, I sat on the living room couch and gazed out the windows into the dark night, thinking about revenge.

I didn't have long to wait. Tires crunched on the driveway, then a car door thunked shut. The car drove off as keys rattled in the entry door, and Kenny came in. He paused, as I had, listening. Evidently deciding he was alone, he closed the door behind him and took the spiral stairs two at a time. I rose through the ceiling and watched as he pulled a suitcase from his large closet and scooped clothes into it.

He's running, I thought. "Where can you go without a passport?" I asked, not expecting an answer. "You remember the detectives took it with them, right?"

Kenny zipped up his suitcase and went back into the closet. When he didn't emerge immediately, I followed him. He had removed a pile of sweaters from a low shelf and was fiddling with something. I slipped around to peer over his shoulder. He'd removed a panel in the wall and was keying a combination into a safe.

You wily paskudnyak, I thought.

He grabbed a knapsack from an upper shelf and crammed it with stacks of bills. "That's got to be at least a million bucks," I commented. He took out a passport and shoved it into his pocket. It wasn't the blue of a US passport; it was reddish-brown, the color of dried blood.

He zipped the knapsack closed and hurried out of the closet, grabbed his suitcase, and trotted down the stairs.

I met him in the garage. He hurled the bags into the trunk, climbed in, started the engine, and punched the remote to open the garage door. Spinning the car in a wide U-turn, he roared out and down the driveway, leaving the garage door open behind him.

I sprang into the air and followed, flying above him as he sped through the unlit streets of Pebble Beach. I was pretty sure I knew where he was going, so I wasn't surprised when he got onto the little highway that headed east toward the freeway. I waited until I saw him pull into the long-term parking lot, grab his bags, and toss the keys onto the front seat of the car. He obviously wasn't planning to come back for it. The last thing I saw before I turned toward home and Silas was Kenny walking into Monterey Airport.

As soon as I entered the cottage, Silas stood. "Where is he?" he asked, reading my expression.

"At the airport."

"Kill him, compel him, or talk to him?" he asked.

"Talk."

Silas nodded but looked a little disappointed.

I took his hand and, at the speed of thought, we were at the postage stamp-size Monterey Airport. We were, in fact, in the upstairs men's room.

"Sorry," Silas said, "I didn't want to appear in a public area, and I could hardly go to the women's room."

"Hey, I'm dead," I replied. "I can handle seeing a urinal or two."

We raced to the balcony that overlooked the passenger area. The airport was all but deserted at this hour. None of the passengers were Kenny.

"He must be at the gate already," I said. We trotted down the stairs to the security check area. Silas ducked under the guide ropes while I walked through them.

"Pardon me," Silas said to the few people in line as he passed them.

"ID and boarding pass?" The tired agent held out his hand.

"You'll let me pass," he murmured so no one else heard him.

"You can pass."

"Thank you."

Three TSA agents staffed the passenger and luggage scanners. I hadn't seen Silas use his power on more than one person at a time and didn't know what to expect. He swept up to the woman at the passenger scanner. "You'll let me pass."

"You can pass, sir."

"Hey!" exclaimed the man screening baggage. "You can't go around the scanner!"

Silas turned to him. "It's fine."

"For you, it's fine, though," the man parroted.

The third person, feeding luggage into the screener, didn't look up.

"What do you think?" Silas asked as we entered the gate area. "Left or right?"

"What's boarding first?"

"Right."

"Right it is."

Kenny sat in a corner, as far away from the entrance as he could get, staring at his phone. Silas and I looked at each other. He took my hand and kissed the palm. "And we're off," he whispered.

We navigated the rows of nearly empty seats and sat on each side of Kenny. I studied him, though Silas kept his gaze focused straight ahead, his long legs stretched out in front of him and crossed neatly at the ankles. Kenny glanced at Silas, annoyed that, in a nearly empty waiting area, he had chosen to sit next to him.

"I'm interested," Silas began. "When someone has so much, why would he hunger for more?"

Kenny looked around, trying to see what Silas was referring to. He stole a quick glance at this exotic looking stranger, then turned back to his phone.

"I mean to say," Silas went on, "a man has an excellent education, a challenging and lucrative career, a wife who is intelligent and charming, not to mention beautiful, yet none of this is enough. Why?" He turned a steady gaze on Kenny.

Kenny tried to ignore him, but as Silas continued to pin him like a bug, he couldn't help looking over. "I couldn't say. I have no idea what you're talking about."

Smiling, Silas cocked his head. "I am talking about you, of course."

"Me? What do you know about me? I've never seen you before."

"Those two statements don't logically follow. You may not have seen me before, although, to be accurate, you have, but I certainly know a great deal about you."

Kenny laughed. "Man, if you're trying to weird me out, I've known a lot of guys who are way scarier than you could ever be."

"Ah, you have no idea how frightening I can be," Silas said, and smiled his most radiant smile. "But tell me," he went on with sincere interest, "did you honestly kill her for her money?"

The sneer slipped from Kenny's face. "Who?"

"Sarah, of course. Sarah Sommers."

Kenny started to stand, but without the least effort, Silas pulled him back into his seat, perhaps with a little more force than necessary. "You'll stay here," he said.

For the first time, Kenny looked shaken. "Look, I don't know who you are, and I have no idea what you want, but if you don't leave me alone, I'll call the police."

Silas's smile was almost kind. *Almost.* "I don't think you will. I think you would rather not see the police at all, given your circumstances."

"What are you talking about, man?" Kenny responded, trying to sound offhand, but I noticed he was sweating. Silas made no response. "Look, I have no idea what you think you know, but the police investigated my wife's disappearance, and they cleared me of any wrongdoing."

"You mean they did not find enough to charge you. There is a difference. But that is because you sent them in the wrong direction."

Kenny's face went white. "What are you talking about, man?"

"You know, that's getting to be a tiresome response. Might you vary it next time? What I am talking about is you told the police you went to the Cleveland Forest, but you took Sarah much farther north to the Santa Cruz mountains."

As his strained expression cleared into understanding, Kenny said, "Are you kidding me? You're from Dmitry? My debt is paid. You know what? You tell him I still have the list. And I can still get it to the FBI."

Understanding dawned on me. "The list in the safe. That's what that was. Insurance against the oligarch."

Silas gave me a subtle nod. To Kenny, he said, "But you don't have it anymore."

"What?"

"The police took it from your safe this afternoon. And you don't have it in digital form. You're far too cautious for that."

I knew this last was a gamble on Silas's part, but it was a good one given Kenny's penchant for paper bank statements and checks. I was relieved when Kenny responded, "How do you know that?"

"I told you. I know a great deal about you. I know, for example, your tearful performance this afternoon was, in the vernacular, utter bullshit. One need not know as much about you as I do to understand you feel no remorse for killing Sarah Sommers. What do you think— are you a narcissist? A sociopath? In your case, is there a difference?"

"What makes you think I killed her?"

"Because she told me." It was a simple statement of fact. There was no triumph in Silas's voice, perhaps a tinge of sadness.

Kenny gazed at him, slacked-jawed, for a long moment. When he found his voice, he stammered. "You're fuckin' crazy."

"You suspect I'm not. You saw her yourself last night."

Kenny tried to stand again, and again, Silas pulled him back into his seat. He looked around, wild eyed. Their conversation hadn't drawn the attention of the other three passengers, all nodding in their separate sections of the waiting area, and the gate attendant hadn't yet arrived. He turned back to Silas. "Look, what do you want?"

"What I want is to kill you. We believe it is what you deserve."

"Silas, wait," I broke in.

"One moment," Silas said, holding a finger up to Kenny as if to mark his place in a story. He turned his attention to me.

"I've been thinking tonight. About revenge. I don't want it anymore." Silas tipped his head and waited for me to go on. "Maybe I mean I don't *need* it anymore."

"Why not?"

Kenny looked from Silas to the empty chair he spoke to and back, his eyebrows raised.

I searched for the right words. "Because I found you. And because, I guess, all that anger feels like the old me. I'm so lucky to have gotten to love Luna. To …" I hesitated, then finally released the last of my fear. "To love you. I'd like to spend the rest of our existences together, if you're willing."

"I am willing," Silas said, almost before I finished my invitation.

"Good." I felt my heart, or what used to be my heart, cast away its defenses. I smiled. "Then all I care about is justice. He needs to admit his guilt and go to prison. I don't want to kill him anymore."

"Very well."

Kenny, who'd been quietly staring at Silas, erupted. "You're a fucking lunatic." The other waiting travelers, their snoozes interrupted, looked up and glared at him, but he ignored them. "I don't know what game you're playing, but you better leave me alone."

Silas regarded him, his expression peaceful, unaffected by Kenny's outburst. "You are being offered clemency you cannot fathom. I would have chosen to kill you, but Senka—but Sarah has had a great deal of time to think about death. I am not alive, no more am I dead. She has a far more profound understanding of death than I will ever have." He looked at me with such tenderness, it was like a balm that healed every pain I'd borne in life. "So it is what she wants that matters. That is not revenge but atonement. She wants you to spend the rest of your hours and days in prison. She wants you to turn yourself in."

Kenny, who'd been staring at Silas open-mouthed, looked at him for a moment longer. I hoped he was considering Silas's words, that he would agree and go back to the police to confess. Then he laughed. It wasn't a chuckle. It wasn't a polite chortle. It was a long, raucous howl of merriment. The other passengers renewed their glares. Silas and I watched him with distaste. After much too long, he wiped tears of laughter from his eyes and said, "That was good. Turn myself in! You're funny. Why would I do that? Do you think I haven't planned for this? I already own a house where I'm going."

"I see. And where are you going? Somewhere without an extradition treaty with the United States, I imagine."

"Somewhere I won't be found. And where the money I already have stashed buys a lot of goodwill."

Silas looked at me for my thoughts. I shrugged. "I wanted to give him one last chance to show remorse."

"May I kill him then?" Silas looked so hopeful I couldn't help but smile.

"Thanks for the offer," I said, "but I stand by my original statement. I need justice, even if we have to manufacture it."

"As you wish," Silas responded with a wistful smile. He turned back to Kenny, whose face warred with itself, unable to choose between a frown of confusion and a sneer of superiority. "She says she chooses justice over your death. I don't find those actions mutually exclusive; however, we will do this as she chooses." As Silas spoke the next words, I felt the surge of power wash around me. "You will go immediately to the police."

"I'm going— What? No!"

I was alarmed, but Silas raised his hand, unflappable. "Of course he would be problematic at this moment too."

To Kenny's mounting horror, Silas extended his eyeteeth, raised his own wrist to his lips, and bit. Two puncture wounds oozed rich red blood. Silas stood and stepped in front of Kenny, masking him from the other passengers and the gate attendant, who had arrived a moment earlier. With a vise-like grip, Silas grabbed Kenny's cheeks and forced his jaws apart as if he were giving medicine to a dog. Kenny struck out at Silas and screamed inarticulately. Silas raised his dripping wrist to Kenny's mouth and forced the blood into it. Instantly, Kenny's hands dropped to his lap, limp, and he was silent.

"Is everything all right here?" The gate attendant had appeared next to Silas, who straightened up and retracted his eye teeth, then looked around. The few gathered passengers gawked at him.

"It is now, thank you." He sighed, tucking his still-bleeding wrist out of view. He raised his voice so the passengers could hear him. "My friend had a seizure. It happens sometimes when he is overly excited. He is fine now, though he has decided not to travel tonight. We apologize for the commotion."

"Oh, I'm so sorry." The gate attendant turned a kind smile on Kenny. "You're lucky to have such a good friend to take care of you." She smiled up at Silas and went back to her desk.

"What did you do?" I asked once we were alone again. "He's not going to become a vampire is he? I couldn't stand having him around for eternity."

"Neither could I. No, feeding him my blood makes my power over him complete. To make him a vampire, I would drain nearly all his blood, and then he would restore himself with mine. In either case, there is a sacrifice the vampire makes for power, as there should be. For the power I have over him now, I must experience pain and the loss of some blood."

"Will he be this passive for good? That could be weird at the police station."

"This phase is temporary. It will pass in a moment." He returned to his seat next to Kenny. "You will immediately go to the police."

In a dazed tone, Kenny answered, "I'll immediately go to the police."

"You will confess to killing Sarah Sommers."

"I killed Sarah Sommers. I'll confess to them," he droned.

"Yes. You will tell them exactly how it happened."

"I'll tell them how it happened."

"Good." He turned to me. "What about Jeremy? Would you like him to confess to his murder, as well?"

"We can let that unfold on its own."

"I agree." He looked at Kenny again. "By the way, where were you going to go?"

"Andorra. No extradition treaty."

"A lovely country." Silas nodded his approval. "Show the police your Andorran passport."

"I'll show the police my Andorran passport."

"One more thing." Silas glanced at me with a marked twinkle in his eyes. "Tell your lawyer to set up a trust fund for Dolores Sanchez with an income of, shall we say, ten thousand dollars a month?"

I grinned at him. "Sounds like a good sum."

"Good. See that it is done, Kenny."

"Yes. A trust fund for Dolores. Ten thousand dollars monthly income."

Silas rose. "Time to go."

The three of us walked out of the airport and up to long-term parking where we climbed into Kenny's McLaren, me sitting on Silas's lap as there were only two seats. Now and then as we drove to the police station, I poked my head up through the car's roof to feel the fresh, cool breeze blow through me.

Silas and I stayed as long as we could, until the first thin rays of sunrise lightened the horizon. It took some time to wake Detectives Washington and Velasquez and get them down to the station. Kenny's lawyer, unshaven and disheveled, beat them there by a minute.

Silas used his powers to convince the detectives and the lawyer he should be allowed to stay, so we were able to hear a good portion of Kenny's confession. We didn't learn anything we hadn't already figured out, except Kenny had grown to resent my fame and the accolades I'd earned.

Seeing my sad expression, Silas whispered to me, "Anyone who fears their partner outshines them is too contemptible to expend energy on."

I slipped my hand in his and leaned my head against his arm for a moment. "Yes. Thank you for saying that."

As the sun rose, we entered the keeper's cottage. Fog shrouded the protrusion of land in a soft blanket. With the sun's first watery rays, sandpipers ran up and down the beach on little stilts, calling to each other in greeting. Seagulls clucked and cackled on the roof above our heads. For the first time since we'd met, we felt completely at ease. We sat on the loveseat, arms wrapped around each other, and watched the world outside our window come to life.

"What do you want to do today?" Silas asked.

"Ignore the news, look for real estate, and read a novel for the first time in over a decade," I said without a pause.

Silas laughed. "I see you have been thinking about this already."

"You have no idea," I said, and leaned against him, feeling content.

I stop speaking and Finn gives me a satisfied smile. "Is that the end?" he asks.

"Not quite. There's a little more to tell."

He nods. "What happened with Jeremy?"

Even after years, I feel a stab of guilt thinking of the boy. I wish I'd been strong enough to save him. "He and Bink are fast friends. He's an excellent flier." I answer the second part of Finn's question, the unspoken one. "His parents buried his body in Mrs. Wang's cemetery. It's been seven years since he died, and they still grieve for him, of course. Human beings are resilient, though. They've designed ways to honor him and to find happiness, both. But it took time."

"I'd want that for my mom. Remember me but find happiness." He takes a deep breath and lets it out. "Did Kenny go to jail?"

"Mm-hmm. He did." I sit back in my chair and swing my feet up onto his bed. "He was tried separately for my murder and for Jeremy's and was found guilty in both trials. He was sentenced to two life terms, served concurrently."

"Seems fair." Finn's voice has gotten hoarse, the chemo affecting his throat.

"I think so."

"Senka?"

"Yes?"

"Will the story be over tomorrow?" Again, I know he's speaking only part of his question.

"The story will, yes."

"Then what?"

"A few more days beyond that."

"Okay." Once more I hear nothing in his tone but acceptance.

"I wish it could be longer."

"It's okay."

We hear the sound of the door handle turning. "Here's your mom," I say.

He nods.

CHAPTER FIFTEEN

I walk the hospital halls, beyond the pediatric oncology ward. I know the layout well; I've been here many times. I make a circuit of the cafeteria. On television, writers always depict anxious family members pacing outside the surgery center as they wait for word, but in my experience, most people go to the cafeteria; sipping coffee or eating gives them something to do. Two older women sit at a table scrolling through their phones, occasionally sharing what they find. They're reading scientific articles about a certain type of cancer neither of them has heard of before. Against the wall, a twenty-something man reads *Northanger Abbey* and spoons tapioca pudding into his mouth. By the window, a young couple shares a piece of lemon meringue pie. Even as they eat, they continue to hold hands. At the center table, a teenager rests her head on her arms, crossed on the table. She is sound asleep despite the noise.

I've been sitting with Finn and Moira for hours, though Finn has been asleep and doesn't know I'm there. The hospital chaplain stopped by to talk with Moira. She seemed to get some comfort out of the conversation.

I go back to Finn's room and find him awake. He manages a smile, though it's obvious he feels terrible. I think his organs have begun to shut down. Tears threaten, but I smile back.

"Where's Mom?" he whispers. I can't tell if it hurts him to talk or if he wants to keep the question between us.

"Asleep there," I say, pointing to the couch under the windows. He nods. I reach over the bed rail and take his hand. "Shall I start?"

"Yes, please," he whispers.

You remember where we were?"

He nods again, his eyes fixed on my face.

"Okay, good. Here we go."

Silas and I sat together, enjoying each other's presence and the sound of the distant waves. We watched the colors in the sky change as the sun rose over the continent behind us. The birds woke and started their days, calling to one another to proclaim their existence and their pleasure at being alive. A cool breeze wafted through the open window, carrying salt air that hadn't seen land for more than five thousand miles. Silas and I were here, in the middle of our own universe.

At length, Silas reached for the laptop and opened Google Maps, going to a street view and turning the image so I could see it. "What do you think?" he asked.

I took the computer from him and looked at the picture. It showed a cream-colored cottage with a light-blue door. The house was set back from the street and surrounded by a riot of lavender, milkweed, hummingbird sage, California poppies. It was as though the house had been designed by fairies with a sophisticated aesthetic sensibility. I loved it.

"It's gorgeous," I answered. "Are you thinking we should make an offer on it?"

"I bought it yesterday while you were out." His smug smile was one of the most charming things I'd ever seen.

"You're so sly!" I looked at the picture again and felt a surge of excitement. "Where is it?"

"On the street fronting the golf course. We'll be closer to the cemetery than we are now."

"That's wonderful! How did you find it? Where was it listed?"

"It wasn't precisely listed."

My excitement waned. "What do you mean?"

"I persuaded the owners to sell."

He persuaded someone to abandon their home! The thought turned my stomach. "How?"

"I made them an offer they couldn't refuse," he said, shrugging.

I was on my feet. I thought I knew him, but I'd misjudged, just as I had Kenny. "Oh, my god, Silas. What did you do? Kill a deer? Take its head?"

"What? No! Why would you think that?" He looked appalled, disgusted.

"Jesus, Silas! Haven't you seen *The Godfather*? 'I made him an offer he couldn't refuse'? That's what Don Corleone says after he chops off a racehorse's head and puts it in a guy's bed."

"No! I merely talked with them."

That sounded no better. "Compelled them?"

"No. *Conversed.* Here. Please sit." I lowered myself into the rocking chair farthest from him. He met my eyes. "Senka. My love. I have always been honest with you, though I was afraid it would mean losing you. That you would be repulsed by what I am."

The truth of his statement penetrated my panic. I nodded.

"Tonight I witnessed *why* you have every reason to be wary. My love, you have a way to see who I am, nothing hidden." He stopped, looking at me.

Butterflies stirred in my stomach. So far, I'd felt the twisting maggots of Harou and the rat-filled basement of Kenny. If I melded with Silas, nothing would be hidden.

But if I can't trust Silas enough for that ... I couldn't bear to finish the thought.

I stood, my hands in tight fists. I forced myself to relax them. Silas stood with me. I inched forward until we were touching. Only then did I look up into his eyes—liquid brown, warm, the corners creased by a slight smile. His arms rose to encircle me. I rested my hands on his chest. At last, I allowed myself to become insubstantial and stepped forward into his body.

I was first conscious of the quiet, the unruffled stillness of him, no heartbeat, no pulse. Then the essence of Silas, the spirit of him, filled me. It felt like standing in a redwood forest, dappled sunlight all around me, the springy ground of centuries of fallen needles under my feet. It was peace and possibility and hope.

His memories flooded me. I felt more than saw the times when despair spread a pall of ashes over that forest, misery with his father, later with Harou. For hundreds of years he had continued to fight. I felt his tenacity wane, not from weakness but from weariness.

I sensed, too, when the ashes gave way to fresh breezes restoring the forest. I felt his profound capacity for love, how he had once loved his sister, how he had loved the Lunas for each cat's unique qualities. I saw myself through his eyes and was aware of the resurgence of his optimism, his desire to continue his existence. I was bathed in his love for me.

I lingered, feeling a bliss I'd never known, but at last stepped back, separating once more.

Our eyes met again, and Silas wrapped his arms around me. I held him close and pressed my cheek to his chest. "Did you feel me?"

"I did."

"Was it cold and weird?"

"No, my love. It was like standing by the ocean between tides, when the sea is blue glass. The surface of the water is still, but you know, just beneath there is so much ... life."

I tightened my arms around him. "Can we do that again sometime?"

"Anytime you like." His laugh was a low rumble against my ear.

"Good. Okay, tell me about our house." I pulled him toward the loveseat where we sat together.

He grinned at me. "The other night while you were out, I took a walk by the graveyard and looked at the houses. I thought you would like this one. I knocked on the door and introduced myself to the residents. They're a very kind couple who have recently retired. It has been their dream for decades to leave the Monterey Peninsula behind and travel around the world, but their retirement funds wouldn't allow them to. In return for their house, I have subsidized their travels. It's far more than the house is worth, but I didn't feel that mattered. It's only money, after all. I told them I have seen much of the world, and my concern was they would grow tired of traveling and want to return. I promised I would gift them the house of their choice, should they want to come back."

"A house of their choice? What if they choose some twenty-five million dollar mansion?"

"My love, I am three hundred years old. I have invested well. The cost is immaterial."

"Oh! I see. Well, good. So how soon can we move in?"

"Next week. They are eager to start their new adventure. I have hired someone to tint the windows—I hope that's all right."

"It's safer for you, I'm sure."

Silas nodded. "Much."

"Do we need anything else? Furniture or whatever?"

It felt strange to be talking about home furnishings after our usual conversations consisting of plots to end Harou or plans to bring Kenny to justice. Strange but very good.

As the night came on once again, Silas and I wandered to the cemetery to see if our friends were around. We found Mrs. Wang, Signore Peluso, Bink, and Jeremy sitting together by Mrs. Wang's grave. Well before we reached the group, we heard Bink's excited voice and saw him gesticulating. As soon as he noticed us, he jumped up. "Dude! Senka! I can't wait to tell you." He turned to Silas and held his hand up for a high-five. "Silas! How's it hangin', bro?" Silas looked perplexed but knew enough to slap Bink's palm.

I rested a hand briefly on Jeremy's shoulder, and he smiled up at me. As Silas and I sat on either side of Signore Peluso and Mrs. Wang, I asked, "What's up, Bink?"

"Catch this. You know how the police went door to door asking questions, and all the time me and Jeremy were right here? Like, we could have answered everything they needed to know. So I realized! We could help them solve crimes!" He looked at Jeremy who nodded with such enthusiasm his hair seemed to come to life.

"So, what? You're going to haunt the police station?" I smiled at the image.

"Oh, dude! You make it sound even more rad!"

Jeremy crowed, "We're gonna haunt the police station."

"We're gonna interview any ghosts that are around. Then we're gonna find a way to lead the cops in the right direction. Right, little dude?"

Jeremy offered his enthusiastic nod, then looked at me. "What d'ya think?"

"I think you both sound super excited about it, and it's a terrific idea." I wasn't sure how terrific an idea it would turn out to be in practice, but the plan clearly thrilled Jeremy. At the moment, that was all that mattered.

Mrs. Wang leaned in to me and whispered, one conspirator to another, "Let's go for a walk." We stood, and she sang out to the others, "We'll be back." As we ambled toward the far corner of the cemetery, she tucked her hand into the crook of my arm and smiled up at me. "How are you, Senka dear? It's been a difficult few days."

I felt grateful for her sensitivity and care. "It has, to be honest. You know, Mrs. Wang, I keep thinking about how blind I was. Willfully blind. I married someone who was so clearly not a good person. I ignored the signs because all I cared about was that he seemed fascinated by ... well, by me. How could I have been so stupid?"

"I think you're asking the wrong question, dear. To be 'stupid,' as you put it—though I think I'd say 'flawed'—is to be human. A question that might give you a useful answer is: what have you learned from this recognition of your flaws? People say it's 'learning a life lesson,' but I think it's a question at the heart of existence: how can we always strive to be better?"

We walked in silence for a bit, turning onto the golf course and passing the place where Jeremy had died. A chill lurked there—a place where a vicious, inhuman murder had occurred. We were both lost in thought until I spoke. "When I was alive, I always believed death was an ending. But it's not, is it?"

"It doesn't have to be. Some people never allow themselves to live, so death doesn't change much for them. Some people choose to move on, but we won't know if that's an ending until we decide to leave ourselves, will we?" She patted my hand. "And of course, those like us decide to stay and allow death to be a change but hardly an end."

"Mrs. Wang?"

"You've been very polite to call me that for so long. I think we're going to be great friends, so I would prefer you call me Grace."

"Grace. That's a pretty name."

"It's short for my parents' name for me, Ai-Xiu. It means graceful love. My parents were very hopeful."

"Prescient, I think. Grace, is Mr. Wang still alive?"

"Ah." A sadness crept into her expression. "No, dear. He died twelve years, two months, and four days before I did."

"Did he stay? Did you see him when you got here?"

"I don't know if he stayed; he was gone by the time I arrived."

"I'm so sorry. You must miss him."

"Every day, Senka dear. Every day since the moment he died."

"Why do you think he chose to move on?"

"I don't know for sure. I believe, though, he lived his life with such—what? Joy? Zest, maybe—and he was always so curious and excited about each new adventure that he decided he was ready to move on."

"And you're not hurt he didn't wait for you? I'm sorry if these questions are too personal. Please tell me if I'm being intrusive."

"I've existed too long to be concerned about privacy, dear. Not hurt, no. I would have liked to have seen him again. You know, we were in love and devoted to each other for more than sixty years. Even so, we weren't joined at the hip. I was very fortunate to find him and to have him with me as long as I did. And now!" She giggled and looked up at me, her eyes shining. "Now, I am very much enjoying learning Italian!"

I laughed. I thought about Silas and felt grateful again that he, of all beings, had stumbled on me in the cabin in the woods. An uncomplicated happiness suffused me as I considered we had eternity to spend together. We could look forward to days and years of peace. Unless a vampire hunter materialized in our midst, of course. I smiled to myself at the absurdity of the thought.

When we returned to the others, I sat next to Silas, and he wrapped an arm around my shoulders. I leaned in and kissed him on the cheek, and he turned a beaming smile toward me.

We sat together, taking in the night air, Jeremy lying on his side in the grass, Bink next to him, grinning goofily at the rest of us perched like birds on a wire on Grace's wall. Suddenly Bink leaned forward and peered into the darkness. "Hey, guys. Look at that." He pointed in the direction of the lighthouse.

Small, disembodied smudges, glowing in the moonlight, rose and fell, approaching us across the grass. Above the smudges hovered two shining disks. As we watched, the smudges and disks developed a shadowy outline. Coming toward us out of the darkness was a small black kitten with white paws, its tail held high in the air.

It announced its arrival with a high-pitched mew-let, then trotted to Silas, jumped into his lap, sat, and gazed at him, saying nothing. Silas held out his fingertip and the kitten stretched forward to touch it delicately with its nose. Formal greetings accomplished, it resumed its study of the handsome features. Silas scratched behind its oversize ears, and the kitten responded with a deep purr.

"Oh, my goodness!" Grace exclaimed. "That's the loudest purr I've ever heard. Why, I'm sure they're hearing that purr all the way to San Francisco!"

Silas leaned down toward the kitten. "Hello," he whispered. "Did Luna send you?"

The kitten blinked.

"I believe that is a yes." Taking an uncharacteristic breath, Silas blew a soft stream of air into the kitten's nostrils. It shook its head as if to dislodge a fly and sneezed.

"Why did you breathe on him?" I asked.

"It allows him to understand us."

Recognition dawned on me. "I always thought Luna was an especially good listener."

The kitten yawned hugely, showing his pointy teeth and tiny pink tongue, then picked his way over to my lap and curled up, turning his head upside down. "Oh," I crooned. "He's perfect. Look at the white band across his little chin! It looks like a strap to hold his ears on!"

"How do you guys know it's a boy? It could be a girl," Bink said, sounding proud of his scientific knowledge.

"No, he's a boy," I answered, stroking his chin with one finger.

"Don't you have to check, though?" Jeremy asked. "You know, to be sure?" He turned to Bink, who nodded.

I shook my head. "He told us."

"He speaks English?" Bink asked.

"No. I ... it's just there." I tapped the side of my head.

"Cool!" Bink and Jeremy exclaimed at the same time.

Silas put his arm around my shoulders again. With the other, he reached over to pat the kitten. "Hello, Luna the twenty-fourth," he said.

"Silas?" I began, hesitant to intrude on a ritual hundreds of years old. "Do you think we could try a different name? I mean, maybe Luna has run its course."

He considered. "You're right. The name Luna belongs to a different era. An era of fear and running. An era before you."

"What name should it be, do you think?"

"Maybe the cat already has his own name," Bink suggested.

They looked at the kitten in silence. "No," Silas and I said together.

Silas added, "He is content with whatever we choose."

"*Sole*? Or Sol, god of sun?" suggested Signore Peluso.

"There is a kind of bookending quality to that name," Silas considered.

Grace took Signore Peluso's hand. "It's too tidy, I think. And it would be a heavy load for a little cat to carry."

They all studied the kitten.

"Hang Ten?" Bink said hopefully.

"Mrow!" The kitten put a stop to further discussion of that name.

I thought of the thing that had been with me at my most troubling times, that had first brought me some ghostly powers, that had allowed me to feel safe, and from which I had taken my own name. "How about Shadow?"

"Shadow." Silas seemed to taste the name. He looked at the kitten. "Shadow?"

"Mrrrrp." Shadow started to purr and his tiny paws made biscuits of contentment.

"Very good." Silas stood. "Now who would like to see our new house?" The others responded with surprise and excitement, and we all stood, ready to follow.

Silas turned to Shadow. "Ride or walk?" he asked. The kitten stretched out a paw toward him, and Silas scooped him up and deposited him on his shoulder. "Try not to dig your claws in, please."

We set off across the cemetery and along the golf course until we stood before the real-world version of the Google Maps street view. Silas, Shadow, and I, along with the others admired the little house and garden as the lights from inside cast a warm glow into the night.

I considered what a sight we would be to any passer-by. Or rather, that Silas would be: a tall, well-dressed man with long, black hair and chiseled cheekbones, a black cat perched on his shoulder, laughing and talking ... to himself. I smiled at the image, then noticed Silas looking at me. He grinned back, his eyes warm as candlelight.

When the group returned to Grace's wall, Silas, Shadow, and I said good night and continued on to the cottage.

"I've been thinking," I said as we walked.

"Mmm?"

"After we got back from saying goodbye to Stanley, Grace asked me how it was. I told her I thought it was the most important and meaningful thing I'd ever done."

"Yes, I can imagine."

"Silas, I think that's what I want to do."

"What do you mean, my love?"

"I want to keep people company as they die." We reached the cottage and went in. "I think for so many people, dying can be a lonely process. It was for me. I want to help people not be lonely or frightened, as I was. I'll go up to the hospital and choose someone who's dying. I'll help them enter the shadow world."

Silas sat in one of the rocking chairs, and I joined him, sitting in the other. Shadow leapt the gap and curled up in my lap. Silas said, "You could tell them a story. Everyone loves stories."

"I could tell them a story about death, help them see it's not as frightening as they might think."

"You could tell them about us." He looked at me and his eyes softened with tenderness.

I stroked Shadow's chin. "I'll tell them about Shadow too. And our Luna. And the times we were scared or brave or happy. About hope. About falling in love."

"It's a wonderful idea, my love." Silas reached over and I took his hand. We rocked in contented silence. "Woman of shadows and Shadow the cat," Silas said. "We are perfect for each other, are we not?"

"In so many ways."

"That's why you came," Finn whispers. "To keep me company. You knew I was dying and you wanted to help me be ready."

"Yes. I walked through the wards looking for the person who needed me next, and I chose you."

"Why me?"

"I could see you knew you were sick, maybe not that you were dying but very sick, yet you were engaged in life. Your lights were on, you were reading. I watched your face as you reacted to the book. I thought, *This young man would dance the tango if he could*. What I didn't know was how much I'd come to love you."

He looks at me, so serious. For the first time, I can hear that his breathing has become labored. "Thank you for coming. Telling me about you and Silas and Luna. And Shadow." He reaches for my hand. I put the bed rail down so he'll be comfortable as we hold hands.

The door opens and we both look toward it. A tall, elegant man with long black hair and prominent cheekbones enters the room. On his shoulders rides a large black cat with white socks and yellow eyes. The man—the being—smiles at Finn and me.

Finn's eyes grow wide. "Silas?" he asks in a whisper. "And Shadow?"

"Good evening, Finn," Silas says. "We wanted to drop by for a moment and say hello." Silas makes a little bow. "Senka has told me so much about you."

Finn looks at me. "Oh, wow," he mouths, grinning broadly. He looks back at Silas. "Is that Shadow One?"

"Yes," he answers.

Finn glances at his mom, who's still sleeping soundly. "I wish Mom could meet you. Probably better she doesn't."

With a whump, Shadow jumps from Silas's shoulder to the foot of Finn's bed. He picks his way up Finn's body until he can look him in the eyes. Finn gives him the slow double blink, and Shadow purrs.

"Wow!" Finn says. "He really is loud. Mrs. Wang was right." He pats Shadow, making the purrs ramp up another notch.

As always, my mind returns to the first time I kept vigil. To Stanley. I think of my parents. I remember each death I've attended. I miss those people. When he no longer needs me, I will miss Finn. I will miss him keenly. I'll remember him for his humor and caring, his kindness and wisdom.

"Finn?" I say, "Do you remember when you told me you thought Stanley was lucky to choose how he died?" He nods. "Would you like the same choice?"

He looks from me to Silas. "You'd do that for me?"

Silas nods. "You are important to Senka."

Finn looks back at me, and his lips crook in a smile. He gives me the slow blink.

"Thank you, Finn," I say, smiling back. "I love you too."

When he returns his gaze to Silas, his face becomes serious. The crease between his eyebrows tells me he's thinking hard. At last, he says, "Thanks, Silas. I know this next part won't be easy." He looks at his mom, and I can sense the love that rises in him. "I want to stick around for her as long as I can." Finn turns to me and I offer a nod of understanding. It's what I expected him to say.

"That is a loving choice, Finn," Silas tells him.

Moira stirs in her sleep. Silas beckons to Shadow, who makes his way up to the crook of Silas's arm.

"Goodbye," Finn says. "Thanks for coming,"

"Goodbye, Finn."

"Prrrow-wow," Shadow adds.

And they are gone.

Before his mom wakes fully, Finn turns to me, the familiar little crease between his eyebrows. "Will you stay?"

"Of course."

"Even after Mom wakes up?"

I nod. "Yes."

"What about ... after?"

"As long as you need me, I'll be here."

"Will you hold my hand?"

"Are you frightened?"

"No, but I want to close my eyes and still know you're here."

Without letting go of his hand, I sit back, stretch out my legs, and rest my feet on his bed. "I'm not going anywhere," I say. He smiles and closes his eyes.

I sit, listening to him breathe and waiting for the time when I will greet him again.

ACKNOWLEDGEMENTS

I started writing this novel thanks to a prompt on Vocal.Media. I intended to write a short story about a ghost and a vampire meeting in a cabin in the woods. Then I fell in love with them and wanted to know more about their journeys—so I wrote a novel. Thanks are due, then, to the creative minds at Vocal.Media.

The folks who faithfully read each chapter as I posted it to that platform kept me writing; I didn't want to disappoint them. Thank you to Jill Jackson, Cammy Torgenrud, and others who cheered me on from the start.

Through her book *Big Magic*, Elizabeth Gilbert infected me with the superstition that if you don't write your book fast enough, the characters will abandon you. I appreciate her for that because the fear of losing Senka, Silas, Luna, and Finn kept me writing through sickness, doubt, and even a vacation in Switzerland.

Rufus and Flacko, you will never read this novel, but without you, neither the Lunas nor Shadow would be possible. Thank you for teaching me the language of Cat and for the snuggles and purrs that fill that cat-sized niche in my heart.

It takes a team to bring a novel to publication. I've been lucky to find the best, thanks to Reedsy: editor Angela Brown, cover designer Candice Broersma, and interior designer Lorna Reid. Thank you all for your professionalism and extraordinary artistry.

Thanks to my faithful writing group, Nicki Ehrlich and Tina Biegel, whose wise questions and incisive suggestions added immeasurably to the depth, honesty, and concision of *Shadows*. Their generosity, friendship, and love astonish me daily. And, Nicki, thank you for your endless patience in guiding me to a published novel.

Kathy Lower and Jan Lower, thank you for reading the chapters as I posted them and giving me unfailing encouragement. Thank you for reading the first draft I thought was polished enough to share with you. Thank you for the high expectations evident in your feedback—they helped me make the next umpteen drafts better and better. You've listened to every permutation of my hopes and dreams for this novel. Thank you for encouraging my storytelling from the moment I could speak. No one could ask for better sisters.

Jackson Sherry, I am so lucky to have found you. Thank you for the humor in hard times, the honesty when I need it, your example of resilience, your indomitable spirit, creativity, advice—and for the number of times you've said, "Now hear me out …"

And John Sherry—you're always my first reader. The person who believes in me more than I believe in myself. My champion. My partner. My best friend in the adventure of life. You give me courage to put my dreams into action. It's thanks to you I know love abides. I'll wait for you.

ABOUT THE AUTHOR

Photo by Anthony Zoccali

Joyce Sherry is a playwright-turned-novelist who writes stories where ghosts speak, vampires brood, and hope refuses to die—even after death. A lifelong lover of the strange and the tender, Joyce once collaborated with Ray Bradbury on a stage adaptation of his novel *Something Wicked This Way Comes* (yes, *that* Ray Bradbury), and her short fiction has been recognized by diverse literary journals. Joyce holds a Master's degree in theater history and literature, which has served her well in all her writing ventures. She's a member of the Central Coast branch of the California Writers Club. She's also a certified coach who helps people navigate life's plot twists with humor and heart. She lives in the gorgeous, foggy, dramatic Central Coast of California with her breathtaking musician husband, her endlessly creative son, two sweet dogs, and two diva cats.

You can find Joyce at **joycesherry.com**, Instagram, and Goodreads.